Heart of the
Diamond

by

Lindsay Delagair

DEDICATION

"Thank you, Lord, it's finished!" With that said,
I'd like to dedicate this book to my wonderful family who challenged me to
see it through to completion; and finally to my friends,
Donna, Ann, and Jan for all of their support and encouragement.

ACKNOWLEDGMENTS

Editor: Ann Beckley

Photo Credits: Jim Kapper

CHAPTER ONE

The rain had been falling steadily, making a miserable day seem even worse. Katie sat in the dining room watching the pattern the raindrops made on the glass. She wondered if they were like snowflakes, no two the same.

The teakettle began to whistle and she headed into the kitchen to put her blackberry tea on to steep. A tear slipped off her cheek and landed on the dark green countertop, leaving a round, wet spot where it landed. It looks like a hole, she thought. "Like the hole in my heart and the hole in my life," she mumbled as a fresh flood of tears welled over her lashes.

Alex and Katie Davidson had been trying to conceive for almost two years. The first year the doctor said they were probably just trying to hard.

"Just take your mind off of it for a while and maybe it will work out okay," he told them.

But after the first year went by without so much as even a false alarm, the doctor began putting them through testing. Katie, he said, had scaring and evidence of uterine fibrosis. Alex turned out to have a low sperm count; though he was convinced the doctor had to be wrong about that.

That was one thing that bothered her about her husband. How could he be so cruel to believe it was all her problem? He was very reluctant to even have himself tested. She assumed it had something to do with diminishing his manhood, but she thought it was damn arrogant of him anyway. Not to get the wrong idea, she was very much in love with Alex; they just didn't always see eye to eye on things—especially things where blame could be laid.

The doctor put Alex on hormones to increase his sperm count and she was put on Clomid to help her ovulate. Doctor Hampton explained that this would dramatically increase the chance for a multiple birth. She thought twins would be fantastic, but what if it was triplets or quadruplets? She told the doctor she wanted a baby or two, not a litter!

When her ovulation predictor showed it was time, they went in for the procedure. Alex was grumbling about having to 'perform' at the doctor's office. And the worst part, he said, was when he had to give the container to the nurse. Katie laughed as she tried to get comfortable on the exam table and asked if he would rather trade places with her? Doctor Hampton and his nurse entered the room before he could respond. Alex held her hand as the doctor carefully placed the sperm in her uterus and capped it off with a diaphragm. Her discomfort was obvious, but she still managed a smile for her husband when it ended.

Though he never answered her question, he decided his job had been the easier.

When her period wasn't on time, as it normally was, she was ecstatic and quickly phoned for an appointment. She even felt nauseous and tender, though she thought it might be too early to start with symptoms. She didn't know all the answers, but she was certain that this time they had finally done it.

Doctor Hampton's nurse, Margaret, seemed just as excited as Katie as they talked in her cubical waiting for the test results. Margaret was a middle-aged woman with a stocky build and an effervescent personality. Her speech was thick with southern charm and grace. She had been there for Katie to confide in the first year when the anticipated didn't occur. She tried to dispel her worries and she always knew what to say to make her feel hopeful again, though the situation continued to get bleaker with the passage of time.

It would only be ten minutes before Katie would get her results, but it felt like an eternity. Margaret checked the test strip and the smile faded from her face.

"I'm sorry, Hon, it's negative? Sometimes these are wrong when it's early like this. Do you want to do the blood test?"

"Yeah, let's do it. I've just got to be pregnant, Margaret. Today makes seven days late; what else could it be?"

"I don't know, Hon, but if this is still negative, we'll have Doc take a look at you, okay?" she said, giving her a sympathetic glance.

2

When the second test came back negative, she was sent in to see the doctor. The examination revealed that, to top off her lousy day, she now had an infection in her uterus. This was the reason for her delayed period, and it also explained the nausea and tenderness. The doctor's mundane attitude irritated her even more and she was starting to convince herself that she needed to find a different doctor—one that knew what he was doing!

But anger did little to overcome the depression that looming over her like the dark clouds that had settled over the sky. Her despair became as evident as the teardrops that stained her face. With a warm and comforting hug from a moist-eyed Margaret, she left for home.

Katie took her cup of blackberry tea and headed for the bed. The soft worn mattress, cozy sheets and fluffy pillows were like the arms of an old friend taking her in and holding her like no one else knew how. Getting comfortable, she sipped the piping hot tea until the toll of her emotional day caused her to put down the cup and give way to sleep.

She jerked wide-awake at the sound of tires in the driveway. It was Alex; he was home. Glancing at the clock in disbelief she didn't realized that she had slept so long. "I didn't set anything out for dinner!" she said aloud as she hurried down the hall. If I can't be a mother, she thought, at least I could try to be a better wife.

Alex was already in the door shaking off the rain like an old hound.

"What's for dinner? All I can smell is blackberry tea!" He had a half smirk on his face until he looked at her. He was unaware that she had gone to the doctor, even though he knew just as well as she did that her period was late. From the look on her face he figured her period must have started or something else happened. "What's a matter, Babe? Are you okay?"

She felt her composure shatter to a thousand pieces, like glass falling on stones. "No, I'm not okay!" The tears began to pour down. "I thought for sure I was pregnant, so I took the day off to go to the doctor's office for a test and—and I'm not pregnant. I've got some stupid infection and… ."

That was enough said as he pulled her into his arms and let her sobs rock through her. He stroked her soft hair and kissed her

3

temple. His kisses were somewhat soothing the beast that had begun to pound inside her head.

"Shhh, shhh. It's okay, Babe, it's okay." He held her just a little longer and then tilted her chin up to his face and kissed the tip of her nose. "Oh man! Have you seen what all this crying does to your face? Wow, look at those raccoon eyes," he said referring to the smeared mascara. He gave her his half-cocked grin hoping to lighten the moment. "Any other bad news you might be holding out on me?" he said, still keeping his screwed-up face.

She smiled only slightly. "Yeah, I don't have anything ready for supper either."

"No supper!" he said being a little too dramatic.

Her lip stuck out in a dejected pout, but before she could say anything, he smiled a softer smile and mentioned going out for dinner. They were on a pretty strict budget so she usually cooked; dinner out would have been appealing, but the thought of going back out in that drizzling rain (not to mention cleaning up her disastrous face) wasn't.

"How about ordering in?" she offered.

He breathed an obvious sigh of relief. He really didn't want to go out, but he felt he should offer. "Whatever you want is fine with me." Then he cautiously added, "How 'bout pizza?"

"Pizza sounds great." She felt the burden of her day lifting and her tear-stained face began to find the smile it had before she went to the doctor's office. "Alex," she said softly, "I love you."

"I love you too, Babe," he responded as he put a tender kiss on her lips that told her he meant it.

~:~

Katie and Alex had been together since high school. They met at a football game. She was a freshman at Vero High School and he was a junior at Port St. Lucie High. The schools were long time rivals, and football was the pinnacle of the rivalry. They met at the concession stand. Katie was getting a coke when Alex, busy fixing his hot dog, tried to open a ketchup baggie by squeezing it. Instead of getting it on his hot dog, he got himself and Katie. In an instant he had a cute little auburn-haired girl very angry. She called him a jerk and a few other choice words, but he turned on the charm.

4

Her anger melted away and she felt as if she had just met the cutest and funniest guy on the planet. He wanted her home phone number, but she didn't think her parents would approve. Alex was undeterred; by the fourth quarter he talked her into it.

She was an only child and often felt she couldn't have chosen better parents if she'd been able to pick them out herself. Her mother, Elizabeth, was a petite, elegant Irish woman with blazing red locks and emerald eyes. Her father, Lawrence, was of Italian-French descent. He was tan and rugged-looking with coal-black hair and deep brown eyes. Katie was a perfect blend of both. Her long, silky hair was a deep coppery auburn, and her eyes were an unusual shade of hazel. She was five foot eight, with a slender yet full feminine build that turned quite a few heads

Alex, though he wouldn't admit it to anyone, was insanely jealous when other men took second glances at his wife. She, as far as he was concerned, belonged to him. He knew Katie didn't think of herself as a beauty, and he never lavished praise on her looks. When she looked in the mirror she was overly critical; he kept his mouth shut. He was afraid that if she realized how very beautiful she really was then she never would have stayed with a flirtatious, self-centered guy like him.

Her parents liked Alex from the start, and after five years of dating, they gave their blessing for marriage. Katie decided to start working right after high school though her parents would have preferred college to employment. She started as a keypunch operator for a major computer corporation, and then moved up into the secretarial pool. The pay could have been better, but the benefits were excellent.

Alex started working his senior year in high school at a boat manufacturing plant. He called his position a 'gopher,' go for this and go for that, but he was actually an inventory clerk. It was his job to be certain there was a constant supply of fiberglass and resin, which he called 'itch and bitch,' because the fiberglass would make everyone itch and the fumes from the resin made everyone bitchy after smelling it all day. Again, the pay was okay, but nothing to brag on. Their combined income barely kept them above the poverty level and it always seemed they were scrimping and cutting corners.

They managed to save enough to put a down payment on a nice little thousand- square-foot, two-bedroom house on a shady lot in

Fort Pierce, in the industrial part of town where both of them worked. But, it was perfectly located between their parents' homes for visits. It was only after they bought their home that they started planning for a family. They both wanted three children, deciding after number two they would sell their little house and find something more accommodating. That was two years ago and baby number one was still missing from their lives.

Katie believed if she could just get pregnant the first time, it would be easier to conceive the next two. All their dreams and plans hinged at this point, and she was afraid of what would happen to their marriage if they couldn't have children. She had known people with the same problem that eventually divorced. What would happen to her and Alex? Would they grow distant or stronger and more bonded? What would life be like without children, or Alex? She didn't know, but she couldn't imagine a life without him. Only time would tell their fate.

~:~

Several days after the exam, and several doses of antibiotics consumed, her period began. She had still been holding on to the hope that the doctor had been wrong, and now with it started, the depression returned. The volume of work at the office helped to keep her mind out of the rut, but the weekend would start tomorrow and there would be little she could do to keep her thoughts in a positive light.

Alex had a deep-sea fishing trip setup with his buddies for Saturday, but now he wondered if he should stay home with her. He thought about asking her to come along, but the guys were pretty crude and she was prone to motion sickness. Put the two together and she'd be miserable.

But she didn't want to ruin his weekend. "No, you go ahead and go fishing like you planned. You don't need to stay home and hold my hand, I'll be fine."

He looked at her with a sarcastic expression that seemed to say, 'Yeah, sure you will.'

"No really, I'm fine." she said, before his expression could come out in words. "I've been thinking about going up to Mom and Dad's for the day. Maybe do a little shopping or something."

"Hey, now that sounds like a winner. Your parents asked you to come over for the last few weeks anyway and... ."

She interrupted him, "They've wanted to see *us* for the last few weekends. You know they'd like to see you once in a while, too."

"Yeah, I know but... ."

Once again she cut him off, "You're too busy, or too tired, or too I don't know what."

His mood shifted quickly to anger. "If you want me to go with you then just say so and I'll cancel the damn plans I made, okay?"

"Look," she said, putting her hands softly on each side of his face, "I'm sorry for being this way. I don't want to start our weekend with an argument. I want you to go fishing and have a good time. Maybe Sunday we can do something together?"

He relaxed his anger somewhat. "Okay. If you want we could go to your folks on Sunday?"

She smiled, "Nah, Mom and Dad are going to play golf with some friends Sunday afternoon, but we could go to your parents, or over to Bill and Sherry's to swim and maybe cook-out."

He knew his parents would be just as glad to see them as hers, and since it would be Sunday he knew his mom would have something great for dinner. "It doesn't matter to me, Babe, you decide and let me know tomorrow. Call Mom and make sure she doesn't have any other company planned for this weekend. I don't think Bill has to work Sunday, but you could go over and talk with Sherry and see what they're doing."

Ugh! She thought. This meant she had to make the decision. Reluctantly she agreed.

"Let's hit the hay 'cause I gotta get up early."

"How early?" She frowned.

"The boat leaves at 6:00 in the morning, so I'll have to leave by 5:00. Get me up at 4:30, okay?"

She wanted to tell him she'd be sleeping at 4:30 and he should get himself up, but that just wasn't her way. She nodded gravely and headed for the bedroom.

He sensed her displeasure with his schedule and added that you have to take the good with the bad, then quickly caught up with her, pinching her rear-end all the way down the hall.

"Ouch! Stop it you big jerk!"

Alex laughed as they tumbled onto the bed. Kissing her, he pulled her under him and pinned her with his weight.

This was common fare for him, and sometimes she wondered if he was truly interest in lovemaking or wrestling matches. "Not tonight," she said with a fake smile.

"Why not?"

"Because—you know…" Without any look of comprehension, she had to remind him of a sore subject, "…my period."

"Oh." he said, suddenly wishing he had been more mindful and she didn't have to tell him. "Well we could take a shower and… ."

She stopped him with a glance.

"Then again," he said, "maybe we should just get some shut-eye."

"That sounds like a good idea."

"Good-night," he mumbled as he turned out the light.

She woke to a blaring alarm at 4:30 in the morning and nudged to life a solidly sleeping Alex from his pleasant dreams. "Get up. Hey you, get up," she said, in a groggy voice. He moaned a little, but nothing more. "Hey Alex, do you hear that?" she whispered in his ear.

"Huh, wa? Do I hear what?" he said, half cocking an eye open to look at her.

"Those fish, do you hear 'um?" She grinned at his puzzled, sleepy face.

He wasn't sure, but he thought his wife must have gone off the deep-end because she wasn't making any sense.

"Those fish," she repeated. "They're calling out to you. 'Alex, Alex, come catch us, if you can.'"

"It's that time already?" he said, casting a disbelieving glance at the clock. "Oh man, I could use some more Z's!"

She gave him a shove as he rolled out of the bed onto his feet. She was already snuggling back down, grabbing his pillow for extra comfort.

"Katie," he said, suddenly smiling, "I could use some breakfast, a couple eggs over-easy, some toast and a big cup of black coffee." But he didn't get a response. "Hey, Sweet-thing, do you think you could get that for me while I get dressed?"

She propped herself up on one elbow and brushed the hair out of her face, "At 4:30 in the morning I ain't anybody's *sweet-thing.*

Ronald McDonald can fill your order, not Katie Davidson. See ya big guy!" Then she plopped face-first back down onto her pillow.

He snickered to himself. Boy! If she could only talk like that to everyone else in the world, he thought, man look out. Katie Davidson would go straight to the top! He pulled on his clothes and kissed his already sleeping wife on the head and whispered goodbye.

When she next stirred it was 8:15 and the sunshine was crowding through the cracks in the mini-blinds, filling the room with a striped illusion. She instinctively reached for Alex's side of the bed—gone. Oh yes, she vaguely recalled her 4:30 comments. She grinned to herself as she stretched and yawned on the comfortable sheets. "The big yo-yo! Asking me to fix him breakfast at 4:30 in the morning—give me a break!" She knew he really didn't expect her to get up and fix him breakfast at that hour, but he always said he liked the funny things she said when she was half-asleep. "Too bad I don't talk in my sleep all the time," she said to the ceiling. "There are a few people I'd like to tell a thing or two, if I had the nerve!" The thought of a bold, brazen, unfettered Katie was amusing to her.

After a shower, a cup of coffee and a piece of toast, she took off in her little Fiesta and headed for her parent's house in Vero Beach, thirty-minutes away. She knew they would be glad to see their 'little-girl' and she wondered if that was how they would always perceive her. Probably so, but in all honesty, she really didn't mind; she loved her parents.

"Hi, Sweetheart, how are you?" her mother asked as they embraced in the driveway.

"I'm okay, I guess."

"It didn't work?" She could see the look on Katie's face before she answered. Katie just shook her head and accepted another hug. "Let's go inside, Honey, I've got a nice breakfast ready for you."

"Awe, Mom, you didn't have to do that." she said, suddenly sounding like a teenager again.

"Well it was no trouble," her mother stated. "I had to fix breakfast for your father anyway."

Her father was in the living room reading the morning paper, just as he did every morning for as long as she could remember. She always had a sneaking suspicion that he only held it in front of his face so no one would catch him taking a morning catnap. He quickly dropped the sports page and met her halfway in the living room, pulling her close for a warm and caring hug.

"How's my little Kat?" he said. He always called her Kat when she was at home.

"Fine, Daddy, and you?"

"Couldn't be better. Where's that husband of yours? Sleeping in on the weekend or what?"

"No, Dad, he went deep sea fishing with some of his buddies earlier this morning—like up-at-4:30 kind of early."

"Four-thirty!" he exclaimed, "Boy, I'd say off-hand he takes his fishing pretty seriously."

"I guess," she smiled.

They sat at the kitchen table enjoying breakfast; her dad filling her in on the latest goings on at the rail station and her mother telling her about a call from Uncle Patty. Katie didn't say much, she just listened mostly. Being there was an experience she savored; the smell of her mother's perfume, the aroma of the house, and in general all the great memories surrounding that wonderful place that would always be home in her mind. She also enjoyed watching her parents; her father's hand resting on her mother's, the looks between the two of them, the kiss her mother would put on the top of his head as she would get up to dish out second helpings. This is what love really is, she thought.

Her parents met in Canada where Elizabeth lived. Elizabeth's family was very protective—she was the only girl. She had five older brothers who were ready to drill-and-grill any would be suitors. Lawrence was from Montana, where his family had a ranch on the Canadian boarder. When he met Elizabeth he had a lot of convincing to do before he was able to date her, and even then it was under the watchful eye of her oldest brother, Patrick.

Katie always loved listening to them talk about their dating adventures with Uncle Patty tagging along. Somehow, Uncle Patty always managed to get between them by the end of each date to make sure there was no goodnight smooching going on. Her father often joked that the first time he got to kiss Beth was on their wedding day. He said he was so nervous that Patty would dash between them that it was more of a quick peck than a proper kiss.

After they wed, they moved to Florida where he had a good job waiting with the Southeastern Coastline Railroad. It wasn't easy adjusting from a northern climate to a tropical one, but before long they couldn't imagine living anywhere else.

Katie was glad that they lived in Florida because she had a strong dislike for cold weather. Mother often told her stories about some of the harsh winters she endured in Canada and that sealed the thought in her head that the north was not where she wanted to go.

Though Katie remained unusually quiet during breakfast they didn't press her to join in on the conversation. Her father was concerned, but he knew better than to question it. Beth would fill him in when Katie went home, but he had a good idea it had to do with female issues.

He and Beth wanted grandchildren with all of their hearts, even though they never made a fuss about it. It was an unspoken wish that surrounded the three of them and they deeply understood Katie's anxiety about getting pregnant.

Lawrence and Beth had been together for four years before Katie was born, and they had begun to think that they would never be blessed as so many of their friends had been. Birthing Katie was extremely difficult for petite Beth, and after being terrified of almost losing her during Katie's birth, they decided she would remain their only child. They poured all the love they had into their single child and would love and support her through good times and bad for as long as they were living and able.

"Oh Katie, I almost forgot! There was a young lady who called the other day, she said she was a friend of yours from junior high school and wanted your number. I told her I'd take her number and you could give her a call." Her mother got up and went to the kitchen phone, rummaging through a pile of notes. Katie thought about saying that she could have told the woman that she was listed in the phone book, but her mother would have thought that sounded rude.

"Here it is!" Mother said, looking satisfied at finding it in the stack, "Rhonda Johnson. She said you'd know her by her maiden name, Rhonda Carver."

"Wow! I haven't seen Rhonda since junior high. Remember Mom, she was the one who came to the house that one summer and asked me to watch her pet mouse while her family went out of town?"

"Oh yes," Mother said with a disgusted look on her face. "I didn't want that animal in my house, and you promised me it wouldn't get loose."

"It didn't."

"It didn't get out, but if you recall, I was the one who ended up feeding and watering the little rat because you decided going to camp that summer would be fun."

She had forgotten about that. "Sorry, Mom." The apology was ten years over due, but sincere none the less.

"That's all right, Honey. I *almost* learned to like mice that summer."

Katie smiled at her mother. "We were best buddies in school," she said looking at the piece of paper and thinking back as if she could see Rhonda's face. "I can't wait to talk to her." For a moment she thought about using her parent's phone to call her, but this visit was to them, not Rhonda. Looking at the number she realized it was a Fort Pierce exchange. Fantastic, she thought, she must be living in Fort Pierce, too.

Later, as she headed home, she rolled down the windows and let the summer breeze billow through her long hair as she zipped down the highway. Her depression had blown away with the wind. The visit to her parents had lifted the weight of feeling sorry for herself and put things back in their proper perspective. Her problems would work out if it was meant to be and no amount of worry or depression would change it. She stopped off at the grocery store before going home; without being depressed she felt like going out in public again.

When she got home, after putting everything away and starting supper, she sat down by the phone to call Rhonda. It was funny to be nervous about calling someone she had been such good friends with, but that was when they were kids and now they were grown. She wondered what Rhonda would look like now? What would they talk about? The old common interest of rock bands, boys and clothes would be gone. Then she wondered if Rhonda had children. No, she thought to herself, I'm not going to start thinking about that again! With shaky fingers, she dialed the number.

A man answered.

"Hi, is Rhonda there?"

"Yeah, hold on a second."

She heard him muffle the phone and call out to Rhonda. Katie heart began to race with excitement.

"Hello?"

"Hi, Rhonda? It's me, Katie—Katie Danor. Well, it's Katie Davidson now."

There was a pause on the other end of the phone, Rhonda had nearly forgotten about calling Katie's parents. "Katie! How the heck are ya! God, it's been a long time!" She was clearly as happy as Katie was.

"I'm great, but what are you doing back in Florida? The last time I saw you your family was moving to Louisiana."

"Yeah, that's right. I just moved back to Florida three months ago with my husband, Ricky. He got transferred from Tri-Maris in Louisiana to the one here in Bradfield, so here we are."

"That's fabulous! I'd love to get together and see you after all these years. When will you have some free time? Are you working?"

"I'm a secretary over at Silver Craft Boats. How about tomorrow? Are you doing anything?"

"Silver Craft?" Katie repeated, "My husband works at Silver Craft."

"Really?! Maybe I know him. You said your last name was..." She paused for a long moment then finished her sentence slowly, "...Davidson?"

"Yeah, my husband is Alex Davidson. He works in inventory on the first floor. He has curly blond hair and baby blue eyes, and he's nuts. If you've met him, you'd remember him."

Rhonda was quiet for such a long time that Katie thought they had gotten disconnected. "Rhonda, are you still there?"

"Yeah—I'm not sure if I know who he is."

Katie remembered about their plans for Sunday, so she asked Rhonda if next Saturday would be okay.

"No," Rhonda said flatly. "I think we're tied up next weekend. Let me check with my husband and call you back. What's your number?"

Katie gave her the number, but wondered about the change in the tone of the conversation. "I can't wait to see you," she said before they hung-up.

"Yeah, sounds good. See ya."

13

Katie had a dull feeling that Rhonda wasn't as enthusiastic about seeing her anymore. She wondered what she had said that was wrong. She wished she had let Rhonda mention about seeing each other first, but it was too late now.

Rhonda hung up the phone, wishing desperately that she hadn't tried to find Katie. She knew that they would have to meet, Katie would make sure of that, but what would she say when the conversation turned to the subject of Alex. She was starting to get a sick feeling in the pit of her stomach. This was a problem.

Alex came breezing in around 5 p.m., slightly sunburned and ravenously hungry. Katie was in the kitchen just taking a hot pan of lasagna out of the oven.

"Oooo, Lasagna! I'm starving!" he said as he came around and kissed the back of her neck.

"How'd your fishing go? Catch any big ones?" she asked as she pulled him close for a proper kiss.

"Nah, George got a fantastic grouper though, close to a forty pounder."

"Oh he did?" She said with a surprised look, "Well, is he going to have us over for a fish fry?"

Alex laughed, "Get real, Babe! George is so tight, he'll probably cut it into forty one-pound pieces and have it in his freezer for the next two years."

They laughed at the thought of George hoarding his catch. Katie dished out his plate of lasagna and tossed salad and sat down at the table to watch him eat. He had gulped down half his dinner before he noticed she wasn't eating.

"Aren't you hungry, Babe?"

"Are you kidding? I snacked so much while I was making it that I'm stuffed." And she puffed out her cheeks as if to show how stuffed she really was then giggled at herself.

"You're back to your old self again," he said with a smile. "You must have had a really good time at your parents."

"Yeah, I did. It was just what I needed to pull me outta the dumps." She came around and seated herself on his lap.

"Did you decide what we're gonna do tomorrow?"

"Yes. We're going to your folks."

"Great! What's up for Sunday dinner?"

"You just finished stuffing yourself with lasagna and you wanna know what's for dinner?" she responded incredulously.

"I'm praying for pot roast," he said with his hands clasped together, "and maybe banana pudding for dessert." His face had a blissful smile as if he could already taste it.

"Sorry," Katie said as she threw her hands up, "I told your mom not to change her plans for us—we're having liver."

Alex's face contorted into an awful prune shape and he hung his tongue out, "Liver! Please, tell me you're teasing."

"Hey, you've gotta take the good with the bad, Babe," she said as she got up from his lap.

"What do you mean 'the good with the bad'--liver is all bad."

She kissed his forehead and started loading the dishwasher. Alex, still grumbling about liver, headed to the living room to watch television. She was laughing to herself, "How the heck did he guess it right? Oh well, he thinks he's getting liver now."

That night as they lay in bed, comfortable in each other's arms, she wondered what their lives would be like in the next several years. Would they finally have a family started? Would they still be happy and in love? She pulled away from his embrace and propped up to look at his face. "Alex," she said, softly, "I've been thinking today… ."

He smiled as he cut her off, "You know that's a dangerous thing to do."

"No, be serious for a minute," she said, gently slapping his bare chest. "I know I said I wasn't interested before, but maybe we should see about filling out adoption papers."

He looked at her with a surprised expression. She had always said that if they couldn't have a child of their own they would remain childless. He mentioned it to her before, but she said she was afraid she wouldn't be able to give the same love to a child that wasn't her own. He knew she would be a good mother, natural or not, but she was the one that needed to be convinced.

"I've heard," she continued, "that it can take a couple of years to adopt, and we could stop the paperwork if I get pregnant."

"Sweetheart," he said, pulling her close, "I think it's an absolutely wonderful idea." He kissed her soft and inviting lips.

Tears of happiness began to brim up in her eyes, "Oh Alex," she whispered, deep in his embrace, "you're going to be a fabulous

15

daddy." They held each other for a long moment then turned out the light.

The next morning they slept in, comfortable, secure and happy. Alex was the first to stir. He slipped quietly out of bed and went to the kitchen. Mrs. Davidson, he thought, is going to have a pleasant surprise this morning. He whipped up some scrambled eggs, link sausage, toast, and a pot of coffee.

Katie woke to the smell of breakfast. She thought she must be dreaming because Alex would not cook his own breakfast. She tiptoed quietly down the hall and peeked into the kitchen. There was Alex fixing the breakfast tray to take to the bedroom. She went softly back and pretended to be sleeping; it would really burst his bubble if he thought his surprise was ruined.

He came into the bedroom feeling quite smug that he hadn't awakened her with his kitchen clatter. "Sweetheart," he said, "wake-up, I've got breakfast ready."

She stretched and yawned as if she had never been disturbed. "Oh Alex, this is so sweet! Crawl in and let's eat," she said, patting the bed. She had made breakfast in bed for him numerous times, but this was a first for her. After breakfast, he took the tray back to the kitchen and came back and caught her trying to get dressed.

"Oh no you don't," he said, "I'm not letting you get out of this room that easy!"

She smiled. "You mean you want something for cooking me breakfast?"

"Uh huh," he said, pushing her gently onto the bed.

"I knew there had to be strings attached!" she told him. "I don't want sex from you every time I cook you breakfast." Then she gave him a seductive smile.

"Oh, Baby," Alex moaned, "I'll be sure you get it from now on and I'll even catch up for all those mornings I forgot." They both began laughing.

~:~

It was a gorgeous Florida Sunday with plenty of sun and blue skies. The air was fresh and inviting. Katie was secretly wishing Alex would turn the car and head for the ocean, but his parents were expecting them so there was no need to mention it, only wish for it.

His parents had moved to Jupiter a few years earlier so it would be a little bit of a drive, but traffic was light and they made it by one o'clock.

As they walked in the house, Alex exclaimed, "I smell pot roast!"

"Of course you do," his mother smiled. "Didn't you ask Katie what we were having?"

"Oh, you," he said, pointing to Katie, who was beginning to laugh under her expression of innocence. "She said we were having liver!" He sounded like a little boy tattling on his archenemy. His parents joined in on her laughter.

"No, but I could fix you some liver if you want?"

Katie excused herself to the bathroom. Alex's parents were always so great, and she felt fortunate to have good relations with her in-laws. She knew Alex felt the same way about her parents. Often he would remark that he felt more like a son than a son-in-law. He was already fixing his plate when she returned to the kitchen.

"Gee whiz," she said, "so much for conversation! Your mom is going to think I never feed you."

"She doesn't, Mom, really she doesn't," he said, trying to sound serious.

"Oh, you big turkey!" she exclaimed. "Just what did you have for dinner last night, huh?

Still looking at his mother, he said, "I had to go to bed hungry, Mom. In fact, I had to cook *her* breakfast this morning."

Katie smacked him hard on the shoulder, nearly making him drop his plate, "Oh you sorry dog! I feed him darn good!" she said, turning to his mother.

Alex was snickering; it was so easy to get her going.

She knew he was getting her back for the liver business.

His mother spoke up, "Well, Son you certainly don't look like you've been missing any meals."

Katie grinned a triumphant smile as she watched him make a beeline for the dining table.

His parents were in their early fifties. His father was a tool and die man and his mother a cafeteria worker in an elementary school. They didn't make a lot of money, but they were rich in other ways. Humor, for instance, was in abundant supply in their family. No wonder Alex is such a card, she thought, as she filled her plate.

The conversation moved along smoothly, even over questions about their attempts at having a baby. Alex shot a glance to Katie at see if he needed to buffer the question, but he quickly realized her upbeat mood was unscathed. She even spoke up and mentioned that they might go ahead and fill out adoption papers.

His dad looked concerned. "Are you sure you kids want to do that? I mean, you don't know what you might get into, what kind of background the kid might have. Know what I mean?"

"Yeah," he answered his father, "but they give you a lot of information nowadays and you pretty much know everything, except for the natural parents' names."

"I hope it doesn't come down to adoption, but if it does I'm sure you two will make wonderful parents," his mother said with a smile that could warm the most cynical heart.

"Thanks, Mom," he said, squeezing Katie's hand under the table.

His father was still shaking his head. "But would you tell the kid it's adopted or would you just let it think you were the natural parents?" He said it as if he was debating the problem with his own conscience. "What if it wants to search for its natural parents?" he continued.

"I don't know, Dad. We'll just cross that bridge when we come to it." Alex's tone of voice made it clear he didn't want the issue pressed, for Katie's sake. Though she was silent through the conversation, it didn't seem to bother her; it just seemed to bounce off. Nothing could ruin this day.

They finished their meal and went into the living room. His parents were still in the other room when she remembered about Rhonda. "Oh, I almost forgot to tell you what happened yesterday when I went to Mom and Dad's."

"What's that, Babe?"

"One of my old girl friends from junior high called because she's back in town. It's been years since I've seen her. I called her when I got home and found out that she's living in Fort Pierce." Her voice couldn't mask the excitement over finding her long lost friend.

"That's great. Is she anybody I know?"

"Well, you might know her. Her name is Rhonda Johnson and she is working in the office at Silver Craft."

Alex felt a sudden pain hit him hard in the chest. Katie went on about the things she and Rhonda had done when they were kids, but he wasn't hearing what she was saying, he was fighting the nausea that quickly engulfed him.

She stopped talking when she realized he looked ill. "Alex, are you okay?" She gently touched his arm; his face had turned pale. His parents came into the room just as she asked him if he was okay.

His mother knew immediately he looked sick.

"I don't think my dinner is agreeing with me," he said as he got up and headed for the bathroom. By the time he reached it, his dinner was ready to come back up. He splashed water on his face and tried to calm his shaking hands. "How the hell," he whispered, "am I gonna get out of this one? How can I keep those two apart? I've got to talk with Rhonda before Katie does." He rested his head against the sink and prayed silently that she wouldn't find out what an utter fool he had been.

Katie knocked softly at the bathroom door, "Alex, are you okay?"

He opened the door, unable to hide how shaky he felt. "Katie, let's go home," he said weakly.

"Sure, Honey, if you're up to the drive."

His mother came around the corner and felt his head; it was cold and clammy. "Son, what's the matter? Is it your stomach?"

"Yeah, Mom, it must have been something I ate on the boat yesterday." He knew it wasn't, but it would be enough to satisfy his mother and Katie.

"Katie, maybe he should lie down for an hour or so before you head home."

"No, Mom," he said, wanting to sooth her worried expression. "I'll be okay. We're going to head back home." He kissed his mother on the forehead and she gave him a hug. "Sorry Dad that we didn't stay longer."

"That's all right, Son. You go home and let that little lady take care of you. You'll be fine by tomorrow."

His mother wasn't so sure. "If he keeps throwing up or starts running a fever, you might want to take him to the emergency room. If it's food poisoning he'll need a doctor."

"Okay," Katie nodded.

"I don't need to go to the hospital," he rebutted, "I'll be fine in a little while."

Katie drove home with the windows up and the air conditioner on. Alex was silent. When they got home he headed for the bedroom. She followed to see if he needed anything. He stretched out as she searched in the bathroom medicine chest.

"Do you want some Pepto?" she said, holding up the pink bottle.

"No," he replied, "I only need one thing."

"What's that?" she asked, ready to get him whatever he wanted.

"You," he said, and motioned her to the bed. He pulled her into his arms and held her tightly, his mind racing, wondering if he should tell her the secret that would break her heart. He decided he would wait until he talked to Rhonda then he would know if he could trust that his secret would be kept.

He was so quiet for the rest of the afternoon and evening that she was certain he must have been feeling really rotten. She kept trying to offer any remedy she had in the medicine chest, but he turned down each one. She got him to drink some chicken soup before he went to bed, which made her feel better.

He was actually starving, but he had to keep up his façade of illness and he realized it would be hard to look sick when he was stuffing his face.

In the morning she dressed quietly, trying not to disturb him. She decided not to wake him for work since he was so sick the day before—surely he would stay home. But he did wake up; in fact he didn't sleep very much during the night because he was mentally reviewing what he would say to Rhonda in the morning.

"Ah, shit!" he exclaimed as he sprang from the bed. "I'm gonna be late for work! Why the hell didn't you wake me up?"

His words were strong and stung her a little. "I—I thought you'd want to stay home after yesterday," she stammered.

He realized he could have been a little kinder first thing in the morning. "I'm sorry for yelling at you, Babe. I feel fine this morning," he said, trying to smooth over his earlier words. He pulled her to him and kissed her.

The passion that was in his kiss took her by surprise.

"I love you, Katie," he said as he held her close.

She was mystified. "Are you *sure* you're okay?" she asked meekly.

Alex smiled and she knew he was fine.

20

~:~

Rhonda was one of eight secretaries at Silver Craft, but today she was wishing she had never even applied. She now had all the pieces of a puzzle that had troubled her ever since she started there. Office gossip is not for the weak at heart and Silver Craft's office was not immune to such wrenching chatter. She always liked gossip because it was like getting to watch a soap opera at work, but this little soap opera was now involving a long time and special friend—Katie Danor Davidson.

Rhonda became involved only days after she started when she noticed one of the secretaries always had a flower on her desk in the morning. She asked one of the other women who was the Romeo with the flowers. She was told it was a guy down in inventory, a married one.

"But I didn't think Crystal was married," she responded.

"She's not, he is," the woman said with a wink.

Oh boy, Rhonda thought, I've got to get to know Crystal a little better and find out what's going on.

Rhonda and Crystal became friends in short order because Crystal, being young, was eager to have a friend and confidant. And she was more than willing to discuss that handsome and friendly guy down in inventory. One thing led to another and they started having lunch together. She told Rhonda that she started out just wanting to be friends with him, but eventually she ended up with one hell of a crush. It really didn't matter to her that he was married. She wanted to be around him regardless of the consequences.

Rhonda didn't want to be judge and jury; after all he was a good-looking guy and maybe his wife was some hideous woman who deserved to lose him. Surely, she though, he must be contemplating divorce or why else would he be seeing another woman? She was somewhat overlooking the fact that Crystal was a very young, very cute, blue-eyed blond who might have been just a little too eager to have a relationship with someone like Alex Davidson.

~:~

Alex made it to work thirty minutes late and told his supervisor he was having car troubles; another lie. What the hell, he thought,

I'm in neck deep; I might as well keep digging down. He couldn't see Rhonda at the ten o'clock break because Crystal would be coming down to see him. He knew he would have to tell her it was over, but when? Should he tell her at work or would it be easier on her if he met her after work and told her then? His head was swimming, which made concentrating on his work impossible. Swallowing hard, he took a message pad and sent Rhonda a note telling her he needed to see her in the supply room ASAP.

An office runner handed her the message. Her heart began to pound. "What does he want to see me for?" she wondered. She debated throwing the message in the trash and pretending she had never seen it, but she knew she'd have to face him sooner or later. She grabbed up some papers, as if they were important, and told Doris, the senior secretary, that she was running them down to Mr. Menintzer's office. Since his was on the ground floor she knew she wouldn't be expected back immediately.

Doris looked at the stack of papers, then back to Rhonda, almost as if she knew something was amiss. "All right," she said gruffly, "but be sure you're back up here in time for Joyce and Crystal's break."

"No problem," Rhonda replied, hoping that Doris wouldn't see how nervous she was. "I should be back up here in ten or fifteen minutes."

Alex waited, watching the hall doors. "Rhonda! Over here."

She walked over trying to gain her composure and trying to sound as if she didn't have any idea what he might want. "What do you need? I've got to get back upstairs in a few minutes."

He took her by the arm and led her to his office and closed the door behind them.

"Rhonda I have to talk to you about Crystal—and my wife Katie." He watched her reaction as she began to stiffen in her chair. "I know Katie called you Saturday—and—and—damn, I didn't know you were old friends. I've been rehearsing and rehearsing what I could say to convince you not to tell Katie about me and Crystal, and now I don't know what to say. Just please believe me when I say I didn't want this thing to go on like it has with Crystal. I certainly didn't want to hurt Katie; I love her. I know," he said, throwing up his hand in the air as if in defense, "I shouldn't have done what I did if I really loved her, but... ." He left he sentence unfinished and plopped down in his chair, covering his face in his hands.

Oh please, don't start crying, she thought. Is he crying? She couldn't tell and silence fell between them. Finally she broke the quiet, "What about Crystal? You've got to end it, Alex." She felt funny calling him Alex; it seemed too personal in a relationship she wanted to keep at a distance.

He looked up from his hands, his eyes were dry. "I'm going to tell her it's over today."

"You're not going to tell her at work are you?" She said, raising her voice. "She'll be a basket-case all day!"

"I know. I'll tell her after work."

"Alex," she said, "You're going to have to let her down as easy as you can. She's crazy about you. You know that don't you?"

He nodded. "I've made a hell of a mess out of things. I can't lose Katie—please, Rhonda... ." Again he left his sentence unfinished, but he couldn't have said more if he wanted to because he was in an emotional wringer that was just about to break.

"Look, Alex," she said as she stood up from her chair, "I've got to get back upstairs and... ."

He caught her as she reached for the door.

"Please, Rhonda," he begged.

"Okay, but just be sure you break it off *today* with Crystal. And Alex," she paused, "don't do this to Katie again." Her words were firm and scolding.

"Believe me, I won't. I can't go through this again." There was a definite sound of relief in his voice. He called out as she began walking away, "Rhonda."

She turned and faced him.

"Thanks. You're saving a drowning man."

She said nothing; she just turned and walked away, feeling like Benedict Arnold, twice over. Damn! No wonder he has women troubles, she thought. He is charming in a demented way.

Doris was drumming her fingers as Rhonda came through the door after being gone twenty-five minutes. "Sorry," Rhonda offered.

Crystal came down to see him on her ten o'clock break, happy and bubbly as usual. He made an excuse about getting to work late and having to work through his break. At least he wasn't lying about that. She was disappointed but, looking around the inventory racks to make sure no one else was around, she grabbed his belt loops and pulled his body against hers. She kissed him hard and erotically, biting his lip when he didn't reciprocate immediately. He'd always had a hard time controlling his desire for women, and Crystal was so willing and wanting. He pulled her closer, and returned the hard kiss letting his hands slip from her waist to her buttocks and pinching her roughly.

"Ouch!" she said, but then she smiled.

"Can you meet me after work at the Sweet Harmony?" He asked, his breaths were short and quick.

"Yes," she whispered then she returned the pinch and walked away slowly, with a little sway to her hips.

Suddenly the inventory room seemed too hot, even though the air was blowing full blast. "How am I going to tell her it's over?" he questioned himself. "I can't even tell her I'm busy without screwing it up!"

He walked back to his little office. His palms were beginning to sweat as he dialed Katie's work number. The phone suddenly seemed slippery.

"Hello, ATI, may I help you?

"Hi, Babe, how's it going?"

"Fine Mr. Davidson, but the question is how are you doing?"

He wanted to say not worth a damn, but he didn't. "I'm doing great. Hey listen, I've got to finish cataloging in some new parts that came in today. It's a pretty big order so I'm gonna be a little late getting home." Another lie. "Is that okay with you?"

"No, it is not!" she said.

His heart jumped a beat.

"But if you have to I suppose I can forgive you."

"Thanks, Babe, see you tonight." And he hung up the phone.

~:~

At five exactly, Crystal was heading out the office doors for the Sweet Harmony lounge. She had been thinking about him all weekend and knowing she would be with him made her body sizzle with excitement. She told Rhonda several weeks earlier that she wasn't positive if she was in love or in heat because thoughts of him made her crazy. She spent many nights fantasizing about never having to let him go. Once she decided she couldn't stand it and dialed his home number. This was an absolute no-no according to Alex, but she just wanted to hear his voice and then hang up. But it wasn't Alex who answered the phone; it was Katie.

"Hello?" Katie said.

Crystal paused, wondering if she should hang up or blurt out that Katie should divorce her husband because he was having an affair. She knew if she did Alex would never forgive her, and perhaps she would never see him again.

"Hello? Anybody there?" Katie was almost ready to hang-up when she asked if Chris was there.

"Chris?" Katie repeated, "I think you've got the wrong number. What number were you dialing?"

Crystal repeated the number, one digit off, told Katie she was sorry and hung up. She was intensely curious about Katie; Alex never said anything bad about her. He never poured out his problems about his marriage like she hoped he would. Surely, she thought, he is unhappy with his wife. Surely they don't get along very well. Why else would he be seeing me?

Alex came into the lounge looking for Crystal, yet dreading what he had to say when he found her. He saw her sitting in a booth in the back corner. She hadn't seen him come in; she was lost in thoughts about him. He stood by the door for a while, looking at her profile. She was only about five foot five with a petite almost tomboyish figure but, then again, she had only just begun to bloom into womanhood. Her hair was so blond it almost seemed white and her skin was tan and taunt. As he looked at her he called himself a fool for ever thinking he could balance the woman he loved and a girl who now loved him.

Truly, he had convinced himself at the start of his flirtatious relationship with her that it would not go further, and that it wouldn't interfere with his marriage. He and Crystal started out just having some fun together, but things quickly progressed from *fun* to serious. She was very willing and he was very weak. He wanted to blame it on those damned hormones the doctor put him on because ever since he started taking them he was checking out *every* woman within ten feet. But no matter what he was taking, the choice was still his to make; and he made the wrong one.

Crystal didn't need hormones to make her want him. She liked to flirt too. She always taunted him with her sexy glances and occasional peeks at her breasts when she would bend over in front of him at work. It was a fire that consumed him and now threatened to burn to cinders the life he made with Katie. He didn't realize at the start just how vulnerable she was to his friendly advances, forgetting how easy it was for him to get turned on as a teenager. Crystal had only been at Silver Craft for a year. Right out of high school, she was only eighteen—Alex was twenty-six.

By this time she spotted him and was motioning him to the table. His walk felt mechanical and stiff; he knew this was going to be hard. She slid into the booth to make room for him, but instead he sat opposite of her.

She smiled, not quite sure why he didn't sit beside her. She reached under the table for his leg, but he pulled away from her touch. There was a roaring that was starting in her ears, her heart leaping as she realized he was getting ready to end their relationship.

"Crystal," he began, "I—we can't see each other anymore."

The cool barroom suddenly seemed very hot. She could feel the heat building over her body. "Alex, what's wrong? What did I do to… ."

He raised his hand to stop her from going further. "You didn't do anything wrong, I did. I never should have let our relationship get started. God, what an idiot I've been!" He was looking down shaking his head.

Her eyes were beginning to swim in a sea of tears, "Please, don't do this, Alex. Why now? What's different?"

He started explaining to her that Katie told him Sunday about her old friend who was living in Fort Pierce and working at Silver Craft—Rhonda Johnson.

She was instantly furious that Rhonda might have only become friends with her so she could inform Katie about the two of them. But he explained that Rhonda didn't know who he was or whom Katie had married after they parted so many years ago. Rhonda was simply caught in the middle, a very bad position. He told her what he had asked Rhonda earlier that day about not telling Katie about their relationship.

"Good," she said, matter-of-factly. "Then she can keep her mouth shut and we can keep seeing each other!"

"No, Crystal." His gaze was firmly fixed on her. "I can't keep seeing you. This was too close for me. I know you don't understand, but I really do love my wife."

Her eyes were searching his face for something to tell her he was lying, but he wasn't. "Then why did we… ." her voice trailed off.

"I don't know why," he answered, swallowing hard. "I don't know why. I wasn't thinking with my head. I didn't mean to hurt you and I do care about you."

She looked away.

"Crystal," he said, gently reaching for her chin and turning her face toward him. "I *do* care about you." There was only silence, the sounds of the bar fading out in the background. "Please help me end this as friends. If you care about me then try to understand how hard this is. Please help me end this without," he paused, "without hurting each other."

She knew what he meant. He didn't want her to run to his wife and tell her what happened between them.

"I'll let you go today and never again mention what happened between us, if…"

He looked at her, frightened at the words she might say.

"…you give me tonight," she finished. She reached out and took his hand.

"No, Crystal." But his resolve sounded weak.

"Alex, I want one more time in your arms and then I promise I'll never, never come to you again as a lover."

The motel next to the lounge always had a vacancy. Crystal and Alex had been there several times. He paid for the room with shaking hands, signing the register as Joe and Julie Brown.

The man behind the counter had seen enough Joe's come through before to know a cheating husband when he saw one. He smiled a filthy grin. "Have a nice night," he snickered.

Alex wanted to grab him from behind the counter and put his head through the window, but instead he took the key and walked away.

Crystal waited in her car and he motioned to her which room. Her body was aching and hot, passion and desire filling every fiber inside her. This would be her last opportunity to convince him that he really didn't want to end what they had together.

Usually when they were together they would rush to undress and slip into bed. But she didn't want to be rushed, not if this was to be the last time. He was unbuttoning his shirt when she came to him and began removing his garments, one by one, until she alone was dressed. She kissed and caressed his body, sending his mind far away from anything other than the moment. She had never been so carefully focused on his pleasure instead of her own.

And it felt too much like lovemaking instead of what he told himself that it had been all along: sex.

"Take off my clothes," she whispered.

He obeyed with slow and passionate deliberation. "Oh Crystal," he moaned as she seated herself on him. "I'm sorry…."

"No, not now. Don't be sorry; just be mine tonight." Carefully she lowered her body to his, connecting them with a bond of pleasure. They moved as one, felt as one, and no desire at that moment was stronger than to be one. Her body was coursing with the pleasure of him, calling him and whispering what was forbidden. They had never said 'I love you' when they were together, but this was sweet, tender love and wouldn't be denied those words.

Holding her close to his body, he rolled her on to the bed, and assumed command of the moment. They cried out together, losing themselves in each other as their bodies peaked.

Lying still in each other's arms she whispered, "Please Alex, please don't end what we have together."

He lifted himself up and wiped the tear that trickled down her temple. "You promised me this would be the last time," he said, emotion rising up inside him. "I wish it didn't have to end, but it does." He rose from the bed and looked at her, wishing there was something else he could tell her to stop the hurt. He felt more for her than he was willing to reveal, yet he pondered how a man could be honestly in love with two women.

He had to leave; the moment she asked of him was past, just as their relationship was also past. He left the key on the table. He dressed and looked back at her, but she had turned away. Stepping outside, the door automatically locked, closing a door between them that he wouldn't open again. He walked past her car and headed back to the lounge to get his truck and head home.

He pulled into the drive at seven o'clock. He was guilt-ridden about the encounter with Crystal, but he kept thinking, it's over, it's finally over. He was making a pact with himself that he would never again jeopardize his marriage over sexual urges that, at times, seemed greater than his own will. He would build his relationship with Katie from this point on with honesty and love. He walked in the door and headed straight for the shower before she smelled the smoke from the lounge or Crystal's intoxicating perfume.

Katie was in the bedroom putting away laundry when he walked in. "Hey," she said in a warm and friendly way. "You finally made it home."

"Yeah and boy am I beat." He closed the bathroom door and quickly striped and climbed into the shower. Water is an amazing thing. Something as simple as having it rush over your body can make you feel like it's taking away all of your problems, all your sins. Alex was experiencing that feeling as he washed his encounter with Crystal down the drain.

The next few days at Silver Craft were strained. Alex was trying to avoid Crystal. He caught a glance of her in the parking lot and noticed the bags under her eyes from crying. Her skin had a pale yellow tint to its usually tanned complexion, revealing the lack of sleep. She started to come to him and speak, but he turned and walked away.

Her initial reaction to Rhonda was one of anger, not so much directly at her, but at the situation that occurred because of her. But the anger faded because she really needed a friend's shoulder to cry on, and someone to share her feelings with. She didn't have anyone at home to talk to about the pain inside her. Her mother had been divorced twice and was a bitter cynic when it came to men.

At first she thought she could understand why her mom was so bitter; look at what Alex had done to her in the short time they were together. But, she realized that she had gone into this relationship with her eyes wide open; it wasn't entirely his fault and her mother just wouldn't understand that part.

Rhonda proved to be a very sympathetic ear, understanding Crystal's pain and still wanting very much to be her friend. Though short in time, their friendship was much like she and Katie's had been so many years ago.

Katie still wanted to see Rhonda and had called her again to see if she had some free time to meet. Rhonda was feeling a little more at ease since Alex was no longer seeing Crystal, so she agreed to meet her for a drink at a local restaurant on Tuesday night.

"Do you think your husband might like to come with us?" Katie asked her, hoping she would say yes so Alex could come with her.

"No, that's his bowling night so he'll be out with the guys."

Katie felt a twinge of guilt at leaving Alex at home, but she made up her mind that she and Rhonda would have a better time without him tagging along.

"Is your husband coming?" Rhonda asked, cringing at the thought that she might say yes.

"No, he wouldn't like going out with two women," Katie stated.

Rhonda wanted to laugh and say that two women were more his style, but she held her tongue and her laughter.

Alex was relieved when she told him he didn't need to go. He really didn't want to have Rhonda looking at him the whole night, knowing the truth about him and then having to pretend to be the perfect husband, as Katie would say he was. Then again, he wished he could be there to make sure she didn't decide to tell Katie the truth. He had to trust she would keep her word, but it was very hard knowing she could destroy his marriage in a matter of minutes. He would pace the floor until she came home, and only then would he know for sure if he was safe.

When Tuesday night arrived, Katie dressed and left without him saying much at all, except not to be out late. She was mistaking him being quiet for being upset at not getting to go, but in reality his nerves were making him sick inside.

The women met in the parking lot of Flannigan's restaurant and lounge, recognizing each other immediately. Katie wondered how different Rhonda would look, but she was the same brown haired, green-eyed friend she had parted from so many years ago. The only difference, besides aging, was that Rhonda was heavier than she'd been in school, but everyone is heavier after eighth grade.

Rhonda on the other hand was surprised at the changes in Katie. Her figure certainly had filled out since junior high. She used to complain to Rhonda that she thought she would stay flat-chested forever, but Katie was a late bloomer. But did she ever bloom, Rhonda thought, looking at her c-cup chest and her curved hips. Alex had to be an idiot to have cheated on her, Rhonda said to herself.

They slipped easily into the old groove of friendship, and the conversation flowed. They picked up from the last time they saw each other to their present day lives and before they knew it, it was two in the morning and the bar was closing.

"Oh, gosh!" Katie said, looking down at her watch, "Alex asked me not to stay out too late and here it's two a.m. He'll be worried sick."

"Yeah, I've got to get home, too. I don't think Ricky will be waiting up for me or anything like that, but tomorrow is a work day," she laughed.

"Now that you're back in town," Katie said with a serious face, "we've got to get Alex and Ricky introduced. I know they'll become friends."

"Yeah, sure that sounds good." She looked away then looked back to her old friend, "Katie are you and Alex happy together?"

She was surprised at the concern in her friend's voice. She must have problems with her husband, Katie thought. "I couldn't be happier. We have a fabulous relationship and best of all he isn't just my husband, but he's my best friend, too." There was something in Rhonda's expression that disturbed her, though she didn't know what it was. "Why?"

Rhonda's mind started racing. I should tell her, she thought. She should know what he's been doing behind her back. She's my friend and... .

"Rhonda?" Katie spoke up; realizing something was troubling her.

"I just wondered," she said dropping her hands and walking away toward her car with an expression that seemed to say 'it was a dumb question.' They said goodbye and then headed for home.

Alex was sure Katie would see the worn spot in the carpet where he had nervously paced up and down for the last six and a half hours. As her car pulled into the driveway he wondered if he should make a dash for the bedroom and pretend to be sleeping or face her when she came in and beg her to forgive him. He decided to stay and find out the verdict.

She was surprised to see him standing in the middle of the living room when she opened the door. "Have you been up this whole time?" she asked in a very surprised, but apologetic voice.

"No, I…" he started to lie, but then he remembered the pact with himself. "Well actually, yeah I have been. I was worried about you being out so late."

She felt the flood of love rush over her. He can be so sweet, she thought. "Come on you big nut, let's go to bed."

He was happy to oblige her. Thank you, Rhonda! Were the last words on his mind as Katie turned out the light.

~:~

Weeks passed and everything seemed to be going so well in their lives that Katie wondered if it could get any better. They had gone to an adoption agency in West Palm Beach, since there wasn't one locally, and filled out the papers to put them on the adoption list. It was a very complicated process and would cost them considerable money when their name reached the top of the adoption list. They had to disclose everything about themselves, whole histories on both their families, questions about their moral values, their income, present health, etc. The list seemed to go on forever as to what was needed. But it didn't matter to either of them because they had just taken the first step in getting a child. They couldn't be happier.

Alex spent less time at work dodging Crystal simply because she was staying put in her area of the building. He was relieved when Rhonda stopped him one day in the break room and told him that Crystal was doing great; she seemed to be coming off the emotional roller coaster of ending a relationship.

He never wanted to hurt her, foolish as it was to begin a relationship with her in the first place, but the thought of causing her pain felt like a knife to his heart. She was getting back to being her old self, which helped him remove the knife that caused him discomfort. The mistakes he made that threatened to make a disaster out of his life were being neatly erased, and his life was getting back in proper order.

The only problem was that, just like the calm eye of the hurricane, the second side of the storm was getting ready to hit and send this delicate illusion shattering to the four winds.

~:~

Katie was leaving work early this Monday afternoon to go to the doctor's office for a check-up. It had been six weeks since her infection and the doctor wanted to give her a thorough exam before she and Alex resumed their attempts to conceive. It had been a great weekend. They had gone to her parent's house that Saturday and then spent Sunday walking along Daytona Beach, exploring the shops and lounging on the sand. It was wonderful how much time he had been spending with her instead of 'the guys' from work, but it also perplexed her. What triggered it? She didn't know for sure, but she suspected the visit to the adoption agency may have been the catalyst. She felt he was maturing into a family man for the time when they would be sharing their lives with a child.

On that same Monday, Crystal came into work desperately ill. She told Rhonda she had been nauseous and weak all weekend and all she did was sleep. She came to work because she didn't want to tell her mother she was sick. Rhonda had to ask because the symptoms were too plain.

"Crystal, did you get your period this month?" Her eyes were locked on her. "Did you?" She was hoping and praying she was wrong.

Crystal's knees gave out and she collapsed into her chair. Propping her head up with an unsteady hand, she wouldn't return Rhonda's gaze. "Help me get to the bathroom and we'll talk in there."

Rhonda guided her to the ladies' room and locked the door behind them as Crystal headed for a stall. When she came out of the stall her eyes were watery and her make-up askew.

"Do you think you're pregnant?" Rhonda asked. There was no reason to soften the question; she had to know.

Crystal began to cry.

"Damn it, Crystal! Did you use any protection at all when you were sleeping with him?"

"Not every time," she sobbed. "There were a couple times we didn't."

By this point Rhonda was near an angry rage. "Why the hell not? Girl, what were you thinking? Didn't you realize it might only take one time to get you knocked up?"

Her eyes flashed anger; Rhonda's words sounded like accusations. "Well, I wasn't trying to corner Alex into making a decision between me or his wife, if that's what you're implying! I didn't intend to get... ." she couldn't finish her sentence.

"I'm sorry," Rhonda said as she slipped her arm around her friend. "Hey, we don't know for sure. This could be the damned flu virus or something. When did you have your last period?"

She was shaking her head, still sobbing, "I don't know. I lost track of things when—when Alex and I quit seeing each other. Oh, Rhonda, if I'm pregnant what will he think? What will he do?"

"Let's not worry about Mr. Overly-Active-Hormone right now. Screw him!" Her choice of words was entirely wrong, but they slipped out before she realized how inappropriate they would sound.

"I did, remember? That's how this happened."

They both laughed weakly.

Rhonda thanked God that the moment had lightened. At least, she thought, she still has her sense of humor.

"Do you have a gynecologist?"

She shook her head no.

"Well, we'll just use mine. I'll call and see if they can get you in today."

"But what about work? Doris won't like both of us leaving early?"

"I don't want you to go alone," Rhonda said, leaving no room to discuss the matter. "Screw Doris!"

"No thanks," Crystal replied, as she mopped up her face. They broke into laughter again.

Back at their desks, Rhonda called and made an appointment for a pregnancy test for Crystal. The nurse could administer the test, so they could squeeze her in that afternoon. Rhonda's doctor was Marvin C. Hampton.

~:~

Katie pulled into the medical complex and parked down on the far end to get under a shady oak tree, then headed for her doctor's office. She walked into the expansive lobby that was the central hub for four physicians and signed in at the patient register, saying hello to the office staff as she did. She turned and headed for a chair when she noticed Rhonda. She was going to say 'hello,' but Rhonda seemed absorbed in helping the young girl beside her with patient forms. She wanted to talk with her about when they could get together and introduce Alex and Ricky, but it would be rude to intrude on their conversation. She took a seat on the same row, near Margaret's workstation, but a large potted ficus blocked her view of them as she settled back in the seat with a magazine.

Rhonda did not see Katie enter the office. She was filling out the forms for Crystal whose hands were shaking too badly to write. Margaret stepped into the waiting room and called Crystal's name; Rhonda went with her. Margaret's little workstation was an open area just in from the lobby where she took blood pressure, checked urine specimens, weight and other vital statistics. This was the same place where Katie sat and waited for her pregnancy test results only weeks ago and now she was sitting only a half a dozen chairs away from it. She had never been one to eavesdrop, but most of the conversation could be plainly heard from where she sat. It seemed the young girl who was with Rhonda was taking a pregnancy test, and from the sound of her voice she was upset.

Katie thought how strange it was to hear someone upset at the possibility of being pregnant when she had been just as disturbed about not being pregnant. Then again, from the quick glance at the blond-haired girl, she didn't appear to be very old; maybe she wasn't even married. She heard Margaret say the word 'positive,' and a little cry escaped the room, then stifled tears and low voices asking what she was going to do. The voice was recognizably Rhonda's. Evidently Rhonda was comforting the girl, but there was something else in the conversation that caught Katie's attention. Rhonda was speaking low about telling the man who was the father. It was bits and pieces, but it was enough to send Katie into shock,

"...do you want...to work and tell Alex...he's...have to know...if he didn't want his marriage...shouldn't have cheated...he'll have to tell Katie now."

Suddenly she felt as if her body froze. She didn't move, not even an eyelash. She felt like a statue that fate had placed in an awkward position but with a human heart racing beneath a bronze breast. Had she been someone else in the room she would have seen a woman gone pale. Terror and disbelief were painted across her face, and her mouth was slightly agape as if ready to scream. This couldn't be her Alex; no, it had to be someone else. Her Alex was kind and loving, truthful and charming. He loved her; he would never do this to her, would he?

As Rhonda and Crystal walked into the lobby, Margaret told Crystal to take some time and decide what she wanted to do. She told her to think about what would be best for her and the baby and not to make any decisions that she might regret. She wanted her to set an appointment for next week to come see Doctor Hampton with her decision.

Katie realized she couldn't face them, but they would see her when they left. She wanted to run, run long and hard and chase the thoughts out of her mind that were dissolving her love for her wonderful husband into a puddle of molten distrust and anger. She rose and turned her back on them so quickly that she lost her balance, but caught herself before falling and dashed for the door. Bursting out of the office she ran all the way to her car, fumbling with the door lock as if some hideous monster pursued her. She didn't recall starting the car or putting it in reverse, but she knew her foot was to the floor as her little Fiesta screamed out of the parking lot.

Rhonda was taken by surprise as a woman jumped up, almost in front of her, and raced toward the door. For only a millisecond she wondered, but as the blur of a running woman passed the office window she knew it was Katie. Margaret and Crystal had no idea what was going on.

Margaret recognized Katie, but was mystified as to what happened. She paid no attention to the conversation between Rhonda and Crystal, so it didn't enter her mind that these three women were somehow connected. The only thing she knew was that Katie looked terrified, and this concerned Margaret deeply.

They looked at each other briefly, Crystal knowing nothing, Margaret knowing little and Rhonda knowing it all. She couldn't say anything to them; Margaret didn't need to know, and Crystal was already upset enough for one day. They walked to the desk and set the appointment for next week and walked out. No words were spoken between them on the way back to Silver Craft. Crystal would have thought it odd if she hadn't been so deeply enmeshed in her own world of troubles.

As they pulled into the parking lot to get Crystal's car, Crystal looked to Rhonda and said she was going inside to see Alex. Rhonda had enough turmoil for one day, but she knew she had to see him, too.

"There's something you should know before you go in to see him. I didn't want to tell you this but... ."

"What? What is it?" There was concern in her voice as she looked at the expression of anguish on her friend's face.

"The woman that ran out of the doctor's office—she was—I'm pretty sure she was Katie, Alex's wife."

She was obviously stunned; her eyes went wide.

"I don't have any idea how much she heard from our conversation, but from the way she left, it must have been enough."

There was still no response from Crystal and she looked almost comatose.

"How could I have not seen her in that room? When did she get there?" Rhonda was shaking her head at the questions. "Damn it all! What a nightmare this is." She stopped her words, afraid Crystal would think she was placing blame again. "Come on, let's get this over with."

They walked into the inventory area, getting a few wolf whistles as they passed some of the production men. Alex was busy calculating additional fiberglass mat necessary for next month's demand when Rhonda and Crystal walked into his office and shut the door. His office was small and confining, but with the three of them staring at each other it shrank to the point of making a person claustrophobic.

Crystal spoke first, crying softly, "Alex, there's something I've got to say and you won't like it. I'm going to have—I'm preg... ."

He knew what was coming and before she could finish her words, anger ignited in him like a torch. "You're pregnant, right? Am I right?" His voice was hostile and angry.

He didn't sound anything like the Alex she once knew.

His hands were clenched as his fury built. He wasn't going to let her ruin his life. "And I'm supposed to believe you, and believe that it's mine?"

Crystal felt herself cringing, trying to shrink away from his bitter spew of venom.

"Stop it, you son-of-a-bitch!" Rhonda sprang up from her chair as if she was ready to attack him, her fists landing hard on his desk. "She didn't plan this to trap you! I've spent my afternoon with her at the doctor's office and the entire time she worried about *YOU!* What would *you* think. What would this do to *you*! Well, damn *you*! You certainly got what you deserved! She's only eighteen years old! Now at eighteen I can recall making some foolish mistakes too, but I'll be damned if I'm going to stand here and listen to you tell her this is all her fault! You messed up your life with Katie on your own, and you did a hell of a good job too, so don't stand here and blame her for something for which you are equally at fault!" She was breathless as the final words came out of her mouth.

Alex and Crystal both were taken aback at the force and truth of what she said.

Rhonda Johnson didn't ask to be put in the middle of this, but she wasn't going to step back and let him run Crystal into the dirt. She had never been this outspoken in her life, but it was time for it.

He knew she was right. In his heart he didn't believe that Crystal was trying to get back at him. They hadn't always been careful when they made love. Passion and desire made them drunk and unwise. They simply didn't think; they acted on feelings that were strong and compelling.

"Crystal, I'm sorry. I'll help pay for whatever you need to get an... ." His words faded as the thought struck him: she might not want an abortion. "You're not thinking about having this baby are you?"

"I don't know. I haven't decided what I'll do yet."

Anger was starting to flicker again in his eyes. "You can't keep this baby."

"Alex," Rhonda interrupted, "there's more you need to know."

"What?" What else, he wondered, could possibly matter at this point? He really didn't think he would care.

"Katie knows."

Her words were like a bomb going off in his brain, exploding all remnants of the illusion that he could have escaped this affair without consequence, leaving only stark- naked reality. It isn't macho for a man to cry, at least that's what he'd heard his whole life, but now it didn't matter and the tears slid down his face. "You told her?" There was no anger in his words, only despair.

"No. She must have had a doctor's appointment today and," she paused, "apparently we have the same one."

"Doctor Hampton," he stated as she nodded her head.

"Yeah. We were getting the test and she was sitting close to where we were. We didn't see her, but the way she ran out of there she must have heard everything we said."

He began to sob, covering his face with his hands.

Crystal wanted so badly to hold him and ease his pain, but she was frightened that he would reject her, again. She felt Rhonda touch her arm softly and guided her to the door. There was nothing more any of them could say; it was time to go home.

Rhonda questioned her in the parking lot about talking to her mother, but Crystal said she didn't want to tell her mother anything until she had a chance to decide. Her mother would say there was no choice; abortion would be her only solution. She had to make that decision for herself; it wasn't her mother's life.

He wasn't sure how long he sat in his office after they left him, but he finally picked up his courage and headed home. He pulled in the yard and wondered how he could mend what he had done. What could he say to convince Katie not to hate him? He had no prepared speech. The only thing he could offer would be the truth, and it would be like gall in his mouth, bitter and sickening.

~:~

Katie had driven straight home with her heart pounding and her mind reeling. She went over and over the conversation in her mind. Was she crazy? She knew she was acting crazy, running out of the doctor's office like a lunatic and driving—well, she didn't even remember that. There weren't any dents or dings in the car so she assumed she hadn't run anybody down. What was wrong with her? She knew Alex better than that. But who else could they have been talking about? If Alex had been involved with someone at work, Rhonda would have told her—unless Alex swore her to secrecy. Why would he do this to her? He said he loved her just this morning. He couldn't love her and be sleeping with someone else. Her thoughts were blurring and blending like someone had turned on a mixer in her head. She would just have to confront him when he came home. If she was wrong, he would think she'd lost her mind. If she was right—God, she thought, please let me be wrong.

When he walked in she was standing only a few feet from the door and he could see she'd been crying.

She also realized Alex had been crying, his eyes were red and puffy. She knew, in that moment, it was true. "Alex, who is Crystal?" Her words asking the question that her heart didn't want to know.

"Babe, I'm sorry, I... ."

"Who is she Alex? A girl from work?"

He nodded and was wrenched with tears again.

She also had begun to let them run like a river down her face. "Why? How could you?"

He wanted to hold her for the rest of his life and tell her that he was sorry. And, if he had been able to read her mind, he would have known there was nothing she wanted more than to be safe in his arms and for this day to simply disappear.

He reached out to her, calling her name, but she knew she couldn't go to him. She couldn't look at him knowing he betrayed her. She ran to the bedroom and slammed the door.

He heard the door lock and her sobbing beyond it. He couldn't go to her now because she wouldn't let him. He sat on the sofa and let all the emotions come out that had been torturing him for over a month. Holding a pillow over his face, he let his cries overtake him.

Within an hour he heard her open the bedroom door. He was ready to talk with honesty, ready to try to piece their marriage together. But when she emerged into the hallway she carried her suitcase.

"Katie, no! Please you have to give me a chance. We have to talk this out." He tried to block her from the door.

"Alex, I'm not ready to talk. I need some time to think, time to sort out the way I feel." She shoved him hard to the side and opened the door.

He grabbed her by the arm, firmly but gently, "Katie, don't do this to us, please."

"I didn't Alex, you did. Good-bye." She walked out into the early Florida evening. Thunder was rumbling as lightening struck in the distance. It would be a stormy night.

She pulled out of the drive and wondered where she would go. She didn't want to go to her parent's because she would have to tell them why she was there, and she wasn't ready for that. She headed for a small and cozy motel in Fort Pierce. It was raining when she arrived. She ran in the deluge from her car to the motel office, getting soaking wet in the process. The woman behind the desk eyed her suspiciously as she signed the register. Once in her room, she stripped off her wet clothes and slipped into a hot bath. Weeping softly she tried to forget the look on Alex's face as she walked out the door.

Why? It was all she could ask herself. Was it her fault he went to another woman? She slipped into bed, tired of crying and tired of wondering how this could have happened. Her body ached to be held, soothed and caressed, but there was no one in the dark to comfort her.

Alex lay on the bed he'd shared with her just one night ago, hating himself for all the hurt he was putting her through. He imagined she was at her parents, and by now they would know what he had done to their 'little girl.' She was so much like a little girl, trusting, caring and easily wounded by his teasing. But he had never hurt her the way he did tonight. He couldn't let her go. He wouldn't let her go. He would find a way to make her forgive him.

Then thoughts of Crystal flooded his mind. She was carrying his child. He wanted a child, but this was not how he planned it; the wrong woman conceived. She would have to have an abortion because Katie would never come back to him if he had to give up a child to keep her. She would tell him it was over, not for her own sake, but for the sake of a child that wasn't even hers. From his viewpoint, Crystal couldn't make any other decision; she couldn't make it on her own and Alex would not leave his wife.

He tried to sleep, but images of Katie's delicate face haunted him: her hair like dark spun copper-silk, her beautiful body full of graceful curves and tender secrets. Her eyes, even now, were piercing his heart with their anguished look, green-gold pools of broken trust and dreams. "Katie, oh Babe, I'm so sorry."

Katie was only sixteen when he met her and he had been her first and only lover. Memories flooded his mind of the first time he took her. She was so scared, crying and begging him to pledge himself to her. She wanted to know he would stay true to her and love her always before she committed herself to his control. The pain was tearing at his heart as he remembered telling her there would never be another. Twice he had stepped outside that promise. Both times he had gone to parties without her because she didn't care for the party life. Drunk and stupid, he had made unwise choices. They hadn't meant anything to him, but they would have hurt her so badly if she had known. But Crystal was different. He was sober and able to make the right choice, but he chose the wrong many times; that was a crucial difference.

When the sunrise came to the Atlantic coast, it spread purple, orange and blue streaks dancing into a cloudless sky. The storm had cleared overnight and left a fresh canvas to paint. It had always taken Katie's breath away to watch the sun rise and set in the paradise where she lived. Even as a little girl, she would get up early just to watch the Master's hand at work. Too many people take such beauty for granted, but not her; she admired it and relished it. Alex told her once that she was too much of a romantic. He'd said that was why she was drawn to the sunrise, cried at love stories and liked to pick wildflowers on the side of the road. But not this morning; even beauty so gripping and vivid couldn't help her overcome the pain in her heart. She knew her life with him, the only life she knew, was going to end, and no amount of sunrises could bring back the image of the man she had trusted with her love.

In the night, she made her decisions. She couldn't stay with him anymore. The illusion that was their life was over. Her trust in him could never be restored. But it was more than that; this girl was carrying the one thing she might never be able to give him: a child. She would move back to her parents' house and commute to work until she could find another job or an apartment that she could afford on her own.

She went to work trying to act normal, but it wasn't hard for her friends to tell that there was something really wrong with her. She confided in her two closest companions at work and they told her to tell Alex to hit the road and keep the house. The house didn't mean that much to her, but Alex did. When the initial shock faded, she made a call to him and said she wanted to meet Saturday morning at the house to tell him what her decisions were.

He was stunned. "Before you go making decisions, we have to talk out our problems. Please give me a chance."

"I'll see you Saturday," she said then hung up before he said more.

She knew he would plead and ask for forgiveness and, even though forgiving was what she wanted with all her heart, she couldn't change the decisions she'd made. She went to see her parents' Wednesday night and told them what had happened. They were visibly staggered by her news, and yet they felt she should consider giving him another chance.

"There's never been a soul alive that didn't make mistakes. Everyone deserves a chance to correct the wrong they've done. Give him that chance, Honey," her mother pleaded.

"I don't know how I can explain to you," Katie began as she and her parents huddled around the kitchen table, all of them on the verge of tears. "I have given Alex complete and unwavering trust since I was sixteen years old. Never once did I even think he would betray that trust. I just don't know how to put things back together without it."

Her father put his arm around her and kissed her head, wishing he could somehow shelter her from this pain. The decisions she had to make were wrenching his heart and he couldn't tell her if they were right or wrong because he didn't know. "Kat, your mother and I will stand by you no matter what happens to your marriage. You can live here at home for as long as you want or need. We love you, Honey." His words were choked and he had to get up, quickly wiping his eyes and saying something got caught in his throat; he needed some water.

"Thanks, Daddy." She started to cry and so did her mother as she excused herself and went to her old bedroom.

Her room hadn't changed in the years she had been gone. The memories were like a giant feather pillow cushioning her fall from Alex. If I only had the chance to redo everything, she thought. I should have gone to college like Mom and Dad wanted. Alex could have finished sewing his wild oats and maybe we would be at a different point in our lives. She had to force herself back to the present and think about what she was going to say to him on Saturday. The thought of leaving him forever sent a chill down her spine. Her heart was screaming 'No,' but her mind was telling her there was no other way.

As she slept that night, Alex filled her dreams. He was so close, but he wouldn't touch her. She begged him to hold her. He told her this was all her fault; she wasn't a good enough wife and that drove him to Crystal. It was her fault, all of it. In her dreams she begged him for another chance, begged him to hold her and to love her as he always had, but he turned away and faded into the mist. She woke at four in the morning, drenched in tears and sobbing uncontrollably. Her body trembled with the need to feel him beside her in the bed. For an instant, she was ready to get in her car and drive home, her home, Alex's home, ready to say she forgave him and beg him to hold her, but the moment faded and she lay back down and returned to sleep.

Rhonda called her at work on Thursday morning. She wanted to see her and talk with her about what happened and why she had kept silent. She said the guilt of knowing about Alex and Crystal wasn't going to let her go until she told her side of the story. Katie agreed and they decided to meet for lunch.

When they met Katie was quiet, letting Rhonda tell her the entire story from the time she started at Silver Craft to Monday when they knew Crystal was pregnant.

"Katie, I don't know if you can understand the spot I was in. I felt like a traitor when I knew and you didn't. I wouldn't blame you if you told me to take a flying hike. I deserve it."

"No, you don't. I don't think I would have done anything differently if I had been in your place." She reached out for Rhonda's hand, but got a hug from her old friend instead.

"Hang in there, kid," Rhonda said, as she embraced her. "You'll make it through this."

"Rhonda, I'm leaving Alex. I'm moving out of the house this weekend."

Rhonda's eyes filled with tears. "Katie are you sure? I mean, can't you work it out? He really loves you, no matter how dumb this was; I can tell he does."

She tried to explain to Rhonda why she felt this tear in the fabric of her marriage was beyond repair. She seemed to understand, even though she knew Alex never would.

"It's gonna tear him apart when you leave."

"It's the only way." She began to sob, trying to get the words out, "What about—the girl—Crystal? How is she?"

Rhonda was surprised that Katie could be concerned for Crystal when her own pain was so obvious.

"She's really confused. She has a tough decision to make. Hell, she's just a kid and... ."

"How old is she? I know she's young."

"She's only eighteen."

44

She didn't expected her to be that young, and the answer took her somewhat by surprise. "Rhonda, she's not going to get an abortion is she?" There was fear in Katie's heart as she thought about the innocent child whose life hung in the balance. Suddenly her own heartache and problems paled in comparison.

"She doesn't know yet. She lives with her mom and I don't think her mom will let her stay if she decides to keep the baby. Then there is Alex telling her to have an abortion and...."

"Alex! Alex told her that?!"

Rhonda didn't know about Katie and Alex's attempts to conceive, but she knew she just hit a raw nerve.

Katie Davidson blazed with anger and disbelief. How could he tell this young girl to simply snuff out the life that he helped to create? This was not some mistake that could simply be erased and forgotten; this was a child!

"Katie, he doesn't want to lose you and he knows she can't make it on her own."

"I've got to see her, Rhonda. Will you tell her I want to see her? Here give her my parents' number," she said as she quickly scribbled it down on a napkin.

"Katie, you're crazy!" Rhonda said in disbelief. "You are talking about the woman who slept with your husband—and she *knew* he was married! Why the hell should you care if she jumped off a bridge?"

She pressed the napkin into Rhonda's hand, "Please, have her call me. I want to talk with her. I want to meet her. And Rhonda, I do care."

There was little left to say; they both had to get back to work.

~:~

Crystal was amazed that Katie wanted to see her. She had been curious about Katie from the time Alex said he was married, and now she would get the chance to meet her face to face. She didn't want to wait, so she got her work number from Rhonda and called only minutes after getting the message. There was no hesitation; she wanted to meet Katie, too.

~:~

Katie barely got seated at her desk when she got the call. They would meet that afternoon at Rhonda's house.

Neither one had their defenses up when they met; it was strange, but relieving. They sat out on Rhonda's patio, just the two of them, for several hours talking, crying and occasionally even laughing together. Katie told Crystal about trying to get pregnant for two years, not pushing her views, just telling her about her feelings.

Crystal told her that, in her heart, she didn't believe in abortion. She wanted to have the baby, but there were so many obstacles: her mother, Alex, her job and even her ability to be a mother. She was scared and didn't want to end up like the bitter woman she had watched her mother become.

By the time they stopped talking, they each knew they had made a friend. No wonder Alex loves her, Crystal thought, she is so caring, warm and open. There was something about Katie that doesn't occur often enough in people. She possessed a flawless heart, an open mind, and a special sparkle that told you there was something different in her.

Saturday morning Katie sat in front of the mirror in her bedroom looking for signs that she had changed. So much had happened on the inside that she felt there must be some evidence of it in her face. The woman that stared back at her was the same one she'd known for twenty-four years, but within her was a stranger. On the inside was a woman who was not so naïve, a woman who no longer trusted blindly as she had all her life. The love for Alex was still etched on her heart, and would remain there for a lifetime, but it wasn't the same love that had been there almost a week ago. She took several deep breaths, knowing the toughest moment of her life, thus far, was at hand. She picked up her keys and headed for Fort Pierce.

Alex walked out to meet her as she pulled her car into the drive. He didn't say anything as she stepped out, but he pulled her close to his chest for a long embrace. She felt like crumbling in his arms, wanting so badly to stay there, but knowing she couldn't.

"Let's go inside," she said as she gently pushed away. The house was as she left it, except for the dishes stacked in the sink.

He faced her as she entered the living room. Gently holding her by the shoulders, he began. "Katie, what I did was wrong. If I could turn the clock back I swear to you this wouldn't have happened. I love you, Baby. Please, give me another chance." He made no attempt to hide the tears he shed as they fell quietly down his cheeks and dripped softly to the carpet.

There was knot in her throat, choking her words, but she made her decision by weighing all that she felt was right. She cried as she spoke. The words seemed to be coming from somewhere else in the room, not from her. She thought she couldn't say these things to him, but she did. She told him she talked with Rhonda and then with Crystal. She wanted a divorce; she couldn't live with him without trust. She told him how much she loved him, but she couldn't stay. Then, as deeply as it hurt inside her heart, she told him she would like to see Crystal move in with him.

He looked bewildered by her request. "But I love you—you Katie, not Crystal. I want you, please... ."

"Alex, tell me what you feel for her. Don't buffer your words. I want to know what's in your heart for her."

They talked for hours and hours, sometimes both of them breaking down in tears, but it was honest and open. He hadn't lied to Crystal when he told her he cared for her. There was something more than just the passion they shared, but telling Katie was the hardest thing he had ever done. He wanted to lie and say there was no one else in his heart, and no one else on his mind, but lies destroyed what they had and now was a time for truth. In the end, he agreed to give her the divorce she wanted and he would ask Crystal to move in and live with him.

She wondered if she was a total fool for doing what she did. She could have had him back moments after she arrived, but instead she convinced him to leave her for another. She had thought long and hard about Crystal and Alex, and she realized that they should be together.

He admitted that he only told Crystal to have an abortion out of desperation to keep Katie. When all had been said, they sat in the still evening looking at one another.

"I need to get my things. I might as well load up what I can tonight."

"Katie, maybe we should sell the house so you can get your part of the money you put into it."

"No, you keep it. Hey, I would have been paying rent somewhere if I hadn't been here. Besides, you're going to need a place to live and you can't move into your parents' with—with Crystal." The words were still hard to say, Alex and Crystal instead of Alex and Katie.

"I'll save up what I can and pay you back for your part."

"No. There's no more to discuss. If you sell the house after a couple more years of living here, and *if* I need the money, you can pay me back then. Okay?"

He nodded as they took her clothes from the closet. He still couldn't believe this was real; she was leaving. They went through each room and made a small mountain of her things on the living room floor. It was ten o'clock before they finished. The last things to decide upon were the photo albums, filled with happy memories of the times they shared from high school to last Christmas. As they sat together and looked at the photos, they began to question the decisions they made.

"Are you sure this is what you want to do, Babe?"

She nodded, afraid to speak. She knew the decision was right, but something in her heart wasn't convinced yet.

They loaded her car until nothing more would fit. By then it was midnight.

"I don't want you driving all the way up to your parents' tonight. Stay here and tomorrow I'll put the rest in my truck and help you take it up there." He didn't want to face her parents, but he felt he should.

"Did you talk with your folks?" she asked, fighting hard not to yawn.

"No, I—I wanted to wait until we talked. It's not going to be easy, but nothing this past week has been."

She reached for the car door, but he stopped her, "Hey, I'm not letting you drive home, it's too late."

She was exhausted and didn't argue. "I need to call my mom. I know she's waiting for me."

Her mother had been hoping they had made up and that was the reason Katie hadn't come home. When the phone rang at midnight, her hopes were dashed.

Katie plopped down on the couch, but he insisted she sleep in their bed; he would take the sofa. As she fixed the bed, he came in and told her he loved her, and then on impulse he kissed her. The heartaches, headaches and tension of the day melted in one warm moment.

"Katie, if this is forever, I want tonight with you." His words seemed to echo what Crystal said to him an eternity ago. Every ounce of her wanted him, craved him and needed him. He kissed her again, passionate and long. She told him no, but her body was responding with a yes. Deeper he kissed her, until she answered with her own passion for him. His mouth trailed down her neck, pulling her desire to be touched by him to the forefront of her will. She felt helpless as he picked her up and brought her to their bed.

Slowly he removed her clothes. She was breathtakingly beautiful, soft lines of complete womanhood. Once she was a girl in his arms and now she was as lovely as a goddess. Her tender lips were begging for his kiss as her supple body answered every touch of his hands. She needed him more than she had ever needed anything in her life. She stopped whispering 'No,' giving way to moans of ecstasy and pleasure.

Taking her in his arms, he wrapped her in his loving embrace and brought her body to respond with all the passion inside her. Their love, desire for each other and sweet-parting sorrows brought them up a stairway to rapture. With its exhausting completion, they slept.

Waking in the early dawn, lying in a bed with the man she had decided she couldn't be with anymore, she realized she couldn't stay in Fort Pierce. The hold he had over her was too strong. Katie Davidson would have to move far away or she would become weak and find herself back in his bed. She left quietly, not disturbing him, and drove her heavily laden car to Vero Beach.

She was taking the last of the items from her car, ready to return to pick up the remainder, when Alex pulled into the drive. She glanced to the back of his truck, wondering if he brought her things; they were there.

"Katie," he said, "I was hoping after last night you'd change your mind and stay."

"Alex I can't go through this again. The decisions we made yesterday didn't change because of our—my weakness last night." She faced him as she spoke, her eyes telling him she would not change her mind. The conclusions wrought by painful truth would not be compromised by a brief encounter, taken when she could do little to resist.

"It's gonna drive me crazy when I see you around. I don't know if I can go through with this." His words were genuine.

She wanted to tell him it would be equally hard for her. But there was something she had to tell him to remedy any future weakness on either of their parts.

"Alex, I'm putting in for an immediate transfer at work. I don't think I'll be in Fort Pierce much longer."

The words stung with their permanence. "Where are you gonna go?"

"I don't know yet, I'm taking the first thing that comes my way."

There was little left to say. He unloaded the truck, speaking only short choked words to her parents; he didn't want to breakdown in front of them. When he was ready to leave he reached to kiss her, more out of habit than anything else. She backed away from him, whispering "Goodbye," afraid that if she said it any louder she would change her mind. As she watched him drive away she whispered again, but this time, "I love you, Babe."

~:~

The corporation Katie worked for was spread all over the United States, including Canada and Puerto Rico. She could end up anywhere, but she didn't care. Her position was a secretary, but she also trained for a short time in programming. Being a programmer is what she really wanted, but her chance for that would be slim because she didn't have any college education. All of those positions started with a minimum of two years of higher learning. Katie's experience was all on-the-job, and she had worked with several of their best programmers. She convinced her boss that cross training would benefit the staff, but after losing several secretaries who decided they wanted to go back to school to learn more, the cross training was cancelled.

Katie had learned quickly and knew that she too would enjoy being a programmer, but affording college and getting the bills paid were total adversaries. She kept abreast of new programs and techniques through the friends she made in that department. Many times she would work on programs at home and share them with those at work. If her idea was good, it was used, but she didn't get the credit. She didn't mind simply because she enjoyed the computer so much it really didn't seem like work; it was more like a big puzzle. Alex told her she was nuts for doing it. Now when she was looking for another position, she began thinking maybe she had been foolish for not taking the credit she deserved.

ATI was a major computer software and component manufacturer. They were highly diversified from making microchips in California to creating innovative programs in Florida. They were ranked as one of the top companies in the world. Many of the other major conglomerates not only competed against ATI, but also used ATI components under very lucrative re-labeling contracts. This enabled other select computer companies to purchase ATI products and re-label them with their name. She thought it was interesting that many of the choices consumers made came down to the marketing techniques, not the products.

The day after she applied for a transfer, Bob Larkin, the operations director for many years, came to see her about her reasons. He had been there when she first applied six years ago. She was only eighteen at the time and he told her that he didn't expect her to last more than six months. He had a gruff façade that he put on for the new recruits; testing their mettle, he said. She had earned his respect after years of diligent, high quality work. He had faith in her ability and encouraged her to advance when new openings came up. Now he was wondering why she wanted to leave.

He was like a father figure to her, so she spoke candidly. He knew Alex was her high school sweetheart, and her only love. It even hurt an old codger like himself to think about the pain that she was going through, though he would never show it. When she had given him her reasons, he sat silent for a while, then patting her shoulder as he got up, he said he understood and would see if he could help find something worthy of her ability.

That night he made a phone call to someone he had never asked favors from, but knew he was owed several, and by his own standards it was about time to use one. It had been a long time since Bob had made a personal call to Albert Trathmoore, the president and founder of ATI. After talking with several personal assistants, he final got him on the phone.

"Bob?" The voice on the other end questioned.

"Albert, how are you? Hope I didn't disturb you from anything important."

"No, but I was a little surprised when they told me who was on the phone. Is everything all right down there in Florida? You and Irene doing okay?"

"Oh yes, we're doing great. I'm getting grouchy and she's getting gray, but hey that's life isn't it?"

Albert Trathmoore smiled. He had known Bob for twenty-two years and he never changed—he'd been grouchy all his life!

"Listen, I'm calling you on business tonight, kind of a favor I'd like you to do for me."

Albert tuned in sharply when Bob mentioned business; it wasn't a social call after all.

"Go ahead, I'm listening."

"I've got a young woman down here that has put in for a transfer."

"You don't want to lose her?" He jumped to a quick conclusion from the tone in Bob's voice.

"No, actually I don't. But I want her to get a chance for something better than the secretarial pool in Houston, Texas!"

Bob went on to explain how she started there at eighteen and spearheaded a cross-training program, how she worked diligently and never asked for credit on programming projects she developed on her own time. He mentioned her dedication and drive for perfection in her work.

All this was fine and commendable with Mr. Trathmoore, but why was she transferring? He could understand Bob's reluctance to promote her within his own personnel system, that would show favoritism, but there had to be some other reason he was taking such a special interest in this girl. He pressed Bob a little hard over his motives.

"I don't like to talk about her personal life, but it's not like I'm talking to the press," Bob laughed.

Albert laughed insincerely; he'd had enough trouble with the press.

"She's been with this one guy since high school—you know first love and all that—and he recently… Well, let's just say she isn't going to stay married to him. Albert, she's a good person. The sweetest and kindest I've seen in a long time, and I want to see her get something in programming. She needs something that pays better and gets her the hell out of this area before gossip tears up an already broken heart."

Albert was surprised. This woman had quite an effect on his old friend and that was unusual. "What did you say her name was?" He asked as he flicked his computer to the personnel files.

"Katie—I mean, Katherine Davidson."

Without any further conversation, he brought up her records. He looked at the picture scanned into the personnel file, quickly realizing she was a beauty. "You say this fellow was the only love in her life? How do you know?"

"We talked for a long time today about why she wants to leave. She's been like a daughter to me. What do you think? Can you do me a favor or not?" Bob was getting the impression that this conversation had taken a misguided turn somewhere.

He studied the picture for a moment longer. She had attributes that intrigued him. He hadn't had genuine interest in a woman since his divorce twelve years ago, but that was because he hadn't found one innocent enough to suit him—until now.

"Yes, I'll let you have your favor. I can't turn down an old friend like you. I know of an opening that would be perfect for her. I'll have my secretary fax you the transfer offer tomorrow morning."

Bob sighed with relief; he didn't like asking for favors, most grouches don't, but this case was an exception. "Thanks, I know she'll be thrilled. Good-bye, Albert."

Albert starting making notes when he got off the phone. He still had her photo on the monitor. As in any potential acquisition, it was time to do a little research.

~:~

Only two days after she applied for a transfer, she was accepted for employment in another branch of ATI. She caught her breath as she read that the opening was a Level One programmer at the head office in New York City. She would only have forty-eight hours to make her decision. The pay grade was four levels above her current pay. The company wouldn't pay for a Level One's moving costs, but they would help her with living arrangements until she could find a place of her own. If she accepted it, she would be given thirty days in which to make the move.

She went home that night trembling with excitement, but also with fear. This would be the farthest she had ever been from home, and New York didn't have a reputation as the friendliest or safest city in the world. It was a big decision and she wanted to make it on her own.

She didn't say much through dinner and went straight to her room afterward. She lay on the bed and stared at the ceiling wondering what it would be like. She wouldn't know anyone. Everything would be new and different. She looked around her room; everything was familiar. She tried to envision a place where nothing, not one shred, would be known to her. Well, she thought, I guess if I don't like it I can come home. I might not have a job, but... . Then she imagined winter in New York. Snow, probably lots of snow. The idea wasn't very appealing.

She spent the better part of two hours weighting the pros and cons and finally made up her mind. She found her parents in the living room watching television. She looked at them, wondering: What was the secret to their marriage? They were always so happy together. She couldn't remember one fight they had ever had. They sat in the dim lamplight together on the couch. He had his arm around her shoulder and she had her hand on his knee. She often thought that she and Alex would have grown old together as happily as her parents had. That dream was gone now and she stood before them with a decision that would frighten and upset them even more than divorcing Alex.

"Mom, Dad." She startled them. They didn't know she had been standing in the doorway. "I want to talk with you both about a new job offer I got today."

"Sure Darlin,' come join us," her mother said, patting the couch. "We didn't know you were looking for another job. Is it something here in Vero?"

"No, I'm staying with ATI. I put in for a transfer."

"A transfer?" her father said with a concerned look. "ATI doesn't have any other places near here, do they?"

"No, Daddy. I've been accepted for a position in New York."

"New York!" They said in unison.

"Darlin,' you can't go to New York," Mother said. "You don't know a soul there and... ."

"Do you realize Kat that it's not going to be anything like here? It's a big place and... ."

Her mother cut him off. "You can't go there! I realize you're hurt over what happened with Alex, but Darlin' New York is no place for you!"

She knew that their concern for her was from the heart and that leaving them would hurt more than anything she'd ever done. But when her mind was made up, Katie Davidson was a stubborn woman.

They talked until late and still her parents weren't convinced that this was a good idea. Exhausted from trying to explain her reasoning, she finally told them she was going to accept the position. She would let her boss know in the morning and within four weeks she would leave for New York.

"I'm sorry," she said. "I love you both, but I have to do what I feel is right and this job is right for me at this point in my life. I wish there were some easier way to convince you that I'll be okay, but there isn't. Goodnight."

She kissed them both as they sat there, still shocked that their little girl was leaving, maybe for good. Then she headed for bed; she needed her rest because tomorrow would be no easier.

The next morning she stood gingerly knocking on Bob Larkin's door.

"What do you want?" he said in his usual gruff manner, but when she stepped in through the doorway, she saw his face soften.

"Katie, come in. What's on your mind?"

"Mr. Larkin, I received notice of accepted transfer yesterday. Did Lois tell you?"

"Of course she did. I wouldn't have her for my secretary if she let such matters slip my attention." He eyed her carefully. "Have you made a decision? New York is a pretty big step."

"Yes, I know." She looked down to her lap, afraid to look him in the eye. "I've decided to take it." Her gaze slowly returned to his, wondering what scowl would play across his face, but instead he was nodding as if he approved. Still, she wasn't sure because he wasn't speaking. "Do you think I've made the right decision?" she asked, hoping to find out how he really felt about her leaving.

"Katie, when you'd been here for a while I confided in you and told you I thought you had potential. I always said you needed to seek more challenging positions and show everybody what kind of material you're made of. I can't think of a better place for you to do that than in the head office. You've come to a stand still here unless you go back to school for a degree in programming. This job in New York is going to be the only way to circumvent that."

"I thought it was a mistake, but I was going to try to take it anyway," she said as the excitement of a programming job filled her.

"It's the most basic position you can get, but it's a beginning for you."

She couldn't get the smile off her face. "Then you wanted me to go all along, didn't you?"

"No, I didn't," he said sternly, shaking a finger at her to remind her of her place. "I only wanted to see you leave if you could get something decent, something that could give you the start you deserve. If I had given you that kind of job here, someone would have said I was playing favorites."

"Oh, Mr. Larkin, I can't thank you enough!" She was exuberant. "I could just kiss you!"

"No, don't do that," he chuckled as he put his hands up, "or someone *will* say I was playing favorites!"

She realized it was the first time she had ever heard him laugh. He was just as excited for her as she was for herself. "But what if I get up there and they realize I don't have the background for the job and... ."

"Don't worry about that. I've got the path cleared for you. No one will question the man who put you in that position.

"Who?" She couldn't imagine anyone that high up that could bend the employment qualifications.

"Albert Trathmoore, that's who!" He said with a wink.

Katie's mind was racing; he was the president of the company and one of the richest men in the country.

"But... ." Her lack of words reflected her amazement.

"He and I were friends back when he was still a little fish in a big frying pan. How the hell did you think an old grouch like me got to be director of personnel and operations of this place anyway?"

Suddenly, she was afraid of failure; surely he would check on this person Mr. Larkin spoke of so highly.

Bob easily read the expression on her face going from exuberant to worried. "Don't worry, Katie," he said, smiling. "You'll do fine. They won't hang a sign on you that says 'someone called in favors for me to get this job.' You just work like you do here and you'll advance in no time."

His confidence in her was like a warm pat on the back. She knew she'd be okay; she'd do more than a good job; she'd do a great job. She thanked him again. He said he'd call the main office and tell them she had accepted. She walked back to her desk, pinching herself the whole way, wondering when she would wake up from this fabulous dream. Only this wasn't a dream; she *was* going to New York.

When she finished work and headed out to her car, Alex was parked beside it.

"What are you doing here?" She asked with a certain degree of shock.

"What the hell do you think you're doing? You can't go off to New York!"

"How did you know I was... ."

"That doesn't matter. What matters is that you can't leave here. New York is too rough for you. Hell, you're scared to death to go to Miami! What do you think New York is gonna be like?!"

"Mom called you, didn't she?"

"So what if she did? They're worried about you--and so am I. I don't want to see you leave."

"Alex, I told you I was putting in for a transfer. You knew this was coming."

"What? A whole four days ago! This is too soon. You're not leaving for the right reasons."

"Yes I am, Alex. I've got an entry-level job in programming—without college. This is going to be my stepping stone to getting into better positions without going to school first. I may have to go later on, but once you're a programmer the company will pay for additional college. I can't get that here in the secretarial pool."

"Well that's great, but how did you get it? I mean, maybe it's a mistake or something."

She was hurt, feeling that he was trying to say she wasn't smart enough to keep this job. "No, it wasn't a mistake. Mr. Larkin knows

Mr. Trathmoore. He talked to him about my work and he agreed to get me in on the ground floor."

His mood switched from angry to sullen. "I still don't want to see you go," he said softly as he moved toward her, grasping her shoulders and wanting to pull her close, but refraining.

"Alex, I'm not doing this to hurt you or my parents. It's just something I've got to do. You and I don't need to see each other because all it's doing is tearing our insides apart. I'm going to start a new life and you need to start over again, too."

He started to speak, but she softly put her hand to his mouth.

"Crystal and that baby need you, not me. I'll find my way and I'll do it on my own two feet. If I stay here, I'll get weak and maybe even get selfish and try to come between you and Crystal. We never would have had a family. I've kidded myself about that long enough. You've got the chance now to have a family, a real one with someone who loves you almost as much as I do, and a baby that I know will love you more than both of us. I'm going to New York and I hope you understand it's not because I'm confused, but it's because I want to."

He was trying to hold back the tears; Katie's face was already streaked.

"Damn you, Katie Davidson," he said gently, "I haven't cried as much in my whole life as I have these past two weeks."

They laughed weakly and embraced.

~:~

The next few weeks were a flurry of activity as she prepared to leave. She shopped on the weekends to get the right kinds of clothes for where she was going, not only for the climate, but also for her career. She wanted to look like someone who had gone to college, even if she hadn't. Even her parents seemed to soften to the idea of her leaving, though they still asked her to reconsider.

She learned that she would be rooming with a woman from her new department until she found a place of her own, which according to everyone would be a long time because finding an apartment in New York was a nightmare.

She and Alex went down and filed their divorce papers, neither one contesting and nothing being divided. They were told it wouldn't take long to finalize. She went down and had her name removed from the mortgage and the utilities. It seemed hard to comprehend that all traces of their marriage would soon be gone. Even her name would change back to Danor when her petition went through after the divorce. It seemed like a sorry slap in the face to all those years she spent with him, but she knew if he married Crystal, it would be awkward for her to keep his name.

There were farewell parties thrown for her at work and at her parent's house. Alex was there and so was Rhonda. His parents came and told her they loved her like a daughter and wished she wasn't going. Rhonda told her in private that Crystal finally told her mother that she was pregnant, and her mother, predictable as Crystal thought, told her to pack her things and get out. She would move in with Alex over the weekend.

Alex also asked for a private moment to say goodbye. He let his lips softly brush across hers, then held her tight and told her to 'knock'em dead' in New York. He said she would always have a very special place in his heart. She asked him to make Crystal happy because their relationship deserved every chance to make it.

Her parents took her to the Miami International Airport where she would board a plane and fly straight through to JFK International in New York. When they reached the airport there were tears of sadness, fear and joy as Lawrence and Beth Danor watched their only child leave their safe and protective care, delivering her into the hands of the unknown.

"God be with you, Darlin," her mother tearfully said.

Her father was too overcome with emotion to speak.

"I love you both," she choked out as she gave them a hug and then disappeared down the boarding tunnel.

CHAPTER TWO

Katie could feel her apprehension growing like weeds inside her as the plane circled over New York waiting for an open runway. She marveled at the city below, a great gray giant waiting to swallow her up with the masses gone before her.

She had taken motion sickness medication before she left home, but now she was wishing she had taken more than just one pill. "I can't get sick," she thought angrily to herself. "Don't be such a damn chicken!" They were descending to land, the passengers were buckled in their seats and she thought how silly she would look making a mad dash for the bathroom. Surely the flight attendant would tell her to get back in her seat and then she would have to explain, in front of everyone, that she was going to be sick. No, she said to herself, I'll make it through this; I'm just nervous. The wheels landed smoothly on the runway and soon they were taxiing into the terminal to disembark. "Thank you, God," she whispered. "I made it."

She was to meet her new roommate, Ruth Macklin, at the luggage area. Ruth told Katie what she looked like and what she would be wearing, but no one fit the description. She grabbed her luggage and tugged it over to a place near the baggage area and waited. She watched the swirl of passengers going by her, creating more nausea inside her with their undulating movement. One man broke from the continual stream, making eye contact and turning her direction. He had some brochures in his hand and an uneasy look about his face. She shifted nervously in her chair, realizing he was headed for her. Surely this isn't the person who came to pick me up, she wondered. Where was Ruth? She should have been here thirty minutes ago. The flight wasn't delayed, so where could she be? The man sat in the chair beside her and, leaning over in front of her, began talking wildly about some sort of religious group he belonged to. She tried to tell him nicely to leave her alone, she wasn't interested in his cause, but he was insistent that she should give him a contribution. She looked at his arms and could see the faint markings where needles had been jabbed repeatedly into the skin. She wanted to get away from him, but he positioned himself so that he was blocking her from getting up. She thought about giving him a couple dollars just to get him to leave her alone, but she knew that would give him the opportunity to relieve her of all her cash. Panic was edging over her and it seemed as if no one was paying any attention to a distressed young woman with an unwelcome guest.

"HEY!" A booming female voice shouted. "What the hell are you doing, Buddy? Get away from my friend before I call airport security to harass you!"

Katie looked up and realized it was Ruth who had come to her aid. As people turned to see what was going on, the man slunk back to his seat. Seizing the opportunity, Katie sprang from the chair where she had felt trapped only seconds before. "Thank God." she said as she put distance between her and the strange man.

"No, thank city transit or I could have been another fifteen minutes late. Here let me take one of those," Ruth said, removing a suitcase from her grip. "Wow, this is as heavy as lead! I hope you've got cash for cab fare because we can't take all this on the bus."

"I've got plenty of cash. How much do you think it will run?"

"That depends on traffic, maybe forty or fifty bucks." She watched the shock come over Katie's face.

"That much! How far are we going?"

"About fifteen miles."

"That's not far, so how come it's so much?"

They reached the cab area and were fortunate enough to be first in a new line.

"It's not the distance," Ruth continued, "it's the time it takes to get us there."

"Well it couldn't take more than twenty or thirty minutes at the maximum."

"Ha!" laughed Ruth, "Maybe in Florida it only takes that long, but, Baby, this is New York; we won't be there for a good hour or better."

Her face was riddled with disbelief, "An hour!"

The cabby asked Ruth in broken English where they were going. When Ruth told him, he laughed and grinned a near toothless grin at

Katie. "On' hor?" he said as he scratched his scruffy head, "If yu luckee."

The drive to Ruth's apartment in Queens was long and nerve racking. By the time they made it, an hour and fifteen minutes had passed. She was still amazed that such a short drive in miles could take so long, but after going through the teeth-gritting traffic, she understood it a little better. She studied the shabby worn brick on the apartment buildings, the occasional broken windows and scattered bits of trash. On the sidewalks, children played hopscotch and jumped rope, old ladies stood on the steps, undoubtedly sharing the latest neighborhood gossip.

She noticed graffiti in some of the areas that seemed deserted, and unsavory characters lurking around an abandon playground. The neighborhood they last entered seemed to be a mix of old and new buildings. The cab pulled to a stop in front of one of the apartments.

"Here we are, home sweet home," Ruth said as she stepped from the car.

Katie searched her voice for a hint of sarcasm, but there was none. She really likes this place, she thought. She paid the cabby and grabbed two suitcases and Ruth grabbed the other. "Which floor?"

"Number five," she said as she headed inside to the stairway.

"No elevator?" Katie questioned.

Ruth shot her a look as if to say 'get real.'

The apartment was clean and comfortable, but the place reflected her unusual taste. It seemed like some hodge-podge combination gathered from a yard sale. None of the furniture matched and decorations on the walls ranged from country geese to what looked like some kind of African facemask.

"That keeps evil spirits away," Ruth laughed as she noticed Katie studying it. "You met one at the airport, remember?"

She shuttered at the thought of the junkie begging for money. "How's security in your building?".

"We don't have too many problems here. Most of the tenants are either elderly couples or young families. But, the door always stays locked in case any street people get in from down stairs."

Katie looked at the door and saw two dead bolts, two chains and a bar lock. It looked secure enough, she though, but what do I know about security in New York.

"Ruth, where do you keep your car parked?" She asked; she didn't see any parking garage when they pulled up.

"First," Ruth said as she put Katie's bag down in the spare bedroom. "Call me Ruthie—everybody does, even at work. Second, I do not own a car and I don't think you could pay me enough to have one in this town. I ride and let city transit drive."

"Even to work?" Katie asked, clearly amazed.

"Especially to work. Every weekday I hop on the bus and head for Manhattan, and so will you."

"I thought everybody here took the subway?"

"No way," Ruth said waving her hands. "The only reason I ever take the subway is when I've overslept and missed my bus. The bus takes a lot longer to get to work, but it's a whole lot safer."

They spent the rest of the afternoon in the little apartment unpacking Katie's things and getting to know one another. Ruthie was originally from Ohio and had moved to New York with her parents when she was fourteen. After high school, she had gone to college for two years and studied programming. She landed her first job with ATI right after college. She worked with them for a year when her father died from a heart attack. Her mother wanted her to come back with her to Ohio, but Ruthie was hopelessly addicted to New York.

She looked at this curly-headed, flaxen blond with sky blue eyes, wondering how she had survived alone in this place. Ruthie wasn't striking or beautiful, but she was cute. Her frame was larger than Katie's, and she seemed to have a powerfulness to her that must have come from the street smarts she learned on her own in the city. Katie wondered if she too would acquire the powerful presence that Ruthie exuded. The way she walked, talked and gestured all gave the sense that she was very sure of herself.

Over the next month, she learned everything Ruthie could fill her head with about New York: where to catch the bus, where to shop, where to eat, where not to go and what not to say to a New Yorker. She learned quickly, but more than once she managed to stick her foot in her mouth. Ruthie would just laugh at her.

The new job was fabulously exciting. The building was located in Manhattan on Fifth Avenue. It was a beautiful structure of shining glass and modern architecture. The inside was always buzzing with people, everyone from the mail boy to the president moved about the building. This was the hub of ATI and excitement cracked through the air like static. Everything the company was involved with passed through this place. Katie herself felt as if she had been electrically charged when she entered it. ATI owned the building, but leased out the first ten floors. Her workstation was on the fourteenth floor. Ruthie worked with her at the same station, and she felt more comfortable and confident under Ruthie's watchful eye.

Mr. Casller was her immediate supervisor and, according to Ruthie, he was critical of everything and everyone under him. But, to the surprise of both of them, he was very civil to Katie, almost friendly.

"Huh," Ruthie remarked, "He must have the hots for you because I've never seen him act so nice to anybody."

She didn't question his politeness; she was simply thankful for it.

Ms. Rathbone was in charge of the entire fourteenth floor and all fifteen supervisors. She was a very liberal woman, and Ruthie said the current rumor was that she had a live-in lover, another woman. She was a heavy built woman with a masculine attitude. She took charge with great delight and strength, but, once again, she seemed to soften when it came to Katie.

"What's the deal with you?" Ruthie said, eyeing her suspiciously, "Are you related to Trathmoore or what? Everybody treats you with kid gloves. I've never seen them act so nice with a new employee."

"No, of course not," she said quickly. She wondered if Mr. Larkin had something to do with this, but she dismissed the thought and hoped it had something to do with her good southern manners.

The truth be known, it had to do with Mr. Trathmoore seeing personally that she was accepted for the position. It had been many years since he had taken a personal interest in any employee. Mr. Casller and Ms. Rathbone were both instructed to give her some breathing room to adjust to New York and to her new job. If she was so special to Bob Larkin that he would make a late night call to get her this position then he'd make sure she got a chance to succeed at it.

Summer ended and fall came to the city. She enjoyed the cool crispness to the air more than she had thought she would. There was a difference in the coolness of a New York autumn from a Florida autumn, and it refreshed and invigorated her.

Ruthie had been away for the last couple of weekends, spending more and more time with her boyfriend, Tom. Tom seemed like a great guy, but he was a native New Yorker and sometimes his accent was so heavy that Katie had trouble understanding him. He was fun to be around and she could easily see why Ruthie liked him so well. He often mentioned that he could fix Katie up with his older brother Marc and they could go on a double date sometime, but she would graciously decline each offer. Her heart wasn't ready to get involved with anyone just yet; it still had the ache for only one man: Alex. Many were the nights when she cried herself to sleep wishing Alex were there to hold her, to smooth her hair, caress her skin and whisper in breathless ecstasy that he loved her. Those days were gone and she would make sure his memory was well faded before she ventured out into the world of lovers.

She called home quite often. Her mother pleaded for her to come home for Thanksgiving. She was just starting to get over her homesickness and she worried that a visit might start the pain and loneliness all over again, but her mother was insistent.

"Mom, I don't have the money to fly home."

"That's all right, Dear, we'll buy the tickets for you. Please, it just won't seem like Thanksgiving without you here."

She knew her mother was right. The holiday was one she had always spent with her family, even when she was with Alex. Alex's parents could have 'dibs' on any other holiday, even Christmas, as long as they spent Thanksgiving with her parents. She had never missed a Thanksgiving with them and, as it drew closer, she felt depressed at not being with them.

"Okay, Mom, but I'll pay for half my airfare."

"Don't be silly," she retorted, "Daddy and I will pay for the trip; we aren't on a fixed budget you know."

Katie knew that if she did pay for half the fare it would put her in a financial bind; living in New York was quite expensive. The arrangements were made and she would leave Wednesday evening from La Guardia Airport, which was closer to Ruth's apartment than JFK.

After several delays in her flight, she arrived in Miami at midnight. She was glad she talked her parents into letting her take a rental car from the airport to home. She wouldn't have wanted them sitting around Miami International in the middle of the night. She called them as soon as she landed, knowing they would be up and worried. She told them about her flight delays and then headed for the rental desk. She requested a compact, simply trying to save a little money, but all the compacts were taken. Tired, angry, and a little airsick, she let her fledgling New York attitude come out.

"I reserved a compact car for the weekend. This is my confirmation number and I am not paying for a luxury car! I didn't screw this up, you guys did and... ."

"Ma'am, I'm sorry for the mix up. We'll be happy to upgrade your car at no charge."

She was taken off-guard a bit by the accommodating remark. "Well, that's great—thanks. I appreciate that. I'm sorry if I snapped at you. It's been a long flight and... ."

"That's quite all right Ma'am, it was our error."

She slipped behind the wheel of a new Lincoln Towncar and just sat for a moment to soak up the splendor of it. It had that wonderful smell that said 'I'm new.' The comfortable leather seats cushioned her aching bones and muscles. It was amazing to her just how quiet it was inside that car. It didn't even seem like the world continued beyond the exterior. She had never owned a new car. She bought her little Fiesta second-hand, and it was always noisy, even with the windows up and the air on. She left it months ago for her parents to sell, and it didn't bring in much money.

She headed out of the airport for I-95, surprised at the feeling of being behind the wheel of a car again. This was the first time she had driven since she left for New York. She turned on the stereo and glided smoothly down the highway. One of these days, she thought, I'm gonna buy myself a new car. Fat chance, she laughed at herself.

She slept until eleven that morning. Everything was so quiet here compared to the apartment. In New York the streets never really died down because there was always traffic, people's voices, and other noises carried up from outside the apartment. This was so different; the only noises she heard were the sounds of the mockingbirds and jays, and occasionally a car or two whizzed by.

She woke to the aromas pies and rolls, and of turkey basting in the oven. There were also faint odors of bacon and coffee drifting into her room.

"Ah," she said out loud as she stretched on the bed, "I'm home!"

She spent her day helping where she could in the kitchen and telling them about life in the big city. She left out the part about the man in the airport when she first arrived. She didn't want to taint their image of where she was living because for the most part all her other experiences of New York were good ones. Later in the day as the guests began to arrive, she had to repeat her scenario of New York to each.

Uncle Joseph and Aunt Carol had moved to Florida from Canada in the past year when Uncle Joe retired. They vacationed many times in Florida and liked it so much that they bought a house on the oceanfront and rented it out when they were in Canada. It was the same house where Katie and Alex had spent their honeymoon. They had walked on the beach during the day and planned their life together. They had made love on the sand in the moonlight one night and skinny-dipped in the dark ocean as the soft lights from the porch shimmered on the shallow crescent tips of the waves.

She wanted desperately to excuse herself from the gathering to call Rhonda and see how he was getting along, but there would be time for that tomorrow; today was for her parents.

Roberta and Max from next door came over for dinner, too. They had been friends with her parents' back when they first moved there. Katie was close in age with their son Bobby and they played together as children. Bobby died of leukemia when Katie was ten. For almost a year she lived in fear that the horrible sickness that took Bobby's life would come and take her, too. She remembered waking at night crying uncontrollably after dreaming about him. Her parents would sit up with her and sooth her fears until she fell back to sleep. She never really thought, until now, about the fact that she kept them from a decent night's sleep many times; she was simply glad they were there to comfort her.

She looked at Roberta and Max now and wondered if their hearts had ever healed from the pain of losing their son. She guessed they hadn't; losing a child would be a crushing blow to anyone. They had two older daughters that were grown with children of their own, but they both lived far from Florida. Roberta and Max were over often as company, but more like family as mother would say.

She noticed her father seemed tired and thinner than when she left for New York, and he didn't participate in the conversations as he normally would have. She stole a few private moments with him in the living room as he pretended to browse over the newspaper.

"Daddy, have you been feeling okay lately? You look a little tired."

"Oh, I'm okay Kat, I've just had a busy week at the rail station. We're always busy before a holiday." His face looked care-worn and she feared it was partly her fault.

He had been a rock in her life; nothing ever seemed to shake him. He was the dauntless hero of 'Daddy's little girl.' But now he looked as if he had aged ten years in only months. Gray was more prominent in his hair, his hands looked old and thin, and his normal radiant tan looked pale.

"Daddy, you should think about retiring and taking it easy. Heck, you know you've worked hard enough for it."

He nodded his head slightly and sighed, "Yes, Sweetheart, I think you're right. I've even mentioned it to your mother. I think sometime in January I might throw in the towel. I'll leave it for the younger men who are jumping at the chance to take my position."

She was a bit startled, even though she was the one who brought it up. She thought he would hotly contest retirement, as he had numerous times before, but instead he was in agreement. It worried her, but she knew he was ready to retire and spend time with her mother. They had talked about traveling when he retired, and now maybe they would get the chance to do that.

They left the living room and joined the others who were ready to sit down for the annual feast. Lawrence said the blessing and the plates began to clatter as they were passed around to be filled with all of the delicious temptations spread out on the table. Conversation picked-up speed as everyone hurried to tell Beth what a wonderful meal she had made, again. That was something she knew her mother appreciated more than any other compliment, a cooking compliment. That was why she seldom asked guests to bring dishes, even though they offered. She enjoyed preparing the big dinner and getting the rave reviews for herself. At one time, Katie wondered if her mother was being selfish, but she came to the realization that her mother had a deep desire to show her skill; she had always been a housewife and showing her talent was like an employee showing off their capability in front of the boss.

Lawrence joined in the praising, which relieved Katie; he was more like his old self as he rolled his eyes and made moans of approval at each forkful. His approval, more than anyone else's, delighted Beth.

As dinner ended and desserts were being served the conversation turned, rather uncomfortably, to Katie. Questions about Alex and the divorce, the prospect of any boyfriends in New York and such, made the desserts lose some of their delicate flavor. She attempted to answer each question politely, but she kept glancing at her mother for help in turning the conversation elsewhere, but her mother appeared to have been just as interested as everyone else.

The divorce had been finalized only sixty days after Katie had filed it, and her name petition followed shortly after it. The time immediately following the receipt of those papers were some of the loneliest she had suffered through while in New York. She thought she was over the desolation of those days, but the questions only too poignantly reminded her that her wounds were far from healed.

She retired to her room early that evening, full and satisfied physically, but emotionally drained and exhausted. The next morning she called Rhonda and talked to her about Alex and Crystal. Rhonda said that Crystal was starting to show the most obvious sign of pregnancy, even though her manner of dress was not revealing. The baby was due sometime in mid-March, and all the tests showed it was a healthy baby. She said Alex seemed to be holding up fine under the strain of impending fatherhood and the fact that everyone at the office was talking viciously about the two of them.

It made Katie angry when she thought about the ignorance of those who make it their business to stick their noses into other people's affairs. It had been painful to give up her husband to Crystal, but she knew it was the best decision all the way around. Who were these people to think they knew better than she and Alex what was right? Rhonda made mention of something about the pitfalls of human nature, but Katie found little that was humane in human nature when others put themselves in the judgment seat.

Sunday morning she flew back to New York and was surprised to find herself relieved to get back to the hustle and bustle of that busy town. New York is a fast-paced place where so many of the worries of yesterday don't have time to invade one's mind. Especially when that mind is busy concentrating on the worries of the present, like commuting simple distances and enduring the ride that takes you there. She knew when she hopped into the cab to take her to the apartment that New York can definitely get into a person's blood.

~:~

Albert Trathmoore decided, not long after Katie started, that he would go down and casually introduce himself on the pretense that he wanted to know how Bob Larkin was doing, but he stopped short when he saw her. The picture in the computer was good, but it didn't reveal what the naked eye could. She had intrigued him when Bob called on her behalf, but now he was caught off guard by the sight of this very lovely young woman. He lived a life of solitude after his bitter and expensive divorce, but watching her that day began to trigger a painful yearning that had been a void in his life for too long.

He was at the top of the Fortune 500 list. He worked tirelessly to achieve that status, but for all his billions he was an intensely lonely man. Not that he was short on offers; he was not only very wealthy, but he was also a strikingly handsome man. Unfortunately money attracts more admirers than looks. Many were the offers from upscale women, but none had even tempted him. He found these women distasteful, much as his ex-wife had become to him since their divorce.

But the sight of Katie Danor that day increased the thirst he acquired from the moment he first saw her picture and heard of her innocence and naiveté, driving his craving even deeper. He watched from Ms. Rathbone's elevated office area, studying her graceful movements as she worked, her delicate facial features, and the curves of her figure that pleased him so well, creating a fire within him. But he wouldn't be like a foolish schoolboy chasing after a girl; he would stay distanced until all the information came back about her, letting him know what kind of woman she really was.

He hired a private investigator immediately when his interest had been sparked. The reports were exactly as he'd hoped, giving him an edge so that when he did finally intercept his prey, he would be able to tell if she was as honest as she was arrestingly beautiful. He hated dishonesty and deceit more than he enjoyed any female company.

And of course, he wanted to be sure he was getting the kind of woman he wanted: one he could sleep with without the fear of getting some incurable disease. That was also the reason other women didn't interest him; he didn't want to catch something which would end his rein at the helm of his true love, ATI.

With the favorable reports in hand, he had personnel send word to Mr. Casller that Ms. Danor would need another drug test. Drug testing was standard for all new employees, but since she transferred, she didn't need a new test. That was before Mr. Trathmoore told personnel to 'lose' her old results and ordered new ones. There are many things that money and power can afford a person, not all of them legal, but that didn't seem to bother him; he was used to getting what he wanted, no matter what it was. She was re-tested for much more than drugs. He was pleased with the results. He would keep her under the watchful eye of his private detective to make sure these results weren't tainted by some experience she might have before he closed in on the woman he chose as the newest challenge in his life.

The detective didn't mind being hired for around the clock surveillance; he was being paid quite well, more than double his regular fee. He had even gotten a little trip to Florida at Thanksgiving.

As Christmas neared, Mr. Trathmoore called a very nervous Mr. Casller to his luxurious office on the top floor of ATI.

"I have a request of you, Mr. Casller." But from the tone of his voice and the look in his eyes, there was no doubt that this was not a request, but a command. "I want you to see that during the Christmas party this year, Ms. Danor, the new employee from Florida, is brought up to the executive party. I'd like to meet her in person, but I don't want her to know the invitation has been extended by me. Is that understood?"

"Ah—yes—yes, Sir, but who do you want—I mean what do you want me to tell her?"

"I really don't care what you say; I simply want her here. Is that clear?"

"Yes, Sir. She'll be here."

The annual Christmas party at ATI was, according to Ruthie, an event not to be missed. Three consecutive floors of conference areas were cleared out to make room for dining, dancing, and the general hoopla that goes with the season. Catered food would be brought in by the truckload and at least four bands would play everything from big band music to good old rock and roll. Since many employees vacationed over the Christmas holiday, the event was set for a Friday evening, one week before Christmas.

Mr. Casller stopped by Katie's desk to ask if she would be attending the party and was obviously relieved when she said yes.

"Listen Katie, I've been thinking about the good job you've been doing and—and I want to introduce you to the president of the company, Mr. Trathmoore, sometime during the party. Would that be okay with you?" He seemed exceptionally nervous, which in turn made her nervous about responding to his question.

""Well—I—I guess so, but... ."

"Great! Then I'll expect you dressed in something really lovely, something that will make a great impression on the boss."

Relief flooded over him so apparent that she wished she could change her response. What is he up to? She wondered. Could Ruthie be right? Was he interested in more than her work? She knew he was a married man and the thought of him being interested in her that way made her sick to her stomach.

Ruthie, however, found the whole situation quite funny.

"You've got to be kidding me? He is gonna introduce you to Iron Pants!" Ruthie called Mr. Trathmoore that, as did many others, because of his staunch lifestyle and lack of female interest. "Man! He must have it bad for you," she said, giving Katie a wink, "I know good and well he's scared to death of Trathmoore."

She winced at the thought, again, of Mr. Casller being fond of her.

"Well, if you're gonna met the big boss then we've got to get you decked out."

"NO! I am not getting dressed up to encourage Mr. Casller in anyway. Forget it!"

But Ruthie would not forget it. She insisted Katie go with her to some of the gown rental shops and try to find the perfect evening gown.

"Won't I be a little over-dressed?" She asked as she modeled a beautiful emerald gown with sequins and a high front slit with ruffled taffeta trimming on the bottom and up the front. "Or maybe under dressed?" She said, looking down at her exposed cleavage.

"Whoa!" Ruthie said as she gave her an approving thumbs-up. "No, a lot of people get really gussied up for the party. Now spin around and let me get the whole effect."

She wasn't budging, "How many Ruthie, fifty percent or five percent?"

"Awe jeez! Don't be such a stick-in-the-mud! It'll be fun."

"How many?" she repeated, showing her stubborn Irish side.

"Oh, maybe about a third get really fixed-up and the rest just dress in their Sunday best, ya know. Now turn around!"

She reluctantly spun about as Ruthie let out a wolf-whistle. "We want this one," she told the clerk before Katie could object any further.

"And just what, may I ask, are you going to wear?"

"For your information," Ruthie said, pursing her lips and turning her button nose up in the air, "I have a very nice red evening gown hanging in my closet that my aunt gave me last year."

They spent the rest of the day shopping for shoes to match their dresses. Katie had to admit that she felt like Cinderella getting ready for the ball. It was exciting, even if Mr. Casller would be hovering around her most of the evening.

"Now we need to get you some nice jewelry to give you the finishing touch," Ruthie exclaimed as they walked out of the shoe store.

Katie was exhausted and her feet ached, she felt as if she had walked over half of New York City. "Today? Do we have to do it today?" she sighed.

"Hey, we're out and about, so we might as well get it all done in one day so we don't have to brave the streets later."

"Ruthie, I'm spending too much money as it is," she rebutted.

"How many Christmas presents did you have to buy this year, huh? As many as last year?"

Katie knew she wasn't spending as much on gifts this year as in the past. The only things she had bought were Christmas cards, a gift for Ruthie, and a gift basket to be sent to her parents. "Okay, so I'm not spending much on presents this year, but…."

"So," Ruthie continued, "consider this stuff as presents for yourself."

She knew it would be useless to argue any further. "Lead on, great shopper of deals," she said, pointing her finger down the row of store fronts.

Friday after work, they came home and rushed to bathe, dress, get their make-up on, and fix each other's hair. When they finished they each gave the other an approving nod. Ruthie's evening gown was simple, but the simplicity of it seemed to suit her perfectly. Her normally rumpled curly hair was pulled back smoothly and piled in lovely tendrils from the crown of her head to the nap of her neck. She wore a single strand of creamy pearls and a pair of pearl earrings with a diamond accent in each. Her mother had given her the jewelry when she left to go back to Ohio. Ruth didn't wear it often. She was afraid of losing them or having someone steal them, but tonight was special enough to get them out of the jewelry box.

Katie looked stunning in her emerald gown. Her ears and neck were adorned with the look of diamonds and gold, but they both knew they were cut crystal and electroplate; very beautiful, but fake nonetheless. Ruthie pulled back Katie's spun copper hair into an exquisite French braid, leaving only a single tendril loose near each ear. Butterflies were dancing in Katie's stomach, making her unsteady in her high-heeled shoes.

Ruthie looked calm, even now, dressed to kill, she had no outward appearance of tension; she was her same humorous self, day-in and day-out.

Suddenly a revelation hit Katie so hard that she had to catch her breath to speak. "Ooh, Ruthie!"

"What? What's a matter?"

"We can't ride the bus looking like this? How are we going to get there? Sit in the back of a cab while the cabby looks at us like we're some kind of escort women or something?"

"We're taking the subway." She watched the horror spread over Katie's face, then she burst into hysterical laughter. "I'm kidding, I'm kidding!" she managed to say as she tried to gain her composure. "Tom's brother Marc works at a limo service and they are going to pick us up between fares and drop us off at the office. It was kind of an early Christmas present from Tom for both of us."

Katie was washed in relief as her terrifying picture of the subway vanished. "Thank heavens!" she sighed.

Tom and Marc pulled up in the dark navy limousine as the neighborhood kids jockeyed for good positions to look at it. Tom was helping Marc for the next week to earn a little extra Christmas cash. He stood dutifully at the door of the car as any professional chauffeur would do, but he couldn't help making a few 'oo la la's' as Ruthie and Katie slipped into the back seat. He dropped them off at the office, giving Ruthie a quick kiss and a slap on the bottom as she got out of the car.

"See ya later on. Just give me a call when you're ready to leave."

Ruthie smiled seductively and said, maybe.

Katie was relieved to find that many people in the building were indeed dressed in similar fashion. Evening gowns and tuxedos paraded in an endless stream of holiday well wishers. The party was in full swing and it was evident that no expense had been spared to make it splendid.

They managed to avoid Mr. Casller most of the evening, but eventually he found them—to his relief and their dismay.

"Katie, you look wonderful," he said as he took her hand in his.

She winced at his clammy grip, realizing he wasn't going to let go.

"Are you ready to go upstairs and meet Mr. Trathmoore?"

"Well, I... Upstairs? You mean he's not down here anywhere?" She began to think this getting dressed-up business wasn't so wonderful after all. She didn't think he would be escorting her alone anywhere.

Ruthie spoke up, trying to help dispel the worried look on her face, "The executive party is up in the penthouse. Go ahead, you'll have fun." She wasn't worried about Katie's safety. Mr. Casller was a little odd, but relatively harmless. "Go on," Ruthie encouraged.

"Shall we?" He said, slipping his arm under her elbow.

She said nothing as he led the way to the elevator. She swallowed hard and tried to keep a pleasant smile on her face. He didn't say much to her in the elevator, but she could feel him giving her looks of approval; it was giving her goose bumps.

"Are you cold?" he asked as the elevator came to a stop.

"No, I'm fine, thank you," she replied, but he was making her skin crawl.

When the doors of the elevator opened, they were in the massive penthouse office. This was very obviously a black-tie affair. Ladies shuffled about in designer dresses costing thousands of dollars, and suddenly she felt small and childish in her gown that only minutes ago made her feel special. She could feel her cheeks growing pink as they made their way through the crowd. It seemed that everyone was looking and she was certain they knew she didn't belong. The thought never occurred to her that they might have been stunned by the lovely young woman who had entered the room; and they were.

Mr. Casller made his way toward a very handsome older man who seemed engrossed in conversation with some other gentlemen. The conversation stopped as the men turned to look at the approaching pair. Katie's pink face suddenly felt flaming red and she was wishing there might be some way to escape the impending embarrassment. Mr. Trathmoore excused himself from the group and stepped toward them.

"Hello, Ernest." he said, shaking his hand.

"Mr. Trathmoore," he acknowledged.

"I'm glad you decided to come up and join us, and whom may I ask is this lovely woman you're escorting? Certainly not Mrs. Casller, is it?"

"No, no, if my wife was this pretty I wouldn't have even come to the party. This is Ms. Katherine Danor, our—your new employee from Florida. She's been doing such a good job that I thought you might like to meet her," he said, his nervousness and embarrassment were evident as he spoke.

"Oh yes, Ms. Danor," he said, taking her hand warmly in his. A sly smile played the corner of his lips. "I believe you're the person I spoke with Bob Larkin about. He felt you would make the best of your new position, and it seems you have."

She smiled outwardly, but inside she was surprised that, with all the people working for him, he remembered about her.

"Please, call me Katie," she said, even more surprised at how effortlessly she spoke it. Funny, she thought, I don't sound nervous. There was something about him that was devastatingly charming, but powerful. He was nothing like the money tyrant Ruthie had described to her. His medium brown hair was slightly gray along the temples and sides. His eyes were a most disturbing dark blue, like the depths of some unexplored jungle pool. He was a tall man, about six foot-two, and on the thin side of athletic, which only enhanced the powerful nature that emanated from him. They conversed easily, gliding over the awkwardness of speaking with a stranger. Little did Katie know that he knew her better than she could have ever imagined.

She didn't realize how intently she had been listening to him speak until she looked around and noticed that Mr. Casller was gone.

"Is something wrong?" he asked casually.

"No, I just seem to have lost my escort."

"He probably just slipped downstairs to check on the party. Would you mind staying here as my guest?"

"Not at all, thank you, Mr. Trathmoore."

"Please Katie, call me Albert."

His words were lingering in her mind; he said them as if he were already familiar with her. He stopped a server and asked if she would like some champagne. Though she rarely ever drank she accepted the fluted crystal glass of bubbly heaven. She needed something to steady her nerves, but she hoped her trembling wasn't evident as she held it. She drank her champagne a little too quickly, but he only smiled and got her another.

He whispered in her ear, "You might want to sip this a little slower."

He lingered close to her ear for a moment; she could feel his warm breath and smelled his expensive cologne, faint but captivating. His hand was warm on her arm as he led her about the room introducing her to people. She was amazed to find that this crowd was from all over the United States. These were the finest executives from ATI, all assembled for this gala event. He seemed to be guiding her purposely somewhere, but she wasn't sure where they would end up. They stepped into another room where the band was playing beautiful romantic melodies and guests glided easily about the floor. The lights were low and the room was cool and inviting.

"Shall we?" he said, gently removing the glass from her hand and placing it on a tray.

"Yes, that would be wonderful," she smiled shyly. She loved to dance.

Damn, she is beautiful, he thought. He wanted so much to slip her away to the apartment in the penthouse and make passionate love to her, but he had to restrain himself so she wouldn't know what was on his mind.

She had worn the emerald crop jack that went with her gown all evening, a little embarrassed to remove it in case Mr. Casller was leering at her, but dancing with it on wouldn't seem appropriate. She let the jacket slip off her shoulders and placed it on the back of a chair. She thought she heard him give a light sigh as he looked at her in the dim light.

Taking her hand and pulling her close to him as they moved onto the dance floor, he softly said, "My dear, you *are* lovely."

She felt giddy; perhaps it was the champagne, but then again perhaps it was the intoxicating company of this very charming man. They danced for what seemed a long time and with each new melody he seemed to pull her closer to him. She felt a little embarrassed to have her body so near his, but being in strong male arms again was fabulous.

He knew he was going to have to stop dancing with her before his desire became obvious. At the end of the fifth dance, he brought her back to their table. "We've been dancing away and I have even offered you a morsel to eat. Would you like me to get you something?"

"Oh no, thank you, I had something to eat down stairs, but I would like something to drink, not champagne though, I'm a little too thirsty for that."

"I know just what you need. I'll be right back."

She sat at the table alone, glad they stopped dancing. She felt a surge of passion and desire for this man that she had only just met. In her heart she had the feeling of betrayal. How silly of me to be thinking about Alex, she considered. We are divorced. He has someone else in his life, and I don't even know if Albert is really interested in me. She remembered what Ruthie and some of the others had said about his staunch resistance to women. Then again, she thought, he certainly didn't feel very resistant on the dance floor.

She sat there wondering what other surprises her evening might hold when Mr. Casller entered the room and walked stiffly over to her.

"Your friend, Ruth Macklin, is ready to leave and wanted me to come up here and let you know."

She quickly glanced at the clock. She hadn't realized how late it was getting. "Okay, just let me tell Alb—Mr. Trathmoore, I'm leaving."

He had a stupid grin on his face at her near slip. He knew Trathmoore must have had plans for her, no matter what kind of lifestyle he was accused of having.

She picked up her jacket and started to follow him when Albert came around the corner. He was obviously surprised that she appeared to be leaving, and he gave a very steely look to Mr. Casller. Mr. Casller scampered off saying he would tell Ruth that she would be down in a minute.

"Katie, you're not leaving are you? The night is young, and New York parties don't end until the wee hours of the morning."

"I really have had a wonderful time, but the young lady I came with is leaving and I won't have a ride home."

"Don't even think about it. I'll have my driver take you home whenever you're ready—that is unless you want to leave?"

She realized the question was two-fold, not only was he asking if she wanted to leave, but also if she was enjoying being with him enough to stay.

He smiled as she hesitated, then he added, "You are safe here you know. I promise to be a perfect gentleman all evening."

His smile was devastating, melting her inhibitions about staying.

"Let me go downstairs and tell my friend that I'll be home in a few hours."

"Very well," he smiled, happy that she made the choice he wanted, "I'll be waiting for you." There was something in his voice that sounded like he was giving her a command to come back to him, but she didn't mind, she wanted to stay a little longer.

Ruthie was standing downstairs at the main entrance waiting for Tom to drive up. When she saw Katie heading toward her she appeared relieved. "Where have you been, Girl? Old Casller came back down and said you were talking to Iron Pants."

"I have been," she said as if she talked with billionaires every day, "and he isn't anything like you told me he was. Listen, I'm going to stay for a little bit longer. I've got a ride home." She didn't tell her it was Mr. Trathmoore's private chauffeur because she didn't want to hear the whoops and hollers that Ruthie would surely shout.

"Are you sure?"

"Yes, I'll be fine. Go ahead, Tom's waiting."

Ruthie hadn't noticed that he had pulled up.

"Listen, Katie, I'm going to spend the night with Tom, maybe even the weekend, so don't be worried when you get home and I'm not there."

"Okay, have a good time."

"Are you kidding," she laughed, "with Tom? I'm gonna have a great time."

They gave each other a quick hug and Ruthie slipped out the door to the waiting car.

"Hey, isn't Katie comin'?" Tom said as he watched her disappear back into the building.

"No, she's gonna hang around here for a while. She's got a ride."

"Oh, man!" He said dejectedly.

"What's your problem?"

"Marc and I were gonna take you two out before we took her home. He's dying to meet her and I thought this would be the perfect chance to get them together."

"Sorry Cupid," Ruthie smiled, "not tonight."

~:~

Albert was beginning to think he had made a mistake to let her slip out of his fingers. Damn, he thought, I should have gone down stairs with her.

Just then Katie walked back into the room and once again felt her face growing flushed as people turned to look at her. It only took a moment for Albert to come back to her side.

The evening was magical as they danced, talked and strolled among the guests. He reluctantly paid attention to the other guests and never left her side for more than a few minutes at a time.

She had eaten hours ago and she was hungry, but she didn't want to eat in front of him. She sat briefly at the bar as he went off to the side to speak to another man who seemed to have something urgent he wanted to discuss.

"Can I get you something?" the bartender asked.

She was thinking about her empty stomach, so she asked him if he had anything that had any substance to it. She meant something that would help fill her up; he took it another way.

He had a mischievous smile. "Sure I do. Do you like it sweet or sour?"

She looked at him, puzzled for a second, then answered, "Sweet, please."

"Coming right up." He laughed to himself; if she wanted to get smashed, he had just the drink for her.

The drink was icy thick and definitely sweet, but although it was cold, it seemed to warm her insides and fill her up. Unfortunately, what was deceptively mild to the taste was loaded with alcohol, and by the time she had devoured the first drink and almost finished her second, she was feeling wonderful—but she was definitely drunk. She didn't realize how strong the drinks had been until Albert walked back to her and took her arm. Suddenly her knees were weak and the room spun slightly. He steadied her on his arm and looked at her quizzically, then back to the nearly empty drink on the bar.

"I'm sorry," she said, putting her fingertips to her forehead, "I think my drinks were a little stronger than I thought. You see I don't usually dink... ." She started to giggle at her slip of the tongue.

"Would you like to rest some where?" he quietly offered.

The night had been exhausting and she was exceptionally tired, particularly with the added effects of the alcohol. "Please, yes." she said, as he led her carefully from the crowd. She suddenly felt embarrassed being inebriated in front of such a prominent man. She started to apologize, but he reassured her that she was fine; it was that damn bartender he would get after when he went back to the party. He took her to his apartment in the penthouse. The lighting was low, yet even in her current condition she could tell it was lavish, more so than anywhere she had ever been. He led her, without protest, to his bedroom. She knew it had to be his bedroom because it had the same capturing aroma that she smelled when he whispered in her ear; and if the scent of power could be bottled, this was it.

Had she been sober she would have been embarrassed to be there, but she was too tired and groggy to care. He turned on the bathroom light, but otherwise left the room dark for her.

"You rest here until those drinks wear off and then I'll take you home, okay?"

She nodded as her head came to rest on the downy soft pillow. It only took a moment and she was asleep. He stood there for a long time, just looking at her. The soft moonlight showered down on her from the skylight, making her beauty even more compelling. He could easily take advantage of her this way, but he would not. He wanted her wide-awake and eager for his touch when the time was right. Reluctantly, he went back to the party.

When he returned to the room, it was four in the morning. His guests had left and security was locking up the building. He intended to sleep on the sofa, but he stepped in the bedroom simply to see if she was all right. He was stunned at what he found.

She had awakened sometime after he left and, still under the influence and disoriented, she must have thought she was home in her bed. Her gown was dropped to the floor, and her braided hair was pulled loose and lay softly about her face and on the pillow. Her exquisite body was only partly covered by the silk sheet.

He stood there, passion inflicting punishment on his reserve will power. He walked silently to her and gently touched her cheek, but she didn't respond. He knelt beside the bed watching her breasts rise and fall as she took her breaths. He was being consumed; he wanted her so badly, but what would she think of him if she woke and he was taking her this way? With greater restraint than he ever thought humanly possible, he left her there and headed for the shower—a long, cold shower.

Katie didn't wake until noon the next day, but when her eyes fluttered open she had the shock of her life. There she lay in someone else's bed—whose bed she couldn't remember. She vaguely recalled saying she wanted to rest at the party. She looked down at her naked body realizing that someone undressed her, Albert she assumed. Panic filled her like a sickening narcotic, adding to her pounding headache. "What have I done? I must have slept with him and I don't even remember it!" She knew he would think she was an easy woman who gave in to any guy who fed her enough drinks. Oh, I can't face him, she thought. How am I going to get out of here? Maybe he's gone already, but I still have to face the security people. I'm going to have to quit my job. Everyone will know what I did! Crap, what a mess this is!

She pulled on her gown and headed for the bedroom door. Cringing, she slowly opened it and looked out into the apartment. Albert was seated on the couch reading the Wall Street Journal. Dressed casually, he looked considerably younger without the tuxedo.

"Well, good morning," he said as she headed for the door, "or should I say good afternoon?" He met her before she reached it, "Did you sleep well, that bed is... ."

"I'm sorry, Mr. Trathmoore," she said, not wanting to look him in the eye, "I don't know what I did last night, but I'm not that kind of girl. I have to go home." The tears were welling up and spilling over her lashes.

He was touch by her emotion; it was a sensation long foreign to Albert Trathmoore. "Katie, you were a perfect lady last night. You didn't do anything to disgrace yourself. The bartender mixed you some very potent drinks without telling you what you were getting. It wasn't your fault, and as far as where you slept, you were quite alone I can assure you."

"But who undressed... ." she stopped short, too embarrassed to continue.

"You did that yourself. I promised you I would be a gentleman, and I was. I didn't remove your clothes." An easy laugh played on his lips as she began to find the humor in the situation, too.

"Then we didn't... ."

"No, my Dear, we didn't. But I must admit, you certainly tested my ability to be a gentleman."

She was relieved. "I do need to go home. I'd like to accept that ride now, if you don't mind."

"Actually, I was hoping you might consider joining me for the day at a house I have near the Adirondack Mountains. I have a stable with horses. *Though I haven't been in the saddle lately,*" he said, a smile turning the corners of his mouth, "we could take a leisurely ride on some beautiful terrain. It certainly would give you a different view of New York."

She looked down at her gown, not catching the saddle comment.

He quickly added, "My driver could run you home so you could get a change of clothes."

He was so charming, and very impossible to resist.

"I think I would enjoy that."

"Wonderful," he said. "Bring an extra change of clothes in case you get dirty from the horses, and a heavy parka, it snowed in the mountains early this morning."

What a weekend this is turning out to be, she thought.

By the time the chauffeur brought her back to the office building it was two-thirty in the afternoon. She didn't know where the Adirondack Mountains were in proximity to the city, but if it was any distance at all she felt certain they couldn't make it by nightfall. If she had to spend another night with him could he be a gentleman twice? He was for a night, but two in a row? Even if he asked her, she wasn't sure she was ready to sleep with him. She couldn't deny the way he made her feel when he held her close, but it would be a step she had never taken so quickly. She and Alex had dated two years before she decided she was ready to commit to him. She didn't even know if Albert truly was interested in her that way or not. His reputation as a loner who was unyielding to the ways of a woman preceded him, but she hadn't seen that side of him last night.

She walked into the elevator and pushed the button. She would know soon enough if she had made the right decision. She stepped into the massive penthouse office; the custodians were busy removing all signs of the party from the evening before. She made her way quietly down the hallway and took a deep breath as she opened the door to the apartment.

He was talking business on the phone when she stepped into the room, so she went to the sofa and sat.

"Well, are you ready to go?" he asked, as he hung up.

There was no mistaking his eyes carefully looking over her figure in her snug fitting jeans and soft flowing cotton blouse.

"Just how far away is your house?"

"Oh, roughly 250 to 275 miles, as the crow flies," he said nonchalantly.

"You're kidding?!" she blurted, suddenly feeling that she had made a mistake to return. "It takes an hour to go ten miles in this town. We won't make it back by Monday!" Her misgivings were clear in her voice.

"Not if we fly, Katie," he said with a devilish grin. She seemed too stunned for words as he took her arm and walked her to the elevator inside the apartment. In moments they were standing on the rooftop looking at a very large helicopter. He felt her resist his hold.

This is too much, she thought.

"What's the matter? You aren't afraid to fly are you?" Suddenly he could see his carefully laid plans being dashed.

"No, not exactly—maybe a little." she said, her face starting to pale.

He laughed out loud, "You'll be fine. I think you'll find flying in a helicopter pleasantly different from an airplane."

They boarded the lush cabin as he instructed the pilot to take off. The engines whistled to life and slowly the blades began to turn. She still looked a little panic stricken, so he put his arm around her and pulled her against him.

She was so surprised at his move to hold her that she didn't even realize they had lifted off and were swooping gracefully over the city skyline.

He felt her relax. He loosened his embrace on her as she cautiously leaned toward the cabin window.

"Isn't it magnificent?" he asked her as she peered out.

"Yes, it is." She felt breathless with awe as she looked at the town below them. "Do you fly much?" she asked, turning to him.

"Yes, I do. I go just about everywhere in this helicopter, unless it's in the city then I take the limo. Of course there are some destinations in the city that I fly to if they have a heli-pad.

"It's beautiful, isn't it?" she said, continuing to look out the window.

"Yes, it certainly is," But Albert Trathmoore wasn't looking at the city; he was looking at the beautiful woman seated beside him.

They flew over the Catskill Mountains, the peaks covered in a soft blanket of fresh snow.

"Is this the Adirondacks?"

"No, these are the Catskills. They have some fabulous resorts down there. Do you snow ski?"

"Are you kidding?" She laughed. "I've lived in Florida my whole life. I've never seen snow.

"Well then," he said with a pleasant surprised look on his face, "I'll have to teach you sometime."

She swallowed hard. There was no mistaking it; Albert Trathmoore was very interested in her.

They landed gently on the pad at his home and then walked to the house as the servants stood at the entrance to welcome their employer home.

They were astonished to see him in the company of a lady, but they knew better than to show it.

He introduced her as one of his programmers from the Manhattan office and then instructed one of the men to get two horses ready for an afternoon ride. He handed her bag to one of the women and showed her inside.

The house was a large rambling ranch style, rough-sawn beams graced the cathedral ceiling in the great room and a magnificent stone fireplace took up most of one wall. The furniture was made of heavy, white oak logs, but the cushions were covered in the softest kid leather. A very large bear skin rug lay in front of the fireplace, authentic, she was sure. The floor was Mexican tile with large Indian rugs in several areas. Paintings and bronze statues of horses, Indians, and cowboys tastefully decorated the room, along with Indian pottery.

"You must be originally from out west?" she said, as she took in the beauty of the room.

"Actually, I'm originally from Kentucky. That's where I acquired my love for horses. My grandfather filled my head with stories of cowboys and Indians, and the Old West. I decided to dedicate one of my homes to the preservation of those old memories."

"How many homes do you own?" she said feeling a little forward for asking, but her curiosity was too much for her mouth to stay in check.

"Only four," he said without much ado. "Two in New York, this one and one in East Hampton, one in Chicago and one in Hawaii; though the one in Hawaii is more of a vacation stop than a home."

She felt the need to find a mirror so she could make sure her mouth wasn't hanging open.

"I'm sure the horses are ready by now. Shall we go?" he said extending his arm.

They rode along a mountainous area that he said would lead to something special. It was so quiet and peaceful on the trail. The smell of the forest filled her lungs with cool freshness, and the only sound she heard was the steady rhythm of the horses' feet as they walked through the mixture of brightly colored leaves and patches of snow.

He didn't say much, only glancing back at her once in a while, and each time he would catch her smiling. They stopped and tethered the horses near a rock outcropping and he took her down a foot trail that led to a small, but splendid waterfall cascading into a clear pool below it.

"Oh I love it!" She exclaimed.

"I thought you might." He smiled as he watched her face light up. "You'll have to come back here with me in the summer," he said as casual as possible. "There's nothing quite like taking off your clothes and swimming in that pond. You can even stand under the waterfall over there," he said, pulling her close to him and pointing to a stony ledge that jutted out from behind the falls.

She loved to skinny dip, but how could he know. "Oh, that would be—so... ." her expression finished what her words could not.

She seemed just as taken with the idea as he had been when he came across this spot long ago. "Then," he said, gently turning her so that she faced him, "you might like to come here again with me—another time?" His words lingered around the question, waiting for her to respond in a way that would let him know if she wanted to be with him.

"Yes, I would," she fairly whispered.

Slowly and ever so gently, he took her face in his hands and kissed her, waiting for her to answer the invitation of the kiss.

Parting her lips, she returned the warm and passionate kiss.

His arms encircled her and pulled her body to his. He had been waiting months for this moment and now he knew it was worth the wait.

"Albert, I—I... ."

"What's wrong?" he whispered still holding her against him. "Does this frighten you?

"I've never been with another man. I mean, I was married, but he was the only one I ever... ." She had begun to tremble against his body as the power of the man who held her overwhelmed her senses.

"I won't do anything you don't want me to," he said in a low and even tone. "You're shaking terribly," he noticed, as he caressed her, unsure if it was the effect he was having on her or the cold. "Let's ride back to the house. If we stay here much longer it'll be dark before we get there." He released her slowly and guided her back to where the horses were tied.

It was dusk when they rode into the stable and turned their mounts over to capable hands. Once inside, he left her with Maria, who had been his housekeeper for as far back as he was able to afford one.

Maria had been through his first marriage and helped raise his two daughters before the divorce. She was glad that he was seeing someone. She knew he had been lonely too long, but she was also worried. This girl was so young, maybe even half his age, she thought.

Katie was taken to a beautiful bedroom, filled with Victorian finery, a brass bed and lace curtains. Her clothes from her overnight bag had been brought in and were hanging neatly in the closet, placed there she guessed by a maid. She went into the private bath and began filling the antique ball and claw tub with hot, steamy water. The bathroom was stocked with all the finest toiletries and it was easy to select a fragrant bath oil to use. She relaxed in the tub, losing track of the time, until she heard a gentle knock at the door. Her heart began to race as she thought of him walking in on her in the bath.

"Miss Katie," said Maria. "Dinner is ready, when you're through."

She breathed a sigh of relief then dried and dressed quickly.

As she entered the dining room, she overheard him tell Maria that she and the other staff would be excused for the evening immediately after the meal. He turned to Katie as if he had known she was there all along, "Are you ready for dinner? I know I'm starving, so surely you must be as well."

"Yes, I think riding gives me more of an appetite than usual."

The meal was splendid: seafood gumbo, lobster tails and drawn butter, rice pilaf and spinach salad with hot bacon dressing. Though she should have felt embarrassed to eat so much in front of him, she couldn't help herself. She was ravenously hungry and the food was prepared to absolute perfection.

He chuckled as he watched her eat more than he could hold; "You were hungry, weren't you? I have to admit, my kitchen staff is skilled beyond most culinary expectations."

"I don't think I have ever tasted anything as good as this meal," she said genuinely.

The staff cleared the table, smiling as they worked; it had been quite some time since they had received such lavish praise.

Albert gave a nod to Maria, and the staff vanished. "Would you care to join me by the fireplace for champagne?"

She didn't answer, but simply followed him to the other room. The fire was burning brightly on the hearth. The champagne was waiting in the ice bucket and two fine crystal glasses sat nearby.

They talked for a while about her life before New York, and then he reluctantly spoke about his first marriage. Though he put on a front of iron, she could tell he was secretly still hurting from his divorce, just as she was hurting because of Alex. She had slid beside him on the sofa as he spoke, no longer afraid to be near him. He talked about his life, not realizing how close she had moved to his side. He seemed almost startled by her presence when he finally noticed. They sat together in the firelight, silent in the pleasure of their closeness.

He put his arm around her and pulled her close to his chest, smelling the sweet fragrance in her hair and on her skin.

She slipped her hand into his as he held her.

"Katie, I... ."

She was surprised by his lack of appropriate words; it was the first time he had faltered in her presence.

"I want to be with you tonight. I want you more than anything I've wanted in a very long time, but I am not going to lie to you and tell you that I love you. I can't even promise you that I ever will. I don't want you to fall in love with me. I just know the honest truth is that I want to make love to you." He searched her eyes for the response, hoping it would be a yes.

"I'd be lying if I said I didn't want to be with you tonight. But I have to tell you I'm scared—oh Albert, I'm scared. I've never made love for anything other than love. I want you, too, but I can't promise that I won't fall in love with you."

He began to kiss her tenderly as he unbuttoned her blouse to reveal the woman inside it. Kissing down her neck to her breasts, sending them both into moans of pleasure, he pulled her down from the couch to the bear skin rug. The fur was hot from being close to the fire, its strands silky yet coarse against her back. He finished removing her clothing, kissing and caressing her body with skilled deliberation. She lay nude in the firelight more beautiful than he imagined she could ever be.

She helped remove his clothes, caressing the soft hair on his chest as she unbuttoned his shirt.

He saw a tear glisten against her face in the firelight, and it touched him that she was frightened, yet willing. His body, warm and inviting pressed to hers, as he wiped back the tear; "Do you want me to stop?"

She looked into his disturbing dark eyes. There was a distinct feeling that she was getting ready to step across a threshold; a threshold that would mean becoming a possession of this complicated and commanding man.

"Katie, do you want me to stop?" he repeated. For a moment, he thought she might say yes, but she pulled his mouth to hers kissing him with the need that was consuming her.

"No, I don't want you to stop, Albert. Make love to me."

Her body was on fire for him to touch her, to envelop and control her. She submitted to him and he cried out at the tenderness of her.

Her body was accepting him, and he had never felt such an exquisite experience inside a woman. He lost his ability to be timid and his powerful presence surrounded her, bring her to heights of pleasure beyond her experience. He was well skilled in the art of love making, even if love was not his motive. He cried out as the tender passion within her captured his will and forced him to submit completely to her.

They lay breathless in the firelight, trying to understand the magnitude of where ecstasy had taken them. He lifted her into his arms as she held tightly to his neck and he carried her to his bedroom. He would not be sleeping in solitude tonight.

He pushed open the doors to his massive bedroom and laid her down on his four-poster bed. The room was only illuminated by the soft, flickering light of another fireplace.

She didn't expect more from him, but again he began to caress her body, whispering words that sounded like words of love, but he said them so softly she couldn't discern them. His appetite for her seemed only slightly kindled from their lovemaking in the great room, and again he took her. This time, he spoke louder, telling her the pleasure he felt in being one with her. His need was great and deep, and she wondered what she had done by unleashing his passion.

He commanded her body to the pinnacle again and again, until he could no longer drink from the cup of passion long denied to him. Weakly, he kissed her and whispered, "You're beautiful Katherine—simply beautiful." Then he fell into a deep and restful sleep.

Lying in the darkness, the fire long since burned to ash, she questioned what she had done tonight. Slipping quietly from the bed, her legs weak and shaking from his skilled lovemaking, she walked to the master bath and closed the door behind her. In the center of his oversized bath was a large marble spa filled with hot, gently circulating water. She slipped into the tub and turned on the jets, letting the water pound against her flesh.

She thought of all the twist and turns her life had taken in such a short time. She thought, again, of Alex. Bitter tears welled up within her as she wondered what he would think if he knew what she had done. He had been the only person who knew her body, but she would never again be able to say that because now there had been another.

What would her future hold with Albert? Would he make working for him impossible, expecting her to be at his beck and call whenever he wanted a companion for his bed? What did he really think of her? Would his interest in her end with this weekend? The thoughts were disturbing and beginning to make her head ache. She dried herself and silently slipped back into his bed. It was three in the morning and the wind had picked up outside. A winter storm was moving in as she drifted into an exhausted and worried sleep.

When she awoke, he was gone from the room. She could see flurries of snow cascading beyond the bedroom window. She suddenly realized she had no clothes to wear; she left them in the great room the night before. She wondered what the servants thought when they came in that morning to find their clothes lying on the floor by the rug.

"Great!" she said out loud. "What do I do now? Stay in bed all day until Albert comes back to the room?" Surely somewhere in this room is something I can wear, she thought. Grabbing the silk sheet and wrapping it tightly around her naked form she made her way to a partially open closet. As she reached in to try and find something she could slip into she found her clothes from the Victorian bedroom and from the great room hanging in the closet, pressed and ready to wear. Embarrassment was warming her cheeks.

She dressed and headed down the hall to the dining room.

"Good morning, Miss Katie," Maria said as she entered the room. "Would you like some breakfast, and coffee perhaps?"

"Yes, that would be nice; coffee and perhaps a Danish if you have it."

"Oh, yes Ma'am. Have a seat and I'll bring it out."

But before Maria could leave the room she had to ask, "Where is Albert—I mean, Mr. Trathmoore?"

"Albert is fine, Miss Katie. He is in his office. Would you like me to call him out to join you?"

"No, that's all right. I just wanted to be sure he hadn't flown back to Manhattan without me."

"Oh no, Miss Katie, he wouldn't do that, and besides no one's going anywhere in this storm."

"You mean we can't fly back to Manhattan? We're stuck here?" Now Katie couldn't think of a more beautiful home to be stuck in or with better male company, but tomorrow was Monday and Ruthie would wonder what happened to her.

"I need to make a call. Could you tell me where there's a telephone I can use?"

Maria showed her to the den and Katie quickly dialed the apartment. There was no answer. Ruthie must still be with Tom, she thought, but she'll be home by nightfall unless she too was snowed in somewhere.

Albert met her as she came out of the den and started down the hall.

"Albert, are we going to be able to go back to Manhattan today?"

He raised an eyebrow with a slight smile, "Are you anxious to leave already?"

She was starting to get embarrassed again. "No, I was thinking about work on Monday and... ."

"Oh, I think I could excuse you from your job for a day." It amused him that he could easily read her facial expression; she was an open book. He knew he was making her uncomfortable at the thought of him personally excusing her from work.

"But... ." she began to protest.

"It's all right. I think the storm will lift by late in the afternoon—so I won't embarrass you at work."

She started to say it wouldn't embarrass her, but she realized he was right. She wasn't ready for the entire fourteenth floor to know that she had slept with him. And to tell Ruthie what she had done over the weekend, and to keep her quiet about it, would be another story entirely.

They spent a leisurely morning together wandering around the large house as he showed her different pieces of his western art collection, all of it originals, including several Remington sculptures. Looking at one in particular, she commented, "That's lovely. Where did you get it?"

"My ex-wife, Dalfina, bought that for my birthday one year. She said original art work was the only way she could be sure it was something I didn't have already."

"Yes, I guess a billionaire would be rather hard to buy for," she laughed.

He smiled. "Most women would have already quizzed me about my financial figures. I find it rather refreshing that we haven't discussed my 'worth' yet."

"It's really none of my business," she stated matter-of-factly.

"Aren't you interested?"

"Should I be?" she replied with a sly smile. She was finally able put him on the spot, and she could tell it rarely happened to him.

"Well, Ms. Danor, it seems I may have underestimated you." They laughed as he pulled her to him. "I think I need to evaluate you more carefully," guiding her to his bedroom as he spoke.

~:~

By two o'clock the storm had stopped, leaving a thick blanket of snow. Katie stood at the bedroom window as she marveled at the white landscape.

"What do you think of your first snowstorm?" He asked as he came up behind her and kissed her bare shoulder.

"You know I didn't think I was going to like snow when I moved up here, but now, to tell the truth, I want to go out and play in it like a little kid."

"Well, let's go!" he said as he slapped her bottom and headed for his trousers.

"Oh, we can't do that! Your house staff *will* think you brought home a kid!"

He zipped up his pants and sat down to pull on a pair of boots. "My staff's concerns aren't mine; neither should they be yours. If I worried about what everyone thought, I wouldn't be where I am today."

She wasn't sure if he was scolding or simply being straightforward. He laughed as he watched her face. He threw her clothes at her and promptly challenged her to a snowball fight, and then he hurried out of the bedroom.

"He's a nut-case!" she laughed. "A rich nut-case, but a nut-case nonetheless."

She dressed and headed outside. The air was sharp, stinging her nose and throat with its first cold inhalation. She stepped out on the snow-covered lawn; it was deeper than she had expected it to be and walking in it wasn't going to be easy. She started to look around for Albert when a ball of snow smacked her in the face. Albert stood not too far away doubled-over laughing.

"Oh, you sorry son-of-a... ."

"Hey!" he yelled. "Don't forget you're a lady!"

"Lady my ass!" she yelled back. "This is war!"

She learned that making snowballs wasn't as much an art as being able to make them in a hurry. She discovered that she had a natural knack for rapid-fire snowballs. Before long Albert was calling for a cease-fire; he surrendered, and that was a concept he didn't even believe in! Once she had her prisoner, she forced him to show her the proper technique for making snow angels and snowmen.

He was, for the first time in a very long time, enjoying something other than business. He studied her as they romped in the snow. She was beautiful, but she was so much younger than he was. He felt a stirring inside him that he had never felt before. Was it her pure innocence, her comfortable body that suited him perfectly, or something else? He wasn't positive the direction he wanted their relationship to go, and to not have a plan beyond this point was disturbing to him. He resigned himself to the 'snow business' at hand and would weigh-out the other decisions when his mind wasn't so intoxicated by her presence.

They flew back to Manhattan that night, tired and happy. It had been a marvelous weekend, but he realized as they entered his apartment that he wasn't ready for it to end just yet. "Would you consider staying with me tonight?"

"I can't take my suitcase to work with me." It seemed a silly thing to worry about, she had clothes in it that she could wear to work tomorrow, but she wasn't sure how she was going to get it home. And it certainly would not be on the bus.

He kissed the tip of her nose, "I'll have it delivered. Stay with me."

She hadn't felt so wanted by someone in a long time, but something in the back of her mind kept nagging her; was this just a fling for him? He wasn't the only one getting enjoyment from their time together, so she wondered if she should even care. She didn't want to leave; being next to him felt as wonderful as it did the first time he had put his arms around her. "I think I'd like that," she whispered.

Dialing the apartment, she wondered what would she say when Ruthie answered, but once again there was no one there to pick up the phone. Ruthie rarely spent Sunday nights with Tom, but apparently she was going to this weekend. Thank Heavens! Katie thought.

Monday morning came too soon. He was an early riser and already out of the penthouse apartment. She showered, dressed and went down stairs to the cafeteria. She didn't usually have breakfast at work, but this morning she made an exception because she was starving and she couldn't possibly last until lunchtime. She headed to her workstation, wondering what Ruthie would say. She was a little early and Ruthie hadn't made it in yet. She jumped right in to the pile of work she had waiting.

"Well, good morning, Katie," came a male voice.

Her heart jumped a beat, but when she looked up Mr. Casller was standing by her desk. "Good morning, Mr. Casller." The dread in her greeting was a little too apparent.

"Did you have a nice time at the Christmas party?"

She could tell by the tone of his voice that he knew nothing about her weekend. "Yes, I did. Mr. Trathmoore is a very interesting person. Thank you for introducing me."

"Well, you're doing such a good job, I thought you merited an introduction."

"Good morning, Mr. Casller," Ruthie interrupted as she sat down at her station across from Katie.

"Good morning Ms. Macklin. It's nice that you could join us for work this morning," he said sarcastically as he pointed to his watch.

"Sorry," she said, throwing her hands up. "You know how traffic is."

"Yeah, well your partner managed to make it on time. Let's see a little more punctuality at the desk and less at the coffee pot!"

Katie breathed a sigh of relief; he wasn't smart enough to put two and two together. Ruthie flipped up her middle finger behind his back as he walked away. Katie started to speak, but Ruthie cut her off. "I'm sorry I didn't phone you over the weekend, but Tom had a surprise for me and, well I kinda forgot about you. Sorry," she said again.

Boy! Katie laughed to herself. I thought about her and I had a *really* surprising weekend!

"He took me outta town to a motel that rents cabins by the Catskills. It was fantastic."

"It sure sounds like a great time." Katie was smiling serenely.

Ruthie was quick to become suspicious. "Well, it was. So, how was Friday night? And who gave you a ride home?"

Katie was not a kiss-and-tell kind of person, but Ruth would continue to press the issue, and it was so unbelievable that she really did want to share it with her. She and Ruth may have only been friends for several months, but it seemed like they had known each other all their lives.

"I'm not sure if I want to tell about my weekend."

"Your *weekend!*" Ruthie said a little too loud, causing heads to turn their way.

"Ssssshhh!!! That is exactly why I don't know if I want to discuss it or not. You've got to swear on your life that you can keep it quiet. I mean it Ruthie, not a soul—not even Tom."

Her eyes went wide. Just what kind of adventure did her friend have? "I can do that," Ruth said with a much lower voice.

"I didn't go home this weekend either," she whispered.

"What!" Ruth said, her volume rising again.

"Hush, Ruthie, I mean it!"

"Well, who did you spend the weekend with?" She asked, leveling an eye at her.

"The boss," Katie whispered nearly inaudible.

Ruth's face had a blank expression; then her little button nose wrinkled up, "Oh gross, Katie—you've been brown nosing Casller!"

Suddenly Katie was horrified at what Ruth misinterpreted from what she said. "NO. *The* boss," she said pointing upward.

Ruth's head tipped back slightly as she looked up—to Ms. Rathbone's elevated office. "No, you're not that kind of girl. Rathbone?" Ruthie said in total disbelief.

"No, you big yutz-head, the boss of the whole damn company—Albert Trathmoore."

Ruthie sat there for a moment looking as if someone had hit her with a baseball bat. Then she found her voice, "Get outta here! Iron pants?"

Heads turned at the mention of the nickname.

Katie's face went dark. "Ruthie!"

They didn't say anything for several minutes, each going back to the work they were doing. Katie looked up and Ruth was tipped back in her chair, nodding at her with a smile on her face. She tried to ignore the look and go back to her computer, but with her peripheral vision she could tell the smile on Ruth's face was getting broader. Finally she looked her in the eye and simply said, "What?"

"Girl," Ruth laughed, "I thought you were brown-nosing and here you were gold diggin'!"

"I shouldn't have told you," Katie scoffed.

Leaning toward her, Ruth sighed, "I'm not telling anybody, but I want to know more."

"When we get home, Ruthie," she said, letting her know it was time to drop it.

Ruthie didn't say anymore during the day; she just kept glancing at Katie with a big smile on her face.

They left the office and caught the bus that would take them back to the apartment. They rode in silence all the way home, but that promptly ended when they walked through the apartment door.

"Okay Sister, spill your guts!"

Katie told her as much as she was willing to say while Ruthie listened with her mouth gapped open. She finished with staying in the penthouse last night.

"Well, hell," Ruth replied, "why didn't you go upstairs before we left to see if he wanted you to stay tonight, too?"

"I couldn't do that!"

"Why not?" Ruth questioned. "There is no way I'd let a man that rich get away from me!"

"I don't know; it just wouldn't seem right. It would look like I was chasing after him,"

"Hah!" Ruth laughed, "There wouldn't be any *chase* to it if I were you. It would be more like a flying tackle!"

"Oh, get off it, Ruthie. If he's really interested in me he'll let me know."

Ruth just shook her head, "Personally, I think you're crazy, girl."

~:~

Albert made no attempts to see her on Tuesday, and by Wednesday morning she was starting to think maybe this was just a one-weekend affair for him. But Wednesday afternoon changed her mind. There was a floral delivery lady carrying several dozen long-stemmed red roses in a beautiful vase and everyone seemed to be directing her Katie's way.

"Hi, are you Katherine Danor?" she said, looking back to the name printed on the card.

"Yes, I am." But she still couldn't believe the delivery was for her.

"Here you are," she said as she placed the flowers on Katie's desk. "Have a Merry Christmas."

"Huh," Ruth said, "I wonder who those could be from?" She gave Katie a little wink.

She held her breath as she opened the card. "Merry Christmas!" it read. "Please come up and see me before you leave." Smiling radiantly, she tucked the card into her purse.

Alice Miller from the workstation across from them walked over to see, "Oooh, got an admirer, huh?"

"No. They're from my parents in Florida."

"Well, they sure are beauties." She sniffed a bud and walked away.

"Parents my foot!" Ruthie whispered.

"Hey, it could be from my parents," Katie said with an unremovable smile.

"Yeah, right. Do I look as dumb as Alice?"

This was the last workday before the long Christmas weekend and Katie had worried she would be spending it alone. She had a good idea that she had worried for nothing. Ruthie would be spending the holiday with Tom at his parents. Tom had invited Katie to join them for Christmas Dinner on Friday.

She gave Ruthie a hug and told her Merry Christmas at the end of the day. "Tell Tom and his parents I'm sorry if can't make it to dinner Friday."

Ruthie hugged her back and laughed, "Shit, you're not sorry. You're as happy as last week's lotto winner!"

"Yeah, I am, but don't tell them that. See ya Sunday." And she left for the elevator.

She was nervous as she stepped into the penthouse office. His secretary was stationed at her desk and looked puzzled as Katie approached.

"Can I help you?" Genevieve asked.

"Yes, would you please tell Mr. Trathmoore that Ms. Danor is here."

"Was he expecting you?" she asked, sounding doubtful but looking down at his appointment book.

"Yes, he asked me to come up before I left."

Genevieve was about to ring the intercom into his office, when he stepped out and saw her.

"Hello, Ms. Danor," he said smiling warmly and using a tone of voice that Genevieve had never heard him use before; it sounded—friendly. "I take it you received my note."

"Yes, they were lovely. Thank you."

His secretary looked completely confused.

"Have a good Christmas, Genevieve." he said as he slipped his arm under Katie's and guided her to the apartment. "I was wondering," he began as they walked down the hallway to the door, "If you would consider spending Christmas with me? I have several parties to attend and I would enjoy some company."

Now she knew what kind of parties he would be attending, black tie and evening gown affairs for the super rich. It had taken a whole day to pick out the gown she rented for the Christmas party and she really couldn't afford to rent it again. "I'd love to, really I would, but I don't think I own the right kind of clothes to attend your type of social affairs. I'm afraid I'd be an underdressed embarrassment. I was hoping you wanted some private company—at home."

His passion flared as they closed the door to the world behind them. Taking her in his arms as if he couldn't have waited another second, he kissed her with all the passion and desire that was in him, surprising them both. Breathlessly, still holding her tightly, he whispered, "I want you for both."

"But, I don't…"

"Shhh." He put his finger to her lips. Saying no more he took her hand and led her to his bedroom. There was a look in his eyes that caused her heart to pound hard against her chest; it was the look of a deep eroticism—an eroticism for her alone.

He made no attempt to restrain his need to make love to her. Before she could even regain her thoughts, he was taking her with the same fiery desire that overwhelmed them both the first time they made love.

He hadn't planned it this way, but she had a most unusual effect on his libido. And, for as much intense pleasure as it gave him, he didn't like letting his control slip away.

They lay together, still in each other's arm, trying to let their heads clear from the drug of desire. She whispered how very wonderful it was to be with him.

"I feel the same way," he responded. "That's why I want you with me this weekend. You're going shopping as soon as you can get dressed. Rosemary, my attendant here at the apartment, is going with you to make sure you get exactly what you need for the weekend. One word of advice; don't look at any price tags. Buy everything that makes you look stunning."

"Where are you going?" She asked as he rose from the bed and dressed.

"I have a few business details to take care of so take your time."

She quickly followed his lead and dressed then followed him out of the room. A striking, dark-haired woman met them as they walked into the living room.

"Katie Danor, this is Rosemary Travante. Rosemary will see you get everything you need. Goodbye." He gave Katie a peck on the cheek and dashed out the door.

Rosemary was smiling a broad warm smile. She looked as if she was in her late fifties. Her dark hair was pulled back tightly in a simple bun, and her eyes were a dark, yet sparkling green.

"Well, my Dear, are you ready?"

"I guess so," she answered meekly, "but I feel a little strange. I mean going out and spending someone else's money."

"Don't worry about that," Rosemary laughed. "We could shop for several years before we broke Mr. Trathmoore's bank account."

Katie laughed as she found herself warming very easily to Rosemary.

Rosemary instructed the limousine driver to head for Sacs, and the shopping trip began. Evening gowns, cocktail dresses, a designer pant suit and five pairs of shoes later, Katie felt like a princess who had been given the run of the palace.

"Are we done?" She could think of nothing else that she would need.

"Oh no, Dear, not yet."

"But what else do I need?" She asked incredulously.

"Dear, it's freezing cold and you can't very well wear your jacket with an evening gown." Turning to the clerk, Rosemary said, "We're going to need to see your furs."

She could say nothing. The whole experience was a shock for someone who could take thirty minutes to decide on spending an extra twenty dollars on herself; now she was looking at a $20,000 full-length fur coat with no decision to be made other than the color of the fur! After taking a coat and a lovely mink wrap, Rosemary headed for the jewelry counter where she insisted Katie needed the real thing; fakes could easily be detected by the wealthy. Diamonds, emeralds and pearls would look stunning, Rosemary said. She helped Katie pick out diamond earrings and a simple but elegant diamond necklace, several strands of beautiful creamy pearls with matching pearl earrings, a stunning emerald and diamond necklace with matching earrings and several bracelets.

"We'll need to see your rings, too!" Rosemary said beaming with enthusiasm.

"I think you're enjoying this as much as I am." Katie laughed.

"Oh yes, I am. It's been a long time since Mr. Trathmoore turned me loose with his money. The last time I did this was with his oldest daughter... ." She stopped at the mention of what might be the wrong thing to bring up to someone who wasn't much older than the daughter she was speaking of. "Well, let's just say, it's been a while."

She watched nervously as the final bags were packed into the trunk of the limousine. "I know he said not to look at price tags, but we've spent a fortune just for a weekend."

Rosemary gave her a wink and a reassuring pat on the hand as they slid into the back seat. "It's all right. I don't think you've quite grasped what he can afford to spend. Believe me, he won't even flinch when the bill comes in. Enjoy this weekend and forget the worries."

"I suppose you're right," she said as the lights of Fifth Avenue blurred past her window.

It would be a Christmas she would never forget. Gala events, private parties, and black-tie affairs filled their four days and five evenings with splendor, and passion filled their nights. Though she was dressed as all the socialites were, she still felt like an outsider. The eyes of the elite seemed to look at her and instantly recognize she wasn't one of them. Albert made the feelings of inadequacy bearable by lavishing attention on her. The women who had tried so hard to capture his interest didn't beat about the bush in asking who she was. In fact, sometimes they were quite brash about it. Albert enjoyed toying with them by simply saying either, "She's my date, of course." or "Sorry ladies; you can't know everything."

Christmas Eve they were at an exclusive Manhattan restaurant dinner party given by Mr. and Mrs. Banshaler, some of the wealthiest landholders in New York City. As they ate their dinner, she couldn't help but feel that someone in the room was studying her. When the band began to play, sending couples filing on to the dance floor, Mrs. Banshaler came up and asked Albert if he would join her for a dance. He smiled politely, and accepted the offer with unseen reluctance. He knew she was interested in two things, and neither was dancing: the availability of any real estate he wanted to sell and the identity of the young woman who was his dinner companion. In the real estate arena she was a formidable opponent, but in society gossip she was a grand champion.

Katie watched with a smile as they walked away. She could sense his dread without anything more than the glance he gave her as Mrs. Banshaler led him to the floor. Suddenly, from the shadows, a man came to their table and promptly seated himself in Albert's place. She was startled, not only by his forward sudden appearance, but also by a dark foreboding presence about him.

The man appeared to be in his forties, his hair was black, as were his beard and moustache. His eyes were equally dark and narrow set. Adding to his sinister appearance was the lack of a smile or any registration of friendliness.

"I hope I didn't startle you." he said evenly and low. "My name is Jon Lindquist. I'm the president of Syntec Industries. I couldn't help but notice you're here with Albert Trathmoore."

Avoiding his statement about Albert, she curtly replied, "Yes, you did startle me a bit. Normally, a gentleman would have asked *before* he seated himself."

His gaze leveled at her, giving her the distinct feeling that he could cut her throat at that moment and never bat an eye.

He sighed at the annoyance of her dodging his question, shifted his weight in the chair and then smiled insincerely. "I apologize. I should have asked. May I sit here while your companion is occupied?"

She wanted to say no he couldn't, but as much as she felt an instant dislike toward him, she simply couldn't be so brashly rude, and it seemed he sensed that immediately about her.

"Thank you," she replied, trying to mimic his insincerity. "If you'd like to sit there, please do."

"I haven't seen you with Mr. Trathmoore before. Have you known him very long?"

With a deep breath to reflect that she thought he was making himself a pest, she sharply replied, "A short time."

He suddenly seemed to enjoy their terse exchange; a genuine smile crossed his lips, "Well, I certainly hope I'll see you with him more often." Then, leaning over toward her ear he whispered, "I've heard he's quite a catch."

She drew back to avoid this man she didn't know from having his face so close to hers. "I wouldn't know," she smiled. "I'm not trying to catch him."

His smile broadened, "Touché, Madame."

Just then Albert reappeared at the table; he had seen Jon seat himself beside her and it didn't take him long to excuse himself from the dance floor.

She noticed immediately that his jaw-line was drawn tight and his eyes were bearing down on the intruder.

"Jon, I didn't realize you were here."

The man stood and thrust out his hand to Albert, and, for a moment, she saw a hesitation on Albert's part to accept it. They shook hands in a very cold and unkind manner   .

"That's a very lovely *young* lady you have with you this evening. I enjoyed talking with her. Good-evening," he said, turning to Katie and then walked away.

Albert reseated himself, but his jaw was still tight.

She gently reached out and touched his hand and his expression softened slightly. "Thank you for coming to my rescue. He's a very rude and unnerving person."

She could tell that her dislike of Jon pleased him.

"His company is a competitor with mine—and he's an asshole."

Katie's expression changed to one of complete surprise; it was the first time she had heard him speak so—unrefined.

"I agree," she laughed.

He smiled warmly at her, "Are you ready to leave? I can think of far better things we could be doing than this."

"Me too," she whispered, squeezing his hand.

~:~

Just as she was starting to get used to the idea of being at his side day and night, the holiday was over. Their last several hours together were spent in each other's arms in his bed. She didn't want it to end. In her brief time with him, he had touched her heart strings and she could feel the deep stirrings. She sought his kiss and his touch for more than lovemaking; she had fallen deeply in love with Albert Trathmoore.

Albert felt the change in her response to him; her eyes were very readable and he could tell that it wouldn't be long before she uttered the words he feared. The true problem was that he also felt the same deep emotion welling up inside himself. This wasn't part of his plan. To have the pleasure of a woman whenever he wanted it was his original goal. He never thought anyone could arouse his heart from its deep, cold slumber as she was doing. Lying there, holding her in his arms, his anger with himself for having such a weakness began to kindle. He would need to put some distance between himself and her immediately. He needed to get her out of his system before it was too late.

She had been talking to him, but he hadn't been paying attention; he was wrapped in thoughts of his own.

"...Albert? Are you listening to me?"

"I'm sorry, I was thinking business for a moment. What were you saying?"

"New Year's weekend—would you like to spend it with me?"

He rose from the bed abruptly, pulling his clothes on in an angry fashion.

She wondered if she had been wrong to make the invitation instead of letting him ask her. "I'm sorry, it's okay if you... ."

"No, we can't spend next weekend together," he said gruffly. "I'm spending it in California with my daughters. I'll be working in my western division until mid-January."

"Oh," she said quietly. "Would you like to ride in the limousine to take me back home? We could talk and... ."

"Katherine!" He stopped her short. "I told you from the beginning, I'm not going to fall in love and have a relationship with you. We've had two wonderful weekends together; let's not spoil it by making more out of it than it is."

Her lower lip trembled as she reached for her clothes and began putting them on.

He wanted desperately to apologize for hurting her with his words, but he had taken the first steps in putting himself back in control. He would not weaken himself for any woman. "I hope your feelings aren't hurt, but I was straight forward with you from the start. I'm sure we'll see each other another time. We've each received pleasure from our brief encounter."

She wasn't saying anything; she just dressed and headed for the elevator. He followed her, and pushed the button for the parking garage. She wouldn't look at him, and that suited him at the moment. He didn't want to see her expression; it would be too easily read. He opened the back door to the limousine and she slid inside.

"I'll see you some other time, Katherine," he remarked casually and then closed the door.

As the car pulled away she felt her cheeks turn flaming red and the tears began to sting her eyes. His last words were echoing in her mind as if he was telling an escort 'So long and thanks for the good time; you've been paid, now leave.'

"Goodbye, Albert," she quietly whispered, "You won't do that to me again. I'm not going to be your good-time girl."

He realized he had been curt and cold when she left to go home. She knows I'm not looking for a relationship based on love, he thought. She had been taken to the best parties in New York and she had been given tens of thousands of dollars in clothes and jewelry to keep as a memento of their time together. She had even said that she had a wonderful time this weekend; that should be sufficient for her, he reasoned. After all, he wanted this relationship to slow down before it was more than skin deep. If he could enjoy her company whenever he wanted it and still remain unattached, there would be no need for emotions to get involved.

He was beginning to get the familiar feeling that comes at the close of a fantastic business deal when his driver returned with a worried expression. It seemed Ms. Danor had refused to let him unpack the car. She told him to return the 'gifts' to Mr. Trathmoore; she didn't want them.

It irritated him that she had done that, yet he had to smile when he reckoned with the fact that no one else had ever had the balls to stand up to him before. Still, he felt secure; she would wait for him to call on her again. She wouldn't see anyone else after having a taste of such an opulent lifestyle. He would keep an eye on her but keep his distance until he had total emotional control.

CHAPTER THREE

Winter faded away like the melting snows across the New York landscape, giving way to the breath of springtime. The few trees that there were in Katie's part of the city began to bud with fresh green growth. Her heart felt as if the 'snow' of disappointment over Albert was also beginning to melt.

Spring brought a new energy and zest for life that she had never felt before. She had always lived so careful and cautious, so planned and precise, yet in the last half year she had taken so many incredible leaps into the unknown that she almost felt as if she had walked into another world. She left her first love, moved from the only state she had ever lived in, changed jobs, and fell in love with an older man who just happened to be one of the wealthiest men in the country. Life, she had to admit, was turning out to be very different from what she ever dreamed it would be.

Ruthie had given up on trying to persuade Katie to go after Albert. She also became convinced that, even though it was love for Katie, it was nothing more than an amusement for the season for him. "I guess it's time to get those feet of yours planted back on the earth again." Ruthie teased as she and Katie planned their next few days off together. "If you're not going down to Florida for a little spring break, and you don't plan on jet setting with the rich and famous, how 'bout going to Cape Cod with me and Tom for a little R and R?"

"I don't want to intrude."

"Intrude my ass!" Ruthie laughed. "I wouldn't invite you if you were going to 'intrude.' We've got a three-bedroom cottage rented and that means there's plenty of room for a little intruder—I mean friend."

She did want to see the Cape and she knew Tom wouldn't mind; he was an easy going, fun-loving person, just like Ruthie.

"And besides, we might run into Marc over there and get a chance to do a little double dating."

"Oh, I see. I'm coming along to keep the future brother-in-law happy, huh?"

"Hey, if you wanna be a lonely old maid, suit yourself. I just thought you might like to date a *normal* guy for a change."

"Marc's not staying at the cottage is he?"

Ruthie rolled her eyes. "Please, give me a break. No, he is not staying at the cottage, but he is driving over Friday so we can do some sightseeing together—that's all! I'm not trying to make you two hop in the sack together or anything like that."

Katie sighed in relief.

"But he is really cute, ya know. I mean, I've seen his hairy chest and his tight buns—in his shorts, of course. He's really sweet too."

"Oh shut up, Ruthie! All right, I'm going and I'll be his date—for the day."

~:~

The Cape was beautiful. The cottage, which was a small elegant New England home, over-looked the ocean near Falmouth. It belonged to friends of Tom's family and it had been a favorite vacation spot since he was a little boy.

"Do you like it?" Ruthie asked as she brought a cup of coffee onto the porch deck. They arrived just after dark the night before and, although Katie could hear the tremendous pound of the surf, this was the first time she had seen the beach. It reminded her of home, yet the Atlantic here seemed to be bluer, more restless, and the air definitely seemed saltier. A spring front had bullied its way up from the south and the surf was taking out its frustration on the shoreline. She watched as the dune grasses swayed in the heavy breeze. Terns and sandpipers stood on beach as the wind rumpled their feathers, while a few brave gulls dipped and swooped on the air currents.

"It's incredible!" she practically shouted, as if the wind was trying to take away her words.

Ruthie smiled. "Yeah, that was my reaction the first time I saw it, too. It kinda takes your breath away. This is the tail of the front that came through yesterday. Just wait till it passes. You'll be even more amazed."

"Tom still sleeping?" She asked, taking the offered cup.

"Yeah, he's been here a lot with his family when he was younger so it doesn't seem to affect him much—except the salt in the air." Ruthie said, gesturing to the wind. "He said it makes him sleep like a baby."

"Well, tell him when he wakes up that he snores like a sailor, not a baby!"

"That's the truth."

They both laughed.

"Marc is supposed to be here around ten or eleven this morning. We're going to do a little sight-seeing and shopping in town. We'll probably go out to eat for dinner tonight. Sound good to you?"

Ruthie watched Katie's reaction to see if there was any reluctance about being Marc's date, but there was none. Katie just smiled and nodded, looking back to the breath taking view of the ocean.

Marc arrived by eleven. After rough housing around with his younger brother, and making polite small talk with Katie, they took off. Marc had rented a convertible and what a day to be in one. With the top down, the sun shining, and the cool breeze billowing, they drove through the local towns, exploring the shops and sights.

Marc, with his New York brogue just like his brother, was a charming host. He had Italian written all over him. From his thick head of jet-black hair, to his deep brown eyes, and olive skin, he was decidedly a very nice looking man. He had a raucous sense of humor and embarrassed his brother and Ruthie with every opportunity. The day was filled with laughter and fun. By twilight she knew she had made the right choice to come along.

They found a quaint New England restaurant that, according to Marc and Tom, served the best food around. And, if the chowder was any precursor to the meal then she felt they must be right.

"You remember the time we came out here to the Cape and Mamma bought all those crab cakes to take back to New York?"

Tom nodded and began to laugh. "Yeah, and she put 'em on the kitchen table at the cottage and left the door open when she came out to see what we were doin'."

By this point they were laughing harder and louder. It was an infectious laugh and she and Ruthie began to laugh along even though they didn't know the outcome of the story.

"Yeah, and when we walked back into the room there were about six cats from around the neighborhood on top the table eatin' those cakes!"

"Dad was in the bathroom," Tom said looking to Ruthie.

Marc leaned over as if he was informing Katie of a secret, "He had *no* idea what was goin' on."

"All he heard was Mama yelling, cats screaming, dishes breaking... ."

"He said it sounded like the worst barroom fight he'd ever heard!"

"The cats scattered through the house 'cause Mama let the door shut behind her when she came in and... ."

Marc was turning red from laughter as he cut his brother off, "Dad came running out of the bathroom with his pants around his ankles, tripped and fell just in time to see a big ol' tom cat barreling toward him!"

The story went on and on and got funnier with each passing moment. She wasn't sure if it was actually as funny as she understood it, or if it was it the inn's ale that helped make the story so laughable.

By the time they finished their meal and headed back for the cottage they felt as if they all had been friends for years. Tom and Ruthie headed straight for the bedroom. Some people might have mistaken that for being impolite, but Katie knew it wasn't intended that way.

"Boy, looks like they abandoned us." Marc said, as he awkwardly fumbled for something to say. "I guess I'd better be heading back to my hotel."

"Would you like a cup of coffee before you go?" She offered, feeling that she could use a cup herself to shake off the effects of the couple glasses of ale. She couldn't imagine driving anywhere feeling this way.

"Sure. I suppose it would help to have coffee on my breath instead of beer in case I get pulled over on the way back," he grinned.

She brewed a small pot and then she and Marc went out on the deck to enjoy the coffee and each other's company. The sky was partly overcast as the stars tried to peek out around the clouds, the wind had stilled, and a sliver of moon managed to sparkle its' reflection occasionally against the ocean.

"Isn't it a beautiful view?" She said looking out on the water.

"Right now, mine is," he said, sipping his coffee.

She looked at him and he was smiling at her. She felt a blush come over her face in the cool night air. It was the first pass he had made and she caught on to it quickly.

They made preliminary small talk and she felt at ease. She asked about his prior marriage, which Ruthie had told her about already. He talked briefly about his former wife, Lenore.

"She was a real scrapper. Man, that woman was rough." He scratched his head as if she still bewildered him. "I thought she'd settle down after our daughter was born, but she just got meaner everyday."

"Do you get to see your daughter?"

"Nah. She sends me pictures sometimes, but they move around a lot. She met a guy in the Air Force after she left me, so they've been stationed all over the place. He's an M.P. or something like that. I guess that's what she needed to keep herself in line."

"So what about you?" He said, turning the conversation. "Your ex-husband must have been crazy to let you get away."

"Over-active hormones got to him," she said, wincing slightly. She hadn't spoken about Alex in quite sometime. He looked bewildered by her answer, so she realized that Ruthie either hadn't told that much to Tom, or else Tom didn't tell his brother what she said. "He had an affair with an eighteen year old girl—and she ended up pregnant."

Marc grimaced as if he'd swallowed something bitter. "Wow, I guess stupid would have been a better choice than crazy. What about this rich guy you been dating? Not that I'm trying to be nosy or anything, I'm just wondering if an ordinary guy like me might stand a chance at seeing you more often."

It was odd to realize that Albert was more of a sore subject than Alex now. Evidently a little of what she said to Ruth made it to Marc.

"Albert? I liked Albert—a lot." She paused, unable to meet his gaze. "But I don't think he was seriously interested in me. I guess he just wanted to have some company for Christmas. I haven't heard from him since." Her face blushed red, but this was a little deeper than just embarrassment.

Marc didn't laugh. He smiled softly and looked out on the night scenery. "Well, I guess he must be crazier than your ex."

They talked a little longer. He was a good person to talk with, but eventually he mentioned it was getting late and he'd better be going. She walked him to the front door and told him goodnight.

"I hope we can go out sometime. Just you and me, without the two love birds along," he said, gesturing toward the hallway that led to the bedroom. "Jeez, you can't take those two anywhere without 'em finding a sack to hop into."

She grinned and rolled her eyes, "That's the truth! Goodnight, Marc."

He opened the door, but then stopped before stepping into the darkness. He looked back into her eyes, "In case you're wondering, I'm not crazy." Pausing for a deep breath of salted air, "Before I lose my nerve; can I kiss you good-night?"

She didn't answer, but smiled and tilted her face up to his.

Softly placing his hand on the back of her neck he brought her gently to his warm chest. Wrapping his arms around her, he kissed her with an erotic and passionate deep kiss.

Surprise was written all over her face. She wasn't prepared for that kind of kiss, but it was so good that she couldn't help give him a shocked smile.

He chuckled lightly. He'd been told before that he was a great kisser and her expression confirmed it. "The French may have invented it," he said with his face reddening a little, "But it's the Italians who perfected it." Realizing she didn't know what to say, he simply said "Good-night, Katie," and left.

She headed for the bedroom, shaking her head the whole way, "If Tom can kiss anything like his brother does, then it's no wonder Ruthie always heads for the bedroom."

That night she couldn't sleep. With the windows open, the salt air flooded the room, clearing her mind to think ahead. She wondered about a relationship with Marc. Was she prepared to fall in love again? In all honesty, she knew that her heart still belonged to a man who had, for all intensive purposes, rejected her. She cried as she remembered the way Albert pushed her away with his last stinging words. She wiped away the tears on the cotton sheet. "I don't know what I did wrong, Albert, but I guess it's time to move on," she whispered in the dark.

She thought about Marc; he was a really nice guy and he was good looking too, but he, in his New York way, was so different from her. He was fun to be around, but....

Suddenly, she heard something that made her jerk around in her bed to stare into the darkness outside her window. She saw a man's face at the screen, and she let out a shockingly loud scream. The figure crashed out of the bushes and headed out onto the lawn. Tom burst into the room with Ruthie close behind.

"What's the matter!" he shouted.

"There was a man at my window!"

At that moment, they heard a car crank up and Tom dashed for the door. Ruthie hugged Katie as they watched Tom racing out across the lawn toward the car that was speeding away.

"DAMN!" They heard him shout.

He came back to the house only slightly winded. "Are you okay? I didn't get a good look at the guy's car. Looked like a tan Buick or something. You know anybody with a car like that?"

She just shook her head; she was trembling all over. It was 4 a.m. and they were all so wide-awake they weren't going back to bed.

"I don't believe it!" He muttered almost to himself as he headed down the hall to fix some coffee in the kitchen. "Twenty years my family's been coming out here and this is the first peeping-tom we've ever had. That's supposed to happen in New York, not on Cape Cod!"

When Tom called his brother to let him in on their plans for the day, he told Marc about the prowler at Katie's window. The girls were outside so he spoke frankly to his brother. "That wasn't you was it?"

"Of course it wasn't me! I'm a little smoother than that little bro. I left around two a.m. and came back to my hotel."

"Well I'm just askin.' I didn't get a good look at the guy. I mean, I know you wouldn't normally do something like that, but she *is* a beautiful girl. If I was you I might be tempted to look through her bedroom window."

"NO! It was not me. Maybe though I'd better stay out there tonight in the spare bedroom just in case our little friend returns for another peek. Do you think she'd mind me being there?"

"I doubt it. She was shaking like a leaf after it happened. I don't even know if she wants to stay here tonight." Tom suddenly changed the conversation as Ruthie and Katie came into the house. "Okay, Marc. Yeah, we'll see you at the restaurant for breakfast. Okay, bye."

He looked at Ruthie as he hung up the phone. "Do you mind if Marc stays here tonight in the spare room? You know, in case we have anymore—ah—visitors?"

Ruthie leveled her eyes at him. "I told Katie he wouldn't be staying here."

"It's okay, Ruthie. I don't care if he stays. There is an extra bedroom. But, I really don't think it will happen again. I'm sure they don't get much crime out here."

"Great!" Tom said before Ruthie could interject. "I'll call him and tell him to go ahead and check out before he leaves to meet us at the restaurant."

Before they left the house for breakfast, Ruthie called the answering machine back at the apartment to check for messages. But, to her surprise, there was only one message on the machine. It was for Katie.

"What's wrong?" Katie asked, seeing the look on Ruthie's face.

"Oh, nothing's wrong," Ruthie said with one eyebrow cocked funny. " It's just that you've got a call to return *immediately*—to Albert."

She handed Katie the number. "We'll wait for you outside."

Tom just stood there looking at her, so Ruthie popped him in the stomach. "Come on Tom! Let's wait outside," she said, making exaggerated motions to the door.

With her hands shaking, she dialed the number. Within two rings, Rosemary answered the phone. "Oh, Miss Katie, it's so good to hear from you. Yes, Mr. Trathmoore has been waiting for your call."

Immediately, Albert was on the phone, "Katie?"

She could feel her mouth going dry, "Yes."

"I need to see you right away. Where are you? Can I send a car for you?" His voice sounded urgent, almost pleading.

She was even more deeply shocked, "I—well, I'm—I'm in Falmouth on Cape Cod with Ruth... ."

"I can pick you up at the Cape Cod airstrip near there in about two hours," he cut her short. "Do you know where the airstrip is?"

"Well, I'm sure Tom does." At once she sensed that was the wrong thing to say.

"Oh, I'm sorry," his voice went cold. "I didn't realize you were there with someone."

"No, I'm not. Tom is Ruth Macklin's boyfriend. We rented a cottage for a few days. But, why do you need to see me so suddenly? Are you okay?"

The sound of relief in his voice was apparent. "Everything is fine. I just need to see you right away." He paused at her silence, "Of course, I guess I couldn't blame you if you didn't want to see me."

There was a lump forming in her throat; the memory of being hurt still raw.

"Katie, I'm sorry for what I said to you. Do you want to see me?"

"Yes," she answered quietly into the receiver. "I'd love to see you."

She walked out into the brilliant early morning sun. The predawn fog had lifted and the day was shaping up to be spectacular, in more ways than one. Ruth and Tom were stunned that she was leaving, yet Ruthie was happy for her because she knew how much she wanted to be with Albert. Tom said he would take her to the airport, which wasn't too far from the restaurant in Centerville where they had planned to have breakfast.

She quickly packed her things and tossed them into the trunk of the car. They had plenty of time to stop at the restaurant for breakfast, but she was too nervous to eat.

Marc didn't say much, and deep down she felt terrible about leaving this way. She knew he was hoping that they might begin a relationship that was more than just friends. Tom teased him about a few things, trying to get him back to his jovial self, yet Marc's laughter didn't seem to have the same sincerity as the day before. When it was time to leave, he looked straight at Tom and, without leaving any room for him to rebut, he said, "I'll take her. You and Ruthie finish your breakfast."

Katie wasn't sure it was a good idea to have Marc as her escort, but Tom made no move to leave the table. Ruthie, who was normally forthright and outspoken, was speechless. Somewhat reluctantly, she and Marc left and headed to the Cape Cod airstrip. He didn't say anything on the way, but as they parked the car and he grab her bags he stopped and looked at her. She looked away as she heard the drone of an incoming aircraft. It was the ATI corporate helicopter. Looking back at Marc, he was still unmoving.

"Are you sure you want to go off with this guy? I mean, ya know, maybe it ain't any of my business, but it don't sound to me like he did you right. Takes you out at Christmas time and then don't call you until April? I—well, I really like you and I just don't wanna see this guy jerk you around. I don't care how rich he is, he needs to treat you right."

The helicopter landed not far away. The engine slowed but didn't stop. Albert stepped out with his valet who headed in Katie's direction to get the baggage from Marc. Albert waited by the door of the aircraft, eyeing suspiciously the man speaking to her.

She looked at Marc. He was a good man and she wasn't going to walk away rudely to Albert's side, remembering for a moment the anger she felt when she and Albert parted the last time. "I'll be careful Marc. And believe me, if he doesn't treat me right, I know who I'm going to call." She looked into his eyes, Albert standing there or not, she kissed him softly on the cheek. "Thanks," she whispered in his ear.

Then she turned and headed to the waiting helicopter. She was grateful that she had to lower her head as she walked under the spinning blades. She knew they were close enough to actually hit her, but at least she didn't have to look at Albert's face at that moment—his stare was hot enough without actually seeing it.

The next thing she was aware of was lifting off and Marc fading into the landscape. To her surprise, and somewhat relief, Albert didn't ask who it was who had brought her to the airstrip, although she knew he realized that it wasn't Tom.

Finally she turned to Albert who was sitting stiffly beside her. He was as handsome as ever, dressed sharply and smelling like some wonderful manly fragrance that a woman could lose herself in. "Albert, why… ."

He turned and met her gaze. Passion was as obvious as if a fiery hot torch was reflecting in his eyes. "Shhh," he said, putting a finger to her lips.

The way he looked at her made her inner resolve melt. He was truly a powerful man, and at that moment she wanted to release herself to his power.

Without saying anything, but wanting so much to touch him and be held by him, she sat there wondering if he knew what she was thinking. The helicopter began to descend near the port in Hyannis and, for a moment, the drop in altitude frightened her.

"It's okay. This is where we're getting off." He reached over and squeezed her hand. His voice sounded so good to hear. "We're taking my boat the rest of the way."

"Where?"

"That depends on you," he answered as he pushed open the exit door.

The valet instructed the men who came to help take the luggage. A short, heavy-set man with gray receding hair came up and motioned to speak with Albert. His face was serious and he didn't smile when he looked at her.

"Come with me," the valet said to her.

Soon she was walking up the gangplank to a large and magnificent ship. This is not a boat! She thought to herself.

She was met by a female attendant who showed her to a well appointed cabin. All the finery was present. She had come to understand that when she was with Albert she should expect nothing less.

"The bath is well stocked, Ma'am, if you'd like to relax. It may be a little while before Mr. Trathmoore joins you."

She nodded numbly as the attendant opened the dressing closet to reveal numerous outfits, shoes, and silky lingerie all neatly placed for her selection. Fine lotions and colognes adorned the bath shelf for her to choose from. She sighed. The attendant left and she was alone to disrobe.

She soaked in the large Roman tub, letting the rush of her morning and the experience of her night before slip from her consciousness. She began to doze in the comfort that enveloped her until she was startled by the revelation that the boat had begun to move. She didn't know how long she had rested, but when her eyes opened there was Albert seated not far from the bath, just staring at her. She let a little scream escape, thinking for a moment of the night before.

"I'm sorry. I didn't mean to frighten you." His voice was soft, almost inaudible.

She started to sit up from the luxurious bubbles when she realized her modesty and settled back down in the bath.

He laughed aloud, "I know what you look like Katie, you don't have to hide from me."

"Well, yes—but... ."

He moved close to the tub, kneeling beside it. He was not accustom to being on his knees for a woman, but he was making a careful exception this time. He reached out to touch her face, but she pulled back from his caress.

"Why did you ask to see me?" She was searching for some resolve, some dignity to resist him. She didn't want to part from him in a few days feeling like she did the last time. "Despite the fact that I came, and despite my—my compromising position at the moment, I don't want to be toyed with."

"Then marry me," he said softly.

"I... ." she stopped. She looked with disbelief into his eyes. *"What did you say?"*

"Katherine Danor, I am asking you to marry me."

She stared at him, trying to let the words sink in. Her world suddenly became surrealistic as she grasped what he had asked her. Her mind jumbled and her thoughts escaped her ability to speak. These were the words she would have been more prepared for lying in his arms their last night together, not the rejection that came as such a complete and utterly crushing surprise. Did she love Albert Trathmoore enough to marry him? She knew the answer in her heart was yes.

"I've thought about you, over and over again," he began. "I didn't want to make a commitment to anyone after I divorced. Then you came along. I've tried to distance myself from you, but it hasn't worked. You've been there every time I close my eyes." He paused a moment; truth can be a hard thing to say. "I expected you to try to contact me, but you didn't, Katherine, you left me alone—as a lady should after the way I treated you. I don't want to be alone anymore."

He reached into his shirt pocket and pulled out a breath-taking diamond ring. Holding it out to her, he asked a third time, "Will you marry me?"

Starring into his eyes, she heard a small and distant voice whispered, "Yes."

He put the ring on her finger. She was crying and laughing at the same time. His hand found the release to the drain, and he let the water escape. Helping her out and handing her a towel, he drew her to him so closely that she could barely breathe. Then he kissed her, his mouth searching her, beseeching her to answer his passion with a passion equal to his own.

"You are the most beautiful woman I have ever known," he said breathlessly, his heart pounding at the thought of the step he was taking with her. He felt her weaken and begin to tremble within his embrace. Wrapping the towel around her body, he picked her up carefully and made way to the bed. "I'm so glad you came back to me. I'm glad you didn't find someone else before I came to my senses."

She was listening to his voice, wondering if he could possibly know how close she *had* come to finding that someone else.

His hand was under her chin lifting her eyes to meet his. "I don't know what I would have done if you had turned me away. I don't want to share you with anyone else. Say you're mine." His mouth kissed down her neck and moved gently to her shoulders. His body pressed to hers. "Say you're mine and no one else's."

"Yes," she repeated over and over.

He kissed her again, but stopped and restrained himself. Her fingers began to unbutton his shirt as he clasped her hands to his chest, stopping her from going any further. "Say your mine. Say your mine."

"Yes, I'm yours, Albert. I'm yours." There was splendor in being with him and ecstasy in being dominated by him. "Make love to me," she whispered as her lips sought his.

He kissed her again, "No. It's not the right time."

Bewildered for a moment, her mind drunk with the pleasure of being near him, she couldn't think clearly, "But... ."

He rose to his feet, deciding to leave now or spoil his careful plans. "I'll be back," he said quietly, and then left the cabin.

She lay there for quite awhile trying to understand the magnitude of what had happened. Marrying Albert was not even a concept this morning. She studied the ring on her finger, but her vision seemed to blur. She had been awake more than twenty-four hours; her subconscious took over and she slept.

When she opened her eyes several hours later, she realized it wasn't some wonderful fantasy dream; she was really on his boat and she had agreed to marry him. The sleep was clearing from her mind, and her thoughts began reeling.

"I've got to call my parents!" she said, sitting bolt upright. She had fallen asleep still wrapped in the bath towel, but it was time to get dressed and let two very special people know about what she had committed to do. She stopped to look at herself in the mirror, fixing her hair in a ponytail and then quickly touching up her make-up. She turned around and ran right into Albert. He caught and held her fast.

"Whoa, Mrs. Trathmoore. Where are you going in such a hurry?" He looked at her with a warm smile.

'Mrs. Trathmoore,' she repeated his words in her mind. "I wanted to call my parents, but then I realized we haven't talked about a date or plans. Where are we going anyway?"

"I had a feeling you'd want to see your parents if you said yes, so I thought we might cruise down the east coast to Florida."

"And if I had said no?"

"Well, then I figured we'd travel to New York Harbor and I'd put you on a ferry for Manhattan and tell you to get back to work and quit goofing off." He smiled a devilish grin.

"Head the boat south," she said, pressing her body against his. "When, Albert?"

"I don't want you to get away from me, ever again. But I have to consult my legal advisors about our—shall we say, merger?" His face turned serious for a moment. "What do you want from me, as far as my company and money are concerned?"

She was stunned. She didn't think about what she wanted from his business. She only though about what she wanted from him.

"Albert, all I want is to know that you love me." Her tone was true and genuine.

"My first wife wanted that too, but later she wanted fifty percent of my company." He looked at her for a long moment. "My chief legal counselor was the man who spoke to me when we arrived in the harbor. He knew I was going to ask you to marry me. He's assembled some of my legal staff to draw up a pre-nuptial agreement. I have to let them know what you'll settle for, financially." She was quiet for such a long moment that he thought she must have been calculating a cash settlement.

"I'm not going to marry you because of your money or your business. I'm not going to have people say that's why I married you. I don't want anything from you, and I'll sign a pre-nuptial agreement without hesitation because I've got to trust you if you're going to be my husband."

He felt an inner wince. There was much about him that this innocent and beautiful young woman didn't know. How he had his eye on her before she was ever aware of it. How he had calculated how he would sleep with her. How he had her medical files lost so she would have to undergo new tests and he could have her checked for HIV/AIDS. How he had her entire prior life examined. How he kept surveillance on her constantly, even up unto last night when his detective reported that she had a man getting a little too close. How his detective peered into her window last night just to make sure the other man in the house wasn't in her bed. How he knew the man's name at the airport was Marc Dunochio, and that he was the one getting too close to her.

What would she think if she knew that he had a night vision video locked in his office with a shot of this same man kissing her? He had decided to ask her to marry him because of that video, it was either that or let her go. He knew she left her first husband over an issue of trust. Now she was willing to give that naïve trust to him; and he knew himself well enough to know that her trust was not something he was worthy to have.

"Albert?" she said, breaking the deep thought he was in. "I have to *know* you love me. That's all I want."

"I wonder sometimes if I know what love is," he began. "I know that I feel something for you I've never felt before. I know when I saw you kiss that man's cheek today I felt a jealous rage unlike anything I've ever experienced. I know that I have had you on my mind unceasingly since *before* you met me at the Christmas party."

He waited for her response. He wasn't sure how much he wanted to reveal. Business had taught him to never give too much exposure to what can hurt you.

Her face showed she was puzzled over his last divulgence.

"Ever since I started talking to Bob about you. I saw your picture in the employment file." He answered her unasked question. Whether he knew it our not, he was building the trust she so desperately wanted. "If this isn't love, then it's the closest I've ever been to it."

"Love," she said, with a tender look, "is the best when you have trouble describing it. Thank you."

"Marry me tonight—on board ship. I'll have a minister flown here and everything prepared for us within a few hours."

She stared into his dark blue eyes; there was a look of urgency in them. She wanted to ask him why so soon, but deep down she wanted it now, too.

He took her in his arms and held her close. His mouth, soft and warm, caressing her with kisses. He brought her gently to the bed, laying her back with his body lightly pressing against hers, he whispered in her ear, "The next time I take you to a bed, I want it to be as my wife. I'll wait if you need more time."

Thoughts tossed about in her mind. When she wed Alex it took months of planning and preparation. She had wanted a big wedding, Daddy walking her down the isle, bride's maids and bouquets, a ring bearer and a flower girl—all the things that go into a wedding because she thought that it made a difference. It was more than they could afford, yet family gifts helped make it possible. Now that part of her life was over and she was lying in the arms of a man twice her age. A man who could afford to let her have whatever she wanted, but it didn't matter. All she wanted was love and the security that comes with being loved.

"Tonight. I don't want to wait."

~:~

Before boarding an ATI helicopter on the ship's deck, she signed her name to the marriage license, which his attorneys would file; the prenuptial agreement would be signed before they took their vows. She left the ship to fly to Martha's Vineyard. A limousine was waiting to take her to an extraordinary shop that had a beautiful selection of gowns, wedding and evening. Then it was on to an exclusive spa for pampering. She would have a manicurist, hairdresser and a cosmetologist waiting for her arrival.

The spa was incredible. Attendants took care of her every need. She felt like a princess in a dream, but it wasn't a dream, instead it was a very beautiful reality. Relaxing in a bubbling mineral bath, she dialed her parent's home. Still unsure of how she was going to tell them. Her mother's quick answer on the other end startled her. "Ah—Mom," she managed to get out.

"Katie, I thought you were off vacationing for a few days. What inspired you to call? Is everything all right?"

"Yes, everything is wonderful, but I'm not at Cape Cod."

"Did you stay in New York, Dear?"

"No. Actually, I'm in Martha's Vineyard."

"Isn't that an island, Sweetheart? Did you take a ferry?"

"I flew over for the afternoon. Then I'm flying back to the ship in a few hours."

The line was silent. Katie could almost see what her mother's face must look like at that moment.

Mother knew good and well Katie didn't have the kind of money it would take to do what she just said, and for an instant she began to think her leg was being pulled.

"Mom, I've got some wonderful news for you and Daddy. Just please, don't—well, just let me start by saying I know what I'm doing."

Her mother felt faint. She didn't know what the outcome of this riddle was going to be, but prefaced like that she wasn't sure if she'd like it.

"Mom, I'm getting married tonight. I know that it's sudden and out of the blue, but he is the most wonderful man. You and Daddy will love him." Although she knew they would be concerned about the age difference. There was no response. "Mom, are you there?"

She heard the phone drop on the counter, banging loudly in her ear.

"Lawrence!" She heard mother yell, "Come here quick! Katie's on the phone saying she's getting married!"

Her dad got on the kitchen phone as her mother went into the bedroom to pick-up on the call. She needed to be in the bedroom because she needed to be seated on the bed for this one.

After several minutes, she calmed their alarmed first fears. It took a bit longer to explain how she had met Albert during the Christmas holidays. She skipped the part about him stepping out of her life until this morning, though; that would only serve to cause them worry.

Her father kept repeating, "He *owns* the company."

"Yes, Daddy. You can see his picture in the last Fortune 500 magazine—or you can just wait for a few days until we're in Florida."

"You're coming home?" They both asked.

She was almost giddy from dropping so much in their laps at one time. "Yes. We'll be in Florida however long it takes the ship to get there from here. I think about four or five days. I'll call you again in a couple of days to let you know exactly when we'll be there. I love you both."

It was well after dark as the helicopter descended in Nantucket Harbor. To her surprise, the valet said she would be meeting Mr. Trathmoore's legal advisors here, and then take a boat to the ship anchored just off the harbor.

She looked stunning. Her auburn hair was pulled back in a French twist with soft tendrils cascading down by her temples and earlobes. Her knee-length dress was a creamy antique lace over shimmering satin, hugging her every curve. The bodice dipped low, revealing her striking bust line. She had always felt self-conscious about showing off her figure, but tonight she simply felt beautiful.

Four men seated at a large table in the harbormaster's office, rose to their feet as she walked into the room. They were surprised at the poise and confidence of this young woman.

"Gentlemen," she said, looking directly to the man she had seen that morning in Cape Cod, "I believe you have some documents for me to sign."

"Yes. I'm Martin Fengale, Mr. Trathmoore's chief legal counselor. This is Mr. Johnson, Mr. Rizzona, and Mr. Carter. They are associate legal advisors."

Katie shook their hands and waited for Mr. Fengale to come and pull out the chair for her.

"Ms. Danor, I'll be quite frank with you," he said as he came back to his chair and straightened his tie. "Mr. Trathmoore is a man of considerable wealth and he has asked that you be certain of the legal arrangement you have requested between the two of you. Normally, I expect the people who deal with Mr. Trathmoore to be responsible for knowing the consequences on their own. It has never been my position to speak in anyway that would jeopardize my client's favorable positioning in any situation. Yet, in this case, Mr. Trathmoore wants to be certain you understand what you *could* request. He has authorized me to negotiate up to certain limits. If you wish to exceed what is set forth, I'll call him for the approval."

"Mr. Fengale, I am not going to change what I told Albert. I'm not marrying him for financial gain, and I won't have anyone saying I did."

"But Ms. Danor, if you'll be realistic for a moment, things change, people change. There may come a time when you'll think your decisions today were unwise and made in haste."

"No. My mind is made up. Do you have the document prepared?" she said as she reached for a pen.

Mr. Fengale was beginning to sweat under his neatly pressed suit. He had never argued against his own client before, yet he was specifically instructed to act on Ms. Danor's behalf. He knew it was in her best interest to request a portion of Albert's wealth. He pulled out his handkerchief and wiped the forming perspiration from his brow. "I'd advise you, Ms. Danor, to wait and reconsider. You could be left penniless in a divorce. A man of Mr. Tathmoore's financial position could easily afford to part with a few million dollars. This agreement leaves you with no money, no financial interest in the company, it doesn't provide for heirs to his estate... ."

"Mr. Fengale, I can't have children," she interrupted. "There is no need for a clause for future heirs." For the first time, she felt a hot blush on her cheeks, but it was more anger than embarrassment.

"Ms. Danor, have you even considered that with Mr. Trathmoore's financial resources, infertility might be an obstacle you could overcome?" Interjected Mr. Johnson.

The redness in her cheeks began to flame. "I didn't come here to discuss my ability or inability to conceive, did I gentlemen?"

Mr. Rizzonna was beginning to smile as he watched his colleague's frustrations rise. This woman had to be either very sincere in her love for Albert, extremely naïve or very foolish. Foolish didn't seem her caliber. He studied her for a few more moments as his partners continued, unsuccessfully, to sway her to see things their way. That was his specialty. He was the one who studied the situation and then, usually, came in to seal the transaction. The others were there to bring to the surface a person's flaws; it was his job to catch them.

Mr. Rizzona cleared his throat and the room grew quiet. "Ms. Danor, you certainly seem to know what you want, or should I say, don't want. We aren't here to embarrass you or upset you in any way. Tonight is going to be a very special night for you and Mr. Trathmoore; we aren't trying to spoil it. If you feel *completely* comfortable signing the prenuptial agreement as you requested it, by all means," he said sliding the agreement to her, "please do. *But*, no one in this room will think any less of you if you wanted to at least discuss the possibilities."

She knew Albert had told them to give her room to change her mind. They were speaking to her about what would be best for her. She smiled for the first time. Mr. Rizzona smiled in return. He thought she was ready to discuss options now.

"Thank you, all of you, for your concern. I'm sure it's difficult to speak to me about someone whose money you're used to protecting, not trying to give away." The tension broke, and there was a brief moment of laughter at the table. "But, I'm comfortable with the original agreement." Quickly pulling the contract to her, she put her signature on it and handed it back to Mr. Rizzona.

"Gentlemen, goodnight." She rose and headed for the valet waiting just outside the door.

The four sat there for a moment, vaguely aware that they had forgotten to rise when she did. Mr. Fengale was scratching his receding hairline, Mr. Carter and Johnson looked on in disbelief, and Mr. Rizzona was the only one smiling.

Boarding a boat in the harbor, she was on her way to the ship. She could see it not too far in the distance; it seemed to sparkle in the moonlight. It was a glorious night to be on the water. She laughed to herself, "I wonder if Albert ordered the weather?"

She was glad to have the agreement behind her. There was a feeling developing within her when she came to New York; it was a feeling of independence. Yes, she was still dependent upon love, but she had a new sense of command over her life that she had never felt before. Decisions that would have agonized her, came easily. Moments of fright became moments of exercising control.

It didn't take long to reach her destination. The boat, which seemed large when she boarded it, now seemed dwarfed by the ship. The second floor gangplank was lowered and an attendant crossed over. "Ms. Danor, Mr. Trathmoore is waiting for you on the upper deck."

With a deep breath, she followed her back to the ship, to Albert, to marriage and to the beginning of a new and exciting life.

Making her way to the upper deck, she could smell the intoxicating aroma of roses and something she could barely make out, yet familiar. Vanilla? The last step on the stairwell behind her, she looked up and her breath was stolen away. White roses were everywhere, hundreds and hundreds of them lining the deck. The area was illuminated, but not by electric lights; candles were placed between each stand of roses.

Albert's back was to her as he looked out over the bay. He turned just as she took a step in his direction.

"I didn't think you could be more beautiful," he said, coming to her side. "You are stunningly exquisite."

She looked at him. His hair was oiled and combed back smartly. He wore a traditional tuxedo, but tailored sharply to show his powerful physique. Tonight he didn't have the look of a cunning and hard-edged businessman; he looked like a lover from the silver screen of old.

Tenderly he took her arm and guided her to the bow where the minister stood waiting and smiling.

They made a wonderful couple.

Quietly and unrehearsed, they pledged themselves to each other. When the minister asked for the rings, Albert opened a dual box with two rings inside, bands of gold, embedded with diamonds. Katie removed the larger band, and repeating the minister's words "…with this ring, I thee wed…" she slipped it on Albert's finger. Albert then repeated the same as he gently placed the other on her finger. She vaguely heard the minister's words, "You may kiss the bride." His warm embrace was surrounding her, pulling her into him, his lips softly enfolding hers, and then as he held her for a moment longer, she heard him whisper, "I love you."

He gave a nod to the minister and, with a quick congratulatory handshake, the minister left them alone.

"Well, Mrs. Trathmoore, are you ready to retire or should I bring up the string quartet that is waiting below?"

"Take me to our cabin," she said looking at him with a fiery light in her eyes, "and do to me what you wanted to this morning."

His eyebrows shot up in surprise. Her body pressed tighter against own and he could feel the heat increasing.

"Mrs. Trathmoore! I'm speechless."

"That's good," she said with a sly smile, "because you won't need your mouth for speaking." And then she kissed him, just as he had kissed her that morning as he pressed her to the bed. He actually looked shocked.

Reaching the cabin door, he swept her off her feet and carried her into the dimly lit room. It too was filled with white roses and candles. Grabbing one rose as he made way for the bed, letting Katie gently down beside it and putting the rose between his teeth.

"I never realized how romantic you are," she said with a quiet laugh.

"I never realized how romantic you make me feel," he said through rose-clenched teeth as he removed the top of his tuxedo. Gently he unzipped her dress, letting it slid down to the floor. Still behind her, he took the rose and softly caressed her shoulders and back with its soft petals. Then dropping the flower he began following the same path with his lips. She shivered with eagerness, moaning his name softly.

Taking her in his arms and laying her back on the bed, he kissed her with all the anticipation and need that had been building in him for months.

Breathlessly, she looked into his eyes, eyes that were hungry for her, all of her.

"Are you really mine?" Came his quiet whisper, as if he were asking himself.

"Yes," she moaned as his body joined with hers, "I love you, Albert."

~:~

Katie's mother and father liked Albert, but she could see the concern in their eyes, too. He was a stranger to them. Alex they had known for years before she married him; but Albert's whole lifestyle and manners were strange to them. He was a commanding man who ran a corporate empire with an iron fist. His demeanor was carefully cultured to deal with people of wealth and stature. It was awkward at first, but eventually they found middle ground.

Age turned out to be a concern that surprised Katie more than anyone else. When her father and Albert shook hands for the first time it suddenly became obvious how much closer Albert was to her father's age than to hers. She was twenty-six; Albert was fifty and her father was sixty. Mother, a youthful fifty-nine, even blushed a little when Albert took her hand.

Two days later, Katie and Albert boarded a private plane for city of Nice on the French Rivera . She had never been interested in being a world traveler, but he insisted she would love it. And she did. They spent a week exploring the shops, museums and restaurants along Promenade des Anglais, sunning on the beach, dinning at the Chantecler each evening, and dancing in the moonlight. Late at night, with their balcony doors open and a warm breeze billowing off the breathtaking Mediterranean Sea, they were wrapped in each other's arms in their presidential suite at the Hotel Negresco.

Yet, even with the splendor around her, she was eager to return to New York. She would not be returning as she left it two weeks ago. She was someone else now, and New York would change with her. No longer would she be hustling off to catch the 6:45 bus for Manhattan; no longer would she live with her friend in their modest little apartment; no longer would she work at her desk on the fourteenth floor, and no longer would she be simple little Katie Danor. Their last night on the Rivera, he reminded her of that.

"You realize when you return with me to New York, you're going to be a celebrity, don't you?"

"A celebrity?" she laughed as if he was teasing.

"I'm serious, Katie. To tell you the truth, I'm amazed we managed to escape the media this far," he said, hardening his expression for the first time since they had come to France. "You're now the wife of a very wealthy man. I'm used to having them bother me, but it's going to be something new for you—and trust me, it's frightening for a while."

She shivered; her privacy was not something she had thought about. Her past life with Alex, her parents, her friends, everything was now going to be under public scrutiny.

He sensed her newly realized fear, "It's all right. We have very good security, and I have ties with enough media moguls to put the brakes on a potential avalanche of inquiries. Yet there are always the tabloids to contend with." He smiled as he looked off in the distant darkness of their room. "I've sued enough of them to make them wary anyway." He stroked back the silky hair from her forehead. "I hope I didn't spoil the mood for our last night here."

She smiled, though it was a little weak. "I won't like the attention, but I feel safe with you. Just don't leave me by myself for too long."

He gently pushed away the satin sheets to leave his bride bare before his eyes. Rising up on one elbow to look at her, he smiled, "I don't think you'll have to worry about that."

~:~

She called Ruth the day after she left Cape Cod, but she hadn't told her that she married Albert the night before. This was something she wanted to tell her in person. He was going to make a public statement to the press Monday morning, so she wanted to tell her before she read it in the paper or saw it on the news. The helicopter brought them to the corporate office from the airport. He didn't want her to go back to her old apartment, but he understood her need to retrieve some of her personal belongings.

"I really don't have much that I want to get, but I do have some photos and personal papers. I guess I really don't need much of anything else. I shouldn't be gone too long and then... ."

"I'll come with you," he stated rather nonchalantly.

"You want to come with me? *To the apartment?*" She tried not too sound shocked, but that's how it came out anyway.

"Yes, then we can leave right from there and go to my—our house in East Hampton. You haven't seen it, yet." He smiled his devilish grin.

She knew he had a house in the Hamptons. She remembered he had told her that during Christmas, but she had come to think of the office penthouse as their home.

"Yeah, right. I haven't seen that yet, have I? You're sure you want to go to the apartment? I mean, it's not exactly—umm—I'm trying to think of the words..."

"High society?" He offered with a smile.

She had to laugh. It definitely was not high society—more like the low rent district actually. "Yeah, that's the truth. But," she offered in defense of her former life, "it was home for a while."

The limousine pulled up in front of the apartment complex. Some of the neighborhood kids crowded around excitedly to see who was inside. Now it was Albert's turn to feel uncomfortable.

"Come on. They don't bite. I promise—I'll protect you." She offered with a laugh.

His response to the five flight climb was the same as hers had been so long ago when she first saw the apartment. "No elevator." Although for him it was a statement instead of a question. "No wonder your figure is in such good shape!" he mused.

Reaching the apartment, she could hear Ruth's unmistakable laughter beyond the door. With a deep breath held in her chest, she unlocked the door and Albert followed her inside.

"Hey, Katie! Is that you?" Ruth yelled from the hall that led to the bedrooms. "Where the hell have you... Whoa!" Ruthie said, putting on the brakes when she saw Albert. Tom, who had been following behind from the bedroom, crashed into Ruthie when she stopped so suddenly and they both stumbled out in to the living room. Ruth was in underwear and a long tee shirt and Tom was in his boxer shorts!

Perfect! Katie thought. Just perfect!

"Mr. Trathmoore!" Ruthie managed to choke out as she pulled her tee shirt down further. Her face clearly beet red. That was something new; Ruthie never got embarrassed.

Tom sheepishly stepped out from behind Ruth and offered his hand to Albert. "Hi, I'm Ruth's fiancé, Tom Dunochio." After shaking his hand, Tom looked at Katie and then to Ruth, "I'll just go—I'm just gonna get something else on." He motioned toward the bedroom.

"Yeah, me too. I'll be out in a minute, Katie," she said as she hurriedly followed Tom down the hall.

Albert looked at her with a strange expression.

She looked back at him, throwing her hands up in the air. "Oh well, this is real life. They're getting married." She offered, though she knew that part didn't matter to him.

"Does he live here, too?" He asked with a certain amount of suspicion in his voice. From his intimate knowledge of Katie's life he knew Tom wasn't supposed to be living there, unless the person reporting to him had left that part out.

"No. Oh, gosh, no. Tom just comes over once in a while, mostly weekends. Usually Ruthie goes out to his parents for the weekend. He doesn't usually come here—for the night I mean. Have a seat and I'll get my things. I still need to tell Ruth, you know, about us."

Tom passed Katie as she was walking back to her bedroom. Quietly he asked, "What do I do with him? I mean, do you want me to offer him a drink or something?"

Katie smiled, putting her hand on Tom's, "Just go out there and be yourself, you'll do fine."

He looked down and saw the rings on her finger. "You—did you? You didn't."

"Yeah, I did. I've got to tell Ruthie. Go on out there and make small talk for a few minutes, okay?

Tom nodded and headed down the hall, but the whole way Katie could hear him saying "Oh man, oh man, Ruthie is never gonna believe this."

She knocked on Ruth's door just as she was opening it to come out. "I've got to talk to you." Katie said walking in and sitting down on the rumpled bed.

Ruth was about to squeal from the excitement. "You spent two weeks with him—and he came here to the apartment! He must be getting serious about you, Girl." Ruth practically jumped on the bed beside her. "Man, I can't believe it! You have gotta go for this you know."

Without saying anything, she raised her left hand and watched Ruthie's eyes as she saw the rings.

"You got engaged? That's a wedding band!" She said in pure amazement. "You—oh, no way!" Her voice went into super high pitch. "YOU MARRIED HIM?!"

"Ssshhh!" Katie said, as if it was some government secret or something that the spies were waiting outside to hear.

It took a few minutes to get Ruth to stop jumping. Then she wanted to know all the details. She recounted as quickly as she could the events of the past two weeks. Ruth just sat there and looked at her in disbelief. "And the only bad part is that I'm not going to be living here anymore. I'm leaving for East Hampton as soon as I can gather up a few personal things. I guess you can do whatever you want with my other stuff," she finished. She looked at Ruth's face and saw that she had tears in her eyes.

"Katie, I'm so happy for you." Ruth said, throwing her arms around her for a hug. They just sat there for a minute in an embrace of true friendship. "I'm gonna miss you, Girl!"

"I'll see you around. I got married; I'm not leaving the planet."

Ruth laughed through the tears, "No, but you might as well because you're going to another world, Kido!"

The house in East Hampton was masterfully done in beautiful French provincial. His first wife was the one who selected the décor years ago. Though Albert told Katie that she would be free to re-decorate anyway she wanted, she was happy with the house the way it was. It was a large home with eight bedrooms and ten baths, carefully manicured grounds and a full staff to attend to their every need.

But, by bedtime the first night in her new home she had to ask, "With people to cook and clean, and shop, and to take care of the gardens and the yard, what am I supposed to do to earn my keep around here?" She was sitting gingerly on the edge of their enormous antique cherry bed, watching him as he headed toward her.

"Keep me happy, of course," he laughed. "You're the only one who is allowed to do that."

"Thank God!" She answered. "At least I've got something to do around here."

"Oh, believe me, you'll be busy. Once you get the hang of all the social affairs of the wealthy, you'll be so pressed to find time even I'll have to check your planner to see you," he said as he hung up his robe and went to the other side of the bed.

"Fat chance!" She giggled. "I'm not, how shall I say, a social extrovert? I'll be stored up in the bedroom waiting for you to get home at night so I can be your *love slave*." She flopped back on the bed as if she were tied to the carved headboard.

He loved the way she teased. She was so unlike anyone he'd ever been around, and it was totally refreshing and made him feel more like he was her age instead of his own.

"As much as that thought is incredibly appealing to me," he said, sliding his strong hands up her slender forearms to clasp her wrist firmly. "I'm sure we can discover some ways to help you blossom in other areas."

Had she known at that moment just how extroverted she was going to become, she would have preferred the bedroom. When the news broke on Monday morning, she had instantaneous fame. Everyone from the Wall Street Journal to Time magazine wanted to do a 'Cinderella' story about her fabulous catch of one of America's most eligible bachelors. Offers were coming in for talk shows and news programs. It was a flood of the most unwanted kind.

Invitations to the social affairs of the wealthy and the nosey were just as plentiful. Though she politely declined them all for the first few months, Albert said there were a certain number of affairs that must, for the sake of social graces and manners, be accepted.

"I just feel as if I don't know what I'm doing," she complained to him after they attended a fund-raising dinner for the Mayor. "Who sits where? Which fork do you use? Which glass do you use? When you are supposed to speak and when are you supposed to be quiet? It's all so confusing and, to make matters worse, when I do speak or converse with these people they are talking in circles above my head! I don't know about classical music, Monet and Picasso, world travels, French clichés." She looked over to Albert seated beside her in the back of the limousine. The dark streets of New York were passing by outside the tinted window. He seemed preoccupied and distant. She sighed, when she had his attention she had it all, but when he was like this it was almost impossible to get him to notice her. "And, though I never thought I be saying this, I mean, with all the money available to spend, I'm bored." She just let the words drop flatly from her lips as if it didn't matter whether she had spoke them or not, he wasn't listening. But, to her astonishment, he had been listening.

His mind was working on helping her feel accepted – but boredom? That was a new piece to add to the puzzle. "The

University," he stated as if she would know exactly what thoughts had been running around in his mind.

"What?"

"The University. It's close to home and you can take some classes in the arts and humanities. You wanted to go to college at one point, didn't you?"

"Yes, but now?"

"Why not? The people you're dealing with are college-groomed people. Most everything else is learned by being in their circles. Perhaps this will dispel your new found *boredom*."

Now it was her turn to be the one with the distant stare.

"You need to travel more too, Dear," he added.

Albert traveled all the time and rarely did he want her along on business. He was a different man when business was at hand. He iced over like a steel razor out in a sleet storm. He was truly frightening to be around because he was a man who could simply remove any emotion from the situation. When it came to business, he saw everyone the same (including her); they were opponents.

"I didn't think you liked me tagging along," she said as she continued to stare out the window. She remembered several weeks after they married she had gone with him to Chicago for a meeting with his mid-western executives concerning some trade secrets that had somehow been leaked to Syntec Industries. As the meeting was about to get underway, she asked him if Jon Lindquist knew that his company was receiving stolen technology.

His entire demeanor changed in an instant toward her. There in front of everyone he hit her with a barrage of demands on how she knew who Jon Lindquist was, and how did she learn that he knew about the programs' origins. She told him she'd discuss it with him later as she tried to walk away. He blocked her path and coldly and calculatedly extracted the information he wanted from her. With everyone looking on, he showed no compassion, nor indication that he was dealing with his wife or some stranger off the street.

He had forgotten that she met Lindquist over the Christmas holiday, but he didn't apologize—not then, and not later. He simply said business is business and it might be a better idea for her to stay away from the business aspect of his world.

"I don't mean business trips," he added coolly, bringing her back from her thoughts. "I meant traveling to Florida to see your family.

You might even take your parents traveling. You said your mother is from Canada. Perhaps they'd like to go there for a month or two."

"A month or two?!" She stated with shock. "But—but what about you? Would you want me gone that long?"

"Absence making the heart grow fonder has a ring of truth to it you know."

"Yes, well it could also make the heart 'go wander' too."

"You don't have a thing to worry about, unless you're speaking of yourself and that I'd have to be concerned with you finding someone else."

She shook her head, smiling. "No not me. Relationships are far too complicated with just two people in it. I'm definitely a one-woman man. If Alex hadn't run around on me, I'd have still… ." She let it drop, forgetting for a moment that he did not like mention of Alex's name. Alex had called her not long after the news of her marriage hit the papers. He had a hard time getting in touch with her, but was persistent enough to get through Albert's staff. Albert had come home as she was ending her conversation. He made no point in hiding the fact that he was irritated with her for speaking to him.

"You'd still be married to him," he finished for her. It looked as if, for a moment, he was angry with her, but his mannerisms softened. "Damn lucky for me he thought with his penis instead of his brain!"

He had been so serious that his remark caught her off-guard.

They both laughed. Moments like this together were wonderful.

The laughter died down and once again he put up his serious side. "I haven't had another woman in my life since Dalfina and I divorced twelve years ago. Not that there weren't a lot of opportunities; I wasn't interest. That's how I'd earned the nickname 'Iron Pants.' "

She was surprised; she didn't know that he was aware of what they called him.

"That was until you came along of course." He gently ran a finger down her neck. He suddenly wanted to make love to her in the back of the limo driving through the center of town.

She knew something was turning him on. The familiar flame began to burn in his eyes as he slid closer to her on the seat.

"As skilled as you are at…" She stopped as he began kissing and caressing her neck. "Dalfina must have been an incredible teacher."

"I said there was no one between you and Dalfina. I never said there were no other women in my life."

She stiffened under his caress. *"You cheated on your wife?!"* Her head began spinning and her heart was in a sickening place in her throat. She had assumed all along that he had been faithful to Dalfina, just as she had been to Alex.

Realizing that she was taken aback by what he said, he stopped and looked into her eyes and saw fright. He had seen the same look when he was hard pressed for answers about Lindquist. "Katie, I'm sorry if I offended you by saying that."

"I just thought you were the type of man to be faithful to your wife. I never thought—I mean with your kind of will power, you'd be… You'd cheated?"

His tone became very soft and his hands, instead of seeking her, held her shoulders warmly. "I had other women when I was a teenager." He could see the look of relief on her face, but he wanted her to know the truth. "And I had affairs when I was married."

She wanted to cry. She wanted to be somewhere else where he couldn't see how hurt she was by his shocking disclosure.

"Katie, I was young when I started massing my fortune. I wasn't prepared for women to start throwing themselves at me. I was conceited with the idea that they wanted me, but really they were only interested in money. Dalfina was a good woman, and she stood by through some things that would have sent most women packing."

"Women like me," she softly added. She would never knowingly stay with someone unfaithful to her.

"I recognized the fact that I'd been foolish, but it was when I first…," he paused. He had said more than he wanted to and now she was looking at him to finish telling her why he stopped cheating. "…heard about a new epidemic called AIDS, I knew I could never again take the pleasure of a woman I didn't know. I suddenly realized I could be risking my business, my dreams, and my life for a moment's satisfaction. I stopped cheating and vowed I would never be unfaithful again. And I wasn't."

"Then why did you get divorced if you started being faithful to your wife?"

He pulled away and straightened in the seat beside her. His jaw-line was set hard and the muscle in his cheek pulled taunt. His eyes flashed with a new fire, but it wasn't passion; it was hot anger.

She could tell he was clenching his teeth, and she began to wish she hadn't asked.

"A year or so later, she met a man who swept her into a brief affair." He looked at her with an expression that said he deserved what he got, but he certainly didn't like it. "She cheated on me and I couldn't be certain if she might have contracted a deadly disease. It could have been months or even a year before I would know if I could sleep with my wife. I couldn't take that chance, but besides that I was so *angry.*"

"I suppose it could happen to anyone," she began to offer.

"It was Jon Lindquist," he interrupted her. "He was the man who slept with my wife. He wanted to take my company from under me and thought she was a viable way to do it. He filled her head with so much foolishness that she was ready to leave me for him. She eventually realized he was using her, but by then it was too late for us."

Suddenly it became clear to her: the bristled attitude at the Christmas dinner party, the ugliness toward her question at the business meeting, and the anger on his face in the car. Inwardly she shivered. She remembered Jon from the dinner party, his icy-cold manners and probing remarks. How could someone find him attractive? Not that he was ugly aesthetically, but there was a cold, almost evil air to him.

"I'm sorry, Albert. You don't need to worry about me. I'll be faithful to you. And you can believe me when I say that." She drew close to him, wanting to be in his arms.

He did believe what she said. There was a pureness he had begun to see about this woman's heart that left little room for doubt. He kissed her, warm and anew. "Where were we?" he said with his debonair smile. Pushing her softly down on the comfortable seat, he added, "It's a long ride home. I'm glad we didn't take the helicopter." It had been years since he made love in the back of a limousine.

Katie on the other hand, had never made love in the back seat of anything.

"Are you sure we're safe in here?" she said a little worried.

"Absolutely safe," he said. "And you can believe *me* when I say that."

~:~

That fall she began classes at the local University campus. Boredom was replaced with sheer exhilaration. She signed up for several courses, though Albert warned her not to try to take everything she wanted at once. Still it was hard to resist as she went through the course descriptions. She was registered as Elizabeth Davidson, which was not something she wanted, but Albert said it was either that or she'd have to have a bodyguard go to class with her. The media bothered her some, but she couldn't believe they would send people to the university just to try to get some kind of inside scoop on her. She enjoyed the assignments and class work; it gave her something that she was responsible for doing.

She loved her household staff. Meals were always delicious and healthy, and she never had to do the dishes—which she didn't miss at all. Laundry was another thing that she didn't miss. Their clothes we always washed, dried, pressed or dry cleaned immediately. But she did miss doing some of her own housework, cooking, and yard work (she always loved mowing the lawn back home in Florida). She was welcomed in the kitchen to cook whenever she wanted, but she couldn't compare to the things their chefs Roberto and Louisa prepared, so she didn't try.

She had talked with her parents about taking an extended vacation with her to Canada, but it would have to wait until next spring. She wouldn't be able to take time off from school until her classes were finished in early May. Her mother said that she had been out of 'snow country' so long she didn't think she could take the winter cold anyway. Her father agreed. He had seen his share of blizzards, ice and snow when he was growing up in Montana, and he wasn't eager to see a snowy winter again.

Her father retired that winter and was spending his time fishing and relaxing. His health was a nagging problem. He was tired often and was glad he could take afternoon naps now whenever he wanted. Katie resigned herself to the fact that, all though her father had always been superman in her eyes, he was getting older and it was time to slow down.

Albert had been so busy lately it seemed she rarely saw him. He spent several nights a week at the penthouse because by the time he completed what he wanted to get done it was usually one or two in the morning. His company had absorbed several smaller companies and, even though his lawyers, accountants, and staffers went over every buy-out with careful precision, he still liked to go through each transaction carefully and usually alone.

It was easy at first to be suspicious as to why he wasn't coming home. But, she forced herself to remember the conversation they had that evening in the limousine. She remembered his openness about his prior infidelity and about his commitment to remain faithful. She had to believe and she had to trust; if she opened the door to her suspicions it would tear her apart. She kept herself busy with her work from college, and when that was finished, she worked out in the exercise room or swam laps in the pool. The combination of things kept her mind occupied.

She had taken four courses that fall. Art History, which she was certain would be boring, but turned out to be highly stimulating. Literature and French I, both of which she enjoyed because of the homework, which kept her busy. But, her most interesting and intriguing class turned out to be Textiles and Design. She read the course description which stated that students would learn the basic philosophy of color coordination and balance, and how to tell the suitability of colors and fabrics individually tailored to each person's complexion and body shape. She had loved to sew and design when she was an older teen. She had even designed and made her own dress for prom. It all seemed so long ago; she didn't even know if she would understand the concepts of the class, but it sparked something within her that said, take it.

The class was made up evenly of men and women. All her fellow students expressed their desire to break into the world of fashion design, and the Big Apple was a great place to do that. The instructor was a wonderfully gregarious woman named Bella Anna Lormaster. She was filled with life and ideas that pushed the boundaries, yet made perfect sense at the same time. The students were asked to call her Bella.

Bella took an immediate liking to Katie. Her other students, she said, had their minds made up as to what fashion was to them. Katie, on the other hand, was open and teachable. It seemed each day that class convened the other students were more interested in seeing what strange and unusual clothing someone else wore to class, while

Katie sat riveted to her chair, taking notes and absorbing the essence of what was being presented.

The concept of knowing what color matched the appearance of which person, which coordinated color then affected attitude and mood, what design corrected figure flaws, or enhanced powerful physical assets was fascinating.

As the semester progressed, she began to envision a computer program that would identify categories of people, match them with correctly coordinated clothing, make-up and hair styles to produce striking results with even the most mousy, unassuming person. As she began studying people and the way each person presented himself or herself, she discovered that so many of the people who were considered unattractive were actually dressed, styled or groomed contrary to their natural features, producing an unappealing look.

By Christmas time, she decided what she wanted to have as her present. Albert might not find it agreeable, but she would find a way to convince him. She hadn't wanted anything so badly since she was a little girl and wanted Daddy to build her a big dollhouse.

The Christmas party at the head office was in full swing when she arrived. The only difference was that there were photographers and reporters waiting for her to step out of the limousine this time. Albert had been at the office since the night before and was waiting for her to arrive for the penthouse party. She had two bodyguards since she had chosen the limousine instead of the helicopter. He had asked her to fly to avoid the crowd that would be waiting to get a photograph of the lovely Mrs. Trathmoore, but she still didn't care too much for flying. Besides that, she wanted to make a grand entrance looking like a billionaire's wife. She wanted to look so incredible that he couldn't possibly say no to her Christmas wish.

The company limousine pulled up to the covered entrance. People were streaming in and out of the building. A gathering of reporters and photographers were waiting for the right car to pull up. She called Albert from the car phone just a few minutes before they arrived so he would be waiting to escort her through the building. Rodrick and Simon, her bodyguards, stepped out of the back first then offered her their hands. The main doors opened with Albert just beyond in the foyer. The doormen were keeping back the onlookers as she stepped out.

She wanted to see his face, his expression, and his reaction to her attire. Her gown was a sequined, deep ruby red with black silk peaking out from under carefully arranged sheer places in the design. Her bodice was cut daringly low, and the effect was finished with black elbow length gloves and a black mink wrap. She wore exceptionally high spiked shoes, which not only gave her the power of height, but also brought out the muscled shapeliness of her legs to be revealed from the front slit. And, though she rarely wore much make-up, she made a careful exception tonight. The illusion was that she didn't have much on, but it was actually more than she had ever worn. Her lipstick matched the beautiful shade of red in her dress and her eyes seemed to have become dark and mysterious. Her hair was pulled back from her face but fell loosely down her back in soft cascades. She had never dressed this way in her life, but it was exhilarating. She had struck a careful balance of power and sensuality—with class.

His reaction was as if he had been stunned. Without much thought to the crowd, he left the building to take her arm. Cameras flashed and some questions were shouted out, but neither one heard nor saw anything but each other. All eyes were upon them, but they didn't care.

Once inside the private elevator to the penthouse, he looked at her and breathlessly exclaimed, "I don't know what they've been teaching you in that class you love so much, but whatever it is," and he looked her over again, "it's damned good!"

She smiled to herself.

"I have half a mind," he continued, "to skip the party and just stay in the apartment with you."

"Please, Mr. Trathmoore, you don't need to unwrap your present in such a hurry," she said with a sexy smile on her lips.

He sighed deeply. "I'd kiss you right now, but I'd smudge those sensuous lips of yours."

She laughed just as the doors opened in the apartment. "To the party?" she asked, tempting him.

"Damn!" he said shaking his head. "I think that instructor of yours must be teaching you how to be a seductress."

She turned to face him. In her heels she was almost as tall as he was. "Would you like that?" she asked.

"You're sexy when you're innocent," he said, remembering the party last year when she slept off those drinks in his bed. He could still see her partly nude form with the moonlight caressing her limbs. "And you're sexy when you're sophisticated, too." It would be a very long night to get through.

The party was wonderful just as it had been the year before, except this time Katie was poised and confident, causing more than one man to have faltering speech in her presence. She was enjoying the power play, but she didn't let on that she was. She began to understand how Albert must feel when his powerful presence disrupted people's ability to act natural. On his arm tonight, she was not an innocent little doting wife, but an equally commanding force. Albert seemed to enjoy the havoc she was creating among his executives.

By the time they had circulated through the crowd, she was ready to sit down and talk with her husband about something she wanted. Besides that, the muscles in her legs were beginning to ache. The shoes were a necessary part of the whole effect, but they were not the comfortable flats she preferred to wear. Finding a quiet table near the dance area, the musicians playing a soft romantic melody from across the room, they gladly sat down for a few moments alone.

"It's been a year, can you believe it?" he said, genuinely surprised at the thought.

"Yes, it's flown by. Almost like this *was* the first time," she left it unfinished.

"You know I had to take a cold shower that night," he confessed. "When the night ended and I went in to check on you in my bed, you were nude and only partly covered by the sheet." He took a deep breath, "I'm not taking a cold shower tonight."

She laughed quietly, "I certainly hope not. That would spoil my night, too."

"We're good together. Do you know that?" he said, surprising her with his statement. "I've never laughed with anyone like I do with you. Don't ever change."

But she did want a change. She wanted to create something that was her own. She wanted an identity that was hers alone, just as ATI was Albert's identity.

"Albert, I've been thinking about what I want—for Christmas," she added.

He smiled at her. "Christmas is only four days away. You certainly aren't giving me much time to shop."

"It's not something from a store. I want your approval for something I want to do—a business proposition."

His eyebrows rose. This was not what he expected her to say: diamonds, a new wardrobe, or a new house maybe, but not a business. "Well, you certainly have my attention. Go ahead, Dear, tell me what you want."

It took a while to explain how the idea had begun to take shape. She wanted to use some of his top programmers to help her develop a system that would photographically analyze natural skin tones, hair and body shapes, and to categorize them into one of the four main groups that differentiates people. She explained what she could to help him understand the 'seasons' of people, just like the four seasons of the year. She could tell he was carefully listening, absorbing what he understood and calculating costs.

"When the program and camera system is in place, I want to open a line of stores call 'Seasons.' People will come into the central hub for a personal analysis and then be directed into one of the four shops, winter, spring, summer or fall, depending on their results. Everything in each shop will be tailored specifically to that type of person, from clothing, make-up, jewelry, and even a styling salon. No matter who they are or what they look like, they can come away looking the best they ever have." She paused for the first time, waiting for his response.

"This would be a major investment into a field that I'm not familiar with," his tone indicating that it would not be favorable.

Her heart began to sink.

"But," he added, "you could have the programmers and get started on developing the system, while I have some of my people check the viability of letting you branch out into an actual line of stores. It sounds like something that could take off with the right advertising campaign, but it could cost a fortune—literally—if it fails."

He waited for her reaction. When she remained silent, he added, "It's going to take some one with a hard-edge to make it work. Do you think you could be that kind of person?"

She didn't smile, or even raise an eyebrow as she turned to look at the couples dancing across the floor. She stood up and said, "I wonder if I can find someone to dance with?" Then she turned and walked out of the room before he had a chance to reply.

He shook his head, knowing full well that she wasn't going to go out to the party and ask someone to dance with her. No matter how she dressed, she was still the same timid young woman. Perhaps she had dreams of being a seductress or a hard-edged businesswoman, but she would always be Katie, just as she had been all her life. He would let her dabble in the world of entrepreneurs, but even if her idea was successful, someone else would have to take command to make it work.

He waited long enough; he assumed it was time to go find her. He had probably hurt her feelings and guessed she was in the apartment, in tears. But, just as he was leaving the room, who should enter but his timid little wife walking arm and arm with Hans Letenauer, one of his Swiss bankers! She was being as charming as any cunning New York socialite looking for a financial backer. He stopped and stood there with his fists on his waistline as he watched her gliding across the floor with Hans, who was holding her a little bit close by his standards. She was laughing and smiling, her eyes sparkling even in the dimly lit room. He was barely aware of several other men that had joined him standing there watching her. Just then one of them walked across the floor to where Katie and Hans were dancing; it was John Melenek, president of New York International Bank. John cut in and continued across the floor into the next dance set. Albert looked to his left and there was Justin Sandsbury and Edward Martin, two of the top programmers in the industry, waiting to take their turn dancing with the lovely Mrs. Trathmoore. And what was really a hard pill to swallow was the fact that they barely acknowledged Albert standing right there!

He couldn't believe it. She had combed the room for exactly the men she needed for launching her plan. She was charming the socks off them all! He wasn't sure if he should be angry or congratulate her for the ones she had picked. He had enough though when Lance Anderson took her in his arms. Lance was new to Albert's team, but he was a good choice because his company, AnderAds, had launched the most successful advertising campaign in ATI's history. He was a young hotshot and, by male standards, he was a ruggedly handsome man. Lance was not as tall as Albert, but he had a more muscled physique, and he was closer to Katie's age. She spoke almost the same as when she had danced with the other men, but this time Albert could tell she blushed once in a while at his responses—and he held her extremely close.

Lance felt a tap on his shoulder, and there stood Albert.

"My turn to cut in," he said.

Lance smiled, looked at Katie and reluctantly relinquished her hand to her husband. He said nothing as he skillfully guided her around the dance floor.

She had a sly smile plying the corners of her lips. "I think I made excellent choices in possible business allies, don't you?"

His body stiffened as they ended the dance set.

She looked up to see him setting his jaw. In that moment she felt she might have pushed the desired response a little too far.

He led her back to the table as the music began again. She was glad to sit down, although she never would have said so, but her feet, legs, and hips were aching from dancing.

"I didn't care for your choice of Anderson," he said flatly.

"But you said he was the best ad man in the business." She knew Albert wouldn't have said that about him if it wasn't so.

"Yes, his company is good at what it does, but he likes you a little too much."

She realized the look on his face and the set jaw was jealousy. "There are women here at the party tonight that you work with that are very attractive, but that's all it is, just work. I can work with someone without any other type of involvement."

"You can start your programming and *I'll* explore the business aspect. I'm not ready for you become a businesswoman on me just yet."

"And when it is time for me to become a businesswoman?" she queried.

He looked up from resting his chin on his fist. "I'll find you the best all female group of business associates you've ever seen."

They both began to laugh.

"I've had enough party tonight haven't you?" he asked, undressing her with his eyes.

"But the night is young Mr. Trathmoore," she said, remembering his line he had given her last year. "New York parties last until the wee hours of the morning."

"Not tonight," he interjected. "That is unless you feel the need to find a few more *business partners*?" He looked at her steadily; he was serious about his question.

"No. I have only one partner in this room, and I'd like nothing more than to be in his arms right now."

She got up from the table and held her hand out to him. Tonight she was going to be the one to take the lead.

He was momentarily surprised by her forwardness. She led him from the room and headed to the apartment. He definitely needed to reappraise this woman he married. "I think I might like you as a businesswoman after all," he said, as she opened the door to the pleasure that lay beyond.

~:~

By spring, her program was near completion. On days she didn't have school, she worked at the office with the small team that Albert assembled to help her create the frame work for the computer program and camera equipment. Scanner technology was good, but not good enough to get a true and accurate skin tone analysis. Her crew consisted of Justin Sandsbury, who was helping her map the program; Micca Noddwell, who was versed in the best scanner equipment in the country; and Ruth. Ruth wasn't there simply because she and Katie were friends. She was good at finding flaws in new programs, and Katie knew first hand that she was thorough and meticulous in her work.

They started running test subjects through the program. First they used themselves and were pleased with the computer's recommended course of clothing and make-up, and its methods of enhancing assets and minimizing imperfections. Next they spent several days walking through the massive building looking at people who might be particularly hard to analyze and asking if they would be willing to participate in a simple test.

There were some problems that came to the surface under Ruth's watchful eye, but Justin was creative in finding solutions. Micca's part became the most difficult at the end. The scanner's camera had to pick up minute underlying skin tones accurately or the whole analysis would be off. For the program to distinguish between a complexion having a rosy undertone or a yellow undertone became their biggest challenge. Everything else was completed.

It would be only a few more days before they worked out the last difficulties and then she would present the entire program to Albert. Already he had asked some of his best business planners to be prepared to assemble at a moment's notice to help her develop a business plan to present to prospective financial backers. Although he could be her primary investor, she wanted to find investors independent of Albert. He understood her desire to keep the project to herself. When he first began creating the company that became ATI, he limited the number of investors in order to retain total control. It was a difficult path to travel, but if it he had not done so, companies like Syntec Industries would have taken over his business long ago. It would take a lot of stamina on Katie's part. And, knowing how much she wanted it to succeed, he hoped she could do it on her own.

Thursday night she worked late, alone in her office. She kept making small adjustments to the program. She felt certain she had the key to the problem, but it was a matter of making it happen. She had been thinking all day about the way 3-D glasses worked. By concentrating on filtering out certain colors, some colors could be brought to the forefront and some could be eliminated. She worked with lightly tinted slides over the scanner's camera lens until she started getting the results she had been desperately working toward. She let out a whoop and a yell as she jumped down from her work chair. "I've got it!" she said out loud.

"Got what?" Albert said from the doorway.

She didn't know how long he had been standing there watching her, but he scared the daylights out of her when he spoke.

He laughed at the little scream that slipped out before she realized it was him.

"I did it! I corrected the final flaw in the program. Do you want to see how it works?" She danced about the room with excitement.

"All right," he said with a little reluctance in his voice.

"Okay, you're going to be the test subject. Step in the next room here and take off your clothes."

He practically choked. "What?! I'm not going to take off my clothes for a nude picture!"

"No, no," she laughed. "You won't be nude. You'll be wearing these," she beamed as she held up a pair of grass green underpants. "The computer will not pick up on this color in the analysis. Just like when they do one of those impossible movie scenes. It's fabulous technology."

He looked over the ugly underpants as he removed them from the plastic wrapper. "You've got to be kidding?"

"Pleeeease," she begged.

He entered the windowless room and closed the door. Changing into the underpants he began to dread that he actually told her he'd do it.

She poked her head in. "Great. Now stand in front of the green screen there and I'll run the analysis."

Shaking his head he stepped in front of the screen. Suddenly, something his grandfather told him when he was a young teen came back to him and he began to laugh.

She looked back into the room. "Okay, all done. What's so funny?"

"My grandfather told me once to never be caught with my pants down. I think I've just broken that solemn rule."

He re-dressed and joined her at the computer. She gave him a complete rundown on the program. The program assessed his skin tone, hair color, eye color and physical features, then matched him with a line of clothing colors and styles.

Albert was impressed. "Very good, Mrs. Trathmoore! Now erase my photo so no one else will see me in my skivvies."

With a punch of a button his picture disappeared.

"What do you think, honestly?

"I think you have a program with considerable merit. You should get your business plan set and start your search for backers."

She squealed with excitement.

"Umm—I like squealing women," he mused. "It's really too late to head for home. How about you and I stay the penthouse tonight?"

Friday morning found them wrapped comfortably in each other's arms. It had been a late night so when the alarm went off at 5 a.m., she groggily hit the snooze bar for a few extra minutes. Albert rolled out of the bed and headed for the shower. She had classes on Friday: Textiles at 10, French at 11:30 and Art History at 2. There weren't many sessions left before exams and summer break. Already she had decided that she wasn't going to sign up for any next year because she was devoting herself completely to her idea.

The alarm blaring for a second time, she decided to hit the shower, too. Albert was still enjoying his morning shower when she surprised him by slipping in with him. She loved his shower. It was roomy and elegant with beautiful marble tiles. The large multi-shower heads jetted from all directions giving the sensation of being out in a warm summer rainstorm. There was a lever that could be pulled to direct the water out a long flat ledge from the top of the shower, making a sumptuous waterfall to enjoy.

Albert grinned as she stepped in.

"Care for company?" she asked timidly, as if she didn't know the reply already.

He didn't answer; he just began rubbing her down with the fresh smelling shower gel, his hands working their way warmly all over her body. She began to rub the soap on him, and he smiled at her response. Reaching the top of her, he began lathering her hair and kissing her at the same moment. He had an insatiable appetite for lovemaking. He could go for weeks at a time being away from her and return to find her tired from her studies, or not feeling well, and he would show no indication that he needed physical affection. But, when she was receptive, he took full advantage. He made love to her last night, and now this morning it was as if he hadn't held her in days.

"Do you want to go to the bedroom?" she whispered.

"No."

She looked about the shower as he pulled the lever, causing the waterfall to come rushing down on them both. "How?"

Carefully picking her up off the floor, he pulled her up to his waist as she wrapped her legs around him.

"This is how my oldest daughter was conceived," he said, looking into her beautiful golden-green eyes.

It had been so long since she had even thought of conception. She still wanted a child more than anything, but she wasn't going to put herself or Albert through the heartbreak of fertility treatments that didn't seem to work for her.

As the water rushed down on them, pain and pleasure mingled. He gently, but deeply made passionate love to her, both of them reaching the pinnacle near the same moment. Sex was not a loud affair with them, yet neither could contain themselves as they cried out from the pleasure they experienced.

He was still holding her as she smiled at him, "Don't you want to put me down now? I'm sure I must be getting heavy."

"No you're not," he replied, kissing her to interrupt her sentence. "I think I could do it all over again. How about you?"

She looked to his face for the hint of jest, but there was none. "Albert, we can't! We'll both be late."

"All right!" he laughed. "If you insist on leaving." He eased her to the shower floor and carefully withdrew. With one more kiss he said, "I guess I'll let you go."

"How are you going to get to the University today?" he asked as he put on his dark blue silk necktie. "I was going to take the limousine to meet John at the bank, but I think I'll be taking the helicopter since *someone* insisted on making me run late."

She raised an eyebrow at him. She knew every other Friday, at 8 a.m. sharp, he would meet with Mr. Melenek at the bank before it opened. They would have breakfast together and discuss money—Albert's money. He rarely took the helicopter because the international bank wasn't a difficult commute, but it was 7:15 already and he normally would leave punctually at 7:25. He wouldn't be ready this morning in time. Katie on the other hand was in her comfortable dress shorts and a white knit shirt. She was glad her 'job' was a little more casual than his.

"Go ahead and take my limousine home. My driver is ready to go. Or, if you prefer, you can fly with me to the bank and then Kyle can fly you home." He knew she really didn't care to fly, but he thought he'd offer.

"No thanks," she said quickly, "I'm not in that big of a hurry to get to the house." She always took a car from the house to the school to avoid pulling up in a limo and having everyone wonder who she was to arrive in such style.

Grabbing her purse, she gave him a kiss goodbye and headed down stairs. If she'd had any premonition that her life was about to change forever from that one decision, she might have learned to love to fly.

CHAPTER FOUR

Katie reached the parking level in an uninterrupted descent from the penthouse. She smiled at Charlie and Andrew, the garage attendants, as she made way for Albert's limousine. Donald, Albert's driver, stood patiently by the car door.

"Mrs. Trathmoore," he said acknowledging her. "Will Mr. Trathmoore be joining you this morning?"

"No. Thank you, Donald," she said sliding into the back seat, "He's going to fly to the bank this morning because he's running a little late."

She could see the surprised expression come over his face—Albert Trathmoore was a rigorously disciplined and scheduled man; he was never late.

But Donald would not question her; it would have been unprofessional.

"Please take me to the Hamptons."

"Yes, Ma'am." He quickly closed the door behind her and walked around the car to the driver's seat.

Before exiting the garage, he stopped at the parking gate and waited for it to be raised. A heavy-set man in his late forties came around from the attendant's shack. His black hair was roughly greased back and his face looked as if it could have used a shave. He was not the usual morning guard, and Donald was trying to remember if he'd ever seen him before.

With a clipboard in one gnarled hand, the man pointed to the front of the car as if something was wrong.

Donald lowered the driver's window slightly. "Raise the gate, please."

"Well, I can raise the gate," the man replied in a thick New York brogue. "But you're leaking coolant all over the place. Green stuff running everywhere," he said shaking his head as he looked to the pavement. He walked away from the car and headed into the shack to raise the gate.

Donald hit the intercom, "Mrs. Trathmoore, I'll be right back. I just have to look at the front of the car. The attendant said I'm leaking coolant."

Katie, comfortably concealed by the darkly tinted windows, replied okay.

She watched as Donald exited the car. Looking down for a moment at the note she had been writing in her lap. She heard a scuffle and then, unexpectedly, the door locks released. She looked up and saw the back of an unfamiliar man climbing into the front seat. Before she could think to react, the back door to the limousine was snatched opened. The dark-haired man she had seen from the attendant's shack was staring at her with a vicious look. His eyes didn't even seem to register as human; they were simply the eyes of an angry animal. He appeared equally shocked to see her. In that stunned moment she realized he was holding a gun in his hand. That's when her heart leapt to her throat: this man expected Albert to be in the car, not her! She screamed in terror, but only a strangled sound came up from her throat. As quickly as she the thought entered her mind, she grabbed for the opposite door—it would be the only escape.

She heard his swear words spewing as he reached for her. He was quick, quicker than she had been. Within a split second he was beside her in the car, yanking her down to the floorboard yelling, "Go! Go! Go!"

She felt the limousine lurch forward as the gate crashed across the front of the car. With tires screeching, the car tore out from the parking garage.

She looked at the man who still had her in his grip and realized that if she didn't get away, this man would kill her. Gun or no gun, this was the time to fight. If she could get to the door she was sure she could jump from the now speeding car.

"NO!" She yelled as she used her muscled legs to push herself away from the floorboard and into her attacker's chest.

It was not what he expected, but it didn't matter. He enjoyed a good fight. He grabbed for her with his free hand, intending to take her by the throat, but he missed and had her by the lower part of her jaw instead. She bit down with all her might on the knuckle of his index finger, and at the same time swung her fist at his face, glancing a blow off his nose. The gun in his other hand slipped and fell to the seat.

"Little bitch!" he growled out. Then with all his force, his fist hurled at her face.

Blackness over took her.

~:~

Katie's head ached and her jaw felt as if it had been broken. She struggled for consciousness, but it seemed she couldn't get a firm grasp on it. She could feel that she was lying on something, a bed perhaps, but it was hard against her body. Her mind felt disoriented and disconnected. This is a bad dream, she thought to herself; it couldn't have happened. She made out angry voices yelling about something, her it seemed. But their words jumbled inside her head: botched, Trathmoore, money, job, wife, were the few things she recognized. Faint and in pain, she drifted back to unconsciousness.

~:~

Nick Randall angrily paced the warehouse floor thinking about the twist in his perfect plan. "This screws up the whole damn deal!" he muttered. He had a job to do. He arranged it carefully, tracing this guy's steps for the last few months. This Friday morning should have been the perfect opportunity to make a cool two million dollars. He'd pulled off a lot of heists in his forty-six year life; some of them good and some of them botched. He'd spent five years in the state penitentiary for one that had gone bad. "I sure as hell ain't spendin' any time in prison over you, Baby," he spat at the unconscious woman.

It was supposed to be easy money. Just take this guy out of commission and then let him go in a week or so. There would be no writing of ransom notes and no waiting for the police to nab him at the drop off point. He'd have to get in touch with his contact and let the money-man know there was a snag in the plan. He figured that this money was shot to hell unless the person who ordered the job had an interest in her.

He knew he'd be safe hiding her here in this old fishing warehouse near the harbor. No one came out here except other thugs like himself, and maybe an occasional lost tourist who would quickly turn-face and leave this forbidding place of scrap metal buildings and broken concrete wharves. Lenny, his partner in crime for that last two years, had already ditched the car in Queens. By the time they located it with the low-jack system it surely had on it, it would be abandoned and, unless he missed his guess about the area where they left it, it would be stripped down practically to the frame.

The only thing nagging now at his very small conscience was the remaining problem of his little brother, half brother actually, Donovan, who was (by his standards anyway) a sissy that he was trying to teach to be a hard-nosed thug. He told Donny he was pulling a big job this morning, and to meet him at the warehouse if he wanted a share in a couple million bucks. It was almost time for Donny to arrive. He figured his little brother wouldn't have the stomach for whatever was going to happen to that pretty little thing tied up in the building. He might end up having to kill two people—and Momma would be really upset about one of them.

The sound of a car pulling up outside shook him from his thoughts. He looked out to see Lenny driving up in his old, beat up Monte Carlo. Not far behind he could make out a brown Chevrolet Caprice coming down the weed-ridden, cracked up concrete drive—that, he knew, would be Donny.

"Terrific," he said in a low and menacing tone.

He flicked his cigarette out on the ground and motioned for Lenny to come inside.

"What'd ya gonna tell the kid?" Lenny asked as he looked toward the nearing car.

"He's gotta get some balls sometime. I guess the truth will work pretty good. Least ways we'll find out if he's with us or not."

Donovan stepped from the car and walked up to the two men with caution. His older brother was not the kind of person you approached with your guard down. He wondered what trouble was brewing. When his brother told him he had a few million coming in on a job, he went cold inside. It was a strange feeling really. He knew the kind of man Nick was, and he didn't like him. He tried to stay away from Nick's 'business,' but his older brother was determined to make him into a criminal just like the rest of his relatives.

Donovan had to admit Nick always had money, money for cars, girls, drugs, you name it. While it could take him weeks to scrape up enough money to pay the rent on his little flat by working at a car dealership as a detail man, Nick would pull some shady job and have a few thousand in no time. He thought it really sucked, but maybe, just this one time, he'd accept the request to join them and then when he got his share (if he didn't end up in jail) he'd leave New York, and his brother, far behind.

"So what's the deal?" Donovan asked, but looking at their faces he had a feeling something was wrong.

Nick began to curse about how he'd gotten a job to snatch Albert Trathmoore for a week or so and then let him loose for two million dollars. He'd planned it carefully for over two months, but it was botched when the guy let his wife leave in the limousine this morning.

"You're kidding?" Donovan said with a sick feeling in the pit of his stomach. This was not something he wanted to get involved with; Albert Trathmoore was one of the wealthiest men in the country, and wealthy people had lawyers that put you away for your entire life.

Nick laughed as he elbowed Lenny, "Look at the little sissy! He's went pale on us, Lenny. I think he's gonna faint."

Lenny laughed hard, "What's a matta kid? You think we're gonna make a couple million from snatchin' purses from ol' ladies? This is where the big money is. 'Cept we got us a lit'le problem to work out."

They walked closer to the figure tied up on the filthy mattress on the warehouse's bug-infested concrete floor. Donovan felt a sick churning in the pit of his stomach. This was a beautiful woman, beaten, bruised and unconscious. He wondered at that moment if she was even alive.

"Shit Nick! What'd ya do to her?" Donovan asked as he bent down for a closer look at the side of her face.

"Hey, the little wildcat clipped me in the nose, so I knocked her damn lights out!"

Lenny laughed; he thought of Nick getting a 'love tap' on the nose as hilarious. Besides, he had already started getting drunk after he ditched the limo so everything was becoming funny to him.

Running quickly all the possible scenarios through his mind, Donovan decided to ask what role he was supposed to play in all of this. If this woman were left in his brother's hands there was little doubt what would happen to her. If she had only Nick and Lenny, she'd be raped and beaten worse than she already was. And, if she didn't end up in the bottom of the harbor tied to a cement block, she'd die anyway. Lenny always got his share of the women that Nick was finished with—he was always the last one because Lenny had something called Acquired Immune Deficiency Syndrome.

"What did you want me to do?"

"We need you to help keep a watch on her. Shit, Lenny'll be drunk in a few hours and I've gotta meet with some people to find out if there is any money for the wife instead of the husband."

Donovan looked back at Lenny. Lenny was a skinny shell of a man. He was around five feet ten inches tall and big boned, but he only weighed about 150 pounds. His eyes were sunk in and there were purple blotches on his mottled face. The only thing about him that was large was his stomach. He had a beer belly of sorts that hung out over his belt line.

"Right, Lenny?" Nick said to his companion.

"Damn straight. I'm gonna get drunk everyday 'til I die," he replied with a look of satisfaction on his face.

That shouldn't be too long a stretch, Donovan thought to himself. "If you get any money for her, what's my cut?"

Nick was impressed that his little brother was considering the deal. "Ten percent," he said nonchalantly. "Lenny and me did the hard work."

Donovan looked back at the woman on the ground. His whole face seemed to say that the idea disgusted him. "It ain't worth it," he said, straightening his posture. "Twenty-five percent."

"Twenty-five percent!" Nick blasted. "You ain't gotta do anything but sit your little pansy ass around here and watch the dumb broad! You ought'a be glad you're even getting in on this deal!"

"Glad I'd get to share the prison time if we get caught? I'd be just as guilty as both of you. Find yourself another babysitter, Nick." And he began to walk away.

"Twenty percent," Nick threw out. He knew he'd have to give an equal share to anyone else he brought in on the deal.

Donovan walked back and squared off to his brother. Standing almost toe to toe, Donovan was a good two inches taller, but Nick out weighed him by at least seventy-five pounds. "You always wanted me to be just like you. I guess if I'm gonna do the same filthy work I should at least get twenty-five percent. Anyone else would want a third."

Nick half smiled. Maybe being a pauper was getting old with his little brother. "You'd better not let me down little Bro, or I'll be using some of that twenty-five percent to plant your ass in the family burial plot."

Related or not, Donovan knew Nick wouldn't lose any sleep over putting a bullet in his head.

~:~

It was twilight the next time Katie opened her eyes. Still hoping she had been having a horrible nightmare, it didn't take but a moment to realize she hadn't dreamed up the place she was in. As the light began to fade she could see the mattress underneath her. Sand and pieces of dead bugs littered the surface of its faded cloth covering. She could taste old blood in her mouth. Her cheek and eye ached terribly, and her head pounded. Small gnats were swarming around her face trying to get to the cut on her lip. As she tried to bring her arm out from under her, she felt the rough ropes that were tied too tightly around her wrists. Her ankles were tied equally tight and she couldn't straighten out because her feet and hands were some how connected. Her first truly conscious thought was to cry; she knew it would do no good, but she felt her emotions choking up within her and spilling over into anguished tears.

Except for the buzzing mosquitoes, the building was quiet. Carefully she rolled onto her stomach, trying to find a way to sit up. It wouldn't work and the ropes only seemed to get tighter. She wouldn't be able to do it on her back so she rolled onto her side. Swinging the weight of her head and shoulders, she got one elbow on the mattress. Straining every muscle and rocking with her upper body, she made it upright to her knees. The blood seemed to rush from her head making her feel as if she would pass out again, but she willed herself to stay conscious. She tore at the ropes with her almost numb fingers, but the knots were too tight. The tips of her fingernails ripped miserably loose to the quick. She tried making sense of the knots, but they seemed to be a massive jumble.

"Come on Katie, come on! Think!!" she said in a quavering voice to herself. By now darkness had descended and she was barely able to make out the silhouette of the partly open warehouse door forty or fifty feet way. If I could get my feet flat under me, she thought, I could hop crouched-over to the door. But, as she got her weight over her feet, she lost balance and tumbled off the mattress, hitting her body hard against the concrete. Fighting back the tears, she tried to get her elbow under her so she could make another attempt. Suddenly, something scurried against her hair. She jerked her head as high off the concrete as she could. It let out a shrill squeak and ran through her hair, brushing against her legs as it ran away. She let a scream escape before she could stifle it.

Her heart was pounding wildly as she looked about for any movement in the darkness: nothing. I'm alone, she thought. She couldn't get back to her knees and she felt she had no alternatives left. "Lord," she whispered in quiet prayer, "let someone hear me." And she began to scream.

Her voice wouldn't cooperate at first, but as her adrenaline pumped up, it grew louder until it seemed to reverberate from the walls of the metal building. She heard voices, and then someone was pushing at the heavy door.

"Help! Please! Someone help me!"

Yet above her own volume she could hear a gruff voice yelling, "...shut the stupid bitch up!"

A flashlight cut the darkness and illuminated the place where she was lying. She screamed and yelled with all her might.

"Shut up lady, shut up!" She heard a younger man's voice say. It wasn't the man from the morning, it was someone different.

"Shut her up!!" Came the gruff voice from the darkness.

Quickly, strong hands grabbed her. His hand covered her mouth, but under his firm grip she couldn't open her jaw to bite him. He pulled her by her upper arm to get her back onto the mattress. The pain in her shoulder was excruciating, but the pain in her feet and hands was so strong that it seemed to block her other senses. He was saying something to her quietly, but it was hard to understand him. She stopped struggling for a moment.

"It's okay. I'm not gonna hurt you. I'll help you when I get the chance, just trust me."

His whisper was incredibly low, but she heard him just the same. He was going to try to help her!

The light wavered and swayed closer to her from the doorway. She could almost make out the young man who held her securely.

"Here," Nick said, throwing a long strip of dirty fabric on to the floor, "wad this up and stuff some in her mouth and tie the rest around her head."

"I'll be quiet," she hoarsely said, as the hand left her face. "I'll be quiet. Please don't."

"Bullshit! Gag her!"

"Please! My hands and feet are tied too tight. Please…," she began to cry.

The light flashed to her tied appendages. They were purple and white from lack of blood.

Nick laughed. Two pair of handcuffs hit the mattress. "I thought those ropes might take a little fight out of you. Make sure they're tight enough that she can get out of 'em."

She was rolled to her stomach as the young man untied the ropes. She was so numb she couldn't tell if they were off or on. Then she heard the handcuffs click shut.

"Use some rope to tie… ."

"There are some pipes against the wall over there," the young man said, gesturing to the north side of the room. "We'd only have to cuff one wrist. She couldn't go anywhere."

There was silence for a moment.

"What the hell do you care?"

"It would be easier, that's all. She sure ain't gonna go anywhere chained to the building!"

"Suit yourself. But the first noise I hear outta you," he said, directing himself to Katie, "I'm gonna cram your mouth full and tie you back up with them damn ropes! You got it?"

"Yes," she said softly.

He laid the flashlight down on its side and walked away mumbling obscenities.

"Shhh."

With Katie lying on the mattress, Donovan pulled it against the north wall. Undoing one side of the handcuff, he clipped it to a pipe running up the wall.

"Be patient," he whispered. "You'll be more comfortable like this." Then he released her slender ankles and walked away, picking up the light as he left.

Darkness, like the black unconsciousness from earlier, enveloped her, leaving nothing but tears for comfort.

~:~

The early morning sunlight had begun to beat down on the metal building, making it hot and dry, and with it came a powerful thirst. She'd had nothing to drink since yesterday morning, and now every fiber of her being cried out for something, anything to drink. She looked down at the hundreds of mosquito and fly bites on her arms and legs. They itched horribly, but her fingers were too sore to scratch them so she gently rubbed them with her palm. Her knee and shoulder were skinned from falling off the mattress, and her wrists and ankles bore the raw, red marks of the ropes from the previous day. She had no idea what the mark on her face must look like, but if the rest of her body was an indication, it was probably worse.

She wanted a drink, but yet she was afraid if she yelled out she would get gagged and bound with the ropes again. Most of all, she didn't want to be in those ropes. She took note of her surroundings; the building was basically a shell, devoid of equipment. There was an office not far from the big front door. Its three glass windows cracked and covered with dust. There were signs that the homeless had, at one time or another, camped in the building. Broken bottles and trash were scattered about the interior. A few weeds, struggling for existence, grew up in places were the floor was cracked.

The pipe she was cuffed to was solidly in place. She had pulled and tugged at it during the night to no avail.

She wondered about the man last night that said he would try to help her. Where was he now? Would he come back and try to get her free? She heard a cough and a rustling noise that seemed to come from the office. She saw a figure staggering around inside it. Her heart began to beat faster. Would this be the gruff, dark haired man who had struck her? Was it the man who had bound her so mercilessly in the ropes? The office door burst open and a gaunt man stepped out. She didn't know who he was and for a moment she thought perhaps he was some drunk who had stumbled in during the night to sleep off his liquor, but then he turned and saw her.

"Looks like the little princess woke up," he said as he began sauntering toward her. He looked at her with a hungry look that said he had plans for her. He was an ugly man.

Katie began to shake as he came closer.

"Sure is a shame," he said when he was within arms reach of her, "such a pretty little body like yours all scraped up and bug ate." He reached out to touch her.

She moved as far away as her cuffed arm would allow.

"What's uh matta, Baby? You too good for someone like me to cop a feel? You never know, I might just turn out to be nice to you," he said with a dark yellowed smile. His breath reeked with the smell of alcohol.

"Leave me alone!" she screamed out. "Don't touch me you bastard!"

He stepped up on the mattress and moved nearer.

With her back against the wall, she kicked at him with all her strength, but he caught her leg and began to laugh.

"Hot damn, I got me a wild thing!" he leered as he slid his hand up her leg.

She screamed louder, trying to hold onto the pipe and kick with her free leg.

The door slung open, filling the room with bright light and dank harbor air. "What the hell are you doing, Lenny?" Nick yelled as he quickly approached.

"You ain't got the go-ahead to feel up the goods—least ways not 'til I say you can."

A third man entered the building, younger and taller than the first two. He had to be the man from the night before. His hair and eyes were deep brown and his skin was olive tan. His features were sharp and youthful, in his early twenties perhaps. His eyes locked with hers and she knew he was the one who wanted to help her escape.

"I wasn't gonna do anything, Nick. I just wanted a feel. I ain't gonna hurt nothing by doing that."

"No feels until we find out about the money. And you," he said pointing to her, "ain't gonna do anymore screamin.'" He reached down on the floor for the rag from last night.

"I need a drink, just some water. Please—then you can gag me if you want."

Nick thought about her giving him permission as laughable, "Lady, I don't think you understand; you ain't bargaining. I'll gag you if I want, water or not."

She looked at the young man with a pleading glance.

"Nick, I'll get her a little water."

He turned and glared at Donovan as if to say NO.

"She ain't gonna bring in any money if she dies of dehydration!"

"I guess you're the babysitter, little Bro. Just don't get any stupid ideas."

Her heart sank; they were brothers. She dropped to the mattress, stifling her sobs.

"Lenny you keep an eye on him. I gotta go meet somebody about our guest."

All three walked out leaving her alone, again. She heard a car crank up and leave. Lenny returned, grumbling as he went into the office.

"Here have some water," Donovan said, holding out a half full bottle.

She was startled because she didn't realize he was back, but she said nothing. She took the water eagerly. It tasted stale, but felt good going down her dry throat.

"My name is Donovan," he said, not really knowing what to say to her. He couldn't talk too long because Lenny would surely mention it to Nick.

"Nick is your brother?"

"Half-brother," he corrected her. "I haven't figured out how to get you outta here yet. I gotta get rid of Lenny first."

"You can't overpower him?"

"Lenny is quick as a cat and tougher than he looks; besides that he keeps a gun in his waistband and he ain't afraid to use it."

She remembered how he had effortlessly caught her leg and held it fast in a strong, vise-like grip. "I want to go home," she said, her voice soft and trembling. Deep in her heart she had a feeling she was never going to make it. For the first time, utter hopelessness was creeping into her conscious mind. She wanted to ask why they had done this. Why were they after Albert? Was it just money, or something else? But before she could speak, he left.

Late in the afternoon, Nick returned. She could hear them talking in the office. She strained to listen to what was being said. She only got bits and pieces of the conversation, but from what she understood, they weren't happy. She heard something about not getting two million dollars, having to wait for several days to see if something happened, something about a week or two, two-hundred-thousand if it happened, but if it didn't happen—she couldn't hear what they said. Despair deepened. It would be days, perhaps even weeks chained to this spot. Donovan came out with car keys jingling in his hand. He didn't look toward her, he just walked out and she heard a car crank and speed away.

Just before darkness fell, he returned. The other two men hadn't bothered her; they had been outside since Donovan left. They probably couldn't stand the sweltering heat in the building, she assumed. The late April air was cool when the big door slid open, but those were the only times the heat was alleviated.

Donovan carried in some bags to the office and then came out to her. "I'm moving you into the office building, you'll... ."

"No!" She cried in fright. "That other man, Lenny... ."

"It's okay. He isn't going to be in there. I've got some water and something for you to eat. There is a bathroom in there. It's nasty. The water doesn't work, but it's a bathroom." He could see the yellow stain where she had urinated on the edge of the mattress. It couldn't be helped; she wouldn't have asked the other two to take her to a bathroom. "At least the bugs shouldn't be too bad in there tonight," he said, motioning to the bites on her legs. "I'll put the mattress in there so you... ."

"How long," she whimpered, "will I be here? When can I go home?

For the first time she could see hopelessness in his eyes. "I don't know," he said. But she thought he did; he just didn't want to tell her.

Nick came into the office and made sure she was secured. They clipped one side of the handcuff to her wrist and the other side through a link on a car chain, the other end of the chain was wrapped and padlocked around a metal counter post. When he was satisfied, he took the keys and left. Donovan set out half-a-dozen quart bottles of spring water and a handful of packaged crackers. He said he was sorry it wasn't more, but it was all Nick would allow. She wasn't hungry, but she was thirsty. She took one of the bottles of spring water and settled down on the mattress because darkness was quickly coming upon this place and she wouldn't be able to see in a few minutes. This horrid place was now her home--for how long, she didn't know.

She wasn't hungry, but she was thirsty. She took one of the bottles of water and settled down on the mattress because darkness came quickly upon this place and she wouldn't be able to see in a few minutes. This horrid place was now her home—for how long she didn't know.

~:~

Newspapers and television stations blared the news across the country, "Wife of ATI Founder and President Kidnapped!" The tabloids said inside sources revealed Albert Trathmoore was grief-stricken to the point of incapacity. It was speculated that she was probably killed in the kidnapping attempt because there had been no contact for ransom. The entire country was predicting the fall of his massive empire without his visionary leadership. ATI stocks were being dumped onto Wall Street at an alarming rate.

Albert held a press conference to assure the stockholders that, although he was deeply troubled and concerned about what happened to his wife, he would continue to run his company. He made a plea for her safe return, offering a ten-million dollar reward for information leading to the capture and conviction of those responsible. But, as hard as he tried to dispel fear, more false headlines produced panic in his shareholders.

His legal team began immediate action to stop the flood of misinformation, but there were a multitude of companies to be sued. The task seemed daunting.

Yet in misfortune comes opportunity. Albert had only twenty-six percent of the stock in his company. Dalfina and his daughters held an additional twenty-five percent, but in order to obtain these shares in the divorce she and the girls had to sign proxy consent for Albert to be their voting voice. He didn't, however, have control over their ability to sell the stock. He had always told them to never to sell it; if they needed money, he would buy it from them.

Jon Lindquist hadn't seen Dalfina in years, but now he was on the phone with her and he was terribly concerned for her and the girls. It seemed, he realized, with the stocks selling at such a rapid rate surely, in the end, she and her daughters would be left with something far less valuable. It wouldn't be right to go to Albert and ask him to take the stock off their hands when he was so deeply grieving. He offered a little less than it was worth, but he would compensate with stock shares in his company.

Though Syntec was not the empire that ATI was, when ATI crumbled, Syntec would possibly become the new leader in the field. Already, he told her, some of ATI's top-level executives were looking at his company in case of collapse. She couldn't take too long to decide because stock prices were falling rapidly, so he might not be able to make them the same offer in another day or two.

Dalfina and her twenty-one year old daughter, Mindi, lived on a small, northern California ranch that became their home after the divorce. The oldest daughter, Corrine, who was twenty-four, lived a hundred miles southwest in a beautiful home that overlooked the Pacific Ocean. It was with Corrine that Albert stayed with when he visited the girls.

"Mindi and I are selling, Sweetheart. I think it might be in your best interest to sell too," Dalfina told her over the phone.

"I'm not selling to him!" Corrine said defensively, still remembering that Jon was the reason for the divorce that tore her family apart. "I hate him! I'm calling Daddy."

"Sweetheart, this is not the kind of thing he needs to deal with right now. He knows we're concerned, and he knows we're here for him, but talking to him about business, now? It's not right."

The line was quiet.

"I don't care for Jon anymore, you know that," her mother continued. "But he still cares about us. His offer is fair and reasonable, and I'm not going to burden you father about money when he has—when he has too many other things on his mind."

"I'll keep my eight percent; I don't care if my stock isn't worth dirt! I'm not selling to him—ever. Goodbye, Mom."

~:~

Albert sat in the darkness of his office, his mind deep in wonder about the events that transpired over the last week. His company was going through the worst period in its history. He mustn't loose focus. He mustn't let his guard drop for a moment. He pushed his anger and fear about Katie to the back of his mind. His true love was in trouble, and it wasn't her. Katie was his physical love, and he did love her. But, this company was his soul, and he loved it more. He had to keep it together, no matter what the cost, and it was costing him his personal fortune. It really didn't matter if his fortune had to go back into the company; he would make it again, but only if his company stayed alive.

Genevieve opened the door and looked inside, "Mr. Trathmoore, Corrine is on the phone for you. Do you want to take the call right now?" Her voice was soft and sympathetic.

He had a lot on his mind and Corrine would, no doubt, distract him even further, but he solemnly nodded his head and picked up the phone. He wasn't going to like what she told him; in fact it would enrage him. But now he had keen insight as to why this had happened and who his adversary was. He thought, if it wasn't for the possibility of getting caught, he'd have the son-of-a-bitch killed—and he'd really like to be the one to do it!

~:~

It had only been eight days since the kidnapping, but the stockholders were calling for an emergency meeting and an accounting of shares. New rumors had spread that Albert no longer had rightful control of the company; too many stocks had traded hands in the last days.

He showed no surprise when Lindquist came into the room with a team of advisors. Jon could have just sent his lawyers, but why? He wanted the satisfaction of seeing Trathmoore's face in person. The meeting was called to order and an accounting of shares began. Syntec Industries had accumulated an astonishing thirty-eight percent, seventeen percent of which came directly from the Trathmoore family. Albert was mildly surprised. He knew Dalfina and Mindi sold their shares, but the other twenty-one percent had been carefully held by individuals and companies that were not known as Syntec allies or subsidiaries; that was not revealed until just before the meeting.

Jon's face wore a wicked bliss, as if you say, 'got ya!' His team started to take control of the meeting. After all, they would be running or dismantling the company; it might as well start right now. No one else could possibly accumulate billions of dollars worth of shares. Jon had stretched every financial resource he had, including stock in his own company to achieve such a feat. But it was worth it—anything was worth it to see Albert Trathmoore destroyed.

"I think your actions might be a bit premature," Albert spoke up. The room grew quiet and the remainder of the report was presented. He may have lost seventeen percent of his family's voting rights, but had he purchased eight percent from his daughter and then picked up an incredible eighteen percent in the avalanche on Wall Street. Adding to his existing twenty-six percent, he now personally owned and voted on fifty-two percent of the shares for his company. He was, and would remain, the majority leader.

"Impossible!" Lindquist shouted angrily. "You would have had to spend everything you have to acquire that much!"

"I have plenty to spend," Albert said with a smile on his face. It was the first time he had smiled since the ordeal began. If it had been under other circumstances, his victory would have been sweet, especially when Jon found that the Swiss bankers who helped him by purchasing Syntec stock had already agreed to sell it to ATI Industries as soon as Albert was in a position to transfer the funds. But there could be no sweetness to winning this battle and ridding himself of Lindquist until Katie was home.

The room emptied quickly, the news was already spreading like wildfire.

Jon's plan had started going bad in the very beginning and now it was nothing but crumbling ruins. His company was too far in debt with the stocks he had purchased, and though they still had value, he had no hope of taking ATI away from Trathmoore. New plans were forming in his mind; if he couldn't have what he wanted, Albert would suffer for it in the worst possible way. "Well, Trathmoore," Jon said extending his hand to Albert. "You did a good job keeping the company. I just hope everything turns out for the best with your wife. I certainly was sorry to hear what happened to her. Perhaps things will turn around for you there, too."

Their hands locked together, both of them trying to crush the other.

"I'm sure it will," Albert said with a look of ardent hatred. "I'll catch the bastard responsible and put him away for life."

The handshake broke loose and Lindquist left the room, but with the same evil smile he had worn when he first entered it.

Albert returned to his office on the penthouse floor. He walked briskly past Genevieve with his teeth clenched and his jaw muscle about to snap. He slammed the door.

Genevieve jumped in fright.

He was not one to lose control of his emotions, but now he couldn't restrain them.

She heard him yelling obscenities and the crashing of furniture and file cabinets.

Sitting in his chair, his office helter-skelter, he looked out over the Manhattan skyline. Bitter tears streaked down his face, his pain over Katie would no longer be denied. He knew if she was still alive, Lindquist would be certain to have her killed. He'd made his choice—his company would survive, but it cost him Katie.

~:~

The days had run together. She wasn't sure how long she'd been locked and chained like an animal. She didn't see much of her captors, and she wondered if Donovan would ever find a way to help her. He told her he was waiting for an opportunity when it would be just him and her, but he always had either Lenny or Nick with him.

The news was reporting a take-over of ATI industries had been averted and that Albert Trathmoore was still very much in control of his company. This was not what Nick wanted to hear. If Trathmoore had lost the company, they would have gotten their two-hundred thousand; if not it was doubtful they'd get anything. It was time to meet the contact and find out if they had wasted their time. He was going to call Lenny on the cell phone and let him know the outcome. Nick planned all along that he would kill her simply because she knew his face and his first name, but he wanted to wait until he got his money. She wasn't going to be the first person he'd ever killed, and surely not the last, but it would be a first for Donny. He hoped that his little brother would realize it was worth it if they got enough money.

Nervously, Donovan waited for the phone to ring. It was down to the wire now and if he had to he'd fight Lenny, but he didn't want to. Lenny would surely kill him and then she would die anyway. When it finally rang, Donovan's heart was beating so hard that he was certain Lenny would see it jumping in his chest.

At first Lenny talked low then a broad smile came across his face. "Good," he said. "I could use some money about now. I'm planning a little party for myself," he laughed.

Somewhat relieved, Donovan was certain if they got the money, Nick would let her go. If they hadn't been paid, Nick would kill her. "Are we gonna get the money?" He asked Lenny cautiously.

"Yeah, he got a fifty thousand dollar down payment from the contact. We'll get another hundred and fifty grand when it's over."

His thoughts began to race; when what's over? They were supposed to turn her loose if they got the money. "What do you mean? How come he didn't get it all now?"

"We gotta kill our little friend and dump her body where it can be *discovered* then we'll get the rest of the money."

Donovan couldn't think clearly. He didn't want anything to happen to the woman that trusted him to get her out of there. "I thought we were supposed to let her go to get the two hundred grand."

"That was the original plan, but now she's gotta die. Don't sweat it kid, you'll still get your fifty thousand. And believe me, there ain't no woman worth fifty thousand dollars. Hell, as tight as you are, you'll probably start a whole new life with that kinda money. But me, I'm gonna drink it, coke it and blow it. Fancy whores and good drugs, that's what I want. When Nick gets back, we're gonna have a little party with her. Hell, you'll be the first one to get to bang her. When the party's over, we'll blow her brains out and dump her off in Central Park tonight. That'll be a hell of a fun find for the joggers tomorrow morning," he laughed as he poked Donovan in the ribs with his elbow.

"When is Nick getting back?"

"He'll be here in about two hours 'cause he's got another stop to make."

Donovan had to come up with a plan to get Lenny to leave. He needed it to be good, but most of all he needed it *now*. He knew Lenny's money had run out and it had been two days since he'd had a drink, but could he convince him to leave to get one? Maybe, if he acted crude enough and heartless enough toward Katie, Lenny would believe that he wanted the money and didn't care about her. The problem was that he did care about her, and to be vicious toward her would be hard; he'd never hit a woman.

"I ain't waiting for Nick," he said turning and heading toward the warehouse. "I've wanted a piece of her ass ever since I first saw her."

Lenny was surprised, but still suspicious, "You gonna do her now?"

"Why not? You said I'd be the first, so it doesn't matter when, does it?"

Lenny licked his dry, cracked lips and smiled, "Well hell, pretty boy, maybe you've got a pair of balls after all!"

They both walked into the office. She looked up, frightened at the sight of Lenny, but comforted that Donovan was with him. Donovan walked over to her and knelt beside her on the mattress. He mouthed the words "It's gonna be okay," then he knocked her back on the mattress and swiftly began forcing the filthy gag cloth in her mouth.

She didn't know what he was trying to do, but she wasn't going to let him without a fight. She bit his finger and he yelped in pain. She was kicking and trying to scream, when she felt Lenny's strong hands grab her legs. Panic washed over her. I've trusted him, she thought, and now he's gonna kill me! He lied to me!

He smacked her across the face, open handed and not as hard as his brother, but still it momentarily stunned her.

"Be still you little bitch!" Donovan growled as he undid the chain and handcuffed both of her wrists.

She felt Lenny handcuff her ankle and clip it to the counter post.

"She can't kick you with that leg, but we don't wanna take all the fun out of her," Lenny said, excited over the fracas.

Winded from struggling with her, Donovan stood up and looked at him. "Here," he said opening his wallet. "Go get us some liquor. If I'm gonna do this I plan on getting smashed." He handed him a pair of twenties.

Lenny looked at the girl, now helpless on the mattress and back at Donovan with distrust clear on his face.

"Nope. Can't do it. Nick said you couldn't be left alone. You might decide to turn her loose."

"Shit Lenny, you're gonna take my car. How the hell am I gonna take her outta here, over my shoulder? Get real. Besides, I don't need you watchin' my ass bob."

Quickly, and without warning, Lenny pulled the nine millimeter that he carried in his waistband. He had his own ideas and he wasn't sure if the kid was being straight or not.

"What'a you doin'?" Donovan said, his voice even, but menacing.

"Do her now," Lenny said motioning to her.

"You sick mother… ."

Lenny pulled the back the hammer on the gun and pointed it at Donovan's head.

"You do her now, then I'll go." Lenny wanted a drink, and he wanted it badly, but he was gonna make sure Donovan was convinced he'd go to jail if he tried to run off with her.

"Why?" Donovan asked without unflinching.

"Because, let me tell you something *Donny*, maybe she's told you she'd say you wasn't to blame, but if you do her and let her go they'll nail you for rape no matter what. You'll get plenty of jail time for that, and you're so *pretty*, all them guys in the prison will like you."

His jaws clinched. This was not something he expected Lenny to do. He was certain if he had let him take the car he wouldn't have cared about leaving them alone. And, now that he had said he was going to rape her while Lenny was gone, Lenny would see no reason not to do it now.

He couldn't hit Lenny before the gun went off, and so, in a manner of speaking, he figured they were both screwed. He had to decide; it was easy to think what he *should* do, but it was another thing to stare down the barrel of a real gun—and know the person holding it had no problem with pulling the trigger. And then he wondered: Are you still a hero when you and the person you are trying to save both die? I've got to get him to leave or she doesn't stand a chance when Nick gets back, he thought. He began undoing his jeans.

Katie's eyes went wide in shock and disbelief. It was evident now what her fate would be. With all her soul she begged for her life to end at that very moment. She screamed and cried into the gag, but it was no use, no one would hear her. She kicked at Donovan with her free leg, but he easily held it down. It only took him a moment to pull down her shorts and underpants to her cuffed ankle. She heard Lenny making remarks about what he planned to do when it was his turn. She could feel her insides churning, choking at the attempt her empty stomach made to heave.

Donovan pulled her knit top up under her arms and unclasped her bra. He didn't think he'd be able to go through with it, but no matter how dirty and beat up she was, she was still beautiful and his body responded to what he saw.

Through the gag, he could make out her muffled "No, no, no."

She couldn't look at him. He had betrayed her in the worst way, letting her think he would help her, and now he was simply helping himself—to her.

Humiliation and degradation seized her and death, in her mind, would be welcomed when it came and ended her shame. It seemed an eternity, but soon he was finished with her and putting back on his pants.

"There! You happy? Now go get us something to drink!" He no longer sounded like Donovan; his voice had taken the same commanding tone as Nick's normally had.

"Yeah, I'm happy. I'll be happier when it my turn tonight," he said leering down on her exposed body. "Give me the keys."

"I gave you the damn keys!" Donovan said looking at Lenny as if he'd lost his mind.

"No, pretty boy, the keys to the cuffs."

"Shit Lenny! You really don't trust me do you?!" He dug around in his pocket and fished out the handcuff keys and then followed Lenny out to the car.

"See ya, kid. Don't do anything stupid or you'll end up paying for it, one way or another," he said as he cranked the Caprice.

Donovan watched the car until it disappeared around the last wharf and he couldn't hear the engine anymore. The liquor store wasn't far away, so he knew there wasn't much time. He rushed back inside, wondering what she would do when he released her; he really didn't want to go to jail.

She let out a muffled scream when he charged back into the room.

"It's okay, it's okay. He's gone. We can get outta here now." He slid his hand up under the mattress edge where he had hidden an extra cuff key in the act of taking her.

She was trying to believe it was real. He *was* going to help her? But what he had just done to her—how could she believe him?

The handcuffs came off her ankle and then her wrists. For the first time in nine days, she was free. She pulled off the gag herself and spit out the fabric. "YOU BASTARD!" she yelled taking a swing at him. "You...," but she couldn't say anything else. She felt his strong hands gripping her shoulders, holding her for a moment as she stopped struggling and began to sob uncontrollably.

"Lady, I'm sorry. Please, I didn't want to," he stopped, realizing that physically he did, but he never would have if the situation had been different. "Please, you gotta stop crying," he said, shaking her gently. "We've gotta get the hell outta here before either of them gets back. They're gonna kill you. Do you understand me? *They're gonna kill you!*"

Her legs were wobbly and she stumbled more than she ran trying to get out of the office. Crashing out into the late day sunshine, she was unable to open her eyes. She had been in the dim and mostly dark office for so long that her eyes had grown accustom to shadows, not sunlight. Tears streaming down her cheeks from the painful light, she grabbed on to Donovan's hand and let him lead her blindly down the wharf. They ran, dodging between buildings and down narrow alleys for what seemed such a long time—especially for someone who had been living life at the end of an eight-foot chain.

Her eyes began to adjust as she wondered where he was leading her. "Where are we going? Do you have a car?" she asked, gasping for breath.

He looked around nervously. "No, Lenny took my car, but we can't stay anywhere around here. Nick will find us if we don't get outta here."

"Find a phone, we'll call the police and...."

"NO!" He stopped her. "No police! Not 'til I've had time to figure this out."

"But... ."

They came out of an alley and looked at the road leading back to the skeleton city of abandon harbor buildings.

"There is what we need!" He was pointing to a row of cars parked down a cross street. The warehouses had been condemned and were scheduled for demolition so there was a tall chain link fence topped with razor wire to keep people out, but it also blocked them from freedom. "Come on this way," he said as they cautiously moved down the back of the buildings. "I saw a place in the fence when I drove past here the other day. I think we can get out there."

Debris littered the ground with everything from demolition signs to broken glass. Her heart beat increased as they drew closer to a narrow gate, but it was padlocked firmly shut.

"Shit!" Donovan said as he jerked her down behind a fallen sign.

Her first reaction was to struggle, but then she looked at his face; he was terrified. "Lenny's back!"

"Did he see us?" she whispered.

"I don't think so, but if you hear the brakes slam on, get ready to run."

The car passed by and they watched it travel the two blocks down to the entrance gate. Lying almost flat on the ground, they saw Lenny unlocked, drive in, and re-locked the gate. He hadn't seen them!

It would be only a matter of minutes though before he would arrive at the warehouse and discover they were gone. They were going to have to move quickly if they were to get out of the fence before Lenny started driving around the buildings.

"Here," Donovan said, as they reached the place in the fence that he thought they could get through. The tear in the fencing was small and Katie wanted to be the first to go through, but Donovan stopped her.

"If I can do it then I know you can," he said as he pushed himself through the fence to freedom. The truth was he didn't want her to go first and take off running.

She was crawling through the fence when they heard the Caprice's engine roaring to life and tires burning against the pavement.

"Come on, run!" Donovan yelled, yanking her the rest of the way through the fence. Hearts pounding and feet flying, they ran across the street and headed in the direction of the parked cars a hundred yards away. In her mind she knew the distance should only take them seconds to cover, but when you know someone is planning on killing you, seconds can be a lifetime. A nightmare from her childhood flashed through her mind: she was running down a road, a car was coming, but just when she tried to get out of the way her feet wouldn't move and she was trapped. But this wasn't a dream; she was flying on pure adrenaline and she *was* going to make it. Around the corner, but not yet safe, Donovan's hands were ripping at door handles as they ran down the length of cars. She turned and glanced back at the warehouses beyond the fence, she could see the Caprice speeding down the inner road. Suddenly a car alarm screamed to life.

"AH SHIT!" Donovan yelled.

Brakes were slamming. In terror, she looked back again. The brown Caprice was stopped in an alleyway and Lenny was running toward the fence with his pistol in his hand thrashing the air. She could hear his obscenities as he hit the fence and realized he'd have to go back to the car.

Six cars, seven cars, nothing was unlocked. The Caprice was moving again and it would only be a matter of about a minute before he unlocked the gate and drove to where they were. Nine cars, ten cars; the eleventh one, an older model Ford LTD opened.

"Get in!" Donovan yelled. Reaching up under the dash he frantically jerked a handful of wires down and pulled a connection loose.

"You've done this before, right?"

"I saw Nick do it once!"

She felt faint, "We're gonna die."

In that moment the engine of the LTD turned over and came to life. "No we're not," he said triumphantly. He clipped the car parked in front of them as he pushed the gas pedal to the floor. The city outside her window blurred past. Within a few blocks they were enmeshed in a major thoroughfare and they blended away into New York traffic. For the first time, she felt a sense of relief. It's almost over, she thought.

"You can let me out anywhere. I'll be okay," she said looking out the window.

"Not yet. I've gotta figure out what I'm gonna do."

"Let me out! I want to go home!" Her hand reached for the door handle as the car slowed in traffic.

"No. Please, Lady, don't! I swear I'm not gonna hurt you. I've just gotta figure out what's gonna happen because I... ." He had his hand firmly on her arm, but then he gently released her. "Please, I just need a little time to think."

She could tell he was frightened at the thought of going to jail. She didn't blame him; she'd had a taste of imprisonment and no one would want it.

The tears washed over her lower lashes. "I'm still scared." The impact of everything that had happened was causing her to tremble violently. She put her head down to her knees and began to sob. "Please don't lie to me. Tell me the truth. Will you let me go soon?"

"Yes, I will. I'm sorry for what I did to you, but I didn't have any choice. If he hadn't left we couldn't have gotten out of there. I never would have hurt you—never."

She rocked against her knees, crying softly. Dehydration, starvation and exhaustion from using the last bit of adrenaline her body possessed overcame her consciousness and she passed out.

~:~

When she came to, he was gently shaking her.

"Lady, wake up and come inside."

She raised her head. It was completely dark. She could smell the aroma of fir trees in the night air. "Where are we?" she asked weakly.

"It's okay. It's a little place that rents cabins. We can stay here tonight. I'll take you to the police tomorrow."

"We're not in the city?"

"No, this is a little country place out of Yonkers. It's quiet here."

She could see the porch lights of other cabins in the distance. He unlocked the door and they walked inside. The aroma of cedar boards and fresh linens mixed with the clean night air. The cabin was small and comfortable. There was a tiny living room with a couch, a rocker and a little television that appeared to be ancient. A petite kitchenette with pine board cabinets was only feet away, and beyond it was a bathroom and bedroom. The only thing that was large in the cabin was the queen size bed that took up most of the space in the bedroom.

"I thought you might want to clean-up," he said apologetically as he gestured toward the bathroom.

She didn't say anything; she just stared at the surroundings.

He could understand that she was still in shock from the whole ordeal, and she probably still didn't trust him after what he had done to her. "It's okay, I won't bother you. Lady?"

"Katie," she said. "My name is Katie."

"I heard on the news it was Katherine, but I didn't think you'd want someone like me calling you by your first name."

"If it wasn't for you, Donovan, I'd be dead right now." She was quiet again as they stood and looked at each other. "Thank you for getting me out of there."

She turned and went into the bathroom

Quietly, he left and walked to the office. He got a bucket of ice, cokes and some mini-donuts from the vending machine and walked through the darkness back to the cabin.

She sat in the tub with the shower beating down on her. She was so dirty, her hair hung in greasy strands down her back. It would take the entire bottle of hotel shampoo to clean it. The tiny bar of hotel soap she rubbed into a washcloth and scrubbed herself from face to foot. At that moment she couldn't think of anything that ever felt so good.

She didn't know how long she had been in the bath, but eventually the water began to run cold and she realized she couldn't stay in there forever. She looked at the now-cleaned cuts and scrapes in the mirror and they looked remarkably better without all of the dirt, but her clothes she wished she could burn. How could she put them back on with all the filth and memories of her captivity still on them? Her cotton underpants were the worst and she threw them into the waste can, her shirt, bra and shorts she shook and put back on.

She could hear the television as she came out of the bath. He was sitting on the couch with his head in his hands. He wasn't watching it, and she wondered if he was crying. She walked silently to the living room, listening as she walked; it was the ten o'clock news and they were talking about her. She didn't hear the first of it, but she did hear them say something about the fact that it was going on ten days and the worst was presumed.

He looked up, wiping his eyes with shaking hands. "I'm gonna go to jail. I know they won't understand about what I did."

"I understand—now." She couldn't look at him when she spoke because for that moment she was reliving it. "I remember what Lenny was saying about he wanted to be sure you wouldn't let me go. I remember the gun. You didn't have a choice. If you hadn't, he never would have left us alone." She didn't want to remember the act of being taken, yet it was there in her memory. She had struggled against him during the assault and he could have physically injured her when he took her, but he had been as gentle as the situation would allow. And, in the farthest reaches of her mind, she remembered as she was pressed to the mattress, his breath in her ear saying, "I'm sorry."

"I'll drop you off at the police station tomorrow and then I'm leaving New York."

"You can't do that. They'll catch up to you and then you *will* look guilty for what happened."

"What else can I do? When Nick catches up with me, I'm good as dead anyway."

Her mind began to reel. She needed him to go with her to the police. He could tell them so much more than she knew. He would have to testify against Nick and Lenny; she didn't want to do it alone.

They talked for hours into the night, Katie begging and pleading with him to come with her and help put the other two away. He told her about the fear he had of Nick. He talked about his life growing up in Brooklyn with his mother and Nick. She had become pregnant with Nick when she was only seventeen. Nick's father, Nicholas Stranette, was a local hood who had a reputation with the ladies. Though they never married, Nick's father stayed around and helped raise him to become even worse than his old man.

When his mother was in her late-thirties she met Donovan's father, a local delicatessen owner. Even though she wasn't Nicholas' wife, he was furious about the relationship. When she became pregnant with Donovan, Nick's father went into a rage, shooting her lover and wounding her. Donovan's father died. Nick's father was sentenced to life in Attica State Prison. He was killed in prison riots a few years later. His mother didn't tell him what had happened. He simply thought Nick was his older brother.

As far back as he could remember, Nick was always trying to get him involved in a life of crime. When he was ten, Nick was teaching him petty thievery at the local grocery, how to break into vending machines and get out the quarters, and how to unlock a bike chain to steal the bike. His mother hated it and finally told him the truth about what had happened; Nick was only his half brother. She wanted him to make something of himself rather than just being a copy of his big brother. His father would have wanted him to be a respectable businessman, not a thug.

Things changed. He began to study in school and started avoiding trouble. He got a part-time job at fifteen and started working to help support his mother, but Nick was always there. It seemed the more he tried to do right, the more Nick pushed him to do wrong. Their mother suffered a stroke at age sixty-one, ending up in a nursing home. Donovan was on his own. And it seemed no matter how hard he worked, he never made the kind of money his half-brother did. Now at 25, he'd finally had enough of twelve dollars an hour and never enough hours to make a decent paycheck. Nick told him he'd have a share in two million dollars and, with that kind of money, he would have left New York and made a clean start somewhere else.

"But the job wasn't to get you," he stated. "You were in the wrong place on the wrong day. When I saw you lying there unconscious, I knew the money wasn't worth it. All I could think about was how I could get us both out of there—alive."

"I won't tell anyone about what happened between us," she said honestly. "I'll just say you had to wait for the right opportunity to get me out of there, and that's all."

"What about your husband?" He asked, finally getting the courage to look her in the eye. "He's going to ask. What are you going to tell him?"

"I'll just tell him it was the only way."

"No! If you tell him, he'll have me locked up for good. I know if I had that much money and you were my wife, and I knew someone did that to you, I'd see he was sent to prison."

She thought about Albert, and she knew he was right. He would show no mercy just because she said Donovan shouldn't be punished. But how could she lie to him? She couldn't. I just can't tell him, she thought. Not because of her own humiliation, but because Donovan had risked his life to get her out of there and he didn't deserve prison for that.

"I won't tell him. I promise you, I won't tell him about what happened."

The clock on the kitchen wall showed it was three in the morning.

"Go ahead and get some sleep," he motioned to the bedroom. "I'll go with you in the morning."

Katie lay on the clean, crisp sheets with the pillow cradling her head and she fell into a deep sleep, comfortable and clean for the first time in a long time.

Donovan stayed on the couch. He would eventually doze off, but his mind tossed and turned over thoughts of what would happen when daylight came. She seemed like a determined woman, and he would have to believe that she meant what she said.

~:~

The morning light awakened her with a jolt. I'm going home! She thought. She woke Donovan gently and asked if he was ready. She didn't want to seem eager, but she was. In a matter of minutes they were standing at the door, ready to go.

He stood there with his hand on the knob, but he didn't open it. He turned and looked at her for a long moment. He was shaking.

"It's going to be okay," she said, trying to reassure him.

"I probably won't see you again when this is all over. You'll be back being the wife of a rich man and I'll just be another guy off the street."

"Not in my eyes," she tried to tell him.

"I don't want your last memory of me to be what happened in that warehouse."

He reached out to her and, though the nearness of him frightened her, she permitted the embrace.

He held on to her for a moment. "I've never met a woman like you," he whispered. "I can't believe it had to be this way."

She smiled at him for the first time.

"I want you to remember me this way," he said. Briefly, but tenderly, his lips brushed hers with a kiss that summed up the sorrow he felt over the circumstances of their encounter. "It's time to leave," he said, letting her go. "I know how bad you want to go home."

They drove out of the shaded lot and onto the highway that would take them to the police and end what began an eternity ago.

~:~

The hospital was cold and filled with a clinically sterile odor. The harsh lights were unforgiving on her pale skin as the female doctor checked each abrasion and cut on her body. There was a policewoman nearby taking note of what the doctor was telling her. Two officers stood outside the door to make sure no one went in that wasn't allowed.

"Okay Mrs. Trathmoore, now just relax and lean back. I need to finish the exam." The doctor was pulling stirrups out from the end of the table and trying to get her to lean back.

"No!"

"Mrs. Trathmoore, I must examine... ."

"No! I wasn't violated that way during my captivity and I certainly won't be violated like that here in the hospital." Her voice was firm and commanding.

"Now, Mrs. Trathmoore," the policewoman interrupted, "The doctor is just trying... ."

"Absolutely not!" She snapped. "I refuse to undergo the embarrassment of something like this. I'll go to my own doctor if you need to put something on the report, but you," she said, pointing to the doctor, "are not going to touch me! And that is final. I will sue you, this hospital and... ."

"All right Mrs. Trathmoore," the doctor began, but just then the door to her room swung open and Albert walked in. The doctor and the officer looked at him, realizing who he was from all the times his face had been on the news or in the papers. They left the room.

She didn't know what to say; the tears were building on her lower lashes, distorting the room which had already begun to swim in her vision. She thought at one point in time she would never see him again, yet there he was, just as handsome and in control as always.

He was shocked when he saw her, for an instant he thought he'd entered the wrong room. Her skin was almost translucent, and her right cheek and eye still had the faint remains of the black and purple bruise. Insect bites covered her arms and legs, and she was deathly thin. Other than finding out that she was dead, his worst fears about her appeared to be true; she had been horribly mistreated and he was more afraid of what he couldn't see than what he could. But he had to put those thoughts aside because she needed him more than he needed to know the answers to his fears.

In the safety of his arms, she began to sob and release the pain and torture stored inside her. He held her for a long time, smoothing her hair with his hand, whispering that everything was all right now; he was taking her home.

They boarded the helicopter from the hospital roof and within moments they were swooping out over the city. The helicopter headed north, northwest toward the distant mountains; she looked to him in unspoken wonderment.

"The Adirondacks," he answered. "It's quiet there."

She said nothing, but leaned against his strong arm, grateful that they wouldn't be facing the crowds that surely would be waiting at the house in East Hampton.

After touching down, he gently led her inside. The staff had been reduced to a minimum to help with the transition back to the public.

"Do you want to lie down? Would you like something to eat? I'll bring it to your room."

"I'm hungry, but I don't want to lie down."

She sat at the dining table. Albert returned with a dinner tray. There was a bowl of steaming hot beef stew, small tender biscuits, a salad and a cold glass of ice tea. He placed it on the table and left her alone. She ate what she could. She was hungry, but her stomach had shrunk so small that after a few bites she began to feel full. She wanted everything to return to normal as quickly as possible, so she ate a few more bites before leaving the table. He was in his study, staring out at the woods beyond the stable. She didn't want to talk; she was glad to be here but not ready to tell what had happened, and he would want to know soon enough.

Alone in the master bath, she stepped into the spa, turning on the jets and letting them pulse against the sore muscles and tired limbs. She poured in raspberry fragranced oil heavily and then immersed herself completely. After soaking, she slipped in between the silk sheets of his bed and fell asleep.

Dreams flooded her mind as she tossed restlessly in the bed. Then, in a state that was somewhere between conscious and unconsciousness, she felt the presence of someone in her bed and she woke screaming.

"Katie it's all right! It me, Albert!" He tried to grab her and settle her down, but she seemed to grow wilder in his grasp. "Katie, Katie," he said her name over and over until she stopped struggling and recognized him. "I'm sorry. I didn't mean to frighten you. I should have slept in the other room," he said, angry with himself for being so ignorant. He rose to leave.

"No, please don't leave me. I didn't realize—I was dreaming and you startled me. I don't want to be alone anymore."

Climbing back into the bed, he pulled her to his side. She was shivering a bit so he pulled her in tight and held her, enjoying the raspberry scent that clung to her. The nearness of her body filled him with desire, but he wouldn't partake of the pleasures she held until he found out what he needed to know. Already he had a group of detectives working with the police to assist in the search for the two men who had taken her.

He wondered about the man who took her to the police and assisted in her escape. There were too many questions to consider; for now he was glad to hold her.

In the morning she woke alone. She was ready to put on her robe when Albert came into the bedroom with a breakfast tray.

"Good morning."

"You didn't have to bring breakfast to me. I'm feeling better this morning."

"Well, I did and I guess you'll just have to eat it."

She smiled and leaned back on the bed, propping herself up on the pillows.

"Drink your orange juice," he said, handing her the glass. He sounded like her parent, not her husband. "The doctor said you were dehydrated so you need plenty of fluids."

"When did you talk with the doctor?" she asked in surprise. She knew they left immediately from the hospital and he didn't speak with her attending physician.

"This morning. She said you weren't very cooperative either."

She took the orange juice, but said nothing as she began sipping it slowly.

"You wouldn't let her finish her job," he added.

She was angry with herself as she could feel the flush coming to her cheeks and she couldn't control it. "She was rude," she retorted, and then went back to sipping.

"Katie," he cautiously began, "are you ready to talk with me about what happened? *I have to know what happened.*"

Her stomach began to churn and she had to take several deep breaths to stop the feeling of forming tears. "No, I'm not ready. Not today Albert, please—I need a little more time."

He leaned over and kissed her forehead, "You rest today and when you're ready I'll listen." He turned to go and then walked back to the bed. "Katie, whatever happened, I'll understand it wasn't your fault."

She nodded her head, but she wouldn't look up at him. She nibbled small bites and tried to swallow them, but they couldn't get past the lump that was growing in her throat.

~:~

It had been two weeks since her release, but she still didn't feel as if she was recovering. The guilt over concealing her assault was eating away at her, but she couldn't tell him. She had made a promise and she must keep it or Donovan would go to jail. She knew he was in protective custody and the search was continuing for Nick and Lenny. Albert had left her in the care of his staff and additional security personnel at his mountain home. Security was going to stay in place until the two men were captured and the media attention died down.

She'd spoken to her parents over the phone and assured them she was okay. Her mother offered to come up for support, but she told her no, she was fine and perhaps she'd come see them in a month or so.

Reluctantly, her mother told her that she should call Alex. She said he had gone wild when the news broke about the kidnapping, blaming himself because he was the one who caused her to leave and go to New York. After a few days passed and speculation began about whether she was alive or dead, he moved out, leaving Crystal and their baby girl, Cheyenne.

"I know it's probably not something you want to deal with after everything you've been through, Sweetheart, but—well, it's a pitiful situation. He's staying at his parents' house."

She thanked her mother and then immediately dialed her old phone number. She wanted to talk with Crystal first. It was Saturday morning and she hoped she would be home.

Crystal was shocked that Katie had called her, instead of Alex. They talked for several minutes, mostly about Crystal and Alex, not much about Katie's ordeal.

Then she called Alex's parents' number. His mother cried when she heard her voice. They had all been devastated by what happened, but they were so happy to know she was all right. When Alex got on the phone, he was so upset that he was hard to understand. She had never heard him talk this way before. It took such a long time before he could speak clearly to her. They talked and as they did, her heart ached for him. He was in such turmoil of guilt and anger.

He spoke about the helplessness he felt when he heard the news, then the despair that settled over him when the days passed, and then the depression that hit him when they predicted she was dead. "Katie, I couldn't stay there and let Crystal watch me go out of my mind." He paused and then said, "I decided that if they found you dead, I didn't deserve to live either."

She couldn't believe he contemplated suicide. It would be almost another hour of conversation before they said their goodbyes. He wanted to know what happened and she told him everything, save one. She reassured him that she was doing well and they were close to capturing those responsible for what happened.

"No matter what had happened, Alex, you were the wrong person to blame. It was my choice to leave, and it was my choice to marry Albert. And I love him, Alex." It hurt her to tell him that so bluntly, but he had to return his focus to the other woman in his life. "Just like you love Crystal, and I know you love her. Go home, Alex, she needs you, Cheyenne needs you. I have a husband. They're your responsibility, not me."

"You're right, but that doesn't surprise me. You've always been the one that's level headed. I just didn't realize how much I still love you until this happened. You and I are never going to be together again, but no matter what, I'll *always* love you."

"You've got a spot in my heart that no one will ever take. You'll always be my first, and you'll always be my friend. I love you too, goodbye."

The house was quiet for another few weeks, Albert didn't come back, but she knew he was having problems with the company because of what had happened. Even though she wanted him to be with her, she understood he had to take care of business; business was first in his heart. She knew that when she married him, and she accepted it.

But he had other reasons for staying away, reasons she didn't know. He was learning more about what she couldn't tell him. There would come a time when she would tell him what he wanted to know, even if he had to force her hand before she was ready.

Most of her personal items had been sent from the house in the Hamptons, along with hundreds of cards and notes from friends, family and business associates. She sat on the bed rummaging through the assorted items and spotted her planning calendar. She smiled at the thought that she was the wife of a computer programming giant, and she still hand wrote her calendar instead of using the computer. She opened it and began flipping backward to the prior month. There was an eerie feeling when she came to the days she had been a hostage, the things she would have been doing, oblivious to the evil that was in the world. Going back farther she came across something that caused her pulse to quicken in fear—a little notation she made each month. Flipping through the pages she added the days, twice, three times she counted and then fell back against the bed, sick at the thought, the thought she once wanted more than anything in the world. It had been almost two months since her last period.

It can't be, she thought. I have to know.

She hadn't been out of the house since her return and she was unfamiliar with the area near this home. Finding the chauffeur she said she wanted him to take her to town. They were shocked by her sudden decision to go out in public. The security advisor said he would have to notify Mr. Trathmoore if she left the grounds.

"I'll be damned if you will! I don't need his permission to leave the house! If you're so concerned about my well-being then you can send someone with me."

Reluctantly he agreed, deciding he would go himself.

She put on a silk scarf and sunglasses, and headed for the nearest store.

There was a Supercenter in town, but the fear of the crowds overwhelmed her. To the security advisors relief, she opted for a small drug store instead.

He followed her inside.

She curtly reminded him that he did not need to be glued to her side, but he remained a little closer than she wanted. She roamed the cosmetic isle, picking up things that she didn't need, and then the toiletry isle, but when she went to the feminine isle and started handling the packages of tampons and sanitary napkins, he promptly moved himself to a neighboring row. Quickly picking up a home pregnancy test, she put it in her shopping basket and covered it under a large package of sanitary napkins. She went to checkout.

He said he would wait outside the door for her.

"That'll be $57.93," the teenage boy behind the counter said, smiling shyly at her.

She paid for her packages and took the bag. "I'm sorry," she said. "I really need to use your restroom for a moment." She lifted out the napkins from the bag. The boy's face blushed deep red.

"Over there," he pointed, handing her the key.

"Thank you."

Within minutes her escort was back inside looking upset, "Where is she?" he asked the clerk.

"She needed to use the restroom. She'll probably be out in a minute."

She stepped out of the bathroom feeling faint. Her face was drained of color.

"Are you all right Mrs... ."

"I need to go home," she said weakly.

She wanted to be alone in the limousine, so the security man sat up front with the driver. It was a beautiful scenic drive back to the house, but she didn't notice. She had other things on her mind, like telling Albert she was pregnant, and then wondering if he was the father.

~:~

It was a lonely set of days that followed the discovery of her pregnancy. She was shocked and upset, but she was also being enveloped in the feeling of wonder. Within her body, sheltered and safe, was new life. She would have to be strong to get through the rough days that she knew would lay ahead, but she had a new reason, a new hope to get beyond what seemed impossible.

She had been cooped up so long in the house and the beauty of the woods was so alluring, she decided to take a walk in the evening air. It wasn't dark yet so her troop of security felt it was safe to let her go out—with them close behind, of course. The gardeners landscaped a path through the woods near the house. It was exactly what she needed to clear the plaguing thoughts from her mind. By the time she decided to return home, she had a renewed sense of energy and refreshment in her soul. As she approached the house, Maria, their housekeeper came running out to meet them.

"They've caught them! Miss Katie! The police got them! They're in jail!" she shouted excitedly, wringing her apron with her hands. "Mr. Albert wants you to fly to the city and meet him at the police station."

She was flown to a heli-pad near the station then was met by a police escort to take her the rest of the way. The worst would be over now, she thought, they are finally off the streets. They went into the building directly from the police garage to avoid the throng of reporters that were waiting. She was taken to a dimly lit room where, to her shock, she saw Albert, Martin Fengale, two other men who looked like legal staff (but she didn't know them), three police officers, and Donovan (who looked petrified).

Albert walked over stiffly and pulled out a chair for his wife.

"Mrs. Trathmoore, I'm Chief Perryman. As you are already aware we have two men in custody that we believe are responsible for your kidnapping. Mr. Randall here has identified them as the perpetrators, but we need you to also identify them, okay?"

"Yes," she answered quietly, but in her heart she didn't want to see their faces ever again.

"If you'll come with me we have a place for you to identify them from. You don't need to be nervous because they won't be able to see you, all right? Are you feeling okay? You look a little pale. I don't want you fainting on me."

"I'm scared," she said, though it sounded more like a whimper.

"You don't need to be afraid. They can't hurt you anymore. We're gonna lock'em up for a long, long time, but we need your help to do that."

Albert took her by the arm and led her behind the chief. Mr. Fengale followed, and the rest of the people remained in the room.

They entered a dark room and stood silent as the group of men on the other side of the glass began to file in. Her heart was pounding so hard it sounded like a great rushing in her ears. There he was; staring at the glass with the same mean, animal-look as the first time she had seen him: Nick Randall. Then three more men entered after him and then Lenny's purple blotched, unshaven face appeared. She didn't think she would react so strongly to seeing them, but her knees began to give way. A chair was brought up under her as she crumpled into it. Her voice sounded strange and choked as she told the chief which ones were her attackers.

Then the line-up filed out of the room as she and the others waited in the dark for a moment before leaving, giving her a needed minute to compose. She could feel Albert's tension as he took her arm; he was seething under his cool façade. They returned to the room from where they had come, no one saying a word until they were all seated once again.

"Now Mrs. Trathmoore, I know this it difficult for you, but I need you to recount exactly what happened. I want you to take it slowly so you don't leave anything out that might be important to us, okay?"

"I've already told you what happened the day I was released." She couldn't understand why they were re-questioning her.

"We want to be certain of the facts. Mr. Randall here has corroborated what you told us, but now we have two men in jail that are giving us a different account of what happened."

"Mrs. Trathmoore would be more comfortable if you removed Mr. Randall from the room." Mr. Fengale spoke before she had an opportunity to answer the chief.

"No, he's fine. I don't have any problem recounting my story with him here. If it wasn't for Mr. Randall, I would be dead."

She could see Albert's jaw go tight. She wondered if Lenny had told them what happened in the warehouse. She began slowly and carefully recounting her story. She told how, from the first moment she met Donovan, he whispered he would help her. Every agonizing moment came forth, and with each memory, she told how Donovan never hurt her and always gave her encouragement that he would get her out of that situation. Carefully avoiding what transpired between her and him, she told the police that Lenny left to get liquor and that gave Donovan the opportunity to set her free.

"Did any of the men sexually assault you in that building?" the chief asked straight-out, looking into her face for a reaction.

"No."

"You said Mr. Randall set you free? That isn't completely the end of the story is it, Mrs. Trathmoore? He didn't actually set you free, but he moved you to another location, is that correct?"

She looked to Donovan who was in an obvious cold sweat.

"All I recall at the moment is that he got me out of that warehouse and away from the men who *were* planning on raping and killing me."

"How did you know they were planning to rape and kill you, Mrs. Trathmoore?" the chief pressed.

"Lenny said they were going to have a little party with me before they killed me."

"Did he say specifically that the party included rape."

"Yes," she was fighting the tears, but they came spilling down her cheeks.

"I'm sorry Mrs. Trathmoore, I know this is hard, but... ."

"No, you have no idea how hard this is," she interrupted. She was vaguely aware of the sound of the recorder on the table taping her statement.

"What did he say, specifically."

"I'm not going to use his filthy verbiage; it disgusted me then and it disgusts me now."

"Paraphrase it for us, please."

"He described a number of sexual acts he planned on performing when it was his turn."

"What did he mean by 'his turn,' was something taking place at that moment? I need you to explain it; I'm sorry, I know it's difficult."

She looked at the chief's face and then at the faces around her; they had to know and they were trying to make her say that Donovan assaulted her. Donovan was looking down at his hands in his lap; his eyes were moist and red.

Taking a deep breath and summing her courage she said, "He meant, when they did rape me, he had to be the last one to take me before they shot me because he has AIDS and no one could take me after him."

Now it was Albert who needed a chair. He had been standing the whole time beside her with his hand resting on her shoulder. He had been too angry to sit, but now one of his greatest fears was too close for comfort.

"What happened when you left the warehouse, Mrs. Trathmoore?" the chief continued.

She explained about the stolen car and why they had to steal it. About spending a night at a cabin to let Donovan sort out the emotions of turning in his half-brother and what would be thought about his role in the kidnapping.

"And then he took me to the police," she ended.

"What was the name of the motel or cabin?"

"I honestly don't know. I don't recall seeing the sign."

"Did you have sex with Mr. Randall at some point in time."

There it was the question she feared, point blank. "I don't think you are supposed to be asking me all these questions," she dodged. "Mr. Fengale, am I on trial here or should I be under some legal guidance."

"You're not being accused of anything," Albert interjected. "He is," he said through clenched teeth, pointing at Donovan.

"Then does he need an attorney?" she asked meekly.

"Damn it, Katie!" Albert's fist came down, banging the table with startling force. "Did that son-of-a-bitch rape you? Yes or No!"

Donovan eyes flashed upward and he started to speak.

"NO!" She yelled back at her husband. The lie was spoken; it could not be avoided any longer.

One of the men who had been standing quietly in the backdrop threw a plastic baggie on the table with something white in it. Albert grabbed it up before the chief could take it.

"These are yours, aren't they?" Albert said holding the bag containing the underwear that she had thrown away in the cabin.

"Mr. Trathmoore! I'm doing the questioning here." the chief spoke up, trying to take the bag.

"They're yours. I saw you put them on when you dressed the morning they took you. My detectives located the cabin and took them from a cleaning woman who was suspicious enough to set them aside." Albert was ignoring the chief as he continued, "They have sperm on them Katie, and they match the DNA they took from *that bastard* when they started the investigation. Now tell me what he did to you, stop hiding it!"

She looked up at Albert with tears streaming down her cheeks.

The chief managed to take the bag from his grip. "Mrs. Trathmoore, I'll ask you again: Did Mr. Randall have sex with you?"

It couldn't be hidden any longer. Her heart sank. "Yes," she whispered.

One of the officers immediately grabbed Donovan's arm, pulling him to his feet and putting him in a pair of handcuffs.

"Let him go!" she said, rising quickly from her chair. The chief blocked her way.

Donovan wasn't going to say anything; he felt he deserved what he was getting.

She realized there would be only one way to keep him out of jail now. "I consented! He didn't rape me!" she sobbed out.

The room went deathly quiet.

Donovan appeared to be more shocked than anyone else.

"I'm sorry, Albert," she said, without looking at his face. "I slept with him at the cabin. I was grateful for him risking his life to get me out of there. I didn't intend for it to happen, but he didn't force me into anything."

The officer started to release the handcuffs from Donovan's wrists; he couldn't arrest a man for something he didn't do.

Donovan took a step toward her. He didn't want her to be the scapegoat for his freedom, but as he did, Albert bolted from the chair and tackled him, knocking him and the officer who was trying to unlock the handcuffs to the floor. Albert spewed obscenities as his fists pummeled Donovan's face. Donovan, still handcuffed, couldn't even defend himself and took several hard punches before the police and detectives pulled Albert off of him.

"*You son-of-a-bitch, I want you in jail!* I know she didn't willingly let you...."

Donovan was removed quickly from the room. He wanted to speak up and say it was truly rape, not consensual, but he couldn't form the words. Later, at the hospital, it would be discovered that his jaw was broken in two places from the beating he took. And somehow he realized it wouldn't matter to Trathmoore now anyway; the damage was done and Katie would be the one to suffer for it.

After a few anxious moments Albert said he was ready to leave.

"Mrs. Trathmoore, you don't have to leave with him," the chief said, gesturing to Albert. "If you want, we have a place you can stay."

Looking into Albert's eyes at that moment, she could see the incredible amount of pain and frustration that filled them. Her heart broke, as if she could feel it crumbling at that very moment. "I'm sorry," she gently mouthed the words, but nothing came out.

He looked away, knowing his eyes were showing the hurt he felt.

"I'll leave with Mr. Trathmoore—if he wants me to come with him."

"You don't have to," the chief tried tell her, but Albert took her arm and they headed out the door.

They said nothing on the way to the helicopter. They boarded in silence and took off in silence. As the city fell far behind them and the mountains came into view, Albert reached into his pocket and tossed a paper into her lap.

"Are you pregnant?" He asked with no emotion in his voice.

She was startled by his question. Carefully she unfolded the paper. It was a visa bill.

"That is what you bought, isn't it? I had the store called and the sales receipt checked. You bought a home pregnancy test, didn't you?"

This wasn't the way she had planned to tell him, none of this was. "Yes, I did—I am."

Now she saw the tears on his face, but his expression was like stone, cold and without empathy.

"When were you planning on telling me, before or after you ended it?"

"I've waited my whole life for the chance to be a mother. I wouldn't end it for anything."

"When are you leaving?" he said, his voice like ice.

"Right away, I guess, if that's what you want. This could be your... ."

"Stop it Katie!" he yelled at her. "I don't want to even hear it." He sat without speaking for a moment, then he added, "I never want to see you again."

She tried to talk to him but he ignored her. Using the phone in the aircraft, he called Mr. Fengale and told him to assemble his legal team for tomorrow morning, eight o'clock sharp. He said he needed divorce papers drawn-up for their signatures. She heard him say to follow the prenuptial agreement exactly when they prepared the document.

She understood he was hurt and angry, but what he didn't know was tearing her apart inside. She wanted to tell him that she hadn't betrayed him, but how could he understand. She ended their marriage when she said she consented to be with Donovan.

She slept in the Victorian bedroom that night, alone and frightened at what lay ahead of her. Albert would send her home, she presumed. She heard him shouting orders at his staff regarding her personal effects, not much of it was clear, but what was clear was that he was venomously angry.

She thought of life back in Florida, and having to tell her parents about what happened. They were the probably the only people she would trust to tell the truth to about her ordeal. She knew they would accept her choices, but it would be hard for them to understand why she couldn't tell the same to Albert.

Morning came with little comfort. He wouldn't even sit in the cabin of the helicopter with her. She wanted so badly to at least tell him the sorrow in her heart and that she truly did love him, but he sat up front in the co-pilot's seat.

They landed at the office building and proceeded in silence to the conference room in the penthouse. The attorneys were already seated. They had been forewarned about the state of mind Mr. Trathmoore would be in, and they didn't dare to not be in place. The documents were spread out on the table, ready for their signatures. The legal staff said nothing when she picked them up. She realized they were working completely for their employer and would not offer any legal counsel before she signed.

She looked quickly over the papers, cringing at the reason for divorce: Infidelities of Katherine Elizabeth Danor Trathmoore. No property of any value was to be transferred to her. Any request for alimony was said to be waived per the prenuptial agreement. It stated that she would not seek any support from Albert regarding the impending pregnancy, per their prior agreement. It also said she would be liable for slander charges if she choose to take her story to the media. She was not to affiliate herself in anyway with the Trathmoore name. A petition for immediate name change was lying beside the divorce papers; she would be a Danor again.

It was a cold agreement, devoid of any semblance that they had once loved each other. It would sever their ties forever. She didn't want it to end like this. For a fleeting moment she considered telling him what she was hiding, but it wouldn't have mattered now; she could tell his mind was set. With a heavy heart she signed the paperwork before her.

Albert took the documents and without hesitation signed them with the same cold lack of emotion he exuded during a business transaction. She shuddered as she watched his mechanical mannerisms.

He looked at her for the first time since he confirmed that she was pregnant yesterday. There was nothing but angry emptiness in his eyes.

"The rings," he stated, as he pointed to her hand.

She hadn't even given it a thought, "Oh—yes." She tried to hand them to him.

"Put them on the table," he said coolly. He turned to Mr. Fengale, "Do you have the personal items that I requested be brought?"

"Yes, Mr. Trathmoore."

A small box was produced and put on the table. Mr. Fengale had the unmistakable look of embarrassment.

She was stunned.

Albert rose to leave.

"Where are all my things?" she said in amazement, following him to the door.

He turned sharply. "What *things,* Ms. Danor?" he said acidly. "This is all you brought into the marriage that belonged to you. Your clothing and jewelry were paid for by me, so they are my property."

"You're telling me I don't even get a suitcase of clothing! Just the clothes on my back?"

He smiled cruelly.

She looked back toward the box on the table.

"But, my program? I worked... ."

"No. You worked with my employees to develop it. It's my property."

196

"How could you?"

"It doesn't belong to you."

She was at his mercy now, but there was no mercy in him. It would be no use to argue, though every fiber in her body wanted to tell him he had no right to take the one thing she had worked for so diligently. The ugly vengeance that permeated him was making her sick. How could he have ever loved her and yet treat her so despicably now?

The thought occurred to her that she didn't carry cash. How would she even get a cab to the airport? Was he going to pay her fare home?

"I need at least an airplane ticket to get home on Albert. That much you have to give me."

His eyebrow went up, "Nothing—that is what you'll get from me. Find your own way home. I'm sure there's some man out there who would be willing to help you. Of course, you may have to sleep with him to show your gratitude."

Without a thought, her hand slapped against his cheek.

Catching her arm after she slapped him, he held it in a painfully tight grip and stared into her eyes. "Get out!" He let her go and walked.

The last person to leave the room beside herself, was Mr. Fengale. He was carrying the box of her personal items.

"I'm sorry it had to be this way," he said, apologizing for Albert's treatment of her. "It's not much, but perhaps it will help." He pressed something into her hand.

When she looked down she saw it was a hundred-dollar bill. She wanted to thank him, but she was too upset to speak. Clutching the box, she walked to the elevator and descended to the lobby. The doorman hailed her a cab and she left for the airport. She wouldn't be flying home to Florida; this was more than she wanted to face her parents with. She needed a place to go to sort out her hurts and emotions, someplace far from New York and Albert Trathmoore.

She had to make a call when she got to the airport, but her Visa card had also been deactivated. Albert had been thorough in cutting the ties. She got change for the hundred and then dialed a number from her little address book that she hadn't called in years. The man on the other end of the line answered after a few rings.

"Hello?"

"Uncle Patty?"

"Yes. Is this—Katie?" he said with surprise.

"Yes, Uncle Patty, it's me. I desperately need a favor. Could you wire me enough airfare to come to your house for a while? I'm in trouble and I don't want to go home yet."

He paused for a moment, letting the shock pass, "Of course. Tell me where to send the money and I'll do it right away."

Hours later she was boarding a plane for Canada, and the beginning of a new chapter in her life.

CHAPTER FIVE

Early summer in the Canadian Rockies is a beautiful time of year. It seems the whole earth is bringing forth a magnitude of new life. From the snow-capped mountain peaks to the glistening green tree line, the air seems to have a unique freshness that permeates to the soul. Katie was soaking in this feeling of renewed life as she stood outside the airport lobby waiting for Uncle Patty.

It had been several years since she had seen him. He had come to Florida many times, but this would be the first time she had come here. He was the only one of her mother's siblings that hadn't moved to a warmer climate. He'd said someone had to keep the family homestead alive.

She didn't have long to wait before he pulled up to get her. He was a lover of antiques and collectibles, so it didn't surprise her that his car was a restored 1963 Ford Fairlane. Its beautiful cream colored body shimmered as if it had just rolled off the showroom floor. Hugging her briefly, he opened the passenger's door and she slid in on the chilly vinyl seat. Glancing about she was amazed at the perfect condition of the car, from the chrome push buttons on the AM radio to the puffy ribbed pattern running up and down the door panels.

He thought it odd that she didn't have anything other than a small cardboard box of possessions, but he didn't embarrass her by mentioning it. She had said on the phone that she was in trouble, and from everything he'd heard about her kidnapping ordeal he thought that her troubles should have been over with the capture of those responsible. He would wait though because he knew she would tell him her reasons when she was ready. But for now, he was happy that she was here with him. She was a favorite among all the nephews and nieces his siblings had produced because he'd always said she had a special inner sparkle. Uncle Patty knew a lot about sparkle; he was a jeweler.

She looked at him as the car breezed down the highway. Though seventy years old, he was so spry that he didn't seem his age. With the windows down and the scent of summertime wild flowers in the air, he seemed to be studying the road ahead as if he too were seeing it for the first time. His hair and beard, though once deep red and thick, were completely gray and thinning. His twinkling eyes, a fresh spring green, were still clear and sharp. He was short compared to her father, only a little taller than her mother. Once, when she was about eight years old, she asked him if he were a leprechaun, partly because he seemed too short and partly because he was mischievous; and mother said all leprechauns were mischievous. And, in keeping with his fun-loving nature, he'd said of course he was!

"I'm glad you came, Katie," he stated, breaking the silence. "I don't get too many visitors out here. It seems once everyone moved away, they forgot how to get back to the old homestead," he said, speaking of his other brothers and her mother. "But I guess sometimes it's harder to come home when you've been away for so long."

She realized he was now talking about her apparent reluctance in going home to Florida.

"Or when so much has changed," she added softly with a lump forming in her throat.

He reached down and patted her hand that was resting on the seat. His hand was wrinkled and age-spotted, but his touch was warm and comforting. "It's going to be all right, Darlin.' You've got what it takes to go through troubled times and come out better than when you went into them." He gave her hand a squeeze.

He turned off the highway onto a gravel lane that wound through the lightly swaying poplars to a beautiful open meadow where she could see a large two story, clapboard-sided house with a tin roof, triple chimneys and a white-washed porch all around. There were rockers adorning the porch and hanging baskets of impatiens gently swinging in the breeze.

It was so picturesque she thought they had come to some sort of bed and breakfast. "This is it? This is where my mother grew up?" she said in awe.

He smiled as he pulled the car in to the large barn that he had turned into a garage, "Do you like it?"

"It's beautiful!"

He didn't say much as she roamed about the old house looking at all the wonderful antiques he had collected over the years. There was so much charm to the house that it was hard to believe that a man had decorated it. Uncle Patty had been engaged when he was in his twenties, but after his bride-to-be was killed in a house fire, he never found another love with whom to share his life. She studied the pictures that were carefully arranged on the beautifully varnished bead-board paneling, easily picking out the pictures of her mother. She was a beautiful girl; no wonder Daddy had fallen in love with her, she thought.

"Let me take you to your room," he said, interrupting her reverie. Up the stairs and to the last door on the left, he guided her. Turning the crystal doorknob, he swung the door open to reveal an old fashioned but charming bedroom. The bed was white iron with porcelain bead accents that were painted in a delicate blue and yellow flower pattern. The curtains were antique hand-made lace, tied back with wide pale pink ribbon. At the foot of the bed was a trunk of well-worn, yet aromatic cedar.

"Mom and Dad?" she queried as she walked to the bedside table. She lifted the oval, pewter frame that held the black and white photograph of two young people who looked very much in love.

"Yes," he said with a reminiscent look. "They were always so happy when they were together. Look at the way they're smiling," he said with a chuckle. "This was your mother's room. I haven't changed it much."

She put the picture back on the table next to the beautiful bubbled milk-glass lamp.

"Would you like to rest a bit before dinner?" he asked, recognizing how tired she looked. His face began to beam with the thought of dinner. "I'm quite a good cook! I've made a big pot of chicken stew with dumplings for tonight."

"That sounds wonderful, thank you." She hadn't realized just how tired she was until he mentioned rest.

"I'll get you up in an hour or so and we'll eat and talk some more, okay?"

She nodded. So much had happened that she welcomed some quiet time before telling him why she was here. Slipping out of her comfortable black flats, she put them and her small box under the bed and let her feet feel the soft rag rug. She was shivering a bit, not that the air was that cold, but emotionally she had been through so much, her body simply needed the comfort of warmth. Without wanting to disturb the beautifully made bed, she walked across the smooth tongue-and-groove flooring to the cedar chest. Just as she had suspected there were several quilts similar to the one that graced the bed, and right on top was a knit bed throw of the softest yellow yarn she'd ever felt. Wrapping it around her, she lay down on top of the bed. The iron frame creaked faintly as she wiggled her foot from side to side. Listening to the low sound, she drifted into sleep.

It seemed she'd hardly closed her eyes when she heard a gentle rapping at the door. Rising up to look around her in the darkening room, she realized she must have actually slept quite a while. The sky outside her bedroom window had turned a deep blue gray as the last golden rays of sunshine disappeared behind the mountains.

"You awake?" Uncle Patty asked, peeking from around the door. "I tried to wake you earlier, but you were too comfortable to be disturbed by my knocking."

She rolled over and stretched, smiling all the while, "Yes, I'm awake now."

"Come on down stairs, supper's waiting."

They took their bowls of soup and dumplings and ate by the fireplace, though he said he didn't normally use the fireplace in the summer. The Canadian nights were cool enough that he thought a Florida girl like Katie would enjoy it, which she did. It not only felt good, but the crackling and popping sound of the burning logs was relaxing.

"Well, I guess you're probably wondering why I'm here."

He smiled and shook his head, "I figured you'd tell me when you were ready." Then he paused. "I have a feeling you've been through hell recently, and I don't think it's just what the news reported."

"Albert divorced me," she said, listening to the finality of her own words.

"What for!"

"Infidelity," she said, looking down at the food which lost its delicious flavor of a moment ago.

"*No.* I don't believe that. Not you, Katherine. There are some things you could have said that I would have believed, but I know the kind of person you are, and if you loved that man, I know you didn't... ." He couldn't go on for the shock of what she had told him.

"It wasn't willingly, but I can't change the fact that I told him it was." She talked for a long time, explaining what happened and how, up until the moment she began talking with him, she didn't plan to recount it to anyone but her parents. She didn't blame Donovan, but Albert wouldn't have seen it that way. She had come to believe that he would have rather had her die.

"You chose the hard road, Darlin.' It's not often traveled unless you're a truly honorable person, but," scratching his head, he still seemed mystified by something. "Why did he throw you out so miserably and cruelly, not even a suitcase of clothing or a ticket home? Why was he so vicious about it?"

"I'm pregnant, Uncle Patty."

He gasped before he could contain it. Bracing himself against the arm of the chair, he looked into her eyes. "And it's not his child?"

"I don't know and to tell you the truth, I don't care. I've wanted a baby for so long that it doesn't matter to me if it is or not, I'm just grateful that I am. He wanted me to end it, Uncle Patty—but I could never... ." Her eyes began to flood.

"No, no, shush that talk," he said, coming over and giving her a warm hug. "Of course you couldn't. You've been denied the joy of motherhood too long. I just can't believe that God would grant it at such an awkward time."

She laughed a little, wiping back the tears. "What's your old saying? 'Before Heaven there's always some hell to pay.' "

They talked about her plans and dreams for the future and she found it amazing that she did have dreams for the future. When Albert had cast her aside like some piece of trash, she thought of her life as ending, but she had reasons to plan for a future. She told him about her dream of opening up Seasons and what it would be like. She told him about the work and love she had put into designing the computer program and equipment that would enable her to do what she dreamed.

"Is that what's in that little box?"

"No. The box only contains some personal papers and photos. He wouldn't let me have my program. He said it was designed in his facility with the help of some of his people, so it belonged to him."

"I don't mean to knock your taste in men, but Katie darlin,' he sounds about as cold as a wet rock in Antarctica."

"He wasn't this way before."

"That may be, but he must have had a helluva cruel streak in him somewhere that just didn't show!"

"Business, Uncle Patty. This is how he is when it's strictly business. And right at that moment I was a detriment to him and his business. Detriments are disposable."

"Katie, I've got to tell you something that I'm sure you aren't aware of and, well—it's a difficult thing to tell to someone in your delicate condition."

He face was so grave that she was alarmed to the core of her being. "What?"

"Have you talked much with your mother since you've been back—you know what I mean." There was the sound of dread in his voice.

"A little, but I've kept mostly to myself. What is it Uncle Patty? What's wrong?" She could tell he didn't want to say what it was.

He began to wring his hands.

"Please, Uncle Patty, you're scaring me."

Nervously he rose from his chair and stood at the fireplace, looking at the pictures on the mantle. He cleared his throat several times and quietly asked if she knew how her father was doing.

Her heart felt as if it had stopped beating. The room suddenly seemed hot and airless as she tried to take a breath and ask why.

"Your father hasn't been feeling well the last several months and... ."

"No. Please don't tell me something is wrong with Daddy."

His rough old hand wiped at his cheeks. "Your mother didn't want to tell you because you'd been through so much yourself. But she and I have talked a lot lately over the phone about your father's health."

"Is he okay, Uncle Patty?" She didn't want to hear what he had to say; but then again, she had to know.

"He'd been so tired and your mother couldn't figure out why. She tried to get him to go to the doctor, but you know your dad; he doesn't like doctors." Taking a moment to compose, he went on, "When they found out about the kidnapping, your father collapsed and had to be taken to the emergency room."

"Oh my God," she said, rising to cling to his shoulder.

He wouldn't look at her but just continued to stare at the faces on the mantle.

"What was wrong? Is it his heart?"

Turning slowly, he faced her, his hand warmly resting on her shoulder.

"He has cancer, Katie."

Stunned, she found her way to the chair she had been sitting in. The weight of what he told her was like a ton of bricks smashing out the last of the remnant of her already broken heart.

"Daddy has cancer?" It didn't make sense to her. Her father was not a smoker. And, as far as she knew, there wasn't a history of cancer in the family. There was a long silence, then she asked, "How bad is it? Is he going to have to go through surgery?" There were a million questions that began to run through her mind, but the first thought that congealed in her consciousness was: home—I've got to go home.

"It's skin cancer—melanoma."

"That's good, right? Skin cancer isn't life threatening is it?"

"Melanoma is a bad skin cancer, Honey. It's spread internally."

"Are they going to treat it?"

"Yes, he's been to Shands Hospital in Gainesville, and they recommended a course of treatment. He had the mole that started the whole thing surgically removed a few weeks ago. He's been going in for radiation therapy and they are supposed to start chemotherapy this Tuesday."

"Mom—how is she holding up?" she choked as she tried to swallow down the lump in her throat.

"You know your mother; she's strongest when she's got a fight on her hands—just like you," he added.

"Can you get me a plane ticket to Florida tomorrow?"

"Slow down, Katie darlin,' I know you want to go tearing home to be with them, but first you've got to concentrate on yourself." She started to interrupt, but he put his hand up for her to stop and let him finish what he had to say. "I'll get you that plane ticket home, but you need to spend a few days in preparation, for you and that child you're carrying, and for what you are going to do when you get home."

"But... ."

"Concentrate on the future while you're here and be ready to do what it takes to reach your dream. You won't be happy if you settle for less than the true desire of your heart. Take the time to clear away the useless baggage that's clouding your mind and devote the rest of your time here to knowing, when you step off that plane in Florida, what you're going to do. Your mother has enough to worry about without adding a daughter that's coming home with a heart full of broken dreams." He knew she needed to hear it straight-out. She had to come away from all of this relying on herself.

As much as she wanted to be home, she knew he was right. She had to be prepared to find her own way. The hopes and plans for her life weren't going to end because of circumstances inflicted upon her; she would have to be the one who determined her journey from here.

That night when she went to her room she took a pad of paper and a pen with her. As she leaned back on the headboard, propped up on pillows, she wanted to map out her future but she felt such anger and pain inside that with every positive thought that entered her mind, two negative ones joined it. Uncle Patty's words were echoing in her head, '…clear away the useless baggage…' Anger, pain, shame and fear welled up in her heart. She began to write down the hurts, the reasons why she couldn't have the future she wanted. The shame of being raped and the anger toward two men she had loved deeply; one had not wanted her to leave and the other wanted her crushed to dust.

The pages filled and as they did she felt a release inside, she was letting go of these feelings—they would not be her stumbling block. She finished, almost breathless from the rapidity of the flow with which they left her. The writing was etched hard in the paper, haphazard and stained from her tears as she relived each pain.

Turning down several blank sheets, she came to the place where there was no more impression from the pressure of what she wrote. Tearing off all the pages before it, she took them and quietly tiptoed downstairs to the fireplace. The fire was out, but the coals were hot. She raked them back, exposing the reddest embers. One by one, she sat there putting the sheets on the coals and watching them turn black, smoke and then flame into nothingness. She smiled as the last papers, blank but with impressions, vanished into ashes. Watching the ghosts of her thoughts disappear, left her with emptiness. She would fill this void with her dreams and hopes for the future. No amount of pain in her past would hold her back from forging on to her destiny.

She wrote nothing else that night. Rest was something her body craved since she became pregnant and she would attend to the physical needs tonight, tomorrow the needs of her mind would finish forming.

Her eyes opened with the first flutters of sunlight dancing into her room. The sky outside her window had turned from midnight blue to azure, clear and cloudless. She smiled to herself as she thought about the vanishing darkness like the dark and painful places in her past she'd let go of in the night. Now the way was clear, fresh and unclouded to let her make hopes into reality.

Uncle Patty was just finishing up cooking breakfast when she came down stairs. Immediately he saw a change in her countenance. She was not only smiling her beautiful genuine smile, but she seemed to be illuminated and renewed on the inside and it spilled over to her exterior.

"I want to show you some things in my shop when you've finish breakfast. I thought about it last night and, though you might think me silly, it's a philosophy about people I've developed over my many years in the jewelry business. I haven't shared it with anyone else," he said, pausing for a moment. "But I think you'll understand what I'm talking about."

"Sure, I'd love to. Uncle Patty, I need to get my hair cut off today. Is there some place close that you could take me?"

"Cut your beautiful hair!" He exclaimed. "Those auburn locks of yours are stunning, why would you... ."

"They're also what make me so recognizable as the former Mrs. Trathmoore. I get a lot of stares and questions from people who have seen me on the magazines or the news, and I don't want that wherever I go."

He understood, but he hated to see that beautiful hair go to waste. Then he remembered something he read in the paper sometime ago about a program called 'Locks of Love' that collected donations of long hair to be made into wigs for children who had lost their hair because of medical conditions, usually cancer. It was a local hairdresser that was mentioned in the article.

She was thrilled at the idea of donating her hair for a good cause. It was going to be a big adjustment going to short hair, but this would make it just that much easier.

Breakfast finished, they headed out of the house to his workshop.

"I don't make as much jewelry as I used to," he said, carrying a large silver case.

She followed him on the brick pathway from the house to the barn. He had a huge arbor over the walkway with purple, white and pink wisteria growing in gnarled vines, twisting about the structure. Beautiful, long clusters of flowers draped about everywhere and the bees buzzed loudly as they accomplished their mission of retrieving nectar. Out of the shade they walked into the brilliant morning sunlight. The hummingbirds were flitting to and from the nectar feeders hanging on shepherd crooks in the flower garden. The blue birds and doves were enjoying the seeds that Uncle Patty had put out on the garden statues of angels with outstretched hands, a little girl holding out her apron and a boy with a straw hat that held seeds in the brim. Lichens edged the path in the shade and mountain heather spread its low green boughs along the sunny places. The flowers were varied and numerous. She didn't know them all, but she recognized a few: black-eyed Susan's, cornflowers, foxglove, daffodils and iris.

"You certainly have a way with plants; arranging and growing them in your garden so beautifully."

"I love beautiful things. I guess that's why I became a jeweler. But, God's beauty far exceeds what I can do with His precious metals and stones."

He opened his shop door and turned on the light. It was small, but clean and bright. The air inside had an odor that was somewhat sharp, but not offensive.

She had started becoming keenly aware of smells since her pregnancy. "What is that smell?" she questioned.

He stopped for a moment and took in a lung-full of what was so familiar to him. "I don't know, unless you smell my melt pot or perhaps an electrical odor from my instruments? Maybe I left a piece of sandwich around here the other day?" He was teasing and she knew it.

Placing the silver case on the counter, he pulled up a high-backed stool and motioned for her to do the same. She was astounded when he opened it; a royal blue velvet tray filled with jewels and gold settings in small compartments made up the first layer.

"These are pieces that I've recently finished or I'm near to finishing," he said as he removed the tray to the counter. "Lovely aren't they?"

"Splendid would be a better word for them," she said wide-eyed. She gently touched the golden charms of flowers, birds, animals and even a mountain charm with the letters CRM at the base for Canadian Rocky Mountains. Her fingers trailed over the loose jewels: emeralds, rubies, sapphires and diamonds. She had worn and owned jewels worth hundreds of thousands of dollars, but at the time they were merely objects. These were more than that; they were art, carefully crafted, sculpted works of art. The second layer was divided by compartment also, but they were filled with curious rocks and stones, a baggie of what looked to be newly mined gold and small ingots of gold and silver.

"Can you pick out what reminds me of you?" he said with a twinkle in his eye.

She looked over the items. Disregarding the second layer, she scanned over the charms, picking up a charm of a small bird. "This?" she asked hesitantly.

"No, Katie. This is someone that was beaten by circumstance and molded to fit the plan of someone else's dreams. Try again."

"How about this?" she said, picking up a gold ingot from the second tray.

"Why do you think you're like that?"

Getting philosophical, she reasoned, "Well, it used to be like this," she said, picking up the bag of rough gold mixed with rock and ore, "and now it's been through the fire. You've skimmed off the impurities and it hasn't been cast into an image—except this little block." She laughed as she struggled, trying to give worthwhile qualities to the metal in her hand.

He chuckled at her effort, "No, it's like that little bird. But you had the right idea when you picked up the mined gold, except it is filled with bad qualities to start with. It is someone who doesn't give up those qualities until they are forced out; then they are at the will of whatever mold they are poured into."

"You tell me. What am I like, Uncle Patty?"

The twinkle in his eye seemed to flash like a spark in the night. He reached into the second tray and picked up a rough, crystal and gray rock larger than the others and put it in her hand.

She stared at it, turning it over and examining it. She and this rock shared something in common? "Uncle Patty," she finally said. "This has got to be the ugliest rock I've ever seen!" Her laughter bubbled up without restraint. "Please don't tell me it's a diamond in the rough."

He was laughing with her, but still she could see the same spark glowing bright in his eyes. He didn't answer, but he removed the second tray from the case revealing the bottom layer. This compartment was filled with gold and silver necklaces and bracelets and a black velvet box that appeared to be very old. Their laughter faded as he removed the box. His aged hands trembled slightly as he lifted the cover to reveal an exquisite, large diamond. It was obvious that it was cut to fit a ring, but it had never been set. He tipped the box to let the stone tumble onto his palm. He became quiet as he held it in his hand as if his mind was drifting back to a memory from long ago.

Seeing his eyes become moist, she gently put her hand on his back and rubbed him softly. "Uncle Patty? Are you okay?"

"This was for my beautiful Melissa," he said, his voice dropping low and hoarse. "I saved for over a year to buy this stone so I could make her a ring. I was new at making jewelry so I had to buy one that was already cut because I was afraid I wouldn't do a good job—and she deserved the best. We had planned a spring wedding," he continued. "I was going to surprise her with the ring. She never would have picked out a diamond like this." He clutched his fist about the stone as the bitter memory rushed back.

"Her parents' home caught fire that winter. In the middle of the night, she woke to a blazing house and ran out into the snow. Her mother and her two younger sisters were there, but her father had run back inside because little William, her four-year-old brother was still in the house. Her mother told me the blaze was horrendous, but when they didn't come out, she said that Melissa didn't say anything; she just took off running back inside. Moments later her mother saw her upstairs, dropping William out a window onto the roof. He slid off onto the snowy lawn. He was okay. He had been frightened by the flames and hid in an upstairs closet. Melissa knew he hid there when he was scared or in trouble."

Katie hugged him tighter as he continued.

"Her mother said she could see that the fire had burnt away most of Melissa's beautiful golden hair. She screamed for her to jump from the window, but Melissa choked out that she had to find her father. Then she was gone and her mother never saw her again. We went through the rubble the next day—we found them. Melissa was behind her father with her arms wrapped around his chest. She couldn't carry him out, but she died trying." After a long pause he said, "There aren't many people in this world who are truly diamonds, but she was a diamond—just like you, Katie." He looked at her with his tear-stained face.

She was crying, shaking her head no. She didn't feel she deserved to be in the same class as a woman of such great courage.

"Yes you are," he stressed. "I've know you were a diamond from the time you were a little girl." He wrapped his soft warm hands around hers and the rough stone that she held. "You see, Darlin,' the difference is that inside this stone is the heart of the diamond. The world has clung to the outside, but it can't get into the perfect beauty that is within it. Every heartache, every trial, every lesson life has thrown at you will grind away at this earthly exterior until what remains," he said as he opened her other hand and placed the finished diamond in it, "is a glittering jewel. Every diamond has a place that can't be split because there is no flaw in that perfect place. The stone in your hand will have a place that I can't divide anymore. It's a place of perfection, a heart of diamond that is strong, hard, flawless and beautiful. You have that place within you."

She didn't say anything, she just hugged him for a long moment. The things he told her that day would remain on her mind for a long time as she came to terms with the realization that the flawless heart of the diamond *was* within her.

~:~

Seven days after arriving in Canada, she was leaving. Uncle Patty stood with her as she waited for the plane that would take her to Chicago's O'Hare Airport and then from there to Miami International. He studied her as she looked across the lobby to the boarding corridor. She had aged from that innocent little girl to a woman of beauty and poise. Her hair was now shorter than his own, styled neatly with pert bangs. The new style suited her well, her face losing some of the round look and becoming more angular and defined. She carried a small overnight bag he had given to her with her personal papers and photos and a few items that she permitted him to buy. She said she didn't want him spending a lot of money because she was already indebted for the airline tickets, but she did need underclothing and two changes of clothes. That was all; she would accept nothing more. The loud speaker announced her flight was loading.

With a deep sigh, she turned to him and smiled. "Thank you Uncle Patty, for everything. I'll never forget these past days with you." She hugged him tightly and whispered in his ear, "Thanks for helping me find the diamond under all the rubble."

He returned the smile and kissed her cheek. "It was there all along, I just helped you see it. Here," he said, handing an envelope to her. "A note for you to read on the plane."

She looked at the envelope suspiciously and then back at him.

"Hurry along Katie darlin',' or you'll be late getting on that plane! Tell your mother and that stubborn husband of hers that I love them both."

"I will. Goodbye." She turned before any tears could spill down her cheeks. She didn't know if she'd ever see Uncle Patty again. It would be a long time before she worked her dreams into reality. She could only hope he would still be around to know that she had accomplished them.

Her bag was small enough to be carry-on, and she put it in the overhead rack before settling into her seat. It wasn't long before she heard the engines' high-pitched whine as they came to life and began pushing the plane down the runway. Canada began to fade into the distance below.

She was grateful that the plane wasn't packed to capacity and that she was able to have the privacy of being seated alone. Slowly she opened the envelope still clutched in her hand. As she unfolded the letter, five hundred dollars of American currency slid into her lap. She was upset with him, but then her irritation turned to a smile as she looked at the large print on the note: *Hush your mouth! It's a gift for the baby.* Then at the bottom of the page in smaller print he wrote: *I put a gift for you in your purse.* Taking her purse she unzipped the roomy center pocket and reached inside. She caught her breath as her hand found a velvet box. Pulling out the box, there was a small rolled up paper fastened to it by a ribbon. With unsteady hands, she slipped the note from the ribbon and unrolled it.

My Dearest Katherine,

I know from time to time you will doubt the beauty, strength, and courage that lies within you, but always know it is there. No matter how hard life strikes you, how many times it chips at the outer casing, inside is the heart of a diamond that has no flaw. Just like the stone you held in your hand was once covered by the ugliness of the world, see it now for what it truly is.

Love for always,

Uncle Patty

Opening the box she found an exquisite large diamond of pulse-stopping brilliance. He had cut it in the shape of a magnificent heart, clear and sparkling. His jeweler's tag was attached inside with the printed words, White Diamond, 6 carats, Value $72,000. The tag was dated and initialed PSO for Patrick Shamus O'Brien, and Good Heavens Jewelry, Canada, was in gold lettering on the reverse of the tag.

"Thank you, Uncle Patty," she whispered. "I'll remember, I'll always remember."

~:~

Florida was a welcomed sight as the plane descended in the afternoon sun in humid, sizzling Miami. Her mother had reserved her a rental car using their credit card since Katie's was no longer valid, but Katie insisted on paying the rental charge with the cash remaining from Mr. Fengale's hundred dollar bill. Uncle Patty's cash would be put away until she was settled and could buy some baby furniture and needed items.

Behind the wheel of a little Plymouth Breeze, she headed for Vero. It was good to be so close to home. With the windows rolled down, she let the hot, salty air fill her lungs and clear her mind.

Her mother was expecting Katie, but Katie didn't tell her about cutting her hair. When she pulled into the driveway, she almost didn't recognize her! They clung to each other and cried when she got out of the car. Beth didn't want too much excitement in the house because Lawrence was resting, so they would get through the tearful reunion outside.

The house had an unfamiliar odor when Katie stepped inside; it was the clinical odor of someone on his sickbed. Quietly putting her bag in her old room, she then followed her mother to where her father was catnapping on the couch. His face was pale and drawn, his mouth seemed to droop from the inebriating effects of pain medication, and he looked thin and weak. The fear that had been taking root inside her came into full bloom as she watched him sleeping. For a moment, she wanted to leave. This wasn't the father she knew and remembered; this was a sick man who had somehow taken her father's place.

"Daddy?" she said softly as she slid her hand into his. His hands were cool to the touch, the same hands that had always been warm and strong. "Daddy?" she repeated.

Slowly his eyes opened and began to focus. "Kat?" he said as if he didn't believe it was her.

"It's me, Daddy. I cut my hair. Do you like it?"

"My Kat!" he began to smile. "Help me up, Mom." he said, extending his hand to Beth. He grimaced as they both helped him to an upright position. His speech was slightly slurred which was something Katie had never heard from her father's voice.

"I'm still groggy," he said. "I took a damn pain pill before my nap. I think I'd rather have the pain, but you know your mother." He winked at Katie. Lawrence didn't usually swear, but he was angry at not being able to be fully cognizant when he needed to be.

"It's okay, Daddy, I love you, groggy or not," she said, putting a kiss on his stubbly cheek.

There was a lot to catch up on and a lot to explain. First she let her parents talk about everything that had happened from the day they found out about the cancer, through the surgery, and the current treatments. The doctor visit the day before showed the growth had stopped on all but one tumor on his lung. There would be a lot of painful treatments ahead, but her father said he wasn't ready to turn-up his toes yet. He was willing to fight as long as the doctors said there was hope for recovery. Granted, a thirty- percent chance was not as good as he'd like, but he wouldn't give up. He had always said that if the weatherman said there was a thirty-percent chance of rain, it always rained, so if there was a thirty-percent chance he'd make it, he was determined he could do it.

When the conversation turned to her, she became uncomfortable. Her father was so sick, and her mother was so tired from the strain of caring for him that she tried to convince them that maybe they should put off the things she had to tell them until tomorrow. But both of them, stubborn as they were, said they would rather know now; they had waited long enough.

It wasn't something she could 'flower-over' or disguise as anything other than it was; truth always seemed to have a bitter flavor, but it was the only way to tell it. They sat there stunned at the magnitude of the events that had unfolded in her life, but the final truth was the one that left them dumbfounded.

"I'm pregnant and I think it's Albert's child. It's just a feeling I have, but I could be wrong, it could be—the other man's." Taking a breath she quickly added, "but that part doesn't matter to me. What does matter is that I've wanted a baby for so long, I'm happy."

They didn't say anything for a long moment; Beth and Lawrence stared at her, then at each other.

"You're going to be a grandpa!" Beth rang out, suddenly jubilant.

They hugged her, laughing and crying. The rest didn't matter now, it was over and wouldn't be changed, but this child was the future and they were all happy that the long awaited miracle had finally happened.

The rest of the evening was calm, but joyful. Katie cooked dinner while Beth sat in the living room reading a Louis L'Amour western to Lawrence. Her father had always wanted to read this series of western books, and he had planned to do so when he retired, but now he was too tired to sit-up and read for very long, so her mother decided this was a good chance to spend time together. Beth read with such emotion and vigor that he said he could close his eyes and see the story unfolding in his mind. It was better than television, he'd remarked. They were a pair of lovebirds and she almost felt as if she were intruding, although they would certainly say she was not.

The next day, a home health care nurse stopped at the house. She made sure he was taking his medication properly, took his vital signs, and drew some blood. Later a home health care assistant came by to give him a sponge bath, shave him, change the dressing on the slow-healing, five-inch incision on the back of his left shoulder and listen to them voice their concerns.

Katie was impressed with this system of health care that allowed her father the dignity of staying home. She also realized that this gave her mother the freedom to spend time with him by not using all her time to simply keep up with his needs. With the exception of Lawrence being ill, they were happy.

This is what *true* love is all about, Katie thought as she washed dishes. She had loved and been loved, but what her parents experienced together was a deep abiding love and respect that didn't fade with time, troubles, or circumstances of life. Certainly there were times they had gone through together that stretched the boundaries of that love, but like a strong rubber band, it brought them back to each other in the end.

There was a knock at the screen door that stirred her from her reverie. Looking up from the sink she was surprised to see Alex standing at the porch door. Drying her hands on the dishtowel, she took a deep breath and stepped out of the kitchen into the breezeway.

"Katie?" His voice sounded funny and high-pitched. "Wow! You look great; I can't believe you cut your hair!"

"Alex," she said, as he stepped into the screened breezeway and gave her a warm and very familiar embrace. "What are you doing here? Did Mom tell you I was coming home?"

"Nah, I had to come up here to Grady's to buy a new prop for my boat, so I thought I'd just stop in and see how your parents were getting along." He paused and then added sadly, "I heard that your dad wasn't doing too well."

"They're in the living room reading," she said as she turned to lead him into the house.

"Wait. Can we talk for a few minutes?" he said, reaching out to her.

His hand was warm and tender holding hers. She looked back into the house; she could faintly hear her mother reading. Evidently they hadn't heard the knock at the door.

"How have you been?" he began. "I heard on the news that they caught the assholes responsible for what happened to you."

She slipped her hand from his. "Alex, I really don't feel like discussing it. How's Crystal?" She was trying not only to change the subject, but to also put back up the barrier that was between them. It was a strange feeling as she stood there with him; he seemed so young and she felt so old.

But Alex was just as determined as she was, "She's fine and Cheyenne is growing like a weed—and she's walking now. But how about you, how are you? That husband of yours decided to let you come home for a little bit? I mean, I'm sure he likes to keep you close after what happened, I'm surp…"

"Alex!" She stopped him with such authority that his eyebrows went up. "I don't want to discuss me or *him*." She put a little too much emphasis on 'him' which only served to fuel more questions from Alex.

"What's wrong Katie? Has something happened between the two of you? Did you have a big fight? Is that why you came home? Katie… ."

"Alex, you are impossible!"

"Hey, Babe, can't we still talk—or is it me?" He got up and headed to the screen door. With his back turned to her he said, "I'm sorry. I didn't come here to bother you. I didn't even know you were home."

"Alex, please. I'm the one who's sorry. It's just that," she took a deep breath, "Albert divorced me and I didn't want to… ."

He turned around, his face riddled in disbelief, "What? After everything you've been through! Why, Katie? Did the son-of-a-bitch lose his mind?!"

By this time Mother had heard the last of the conversation and came out to see who Katie was talking with. "Alex!" she said, surprising them both. "What are you doing here?"

"I'm sorry, Mrs. Danor, if I disturbed you. I just came by to say 'hello.' I didn't know Katie was here."

"It's okay Mom," she said, putting a kiss on her mother's worried head. "I'm fine. Are you and Daddy finished with the chapter?"

"No, but I heard voices and… ."

"Go ahead and finish and then Alex would like to come in and see Daddy for a minute or two."

She nodded, but it was clear to them both that she was reluctant to leave them talking. Katie's wounds were too fresh to have Alex rubbing salt in them.

It was enough of a pause in their conversation to let Alex's temper come back down to a reasonable level. "Divorced?" He said quietly as Beth disappeared from sight.

"Someday, Alex, I'll be ready to sit down and tell you the whole story, but not now. Okay?"

Beth returned and said Lawrence wanted to see him now instead of waiting. Alex quietly followed her inside to the living room where her father was propped up on pillows on the couch. It was the first time Alex had seen him since he had heard about the cancer. He was clearly as shocked as Katie had been at first sight of him. They talked briefly, Lawrence still appeared little woozy from the pain pill he had taken after supper.

Smiling up at Alex, he asked quite innocently, "So did Katie tell you the good news?"

Katie's and her mother's eyes both went wide with the knowledge of what he was probably going to say.

Alex looked at him quizzically. The only news he had heard was that she was divorced, but he didn't think her father would announce that as good.

"Daddy…" Katie began, as her mother chimed in.

"Lawrence!"

"I'm gonna be a grandpa!" he spilled out happily.

Alex was literally dumbstruck. His jaw dropped and his head jerked to look at Katie as if she had pinched him. He didn't know what to say; all he could do was look at her.

She turned deeply red, then looking at her father she smiled and patted his hand, "That's right Daddy, you're gonna be a grandpa—and it *is* wonderful news."

Alex, finally finding his voice again, stood up. "Well, I gotta get going. I'll stop by and see how you're getting along another time—if that's okay?" he added.

"Of course it is," Lawrence smiled, "You're always welcome here, Alex." And he meant that; it wasn't the pills talking.

Taking Katie's arm, Alex put on a fake smile, "Walk me to my truck." But it wasn't really a request, even if he did say it that way.

Once outside he turned her to face him, and very slowly said, "You are pregnant?"

She nodded, not wanting to talk.

"Did he know this when he divorced you?"

Her eyes filled with tears as she nodded again.

He wanted to puff up his male ego and say he was headed to
New York to kill the bastard, but that would only make him feel
better, not her. Instead he reached out and took her in his arms. "Oh
Katie, I know you're hurting from everything that's happened, but I
am happy for you. Oh, Baby, you deserved to have a child more than
anyone I know. I only wish it was two years ago—and that it was my
baby." He kissed the top of her head.

She was surprised at his tenderness and the soft-spoken words.
His embrace felt so comfortable, like a good memory from long ago.
Secretly, she was wishing the same thing, but one can never go back.
And then he really surprised her.

"But we can't go back, can we? We just found out the other day,
we're expecting again."

She looked at him, but before she could tell him that she was
happy for them, he said, "Anything—if you need anything, call me,
please. We put the house up for sale and we're looking for a bigger
place. I told you when you left that you've got money coming to you
if we sell it."

"No," she started to rebut, but she knew she was going to need
the money.

"Don't tell me no. You'll get back what you put into it, I
promise." He kissed her tearful cheek and said goodbye.

She was left with an odd feeling as he drove away; Alex had
finally grown up.

That evening after Lawrence had retired to his bedroom, she and
her mother sat in the stillness of the living room talking. They
discussed finances. Katie was shocked at the cost of things that
weren't covered by Medicare, even with an extra supplement that
her father enrolled in when he retired. Social Security wasn't
supposed to start for another year for Lawrence and two for Beth,
unless they wanted to take a cut that would seriously decimate the
pittance due them. For now, they were living on Lawrence's railroad
pension and savings, but at the rate things were going that wouldn't
be enough in the near future. And, as shocking as it sounded, Beth
said they even thought about selling the house and moving into a
small place to conserve their money.

She told her mother her idea for the future, but for the moment it
was only an idea. She was going to need a regular 9-to-5 job very,

very soon. No matter what the law stated about discrimination, she felt her chances might be slim of getting a job after her pregnancy became obvious. She felt there probably weren't a lot of employers out there anxious to get a pregnant woman trained and then have to find a replacement while she was out on maternity leave. And, she knew from the major medical company that supplied the benefits for ATI, pre-existing conditions, including pregnancy, were not usually covered for new employees.

She didn't want to be a burden to her parents; they couldn't afford it and they were under enough stress anyway. Tomorrow morning was her appointment at Doctor Hampton's office and, as soon as that was behind her, she was going to get a newspaper and start filling out employment applications. She doubted she'd have the luxury of picking and choosing; it would have to be the first thing she could get.

It seemed strange being back in the Vero Beach Gynecology Suite after all this time, but she was relieved to find that Margaret was still working there. Many of the office staff had left and had been replaced, but Margaret was just the same smiling, friendly, understanding woman from two years ago. Unfortunately, Doctor Hampton was still the same dry, detached monotonist. After the pregnancy test confirmed what she already knew, they discussed the approximate date of her last period and calculated the due date as January seventeenth.

"That means you are in the end of your first trimester, about twelve to thirteen weeks along. Have you had any problems such as spotting, morning sickness, dizziness—anything like that?"

"I've had morning sickness, but it actually seemed to last all day. I really didn't know what it was. I never threw up, I just felt queasy all the time." She continued talking as he was motioning her to recline so he could examine her, "I didn't feel like eating a full meal, so I just nibbled—a lot."

"Well, that's the best way to keep it down; small frequent meals. Good job," he added, but never changed the inflection of his voice.

Margaret held her hand as he completed a pelvic examination. She was scared and knew Margaret could read it from her expression. She wanted everything to be fine with this baby and she certainly didn't care for the pressure he applied as he examined her body.

"You seem to be moving along at textbook speed," he said, ending the uncomfortable probing. "Let's see if we can hear the heartbeat. Does that sound all right to you?" He smiled.

Katie realized it was the first time she'd ever seen his smile. "Yes," she said excitedly, as Margaret gave her hand a squeeze.

The cold ultrasound jelly was applied to her stomach as the doctor moved the microphone around. He was listening intently, and for an instant, she had the fear that they wouldn't find a heartbeat. He smiled again and turned up the machine as a rapid pulsing sound filled the room.

"There it is. We have a little person rolling around in there."

She let out a little squeal of delight as the tears of happiness flowed.

"Okay," he said, wiping off the jelly, "I'll need to see you at twenty weeks so we can get a picture of this baby. And, if you want, maybe we can find out if it's a little girl or boy." Just before leaving the room, he turned back to Katie, and in a tone she had never heard from him, he said, "Congratulations!"

Margaret helped her sit up on the table, smiling the whole time, "I knew someday you'd get the child you always wanted, Honey. But I can't figure out what you are doing back here. I mean, with all those fancy doctors available in New York why did you come back to Vero Beach?"

"I'm divorced—again," she told her friend. "It's a long story, Margaret."

"Doctor Hampton is leaving for the hospital to do a scheduled C-section. You're the last person for him this morning." She looked at her as if to say, 'I've got the time.'

Katie sighed. Besides her story there were a lot of 'pregnant' questions she would love to ask her.

"I'm not trying to be nosy, Honey. I am willing to listen if you wanted someone to talk with." Then she added, "There's a coffee shop across the way. If you can keep down a donut, I'm buying."

She smiled; a donut actually sounded delicious, "I'd love to."

They talked for the better part of an hour, Katie trying to give as painless a version of her story as possible, but that wasn't easy. Then she talked about her dad and the cancer, her parents' impending money troubles, and her own concerns for the immediate future.

Margaret listened and seemed to be taking everything she said into deep thought.

"I don't want to become a burden on my parents. I've got to find a job and a place of my own."

"I've known you for years, Katie, and I hope you don't think I'm saying this out of pity, but I may have some answers for your immediate troubles—if you're interested that is."

She nodded, shocked really that Margaret cared enough about her to offer help.

"I have a house on the other coast. Now mind you, it's not a fancy house. It's just a little seven hundred square foot, wood-frame house, but it's cute and I'd be willing to let you stay there, rent-free, for as long as you like. It was the first house that my husband and I bought. I worked over in St. Petersburg at one of the largest epilepsy centers in Florida for eighteen years before my husband died, and then I moved over to this coast five years ago to be near my sister." Katie wasn't saying anything so Margaret continued, "That's when I started working here. It was a change, but I loved the idea of obstetrics. I love babies!" she added. "I've tried over the years to rent it out, but it always seems to be a bigger pain in the neck than leaving it vacant; and besides that I can't bear the idea of selling it. The last woman who rented it from me moved out a few weeks ago owing me two months rent. I need to go over this weekend and spend time cleaning it, unless you want it. Then I guess I'll let you clean it."

"Margaret, I'd love to have a place of my own, but I've got to find a job, and I hope one that pays well enough to support my new family," she said, looking down at her stomach.

"I know several of the people at the epilepsy center. It's a big place with a lot of employees coming and going. I could call and see if there is something available. You work mostly with computers, right?"

"Yes, computers, programming, secretary, receptionist—anything like that I can do."

"Let me call over there this afternoon and talk with Dr. Sullivan. He's the center's director, and my old boss." She gave her hand a pat. "Sometimes, Katie dear, problems are just challenges we haven't tackled yet."

All the way home she was excited with the possibility of a job and a place of her own. Yet, she really didn't want to be so far away with her father being sick. Mother had plenty of help with the nurse and the aide coming over, but still it would be a three-hour drive when she wanted to come for a visit.

Max and Roberta, who used to live next door until recently, were at the house when she walked in. They were happy to see her, but were tactful enough not to prod. Max was beaming from ear to ear. Their house had sold recently and they were living in the Sea Crest condominiums.

"Condo life is great!" he said cheerfully. "If I'd have known how good it was, I would have sold our house a long time ago. No yard to mow, no pool to clean, good neighbors our age."

"It sounds wonderful," Katie said, being polite.

"I was just telling your mom and dad that there is a nice one-bedroom unit on the ground floor up for sale. It's tiny, but they only want $27,000 for it. It was recently redecorated and it looks like a show model."

"Max!" Roberta said sharply, giving him an elbow in the ribs. Beth had already told them before Katie arrived that they couldn't sell the house with her returning to live with them; not to a one-bedroom, adult community like Sea Crest, anyway.

"Mom, that sounds like a great place to live. You told me last night you two had thought about selling."

"I know Katie, but—well, it's only one bedroom and you have to be fifty-five or older to live there."

"Mom, you and dad only need one bedroom, and you're both over fifty-five."

"But Katie we want to be here for you."

"And you will be there for me when I need you, just like I'll be there for the two of you, but I've already had an offer to house-sit, rent-free, for as long as I want, and a possible job offer, too."

"There, you see!" Max said smiling at Roberta and Beth. "You don't have any reason not to at least check into it. See how you like it. The manager at the condo has the keys and you could look at it today—if Lawrence feels up to it," he said, lowering his tone.

Lawrence said he would like to get out of the house for a while, but they'd have to go slowly and not expect too much out of him. Katie and Beth helped him dress and they supported him on both sides out to the car. He looked so fragile in the midday sunlight. His tan had faded to pale beige and his hair seemed to have grayed overnight. Everything about him said he was not a well man, except that wonderful radiant smile that he flashed from time to time, that said, 'It's still me.'

She sighed as the car pulled out of the drive. It was hard to see her father lose so much vibrancy and independence, but he was a fighter and this was a battle for life. She barely settled into the recliner for an afternoon catnap when the phone rang. It was Margaret. There were a couple of openings at the center ranging in pay from $9.00 to $13.50 for office work. Margaret said if she wanted to go with her over the weekend, she could see the house and go for an interview on Monday.

Early Saturday morning, Margaret came by and picked her up and they were on the road.

There was a tiny tingle somewhere down inside Katie that told her a new adventure in life was ready to begin. Even though she hadn't seen the house or interviewed for the job, she had a feeling that this was the right direction. Her parents loved the condo and, at Katie's prodding, they contacted a real estate agent about selling their home. If things turned out as planned, even after buying and paying for the condominium unit, they would bank about $40,000. This, in turn, would give them plenty of cushion to reach retirement age without depleting their life savings.

The three-hour drive passed quickly because they spent their time talking about the new baby and the changes that were taking place inside Katie's body. To her astonishment, Margaret had never had children because she was infertile. It seemed to her that working in the kind of environment that Margaret was in would only serve to depress her, but Margaret said no, because with every pregnancy her heart filled with happiness for the woman who was able to conceive.

The town of Terra Ceia, just south of the Sunshine Skyway Bridge, was only twenty minutes away from the epilepsy center in St. Petersburg. It was a small, picturesque community that bordered a large saltwater inlet, aptly named Terra Ceia Bay. The roads were narrow, causing them to drive on the shaded shoulder as occasional vehicles came from the opposite direction. She felt as if she had taken a step back twenty or thirty years to a simpler era. The road wound around the bay, past a development of new, luxurious homes and then back into a section of older homes on the west side of the island. Small cottages sprinkled the landscape between mangroves and inlets. Margaret turned into the driveway of a small, gray, wooden house with blue trim. The yard was overgrown; trash and broken yard toys were scattered among the weeds.

"Well, here we are," she said, pulling the car up under the carport. Frowning at the mess, she looked at Katie, "It's cute when it's all cleaned up."

That wasn't hard to imagine; it was quaint even if it looked as if someone had not taken due care with it.

Katie stood in the shade of the large jacaranda tree in the front yard. It was in full foliage of tiny, deep green leaflets with a smattering of purple blossoms left from the spring bloom. The breeze was cool under the tree with a smell of salt water mingling in the late morning air. The backyard was fenced with four-foot chain link, which would come in handy when her little one was old enough to go outside and play. The house to the south looked to be new construction, but it also was diminutive and quaint. There was a sheriff's car parked in its driveway, which provided Katie with a feeling of security in the neighborhood.

Margaret walked out to where Katie was taking in the scenery. "She left it messy inside, but I think we could get it cleaned up this weekend. Do you want to come in and look around?"

"Sure."

"It's hot in here now, but we can turn on the air conditioner and then run to the store and pick up a few supplies. It should be cool by the time we get back."

Katie ignored the trash left behind and walked through the small house. The walls were pine, as was the tongue and groove flooring. The living room was as wide as the house, but only about ten feet deep. She stepped up two steps into the petite white and peach-trimmed kitchen. The sink was an old double-bowl, white porcelain with the drain board as one unit. An old electric stove and a strange, square, white enamel appliance as big as the stove stood together on the wall opposite the sink. Margaret explained it was an old-fashioned water heater. It worked fine, so she had never replaced it with a more modern unit.

"Besides that," she told Katie, "it makes a great cutting board!"

The only modern-looking appliance was a side-by-side refrigerator that looked too big to fit in the tiny kitchen. It was grossly mildewed inside, causing Katie to gag.

The two bedrooms shared a closet that separated the rooms. The first bedroom was so small that it reminded her of a walk-in closet instead of a bedroom, but a baby's crib would fit with a changing table and a small dresser. The other bedroom had a queen-size bed with a stained mattress, ample space for a dresser, and would still leave some walking room. The back door and the bathroom door were only accessible from the master bedroom. The bath was as messy as the rest of the house, but it was functional with a small linen closet, fiberglass tub and shower combination with sliding glass doors, an antique toilet with the high tank, and a pedestal sink.

"I used to have an old ball and claw tub in here," Margaret said, "But I figured with renters, I probably needed something that would keep the water from getting splashed onto the floor and rotting it out. My husband had to replace the floor in here when we bought it because of water damage."

Katie stepped into the bathroom; the floor was still strong and solid.

They unlocked the back door and opened it to reveal a screened porch which had several panels pushed out or torn. Margaret sighed but didn't say anything. The backyard was grassy and overgrown, but spacious. In the back corner was a metal storage building on an oversized concrete slab. And then there was the orange tree. It was the only tree in the backyard, but it was huge for a citrus. And, according to Margaret's memory, its fruits were delicious when they were in season.

They turned on the air conditioner and locked the house as they left to go to the store. The neighboring town had several big shopping centers where they could buy everything they needed. Besides the cleaning supplies, Margaret bought bedding, towels, a few new curtains, throw rugs and small set of cookware. Ignoring Katie's protests, she said that wasn't going to let her move into a house devoid of necessary items; it would be as close to turnkey as possible. At midday they stopped at the local used furniture dealer and picked out living room furniture, a dresser and a television. All of which the dealer promised to have delivered before six that evening.

Grabbing a bite of lunch, they headed back to the comfortably cooled house to begin cleaning. The remainder of the day was left to throw away garbage, vacuum, mop, dust, disinfect and scrub until that little house sparkled. Margaret disappeared for a while as she went to visit a few of her old neighbors. Before too long she returned with two of the neighborhood boys tagging along. They shyly said hello to Katie and then the smaller of the two began picking up the yard debris while the older one got the high-wheel mower out of the storage shed and began mowing.

The furniture was late arriving, but it worked out well with the completion of the housework. By dusk, both women were exhausted, but fully satisfied with the transformation of the little house from neglected to loved. It still needed work, but it had come a long way from what they had found that morning.

Margaret ordered a pizza using her cell phone. It arrived as the furniture delivery people were pulling out of the driveway. Katie hooked up the television to the antenna and they were able to watch the local stations as they enjoyed their dinner.

"I'm exhausted!" Katie said as she pulled off a slice of hot pizza, catching the mozzarella strings and winding them back onto her dinner.

"I'm sure you are! I hope I didn't make you over do it today."

"No," Katie assured her, then laughed. "I've never seen someone organize and orchestrate such an undertaking in such a short amount of time. You could have been a drill sergeant, you know."

Margaret laughed too. "It's simply a matter of knowing what you want and being single-minded enough to bulldoze your way to it!"

"That's the truth, but we've done all this work and I don't even know if I have a job yet."

"Yes, but," Margaret interrupted, "the work needed to be done anyway and besides that, remember: bulldoze your way to the goal! Don't go to the center Monday wondering if they want to hire you; go there thinking they need you."

She laughed, catching a sliding pepperoni and dropping it into her mouth. "Bulldozer, huh? You're right, but do you want to know something funny? I feel like everything is just coming into place, like I'm at home here, really at home. Maybe it sounds stupid, but it's like this was God's plan for my life all along. It's like driving on a road that you've never been down before, but yet it feels so familiar."

"No it's not stupid, Honey. I think sometimes we stray from the way He intended for us and that's when our life seems to go out of control and crazy, but when we get back on track that little voice inside lets us know it's right."

Before turning in for the night, Katie called her mother to let her know everything was okay and to check on her father. To add to her good feeling about moving into Margaret's home, Beth told her they had signed the listing agreement and by Monday the 'For Sale' sign would go up in the front yard.

~:~

Sunday, Margaret and Katie went out for breakfast and then went to church services in a beautiful church on Terra Ceia that had been built in the 1930's. She had the opportunity to meet some of the people who would become her neighbors and Margaret had the chance to reunite with some old friends. Later that afternoon, Margaret took her all over the nearby town, showing her where everything was, and then they headed out to the beaches to see the Gulf of Mexico. It would only take one afternoon to fall in love with the white sandy beaches and beautiful, calm, blue-green waters of the warm gulf.

"I'll show you my favorite place to relax after a hard week at work," Margaret said with a look of yearning in her eyes. "My husband and I used to come out here to this little park in the late afternoon for several reasons: first, we liked to eat at the restaurants out here; second, because it was never crowded; and third, because it's on the east side of Anna Maria Island which means you are in the shade even though you're sitting on the beach."

They drove over a little hump-backed bridge and came to a park with towering Australian pines lining the beach.

"Wow, I can see where the shade comes from," Katie said, smiling as they walked down to the water.

"That's right, Honey. Everyone goes to the other side of the island to see the sunset in the evening, and it's pretty, don't get me wrong, but I like to throw a chair at the edged of the water, plop-down, wiggle my toes in the sand, and relax—in shade, not sun."

"Margaret," she said, looking down the quiet, white beach, "I never thought I'd like anything better than the Atlantic coast, but this—I—I love it."

"If it wasn't for my sister and her family," Margaret said as they took off their shoes and dabbled in the water, "I'd be back here in a minute, but she's all the family I have left and they aren't leaving Palm Beach anytime soon."

"Thank you, Margaret!" She said suddenly. She had thanked her for her help already, but this was a thank you from bottom of her heart. "I've said it before, but I just want you to know how much I appreciate everything. I hope if I can accomplish my dreams that I can repay your wonderful kindness to me."

Margaret laughed as her stocky frame began to chug down the beach, "Bulldozer, Katie! Remember your goal and push until you get there!"

Monday morning a confident Katie and a reminiscent Margaret walked through the doors of the medical center. Margaret led the way to Doctor Sullivan's office on the third floor. He was a short, heavyset, older man, Katie guessing about sixty, with totally white hair and pale gray eyes. Immediately, she felt comfortable with him as he began showing her around the complex, telling Margaret about changes since she'd left and Katie about the positions available.

"You certainly look familiar to me. Have you ever been here before?" He had an excellent memory for faces and hers was recognizable, but he just couldn't seem to bring it to the forefront of his mind.

She realized he probably recognized her from the news, but couldn't place her with the different hairstyle. "No, I've never been here before. I'm originally from the other side of Florida," she said, skirting the issue that she knew would eventually surface.

He showed her to the patient records center and database room. She caught her breath as she looked at their equipment. They had the most comprehensive and up-to-date computer system on the market. But the thing that caused her pulse to race was the scanner equipment they were using to scan x-rays into patient profiles. It was the same type she had used to bring to life her idea for Seasons.

"Yes, we're proud of our system," he said, pleased at her knowledge of the equipment. "We upgraded about four months ago. It cost us over a quarter of a million dollars, but it was worth it. We can send and receive completely detailed patient information all over the country. You sound as if you're familiar with the system. Do you have specific skills with this type of equipment?"

"Yes," she smiled, "intricate knowledge, actually."

"Really?" He seemed impressed, but curious. "Where did you say you worked before?"

Taking a breath, she answered, "ATI corporate headquarters in New York."

But before she could finish, the look of recognition crossed his face. "Trathmoore. You're Katherine Trathmoore!" He seemed shocked at his own words. He knew he had seen that lovely face and now he remembered it was on the news. But what was the wife of a billionaire doing looking for work, he wondered.

"I was," she corrected him. "My husband and I recently divorced, and to tell the truth I'm surprised it hasn't been in the news yet. If it's all the same to you," she added, "I'd rather not have anyone else aware of my *former* name, if you understand."

"Yes, of course," he said, understanding instantly her reluctance to be known, especially after what he had heard about her life in recent months. "I'd like to offer you the position working with our system, if you don't mind the pay. I'm sure $13.50 isn't exactly what you are used to, but... ."

"I'll gladly accept that," she interrupted. "When would you like me to start?"

"Would next Monday be too soon?"

"Not at all." she smiled, shaking his hand. "I'll be here."

Katie and Margaret walked out to the parking lot together as Margaret smiled at her young friend. "You're learning how to bulldoze quite well," she laughed. "You didn't even fill out an employment application!"

~:~

The months passed quickly as Katie's due date neared. The sonogram revealed that she was carrying a son, and he was plump and active. It was the most wonderful sensation in the world when the baby would kick and bump about inside her body. Each time she marveled at the miracle taking place within her. She wondered from time to time about her son; would he look like a Trathmoore or a

Randall? It was something she thought about at night, as she lay awake unable to sleep. It didn't matter to her; she would love this child no matter what, but she thought of the two men; one knew, but didn't believe it would be his, and the other probably had no idea what had happened to the woman he saved.

The trial had ended recently and, to her relief, she was given the decision of appearing or not. She talked with Chief Perryman, who sounded genuinely concerned for her and said her taped testimony, other evidence and, most condemning of all, Donovan's testimony would be sufficient if she wasn't up to the task. He didn't know she was pregnant, but he did know it had been a harrowing experience, coupled with the fact that when they started to discuss the trial she informed him about the quiet divorce. She had no desire to become the focus of media attention once again, so she was glad that it wasn't something she would be forced into.

Nick and Lenny had both been found guilty. Nick was given one life term, but would be eligible for parole in twenty-five years. Lenny, as an accomplice, received twenty-five years. He would be eligible for parole in eight to ten years, but with his advanced stages of AIDS he would, in all actuality, only live another few years at the most. Donovan entered the witness protection program because he had willingly offered the police vital information on several of the crime families that his brother had contact with, and that could be a death sentence if they found him.

Work at the center was exciting and interesting. She filled her days with the tasks of her job and, with the permission of Doctor Sullivan and Hilda, the systems operating manager, she was able to work each evening re-creating her program. It was a daunting task because before she'd had Justin's expertise to shorten the process, Ruth to check for errors, and Micca to tie in the scanner/camera equipment. But Katie had not been just a fixture in the room; she had been the designer and she had worked through every aspect of the program's creation. She would finish it on her own, but it would simply take more time.

Her parents sold their home and were now living at Sea Crest. Her father was holding his own; the cancer was retreating, slowly. He was able to do a little more each day and depended on the painkillers a little less. They enjoyed the covered pool where he could do water exercises without exposure to the sun. Also, they enjoyed the new friends they were making. Max and Roberta had been right; it was a great place to live.

Her own little home had become a comfortable retreat from the world. She made friends with the neighbors, and found the community to be close-knit; everyone seemed to care about others—she liked that. She had been able to buy some beautiful, second-hand, oak baby furniture through ads in the newspaper and her little man's room was already decorated for his arrival. The office, the little community church, and her parents each gave her a baby shower. She received some wonderful gifts and several hundred dollars in cash.

Being shrewd with her earnings, she was saving about a thousand dollars a month, after expenses. Alex and Crystal sold their house, and after going back through the original purchase and receipts, they sent Katie a check for $4,860. All together, she had amassed close to $11,000 in six months. She wanted the money to go toward the opening of Seasons, but just as she suspected, the health insurance policy at the center wouldn't pay for her pregnancy, but it would cover the baby after he was born. The doctor and hospital would take more than four thousand of her hard-earned dollars.

The due date passed, and still her body wasn't ready to release its miracle. Beth arranged for Max and Roberta to stay with Lawrence for a few days whenever the time came, but the waiting was tedious. She felt like the proverbial watermelon, waiting to burst. She had acquired all the full term oddities: the duck waddle, the missing belly button, and the ankles that would swell into unrecognizable logs.

Dr. Ford, who was her obstetrician now, told her on the last visit on Friday that since the baby was large and the due date was coming up on two weeks late they would induce labor the following Monday. She called her mother and they made plans for her to arrive Monday and accompany her to the hospital.

But babies have their own time schedule and they certainly don't like to follow what anyone else thinks they should do. So, as luck would have it, she woke at two in the morning on Saturday with a terrible backache and a cramping pain that occurred every five minutes. It was time.

She grabbed her already packed bag and tossed it into the back of her little Renault. The car was one she had found in the paper for five hundred dollars the week before she moved to the Gulf Coast, but it needed work. Her parents paid for the new front axle and a brake job. The air conditioner blew cold and the mileage was low, but it was an ugly little car; its red paint job had faded and peeled on the hood and, in general, it was scratched and dented. She couldn't complain about its dependability though because it ran well and got great gas mileage.

She was scared going into labor without someone to help her, but she had gone through Lamaze alone, even though she had neighbors who offered to be her coach. She felt she could do it by herself, but now she had doubts. The nurses were wonderful, and seeing that she was alone, they made extra special efforts to keep someone with her.

Roxy was a nurse who seemed to take special interest in her, telling her that she'd be there for the birth even if she had to do it on her own time. Though Roxy told Katie that she was only forty-six, she also told her that she was retiring after today. The birth of Katie's child would be the last delivery for her because tomorrow she would be on a plane for the Caribbean.

"That must be nice—early retirement," Katie said, taking a deep breath after a long contraction.

"Yes," Roxy said, smiling. "I got a nice inheritance from my Aunt's estate. I'm gonna be dancing in Aruba, Kid, while you're changing diapers."

"Someday—I'll—join you—down there." she tried to joke, but a mounting contraction sent her mind back onto her breathing.

"Well, how's my patient?" Dr. Ford said as he entered the room. Katie didn't answer because she was deep in concentration. "You were just stubborn enough not to let me get this all going Monday. Had to do it on the weekend, didn't you?" He was joking, but Katie was completely ignoring him. "Do you want something for the pain?" he said sympathetically, "You don't have to be a hero and go through this without anything you know."

The contraction eased off and she looked up to him, "I want to be fully aware of what's going on; you're not going to dope me up and…."

"It's okay, I was just asking." he said, frowning at her stubbornness. "I'm going to check you during the next contraction. I think from the progress you've been making you'll be ready to start pushing soon. Would you like to get this over with?"

"You're gonna check me when?" she asked anxiously.

"During your next contraction."

She wanted to cry. "It hurts bad enough without you sticking your hand in there!" She snapped.

"We won't know if you're ready, if I don't."

"Oh, all right! But I'm not gonna be happy about it!"

He tried not to laugh because he knew she was serious, but she was the one who wanted neither pain medication nor an epidural.

Gasping at the pain and loosing her ability to concentrate on her breathing, she swore; *"Get your damn hand outta there!"* She wanted to kick him, but it wouldn't do her any good—but she still wanted to do it.

He smiled as he threw the latex glove into the trash, "You're ready to start pushing with the next contraction. You're at ten!"

"Thank God!" She sighed, and she really meant that, too.

The room was abuzz as the nurses brought in the warmer for the baby and prepared instruments for the doctor. Suddenly the thought occurred to her that she was supposed to have an urge to push, but she didn't have it yet. She questioned Doctor Ford, who simply said to push with the next few contractions and she'd get it.

"Men!" She muttered out loud, getting a few snickers from the nurses.

At 2:32 in the afternoon, with the nurses pushing her stomach and curling her over like a fat toad trying to reach its feet, the baby's head finally burst free from her body. She let out a cry mixed with pain, exhaustion, and delight, as Dr. Ford carefully cleared the baby's nose and mouth. Then she heard it, the cry of a baby who was seemingly just as angry with Doctor Ford as his mother. Carefully he manipulated the baby's shoulders free, and then in one quick motion the baby was out and lying on her stomach.

The rest was a blur to her. Her whole concentration changed from herself to the beautiful screaming boy being attended by the nurses. It seemed to take forever before she was allowed to hold him. She pulled the warm blanket back from his face and tiny hands and gasped with wonder at the miracle that had come from within her own body. He was finally quiet and resting as she looked at him and suddenly felt that she was looking into a familiar face. Tears spilled down her cheeks with the realization that her premonition had been right all along; this tiny face was just like his father's—Albert Trathmoore.

Beth arrived that evening to marvel at her new grandson. She took pictures of Katie and the baby and then mailed them back home from the hospital. Tomorrow she would take accompany Katie and the baby home, spending the week to help her daughter adjust to motherhood.

Before checking out there was a mountain of paper work that needed to be completed. First was the matter of this young man's name for his birth certificate.

"Jordan Lawrence Danor,"

"And the father's name?" The nurse asked matter-of-factly.

Katie paused and then said, "Unknown."

Her mother was astonished because Katie had already confided that it was Albert's son.

"Unknown?" She rarely got that response. "Are you sure you want it to say that on his birth certificate?"

"Yes."

An orderly came to her room with the wheelchair and took her and her son to the maternity desk for final checkout, but there seemed to be some confusion.

"Is something wrong?" She asked, seeing the nurse's puzzled expression.

"They lost some things for your son in the pathology lab. Nothing serious, but they usually give us the report from the umbilical cord before you checkout—and they somehow lost his cord! Don't worry, it won't keep you from going home." Then she added, "It's never happened before; I'm sure they'll find it."

It troubled Katie for a moment and then it was forgotten as the orderly wheeled her downstairs; she and her son were going home.

~:~

Albert Trathmoore sat in his penthouse apartment staring at the paper he held in his hand. He had been wrong. He didn't like being wrong with such a costly mistake. He fully expected to find that Katie birthed Donovan's child, but to his shock and surprise he was incorrect. He swallowed hard as he came to the realization that he had a son, something he had always wanted. It cost him a hundred thousand dollars to Roxy McCulver to have the cord sent to his laboratories for analysis, but for him that was pocket change; the cost of losing his wife and son was astronomical. And now the new challenge presented itself: How would he get his son from the woman he had spurned so terribly.

~:~

Katie was grateful that her mother would be staying the week. It would be wonderful to have someone else doing the cooking and cleaning so she and her son could get acquainted with each other. There was so much to learn how to do: breast-feeding, adjusting to a baby's erratic schedule, diapering and bathing, just to mention a few of the tasks that she was praying she'd master before her mother left.

She thought motherhood was supposed to come naturally, but nothing could be further from the truth; perhaps it wasn't rocket science, but it definitely was an on-the-job-training situation. Nothing proved it to her more so than the crying episode.

The second evening after coming home, with her breast milk not in yet, Jordan began to cry—loudly. He wailed and screamed with his tiny fists battering the air and his lungs getting the best exercising yet. No matter how she tried to soothe him or tried to get him to nurse, nothing would dent his crying.

Beth had stepped out to run to the grocery store and Katie was hit with the sudden realization that she had absolutely no idea what to do. His diaper was changed, she had let him nurse moments earlier, and he had only been up about forty-five minutes, so she was stumped.

"Lord knows," she said above the crying, "the neighbors will think I'm beating you! Shush, baby, shush."

But he stoutly refused.

Relieved to hear the car pull in the driveway, she laid the upset child in his crib (which only served to cause his cries to become louder) and dashed out to ask her mother what to do.

"Good Heavens, Katie! What is wrong with the baby?" Mother asked as she got out of the car. She could hear his incessant shrieking.

"I don't know!" She cried. "I was hoping you'd know what to do!"

Her mother took one look at the upset newborn, picked him up and poked a bottle of sterile water in his mouth. He sucked down the water with hardly a break to give the bottle air, and then promptly pooped his pants.

"You mean all that fuss was because he needed to poop?" Katie said incredulously.

Her mother smiled. "You haven't produced enough milk to give his tummy something to push with, and he had a bell-wee-ache. Didn't you Jordan?" she said, reverting to baby talk in the middle of an adult conversation. He was gurgling happily as he finished emptying his labored load into his diaper.

"My word," she exclaimed, "I thought he was dying or something."

The next day, as she put him up on her shoulder, she felt something warm running down her shirt. "Mom," she said, getting her mother's attention, "did he just pee on me?"

"Oh, he couldn't have; his diaper is on." Then looking down at where his tiny foot was planted on his mother's breast, she happily replied, "No, but I think your milk just came in."

And did it ever. She had worried about it starting and now she was wondering if it would ever stop. Finally, Jordan could fill his eager little belly with more than just the colostrum that had been dribbling out.

With the first week ending, and before her mother left to return home, they went for the one-week check up at the pediatrician's office. Jordan had gained two ounces, which didn't seem like much to Katie, but the doctor assured her that they usually lost weight the first week; he was doing well at a bouncing 8 pounds 11 ounces.

After her six-week maternity leave ended, she began taking Jordan to an elderly neighbor lady named Virginia, but lovingly known to the neighborhood kids as 'Granny.' Granny only wanted fifty dollars a week to take care of Jordan; all the other places wanted over a hundred to care for a newborn. She had to work to keep a supply of breast milk two days ahead, frozen, so he could continue with his favorite food; Mom.

Her days were clicking into a good routine, with the only exception being that he still didn't sleep through the night. Even though the late night feedings were tiring, she relished every opportunity to be with her son. Her life couldn't be any better, she thought. The only thing she would add would be a store of her own design opening in the Tampa area.

It was harder to save now with the expense of diapers, and child care, and all the extras that go with a baby, but she was still putting five hundred a month away, and she still had her diamond. When she got depressed over the speed, or lack of speed, at which her plan was progressing, she would take out the diamond and hold it. She could cash it in and accelerate her plan, bringing her so much closer to being able to have what she wanted, but she wouldn't. Each time she was tempted, she remembered Uncle Patty's words about having the strength to achieve her dreams. She wanted her dream, but she would do it by the strength of her own will. If she ran into troubled waters, the diamond was her reserve. She kept telling herself that it wasn't rough yet; it was just difficult; and difficult was something she could overcome.

~:~

It had taken Katie two and a half years to accumulate $21,000 dollars. Not enough to construct her own store or to even renovate a store to suit her needs. She would have to either start small with only analyzing people and making recommendations, or bring in investors and try to open it as she envisioned her store; clothing, make-up and styling salons all set to cater to the four basic groups that categorized people. Late one night as she sat rocking her toddler she made the decision to start bringing in investors. She mapped out in her mind who she wanted to start talking to about her vision for the future. She also decided it was time to create a business plan to present to the area banks and see if she might find financing through one or more of them. But her decision should have been made sooner, because if she was going to keep her dream alive she was going to have to start fighting for it.

CHAPTER SIX

It was a Thursday afternoon and she had finished up her work at the office. She had spoken with Doctor Sullivan and several other board members during lunch that day about an investment opportunity she was proposing. She was pleased with their response. She had been so nervous presenting it that she expected them to dismiss her idea as nonsense, but to her relief they were willing to meet again and discuss the financial needs for such a venture. Her business plan was drawn up and ready. Monday afternoon she would leave work early to meet with two bankers who expressed interest in her idea.

She stopped and picked up Jordan then drove the two blocks home. As she neared her little house she was surprised to find a car in the driveway. It was a new Lincoln with windows tinted so dark that she couldn't see if anyone was in it or not. She was puzzled as to who was paying her a visit. Pulling in behind the car, yet off to the side so as to not block it in, she gathered her purse and Jordan, and cautiously approached the car.

"Mama who's dat?" Jordan asked in his sweet voice.

"I don't know," she answered. "I... ."

Just then the door to the car opened and Albert Trathmoore stepped out onto the shell driveway.

She gasped in surprise and instinctively held on tighter to her son.

"Hello Katie," he said, as if she should have expected him there.

"Hi!" Jordan beamed.

"Hello Jordan! How are you?" he said looking away from her to the handsome lad she held in her arms.

"Fine!" Jordan shouted at him.

"What are you doing here, and how do you know my son's name?" The shock was fading, and anger was replacing it.

"That's mama," Jordan said, patting Katie's breast.

"Yes, I know that," Albert answered him, ignoring her question.

"Can we go inside and talk?" he asked softly. "I'm sure this little guy wants to get down to play, don't you?" he said, playfully reaching out to tickle Jordan's side.

Jordan giggled as she pulled him from Albert's reach; this seemed like a fun game to play. "Miss me, miss me, you gotta kiss me," he chirped. That was his favorite game to play with his mother.

He laughed at Jordan's antics. "Please," Albert said, looking back to Katie.

"Mama, I wan' down!" Jordan demanded, taking her face in his little hands and turning it toward him. "*Pleeesssee*," he added for emphasis.

She was weighing out the problem in her mind; then reluctantly she went to the door and unlocked it.

"He can talk quite well for a two year old," Albert remarked, following her into the house.

"Okay Jordan, you can go get your toys and play while mama gets dinner ready."

"O-Kay," he said and than he ran up the steps into the kitchen and to his room.

"Why are you here?" She asked, squaring her shoulders and facing him. Her voice was filled with bitter resentment and anger.

"I came to see my son," he said as he looked off toward Jordan's room. "And my wife," he added, waiting for the shock to come over her.

"Your what?" She said as her eyes went wide in disbelief.

"He is my son, and I know that now."

"Your what?" She repeated. Perhaps she hadn't heard him right, but her pulse was beginning to pound in her ears as she remembered the day he divorced her, the day he humiliated her, the day he threw her out like a piece of trash.

"I like your hair short," he said, reaching up to touch her face.

She pulled back, seething with anger at his nonchalant attitude. "I am not your wife! And furthermore, you have no right to come to my home and… ."

"Don't you mean Margaret's home?" he tossed out.

"You sneaking, prying, asshole!" she said, trying to keep her voice low enough not to disturb Jordan.

"I hope you don't talk like that all the time around my son," he said, raising one eyebrow.

She was ready to hit him with the barrage of bitter barbs welling up within her when he added, "I didn't come here to argue with you." She was even more beautiful than he remembered, and he didn't want her angry. Very softly he said, "I'm sorry for the way I treated you."

His sudden apology caught her quite off guard and jumbled up the angry words she was about to say. *"You're sorry?"* Her words reflected her feeling of the inadequacy of his apology.

"Yes, and I want you and Jordan to come back with me to New York." He stepped closer to her, the faint aroma of her perfume was tantalizing his senses, "Katie, I forgive you for what you did."

"You forgive me?!" she burst out. "You bast...you idiot!" She caught herself before she cursed and rephrased what she was about to say, but idiot was more offensive to him. "I didn't do anything to apologize for."

"No?" he interrupted, "sleeping with another man isn't worth apologizing for?"

"Not when it was at gun point!" she said, her eyes going narrow like two fine slits. She had no reason to hide it any more because the trial was over and Donovan was living an anonymous life somewhere out of Albert's reach.

His head cocked sideways as if he hadn't heard her correctly. He knew from the beginning that one of the men accused Donovan of raping her, but he thought it was only an effort to incriminate the man who let her go. "What do you mean?" he said, grabbing her arm as if she might run away before she told him the answer to this riddle.

"Why didn't you come to me about the underwear *before* you asked me to come to the police station?" Her eyes trying to well up with the hurt and pain inside her, but she would not; she swallowed hard and willed them back. "You knew, didn't you? Long before then, but you wanted to crush me down in front of those men. You wanted me to bare my soul in front of the man that risked his own life to get me out of there. And for what, Albert? So you could have the satisfaction of sending him to jail for touching *your* property?

"You said you consented."

She twisted out of his grip. "I had to! I promised him I wouldn't tell what happened at the warehouse. He didn't have a choice; Lenny pulled a gun and would have killed us both. He was ordered to have sex with me so he wouldn't turn me loose."

Albert walked to the couch in a state of shock; he had gravely miscalculated this woman. She had given up everything in order to keep a promise to someone she barely knew. "That was a foolish mistake, Katie." he said, as he slumped down on the couch.

"No Albert, it wasn't. You should have come to me as soon as your detectives told you about what they found. Alone, just you and I, I might have tried to explain why you couldn't send him to jail. You didn't leave me a choice, and you wouldn't listen to me after everything had happened, would you?"

"I made my decision from what you told me." His fingers rubbing his forehead as he spoke.

"You made a decision to decimate me, to grind me into the dust of nothingness. What you did the next morning in your office was more ugly and horrible than anything that had happened to me by those men." The emotion in her was rising, making it harder to control the welling tears. The corners of her mouth quivered as she finished what she had to say, "Because you were supposed to be someone who loved me."

"I didn't divorce you."

He had said it so quietly, but it was like an explosion reverberating the confines of her thoughts. "Yes, you did," she said, reassuring herself. "I signed the papers and so did you."

"I never filed them," he said, continuing to rub his forehead. He had many ways to get his son back; he hadn't planned on being so blunt but he couldn't think clearly at the moment. "Didn't you ever wonder why it wasn't blasted across every newspaper and television station in the country?"

She stood silent, afraid of the thought that he had some right to be there, some right to her son. After gathering her anger back like a sword, she said, "*I am not your wife*. Get out of my house and don't come back. I'll file my own divorce papers tomorrow."

Jordan bounded back into the living room with his teddy and his favorite car. "Mama," he said, pulling at her skirt, "I wanna watch lit'le peep."

Quietly Katie went over and turned on the television and put in the DVD. When she turned around, Albert had picked up Jordan and was holding him. Fright filled her that he might try to walk out the door with him.

"Are you gonna watch lit'le peep wiff me?" He asked, his dark blue eyes looking into Albert's.

She tried to hide the fear, "Your show is on Sweetheart, sit down with teddy and watch it. Mr. Trathmoore has to go home now." She reached to him and he instinctively reached to his mother.

Albert's eyes were moist as he kissed Jordan's ruffled golden hair; reluctantly he let him go to his mother.

Jordan looked back at him as if the kiss was a very strange thing to receive. Then he laughed and ran, jumping up on the couch with his bear.

Albert looked at Katie and said, low enough that Jordan couldn't hear him, "He is *my* son and I'm giving you the choice of coming back with me, or I'll take him from you. You know I can do it, Katie."

"Money doesn't mean you automatically win, Albert. I'll fight you with every ounce of my life"

"I'll win, I always win. I'll be back tomorrow for your decision." Then staring at her with the most intimidating look, he growled out, "Don't make the wrong one." And then he was gone.

The following morning Jordan didn't go to Granny's house, instead he was pleased to discover he was going to work with his mother.

Dr. Sullivan was surprised when Katie walked into his office with her little boy in tow. He could tell by the look on her face that something was terribly wrong. And when she said she wanted to know who the best lawyer in Tampa was, he knew she was in trouble.

Albert knew she'd decide to fight, but his lawyers would tear apart anyone she could find to represent her. Still he'd give her the benefit of the doubt and wait to see what her answer would be. He was stunned when Mr. Rizzona, his chief legal advisor since Martin Fengale retired after the divorce fiasco three years ago, called him and said not to go to Katie's house for her answer because her *team of lawyers* out of Atlanta, Georgia, had already contacted them.

Albert was under a restraining order to prevent him from getting near her or her son.

He went in to an immediate hot rage. No one would tell him where he could or couldn't go! He made it clear to Mr. Rizzona that he had better figure out how to render her little battle charade useless immediately or he would find someone to replace him. But this battle wouldn't end as neatly and cleanly as he had planned; in fact she had forewarned him how she'd fight, but he didn't believe she could do it—no one ever had.

~:~

Doctor Sullivan listened as Katie told him about what had happened the day before, how Albert had shown up at her house, how he told her he hadn't divorced her, and how he gave her a choice to come back to him or lose Jordan. He listened, his expression one of deep thought.

"I know someone who could help you, but he is expensive." He looked over the rim of his dark-framed glasses, "Have you heard of LaBrant, Barner and Stubbens out of Atlanta?"

"Yes, they handle high-profile divorces cases for the rich and famous, but Albert is the one rich and famous, not me."

"True, but I know Carson LaBrant personally. I don't think they'd lower their fee or anything like that, but I'm willing to wager he'd take the case in a moment, if I asked him to. I'm sure we can find a way to help you with some of the fees." He paused for a moment, "Katie, if anyone can win this for you, it'd be him."

"I'm going to need the best no matter the cost. My son is more important to me than anything else in this world."

Carson LaBrant flew from Atlanta to Tampa the next day to meet with her and started gathering as much information about this highly unusual case as she could tell him. His team had already processed a restraining order, which was, more often than not, always the first order of business. This was the kind of case that had propelled his firm to the forefront of the divorce battlefield; and that is what a divorce always came down to, a bloody battle.

He handled the break-ups of movie stars, multi-millionaires, and politicians. The worst by far were the ones involving the powerhouses of the money arena, and Trathmoore would be the most powerful he'd ever tackled. If he could win this case for her, the recovery of the legal fees alone would be astronomical, but he had never had a case quite like this one. If they couldn't prove her case, however, she could lose her child and become the woman with the significant title of the most in debt person in the United States; that would be a black mark for his firm. The key to any case was the legwork, but this time it would weigh more heavily on the detective work.

He rarely encouraged his clients to put their cases in the public eye; he had always been driven to keep things as quiet as possible. But not this time. This woman had the curiosity of the public on her side. She could not only gain the support of the public with her wrenching story, but after hearing about her business venture that Trathmoore tried to strip her of when he threw her out, she might generate enough investors to launch it.

"Ms. Danor, I'm going to be frank with you. If it hadn't been for Dr. Sullivan asking me to take this case," he said, as they sat in the conference office at the center, "I think I would have told you to seek other council."

"Why? Please Mr. LaBrant, I have to know if you think I can win this."

"It's going to be costly, our retainer alone is $100,000, and I can't say what, if anything we'll uncover to collaborate what you know to be true."

"I have $23,000 dollars in the bank that I was saving to open my store, but Jordan is more important than the money."

"You're still a long way from $100,000," he said looking toward Dr. Sullivan.

"Not really," she said, reaching into her purse. "I have something that will help me reach the total for the retainer, but I'd want this back if I win." She pulled out a dark box and rolled the glittering diamond out onto her hand.

Carson's eyes went wide. He'd seen jewels before, but this was an impressive stone. "Real?" he asked, taking it from her hand.

She handed him the jeweler's tag; "It was valued at $72,000 over three years ago, I'm sure it has gone up in value since then."

"This doesn't—didn't," he said, correcting himself, "belong to Trathmoore did it?" He hated the idea of the retainer becoming part of a property dispute.

"No, it's mine. My uncle gave it to me—after." she said, knowing he understood.

"I'll take it to an appraiser and then have it put in a safety deposit box until this is all over." He sighed; there was a lot of work ahead. "I'd like to take you to dinner this evening and we can discuss more of the details," he said, putting his recorder back into his pocket.

She was plainly surprised by his invitation.

He smiled. "It's okay, my wife listens to all my tapes. Besides, client dinners are a tax deduction."

After Jordan's bath and early dinner, he (and all his favorite movies) went to Granny's house for a 'jammy party' which, according to his mother, was a lot of fun.

"You look purdy, Mama," Jordan said with his eyes dancing as he reached over to touch her earring.

"And you look soooo handsome in your Pooh jammies!" She exclaimed as she turned into Virginia's driveway.

Jordan giggled. He liked his Pooh pajamas too.

With a kiss on his little head and a stern 'Be good for Granny,' she was on her way to the Columbia restaurant in Tampa. She was a little apprehensive about meeting him at the restaurant, not because she was afraid of him, but because she was afraid he would decide the case was hopeless.

The waiter showed her to a table tucked in the most private recesses of the restaurant where Carson was already waiting. He smiled warmly as she approached.

"Just in time." he said, standing up as the waiter seated her. "I've only been here about five minutes. Would you like something to drink or an appetizer perhaps?"

"An iced tea would be wonderful."

Carson looked up to the waiter and nodded, and the waiter disappeared.

Dinner was delightful, partly because of the good food and also because of the good company. Carson was easy to talk with, like an old family friend. He told her to take him all the way back to her first meeting with Trathmoore and bring him up to the present, mentioning that if anything in particular stuck out in those memories not to hesitate saying what they were.

His black recorder sat near her with the tape silently recording her every word. Six tapes would be used as she recounted her story that night.

He liked listening to Katie because she didn't yammer on with useless details. He hated useless details. But she spoke eloquently and concisely about her prior relationship with Albert Trathmoore. Several things she mentioned as details that were noteworthy began to paint a picture of who he was dealing with.

"I believe he has had someone watching you, a detective perhaps, since you first met him; and probably still does." He went on to explain what she told him that brought him to that conclusion. Things she once thought were simply fate, suddenly looked suspicious now. It angered her to think he that had been spying on her.

"I would venture a guess that if we have a professional check your home we might find a listening device planted somewhere." Then making a notation on the small note pad he had on the table he said, "I'll have someone over tomorrow to check your house."

Finishing their coffee, he asked her to follow him back to his hotel where they could end the evening in the quiet hotel lounge and ballroom. He had her trust now and she didn't question his motive.

If the truth were known, he was enjoying his evening with this lovely young woman, and though he followed a solemn rule of no personal involvement with clients, she was refreshing and different. But, in addition to her charming company, her story was one of great interest to him; this case would be a challenge, but intriguing nonetheless.

"We've discussed every possible thing about me, how about you?" She asked. "I mean, how do you know Doctor Sullivan, if you don't mind me asking?"

With a small sigh, he looked at her and wondered just how comfortable he wanted to become. Then, deciding she was someone of integrity, he began, "My wife and I have two children, our youngest, Carson Junior, was born with a seizure disorder that started immediately after birth. The doctors in Atlanta recommend Dr. Sullivan."

"Is he all right, now?" she asked with genuine concern. "Are his seizures under control?"

"You can't tell there is anything different from him and any other three year old, except perhaps a fine scar, if you look under his hair. He hasn't had a seizure since the surgery."

She looked at him quizzically.

"Carson didn't have epilepsy. He was born with a brain tumor that caused him to go into uncontrollable seizures that would have eventually led to death. Doctor Sullivan recommended Dr. Phillips from the children's center in St. Petersburg to do the delicate procedure of removing half his brain."

Katie gasped in shock. She had heard of the procedure, but this was the first person she met whose child had been through it. Dr. Phillips was a pediatric neurosurgeon who had made a name for himself as a bright, young prodigy, pioneering new techniques and procedures in his field. She had seen him a few times at the center, evaluating someone that Dr. Sullivan recommended for surgery. He was the kind of man that turned all the ladies heads, but he shared a trait with Albert, and that made her uncomfortable: wealthy, but solitary when it came to his love life.

"Yes," Carson continued, "that was the same reaction my wife and I had when they told us the only way to save him from a short and debilitated life was the surgery. The procedure was lengthy and nerve racking, and the worst part was that we had to wait to see if the remaining half of his brain would compensate for the loss." Then he smiled a large and satisfied smile, "I'll always be grateful for Doctor Sullivan's recommendation and Dr. Phillips' skill. He comes back twice a year now for Dr. Phillips to check his skull growth and make sure the prosthetic brain insert is keeping his head properly shaped as it enlarges."

"I'm sure that was a harrowing experience, but I'm certainly glad he is seizure-free. We see so many patients at the center who live day-in and day-out with them."

Carson talked a little more about the rest of his family and his lovely wife, Tina. In some ways, Katie reminded him of his smart and energetic wife. Ending their evening together, Carson assured her that his firm would do everything they could to win this case, but it wouldn't be easy.

By three in the morning, she headed for home. To her shock, there was a listening device found in her home the next day. It was probably placed there when she'd had a problem with the cable to the television, but for now they couldn't link it to Albert.

The months that followed were stressful, but encouraging. Albert was unable to stop what she put into motion. She had been on the news, in the papers and magazines and on two carefully orchestrated talk shows. Carson kept in constant touch, informing her on each new development. The most exciting thing that Carson suspected was true, and it had nothing to do with Albert; she had offers and investors waiting to get Seasons off the ground.

She continued working at the center, glad that she could keep busy and take her mind somewhat off the events of her now public life. But sometimes the anger and frustration would flood her senses and she would take a break to cry it out and return to the computer to continue her work. Hilda talked to Katie about joining her three afternoons a week for a martial arts class. Katie laughed it off at first, but as Hilda talked more about the release and exhilaration she experienced during class, Katie decided to give it a try.

"Doctor Phillips goes there for class too, when he's not in surgery. He's a bod! Too bad he's gay though," Hilda said, tossing back her dyed black hair.

"Gay?" She said, clearly surprised.

"Well, we all figure he is. He has dated some women I know and they say he doesn't make a move. They said he acts as if he isn't interested in the opposite sex at all. He pretty much avoids women," Hilda sighed. She was a man-chaser at heart, forty years old and still single. "You gotta see him with his shirt off—ummm—too bad though, too bad." She clicked her tongue as if to say it was a shame to waste such a sexy man.

That afternoon Katie went to class for the first time. It seemed inappropriate that the instructor, Dr. Richard Redmond, was a psychologist and a fourth degree black belt.

"I thought psychologist were peace-lovers, not fighters," she mused with Dr. Redmond. He was a handsome man in his mid-forties.

"We are essentially peace-lovers, but that doesn't mean we shouldn't know how to defend ourselves, if the need arises, right?"

"True," she agreed.

The room, which was mirrored on three walls and padded on the fourth, was large and open. Children began to fill the space as the time neared for class to begin.

"I hope there are more grown-ups than just us," she whispered to Hilda.

"The kids get into it more than the adults, but there are a few of us," she replied, nodding toward the door as Doctor Gill Phillips walked in the room.

He seemed to notice Katie immediately, then after a brief moment of locking into each other's eyes, he looked away and greeted Richard.

"See what I mean," Hilda stated matter-of-factly, "He isn't interested."

The session began with a series of warm-up exercises and stretches, and then the basic kicks and punches. She felt awkward at first, but she had a certain amount of grace that covered some of the fact that she didn't understand what she was supposed to do.

Richard worked with her, teaching her the proper fighting stance and the first two basic kicks, punches, and blocks. Then, needing to work with his younger but more experienced students, he asked Doctor Phillips to help her master the rest of the basics.

"Hi," Gill smiled warmly, his amber eyes avoiding hers as he began to instruct.

Hilda had been right about one thing; he was extremely handsome. He was roughly six-foot-four with dark brown hair and a radiant white smile. His demeanor was quiet and gentle; but he didn't act gay, just shy. His voice had a sexy deep rumble to it that gave Katie a shiver.

"Here, kick me with a straight kick and I'll show you which part of your foot you should be trying to hit with."

"Kick you?" She couldn't help but smile when she looked at him.

"Kick gently, but don't worry about hitting me," he was looking into her eyes again, returning her smile.

She assumed the fighting stance and then kicked toward him. He effortlessly caught her foot before it struck him. "Here," he said, holding her heel, "use your heel, not your toes; you'll get more power."

His hand was warm. He was speaking about form and muscle, but she was having trouble paying attention as his other hand caressed the calf muscles of her leg. He was explaining something about thrusting with the hip, but using the power of the calf muscle. Quite unexpectedly she lost balance because she had been thinking about his hand on her leg instead of staying upright.

"Whoa!" he said, grabbing her before she hit the floor, "I didn't mean to make you fall."

She was close enough to smell his cologne; it was fresh, clean, and intoxicating.

"Leave you two alone for a couple minutes and you end up in each other's arms!" Richard chuckled as he walked over to them; he'd seen what happened from across the room. He knew natural attraction when he saw it and these two had it.

Suddenly they both became aware of the fact that they were still holding on to each other; quickly Gill let go of her; his face turning red from embarrassment—or perhaps something else.

By the end of the hour-long class she had the bare basics, and had to admit that it was an effective way to relieve stress. Most of the children had already left with their parents as she waited for Hilda to put her tennis shoes on—and she was putting them on very slowly.

Patience waning, she walked over and quietly asked if she was having a problem with her shoe.

"Shhh," Hilda said, "Don't be in such a hurry! There are some great sights to see if you wait a few minutes." She looked over to the kick bag where Richard and Gill were talking.

Undoing his white top, Gill slipped it off and handed it to Richard.

"Wow!" Katie said out loud without thinking. Gill, Richard and Hilda turned to look at her. "You must workout a lot!" She should have been embarrassed, but his upper body was so sculpted that she spoke before considering how it would sound.

He smiled, "I body build in my spare time—what little of it I have." He turned to face the bag and then with a second thought, turned back and said, "Thanks. It's nice to know someone likes it."

"Well, I like it, too!" Hilda interjected pathetically. "I just never opened my mouth and said anything!" They all laughed, even Hilda. They left the room as Gill and Richard worked out.

"So you think you're gonna like the class?" Hilda said, swinging her sweater over her shoulder.

"I don't think he's gay," she replied, ignoring her question. "At least I sure hope he isn't." It had been a long time since she felt the familiar sensations stirring inside her. If he wasn't gay, she intended to let him know she liked him, somehow.

"Yup, you liked the class," Hilda stated. She'd seen that expression before, she thought, as she glanced at her friend. Heck, she'd had it many times herself; it was the look of a serious infatuation blooming.

To Katie's disappointment, Gill couldn't make it to each class and many times (when he did make it) his beeper would go off and he would have to leave. She enjoyed the class anyway, but she enjoyed it so much more when he was there, and he always managed to take time to help her when Richard was busy.

Each Friday there was time set aside for sparring, and frequently Richard picked Katie as his partner. He was trying to unleash the anger he could tell was just below her calm façade, but she always exercised extreme control, kicking and punching with just enough force to make contact, yet startlingly accurate.

One particularly rough day, she finally turned her anger loose. Carson had called her that morning to tell her that the New York courts had made their ruling on Albert's custody plea. He would be given weekend visitation until the divorce was finalized. Her team made an immediate counter petition to the ruling, but it looked as if Albert might get to take Jordan to New York for visits very soon.

That afternoon as Richard held the kick bag he told her to put everything she had into it. "Think back," he said, "to a situation in which you felt helpless and turn it around so that the bag becomes the person or situation. I don't want you to simply kick the bag, but envision that you are kicking completely through it."

Assuming her fighting position, she began to pound the bag with roundhouse kicks so hard that Richard could barely stand up against her fury. Finally she let out a yell and flew into the bag with a straight kick that sent him up against the padded wall.

Realizing what she had done, she helped him up. "I'm so sorry, I didn't mean to... ."

"That's okay," he laughed, lightly pulling himself up onto his feet, "*That* is what I've been trying to get you to do all along! How do you feel?"

"Great! But I still wanna fight!"

"Slip on the sparring pads and let's do it!" He said, encouraging her. He loved a good match, and he had a sneaky suspicion that today he was going to get one.

She was still controlled and precise, but her kicks and punches were rapid and hard. He believed in equalizing to his student's level, whether it was soft or hard, so he increased the power in his strikes. To his delight she didn't back down. From that day on, she learned to turn loose more of her aggression, holding back less and less each time.

The custody issue was a battle within a battle. Though it was ruled that the father should have the right to custody every other weekend, her team won the issue of where it would take place. Albert had wanted the child flown, by his personal staff, to New York every other weekend, but now he would have to be in Florida; Jordan would not be taken out of the state.

Albert bought a secluded mansion on the west coast of Florida. He would enjoy visits with his son in privacy.

Angrily and bitterly, she thought about the privacy that his money afforded him; she had no such luxury when she and her son were together, save inside their home.

It was a delicate matter, but over several nights of careful discussion with Jordan, he became willing to spend a little time with the man referred to as his father. It was important to Katie that Jordan not hate Albert; she didn't want him hating anyone. So, in his presence, she was always careful how she referred to, and spoke about, Albert.

She had the option of letting Albert's staff pick up Jordan, but that would have been too traumatic for him. She also wanted to avoid the media circus that would thrive on covering a screaming child being forced to go to his father. She made the decision to take him there herself.

With great personal composure, she entered the lavish mansion under Albert's scrutinizing glare. Gaily she spoke of the fun he would have as she and Jordan were shown to 'his room.' Just as she feared, when the door opened Jordan squealed with delight: no expense had been spared. His room was larger than their entire little house. Putting him down she could tell that he wasn't sure which toy to run to first. His smile was infectious and even Albert was forced into a genuine one.

"I already have clothes for him," Albert said dryly, the smile fading from his face as she tried to hand him the small pooh-bear suitcase.

"You know something? I figured you would," she said, forcing the bag into his arms. "His good-night teddy and his bedtime storybook are in the bag with a couple of other things that *he* decided he wanted to bring."

With nothing else said, and Jordan happily occupied with the roomful of new and exciting toys, she left. The tears stained her face as she drove home; Jordan had forgotten to kiss her goodbye. She wondered if he would want to leave that place of store-bought happiness when the weekend was over.

Pulling into the narrow shell driveway to the little house in Terra Ceia, she slumped over the steering wheel in a mixture of anger, frustration, and hurt. Albert had won the first victory. It was small, but it was a victory nonetheless. She didn't want to get out of the car; she didn't want to spend the next days without her son. For a moment, she thought about asking Albert if he would consider taking her and her son back now, and they would end the divorce. She couldn't love him the way she once had, but she couldn't deny he was a good lover, and it had been so long since she had experienced the pleasure of sex. As quickly as the thoughts entered they were dismissed, replaced with the anger that fueled her fight.

Eyes closed and her head resting on the wheel, she jumped as someone tapped on the window of her car. Looking up she expected to see the face of her next-door neighbor, Elaine, but to her shock, and a momentary fright, it wasn't her neighbor at all—it was Donovan Randall.

He gingerly opened the car door, "Are you all right?"

She couldn't say anything; a mix of emotions was clashing inside her.

"I'm sorry, I couldn't get your phone number, but I knew you were living out here from the news. I hope you don't mind me showing up like this, but I had to see you."

"I—I thought you were in the—witness protection program?" she stammered.

"I was, but I wanted to find you. I had some changes in my life and I was tired of hiding," he sighed and stepped back to sit on her front door step. "Maybe it was a mistake coming here. I'm sorry."

"No, Donovan, it's all right. I'm glad you came. Do you want to come inside and talk?"

He smiled at her, "Yeah, I'd really like that."

They talked until well past dark. She made supper for the two of them. He told her that his mother died about six months ago and left him a two hundred and fifty thousand dollar insurance policy that he didn't even know she had. He had heard about her problems with Trathmoore on the news, and watched had her on a talk show. It was then he decided to do two things: open his own car dealership and find her. The only problem was that the life of someone in the witness protection program was supposed to be low key and obscure. If he wanted to pursue those two things, they said he would have to leave the program.

"I decided it was time, so I did it." Then pausing to look around at some of the scattered toys that hadn't been picked up yet, he cautiously asked, "Where's your son, if you don't mind me asking?"

She started to tell him, but then the emotions of the day and the months of battling Albert started flowing out. Her heart was like a broken dam that could no longer retain the flood of pain-filled thoughts. He moved close to comfort her. She jumped at his touch, but then relaxed against a strong male shoulder. She was crying, but as the tears gushed out from the bitter torrent of defeat, she could hear him saying, over and over again, "I'm sorry…I'm so, so sorry…I know you'll never be able to forgive me…I'm sorry… ."

"That's not true," she said, pulling back to look into his dark brown eyes, "I forgave you a long time ago."

He smiled, reaching to stroke her hair, but she pull back slightly from his caress. "See," he said, his hand in mid-air where he had reached for her, "You're still afraid of me."

It was then that she was aware of how she was responding to him. "No, it's not that. I'm not used to any man touching me—not for years now. I know you, but yet I don't. Do you understand?"

"Tell me something, and you're going to have to forgive me for asking you this, but I have to know: is your son—is he Albert's—for certain?" He knew there was a chance that she could have had his child instead.

She nodded her head, "Yes, he is, for certain."

His whole being slumped; he had hoped against hope that it wasn't Albert's child. Ever since he helped her escape, ever since she had put her marriage on the line to keep him out of jail, ever since the last time he had seen her, he knew one thing with all of his heart: he had fallen in love with her.

"I wondered too, at first, but when he was born I knew without doubt. He's Albert's." For the first time she made a move to reach out and touch him, "I would have loved him just the same if he had been your son."

"I wouldn't expect anything less from a woman like you." Then sighing deeply he got up and said, "I hope we can see each other. I know it's hard with everything going on right now, but I'd really love to see you." Before she could answer, he added, "I own a dealership in Tampa; I'd like to show you around there sometime."

"I'd like that," she said, walking with him to the door.

"How about next Saturday? You and your son could come and then maybe we could go to the zoo for the afternoon."

She studied him for a moment. This was not the male involvement in her life she was expecting, but Gill hadn't even offered so much as a lunch date. Donovan was only two years younger than she was, handsome and rugged with his almost black hair, dark eyes and olive skin. She remembered the kiss as they left the cabin, how gentle and sorrow-filled it was. Her body ached for a man who would be gentle and loving, and in that thought she didn't want him to leave, but it would be wrong to ask him to stay.

"I think that sounds great. Jordan loves the zoo." Then surprising them both, she hugged him and thanked him for coming to see her. She held the embrace a moment longer than she should and he responded to the invitation to be in her arms. Turning her face up to his, his mouth found hers for a passionate, warm and long kiss. She didn't want him to stop, but with her knees beginning to get weak she knew they must.

"I've missed you so badly," he whispered, his breath hot and shallow against her hair. "I always wondered what would happen if I had the chance to be near you again—if you would let me touch you."

Then putting his mouth over hers again, he searched out the passion that was smoldering inside her.

The kiss was a moment of perfection. She wanted him, yet she knew the timing was wrong, "It's too soon for this," she said as they broke the kiss, "I think we should go slowly. I've got to think this through."

"I can wait. I've waited this long to find you. I can wait until you're ready—whenever that is."

He opened the door and walked out to his truck parked in the edge of her yard, waved goodbye and was gone.

She closed the door and crumpled onto the living room floor. "What am I doing?" she cried out to the four walls. This couldn't possibly help her in her pursuit to keep her son. In fact, she knew if the press got wind of this it would be plastered on every newspaper from Florida to California: "Estranged Wife Has Affair With Captor/Hero Before Finalizing Divorce." But she couldn't deny the fact that she wanted him to stay. She was only a breath away from telling him she wanted him to be with her tonight. If she hadn't gathered her thoughts she would have and, at this moment, they would have been entangled in each other's arms on her bed.

Tired and frustrated, her heart broken over leaving her son with Albert and her body aching for the touch of a man she only barely knew, she climbed between the sheets and closed her eyes to this emotional day.

The weekend ended and Sunday night a chauffeured limousine with a very blonde, very young and bouncy nanny returned her son. What made it even worse was the fact that Jordan liked her, the house, and the man he was comfortably referring to now as Daddy. But he was glad to be home. They played their favorite games like ring-around-the-rosies and hide-and-go-seek. He was still her little hero when they played hide-and-go-seek. He had always been afraid of the dark, but one evening months earlier, she had hidden in the bedroom and hadn't turned on the light. Jordan wouldn't go back there in the dark, but when she stubbed her foot on the bed roller and cried out in pain, he yelled, "I'm coming Mommy!" and charged through the darkness to find her. They laughed about it and wrestled around on the floor. He was brave when he thought his mother needed him; darkness or not he would come to her. He proudly told her he was her hero and he would fight any monster to save her.

Now as they played hide-and-go-seek, she thought of that brave little boy and wondered if he knew just how much she loved him. He would always be her hero; Albert or not.

The following Saturday they went with Donovan to the car dealership. She was impressed with the business; he was apparently very successful. He wore a coat and tie, and looked like any other dedicated businessman she'd ever seen. One would never suspect he had come through the kind of life he had and made something so outstanding of himself. He showed her around, talking with his sales associates as he and Katie looked around the glass-encased show room.

Later they went to the zoo and Jordan loved it, wanting to see each animal and have someone read the information on each plaque. Donovan was happy to lift him up onto his shoulders for a better view and tell him about seeing the Bronx Zoo in New York when he was a little boy. He was excellent with Jordan, even when it was the end of the day and Jordan started to get cranky from missing his noon nap.

With the evening ended, Katie and Jordan returned home, tired but happy. She was even more impressed with Donovan than she had ever been. A relationship with him would not be out of the question, but it would have to be friends first and eventually evolve into something more meaningful later.

It didn't take too many weekend adventures with Mommy's friend along for word to spread to Albert about the re-appearance of Donovan in her life. In fact, on the weekend that Jordan happened to mention the fun he, Mommy, and Donovan had on a fishing trip, Albert brought Jordan home, instead of the nanny that he had hired for the express purpose of angering Katie.

She was surprised when Albert stepped out of the back of the limousine, and from the steely look he gave her, she figured Jordan had mentioned Donovan's name.

"Why don't you run inside son and put up your bag and change your clothes while I talk to Mommy, okay?"

Jordan smiled a big grin and proudly told her, "I rode a pony!"

"You did, Sweetheart? Did you like it?" She completely ignored Albert, but focused on the shining little face of her son.

"Yup! Daddy's gonna buy me a pony too!" he beamed.

"You silly!" She laughed, tickling Jordan's belly, "Where are we going to keep a pony, in the back yard?"

"No, Daddy says we keep it in York, when I go live with him."

She smiled at Jordan and kissed his head, "You go inside and we'll talk about that tonight, okay?"

"Okay," he said, turning and running to the house.

She watched him disappear behind the front door and then turned and glared at Albert, but he wasn't paying her stare any attention, and before she could even speak about the pony issue he grabbed her arm forcefully and asked her what the hell she was doing.

"What do mean. Let go of me!" she struggled against his hard grip. "You're hurting my arm."

"Don't you ever bring that son-of-a-bitch around my son! If you're going to whore around you better make sure you do it on your weekends off!" He practically spit the words in her face.

Pulling her thoughts together under his painful hold, she came up with a hard upward block with her forearm and broke free from him. He was surprised at the forceful move she made against him and he almost expected her to strike him with her free hand, but she didn't. He wished she had, because then he would have added it to his lawsuit, but as it was she was the only one with a mark.

Rubbing her arm she looked at the bright red impression of his fingers on her skin, "Don't ever touch me again. I've tried my best to keep civil with you where my son is concerned, but not if you... ."

"How long have you been seeing him?" His voice revealing the seething anger and jealousy inside him. "Are you sleeping with him *again*? This time I won't believe it's rape."

"You have no right to accuse me of anything! Donovan is kind and gentle—and he's great with Jordan."

Albert's fist slammed against the side of the car, denting the door and causing his driver to jump with fright. "I don't want him around Jordan!"

Sizing up his intention, she coolly replied, "But you don't care if he's around me?"

"I'm never going to take you back if you've been sleeping with him. I'll simply take Jordan away from you for good. You'll never see Jordan again, Katie, unless you stop it right now."

Leaning her back against the car and looking into the evening sky, she brushed away a tear that struggled free from her determined resolve. With her lips quivering at the tips, she hoarsely replied, "I could never go back with you because I know now the kind of man you are." Then facing him she said with rising emotion, "I just can't believe how much I used to love you. I guess you'll just have to try and take him." She walked away without a backward glance, and left him standing in the drive. He wasn't running her life; no matter how much he tried. She wouldn't permit it.

~:~

Over the next few months her investor list grew and she began to search for the ideal location to build her dream. She was working with a good commercial realtor who contacted her everyday about another possible site. By Christmas, she got a call from a woman named Theresa Ponder, who worked for a large mall management company, with a very intriguing offer for her.

One of the largest malls in Tampa was undergoing a big renovation project that could be tailored to include the first ever Seasons. The offer was for the mall to split the cost with her fifty-fifty in order to get the project and would include a $50,000 advertising bonus to help her launch it. If the project didn't meet projections, she would repay the mall for their investment over a ten-year period.

If the Seasons concept did go the way that it was projected, they would offer her similar deals in malls in Miami, Orlando and Atlanta, to get her started. Other deals in major U.S. cities would follow within five years, or sooner if the business exceeded expectations.

"If this is something you would like to consider, we'll have the contracts drawn up and you can have your legal staff look them over," Ms. Ponder said, her voice quiet and reserved.

Katie felt her insides begin to quiver. This was the ideal set-up to get her started, but it could leave her owing millions dollars. It was a matter of asking herself if this had just been a dream she was chasing or did she seriously believe it could become a reality? She had seventeen investors ready to place $100,000 each into what she had proposed.

"Ms. Danor?" Ms. Ponder replied, wondering about the silence.

"Yes, please by all means, draw up the documents. I'd want to setup a time for us to meet so I can see the building. I'll pick up the contract at that time and have my legal staff make sure everything is in order." She knew her only 'legal staff' was her divorce team, but there was no need to inform Ms. Ponder of that tidbit of information.

"Wonderful Ms. Danor! We'll have them prepared and expect you the week after New Years. I'll call you a few days before and let you know the exact date and time."

The excitement was overwhelming, but she had to gather her thoughts as she got out her list of investors. She would waste no time; she would begin contacting them right away and let them know the project was to be set in motion within a few weeks. The investments would be collected and placed in an account that she would have under her control. The investors would then make up her primary board of directors to help with major project decisions.

The day before Christmas, all the investors had been contacted and $1,700,000 had been deposited into the account. Seasons would be more than a dream at last.

Donovan helped her pick up Jordan's 'big' Christmas present at the lumber yard; it was a play structure with a sandbox, slide, tire swing, regular swing and a canvas-covered fort above the sandbox in which to survey his surroundings for pirates and monsters and such. She was sure it would pale in comparison to the gifts Albert would bestow upon him, but it was the best she could afford and it was a gift from the heart, not the wallet.

Jordan stayed at Granny's while they assembled it. Katie thought it would come pre-cut and drilled, but to her shock, it did not. Donovan brought his power tools and together they labored in the mild December weather. They laughed and talked as they worked on the structure; Katie musing that it was so involved she'd have construction experience for the building of her store by the time they finished it.

By late afternoon, the project was near completion. Donovan was hauling the fifty pound bags of sand into the back yard to fill the sandbox base while Katie tried to drill the two-inch holes in the two-by-four ladder legs for the thick wooden dowels that served as rungs. Every time she pushed the drill through the other side of the wood it would wrench the drill from her grip and swing it around and crack her knuckles.

But she was determined to make the ladder without asking for help.

He was pouring in the last bag of sand when he heard her yelp in pain. "You okay? Let me see your hand." Taking her hand he looked at the battered and bloodied knuckles, "Katie, why didn't you tell me you were having a problem with the drill?"

"I'm fine. I wasn't going to wimp out and ask you to get beaten up by the drill, too."

"Did it ever occur to you that I might be able to hold onto it without getting it jerked out of my hand?"

"I don't think so," she started to say, as he took the drill and started the last hole.

And, just as she had said, when the bit popped out the other side of the two-by-four the drill jerked itself out of his hand, swung around and cracked him in the knuckles before he could pull his hand out of the way.

"Ouch!" he yelled out. "Well I'll be damned! You were right." Then looking at the pieces on the ground for the second ladder, he said, "I'll do the next one."

"No, never mind." She picked up the dowels and headed for the back door, "It only needs one ladder and I need some sturdy props for the windows in my bedroom." Stepping in the room, she slid up the double-hung window and propped the dowel against the frame. "There, just right." She did the same with the other two windows and was left with one extra dowel.

"What are you gonna do with that one?"

"Hmm—I don't have any other windows that need a prop. Security I guess," she said, thumping the solid dowel against the palm of her hand. She looked at him with a sly grin and then put the dowel under the edge of her bed. "Mama always said to carry a big stick."

"Wow, remind me to behave!" He joked, retreating quickly from the bedroom.

She called Granny only to find that Jordan had fought his nap earlier, but had fallen asleep on her couch watching a movie.

"Let him rest about an hour, Honey. Then you can come get him."

She didn't argue; she was tired from putting together the gift and besides that she was hoping it would be dark enough when she picked him up that he wouldn't see it before tomorrow.

Donovan picked up his tools and the scrap materials and then came inside to relax before the long drive to Tampa. It was the wrong time of the year for commuting because of the holiday traffic. They sat on the couch together, Katie talking about the plans for Seasons and about the fact that, if the building looked good and the contracts were acceptable, she would be quitting her job at the center within two weeks.

"I don't really want to quit, but I'm not going to be able to do them a decent day's work with all the things I've got to get done."

"Are you going to use the investment money to pay your living expenses?"

"I don't see how I can." She looked worried though she would have denied it if he asked. "I've got a little more than $3,000 saved; this fight with Albert has tied up the other money I put away."

"Did you ever consider letting someone else pay the bills?" he said without much ado.

"Who? My investors? I don't think they would appreciate the fact that I can't support myself."

"No, me. I could support you while you work on the project." He turned to face her, his dark hair glistening wet from rinsing his face. He was just a little bit sunburned, but the red tone looked good on his skin.

"I wish you could, but, Donovan, if you live here or if I live with you, it's going to hurt my chances to keep Jordan. Albert will make sure it comes up at the trial and I'll look... ." she wasn't sure how to say it delicately.

"I know the kind of woman you are, and so do you. He can't change that."

"Maybe not, but a judge won't see it that way. I'm not completely certain he won't find a way to buy his victory."

"I don't want to live here, but I do want to help you reach your dreams. I've put everything I have into the dealership, but it's starting to make a good profit now. I could give you... ."

"No, Donovan. I'm not going to take your money. You've worked hard for what you have. I will make it through this on my own. I'll find a way."

"I love you and Jordan, and I want to help." He hadn't told her before that he cared for her so deeply, but he felt she probably knew by now. "I guess I'd better head home. If everything is still on for New Year's Eve, then I'll see you next week, okay?"

Tender feelings were welling up inside her for this patient, caring man; feelings she hadn't felt in a long time.

Without saying anything, she leaned against him and kissed him. This was not the kind of kiss he expected and for a moment, he was surprised at the warmth and passion in it.

Wrapping his arms around her, he held her close, feeling the rhythm of her heart pound against his chest.

"I want New Year's Eve to be special for us," she said, looking into his eyes and telling him with her heart what she meant.

His eyebrows went up a little, "Are you sure you're ready to take that step?" He cared so much for her, but he wouldn't want her to do something she would regret. And if Albert found out, she would regret it.

"Yes—I am. I can't lie and say I'm not scared, but I do want to."

He kissed her long and intensely, wanting to be with her more than he ever wanted anything in his life. "It's going to be a long week," he whispered as he rested his forehead against hers.

~:~

After opening Christmas presents the next morning and letting Jordan enjoy his new play structure for an hour or two, they packed up the car and headed to Vero Beach to have Christmas with her parents. It seemed like such a long drive now, but it was always good to be with them.

Her father's cancer was finally in remission and he was able to lead a life free from the sickening treatments that at times seemed worse than the illness. He had lost all his hair, including his eyebrows and eyelashes, creating a different look about him.

Katie had teased him when it was discovered that the hair wasn't growing back, that if he had an earring he'd look like Mr. Clean. He was good-natured about the teasing and said that he rather liked the fact that he didn't have to get a hair cut anymore.

Jordan loved his grandparents dearly. He was the bright spot in their lives and they all wondered and worried about the fate of his custody with the impending divorce. Lawrence said he understood Albert's desire to help raise his son, but he couldn't understand his fixation in having total custody. Katie was doing a wonderful job in raising a caring, loving and stable child; it didn't make sense to try to exclude her from his life.

Christmas dinner was delicious with Beth's careful touch to the meal. She did allow Katie to help cook simply because, since Lawrence's cancer, she said she had learned that the meal was second to the time she could spend with the people she loved. After eating dinner and sharing a few more gifts, they spent the last of the evening swimming in the pool. Katie and Jordan, comfortable and tired after such a wonderful Christmas, made their bed on the sofa pullout.

The condo was still and dark except for the nightlight burning in the bathroom. Jordan cuddled next to his mother's chest, "I love you mommy," he whispered in his angelic voice.

She stroked his golden hair, cradling his small face with her hand, "Mommy loves you, too. You're my little man, you know that?"

He nodded with his blue eyes, big and round.

"Remember that: Mommy will always love you, no matter what." Her throat began to tighten as she thought that she might not win her fight to keep him. And it was so important to believe that he would not forget her, no matter how young he was, if and when that time ever came.

"I always love you," he replied with his most serious face. "I'm your hero!" he shout-whispered.

She hugged him tight, not wanting him to see the tears that had begun to form in her eyes, "Sleep-tight my little hero." Then kissing the top of his head she whispered, "Goodnight."

She didn't have to work the week between Christmas and New Years, so she had extra time to play with and enjoy her son. New Year's weekend was Albert's turn to have Jordan, and she was dreading taking him there as the time grew closer. His ugly stares and quip remarks cut her to the bone. He was starting to get very smug and confident about the way the divorce would end, and she could tell it delighted him in a sadistic way.

After dropping Jordan off, she headed home to dress for her evening at the Gulf Nights beach restaurant. She and Donovan had reservations for a New Year's celebration complete with dinner, champagne and dancing on the gulf front deck. The Gulf Nights was a small and intimate location where the guest list was limited to fifty people for the celebration, so she felt relatively comfortable that they could remain anonymous.

She was excited, nervous, and just a little scared about the commitment she had made to him to make this the night that they would explore the bonds between a man and a woman. She thought about the future and the changes that would occur because of tonight. She had been certain it was the right choice when she was presented with the same situation with her first two lovers, but for once she was thinking with her physical being instead of her head, and she could only hope she was making the right decision. Albert was gaining so much ground in the divorce that she felt hurt and abused. She needed the soft caress of a man who wouldn't hurt her, only love her.

Donovan pulled up in the yard with a Lexus from his dealership. His pick-up truck, though new and quite stylish for a truck, was still a truck. He looked handsome and confident in his traditional tux. She wore a deep coral mid-thigh dress that was covered with luminescent sequins that shimmered as the moonlight reflected against it. Sliding onto the leather seat, she soaked up the aroma of the car mingled with his cologne. They smiled at each other as they pulled out of the drive.

They ate a light dinner and then joined the other couples out on the deck to dance to the live band in the cool night breeze. The Gulf was softly lapping at the shoreline as they enjoyed the comfort of being in each other's arms.

"I have a surprise for you," he whispered in her ear.

She could feel his smile as his cheek was pressed to hers. Her heart began to speed up as she thought about what he might say.

"Let's get out of here."

"But it's only ten o'clock. Don't you want to stay until midnight? We'll miss the fireworks." She had been looking forward to the night display, and she knew the reservations were $150 each and they had only been there a little more than an hour.

"No, let's get out of here and go some place private."

Things were moving quicker than she had planned and she wondered if he was rushing to get her to bed. She nodded silently and they slipped through the restaurant and out to the parking lot.

"You're quiet tonight," he said as he pulled the car out onto the road. "Are you having second thoughts about us?"

"And if I was?" she said, testing him.

"I'd take you home and kiss you goodnight, and that would be the end of our evening." Then with great reserve he asked, "Do you want to go home?"

She was quiet; the car was heading the wrong direction for home. Would he turn it around if she asked? "No," she finally said. "I want to go wherever you're taking me."

He pulled the car into a secluded condominium complex and parked in the covered lot.

"Come on, I've got a surprise waiting."

He unlocked the door to a spacious unit on the second floor. There was an ice bucket with a bottle of champagne resting in it and two glasses on a table near the sliding doors. He slid back the doors and the salted breeze flooded the room.

"We can dance on the balcony, it's beautiful out here." Then stepping back inside he turned on the stereo system and the song 'Penny Lover' filled the room. She loved that song.

"Would you care to dance?" he said, gallantly stepping back out onto the balcony and motioning her to join him.

Her tension eased and she slipped into his waiting embrace.

"I know all the trouble you'd have if we stayed out in public too long and probably the same trouble if we went to either of our homes, so I rented this from one of my salesman at the dealership. I told him I had relatives coming in from New York this week."

Each time a new song would begin playing on the stereo she would give a little sigh because it was another of her favorites.

His arms were strong and warm as he held her and they danced slowly about the balcony.

"Do you like it?" he asked.

"All of it," she replied. "But every song is one that I really like. How did you do that?"

"Every time we went somewhere or did something together, you'd remark about the songs you liked. When I'd get home, I'd write them down. A friend of mine said he could make CD's, so I had him make up a couple. That's part of your surprise tonight."

She looked at him in amazement, "I can't believe you did that for me."

He kissed her softly and whispered, "I'd do anything for you."

It was nearly midnight, and it seemed they had only just begun to enjoy each other's company. Bringing out the champagne and glasses to the patio table, he pulled two chairs away from the table and beckoned her to sit down.

She thought they wouldn't be able to see the fireworks display, but to her delight it began at the stroke of midnight and was well within their view. She had loved fireworks since she was a little girl and her parents had taken her to the city display on the Fourth of July.

"What a perfect way to end the year," she said as the last colored burst faded from the night sky.

Leaning closer to her, he said, "I know a wonderful way to start the New Year."

His eyes were penetrating and he wouldn't break off the stare he held her in. Her heart raced wildly even though she tried to tell herself it was time to make a change in their relationship.

He took her arm and walked with her back inside, shutting and locking the balcony doors.

Instantly he was at her side, his passion no longer was restrained. She was frightened at the depth of his desire.

"Please, don't be scared," he said, holding her body tightly to his own.

"Why?" she whispered, "Why am I afraid?"

"We both know why," he answered, "but tonight I want to change that memory forever. When you think of me I want you to remember tonight, the music, the passion, and the love I feel for you." Then in the moonlit room, staring into each other's face, he said, "I want to erase New York tonight."

His lips trailed down her neck, sending shivers and sensations rushing through her as her dress slipped to the floor. Laying her back on the bed he began to gently caress and kiss her, all of her, everywhere from her hands to her ankles. He kissed her as if she was the most treasured thing he had ever found. Softly and lightly his fingers traced her body. She had never felt so adored in her entire life. She began calling out to him, but he said no, not until her old memories of him were destroyed. Her inhibitions melted and she began to undo the buttons to his tuxedo, her hands finding the man within it. He moaned in pleasure from her touch. She wanted him, at last.

They were searching hungrily for each other's kiss, wanting, needing, and begging for the other. But then he was moving away from her, leaving her on the bed alone.

"Donovan? What's wrong?"

She heard him at the table beside the bed, fumbling with something. "We have to stop for a minute because, as much as I want to at this moment, you can't get pregnant. You'll lose Jordan for good if that happens."

She understood what he was searching for and his concern for her and her son filled her with a sense of heighten desire to accept him as her lover, sealing something in her mind she had known for awhile.

Coming back to her in bed, he whispered, "I love you, Katie," and gathered her body against his.

She pulled him in closer, basking in the warmth of his nearness. "I've wondered what I would tell you when it came to this moment. I wasn't sure until now, but I know—I love you, Donovan."

She felt his tears fall softly against her breast, "I'm ready, Donovan. I want you."

Pressing his body into the private reaches of hers, they each cried out at the pleasure of togetherness. They moved in rhythm with something that didn't seem to be either's choosing; they found their combined rhythm. The night would be long, and the love would be good. Daylight would come too soon and end what they had discovered in the darkness of the New Year.

~:~

Four days after the start of the New Year, she was standing in the enormous emptiness of what once was a stylish Joel Brother's department store. It was certainly larger than she needed and looking at the amount of square footage from the shell construction drawings, she wondered how she would ever fill the space. The first floor was more than ample, but the second floor was overkill.

Theresa Ponder was there to show her around and answer questions, along with Ms. Ponder's boss, John Borderoux, and Red Balsinger, the head of Balsinger Construction who was working as the contractor for the mall. Katie asked Carson if he would be willing to help her and, even though it was not his chosen legal line, he accepted. Also, June Pritchard, her commercial realtor, came along to offer any assistance she could. This wasn't a contact she had made for Katie, but it certainly couldn't hurt her status in the real estate community to appear to have had a hand in the deal.

"Don't be concerned about the second story," Ms. Ponder was pointing out. "The mall has needed to relocate its office space for sometime and we have plans to use this upper story."

"Yes," Mr. Borderoux added, "our ground floor offices are going to be converted into retail space as soon as this upper floor is completed."

Katie couldn't look to Carson or June for advice at this point. It was her dream and determination that would have to fill this place. She would have to draw on the diamond-hard substance deep inside her to forge ahead. Calmly and naturally, she assumed the lead, just as if she had been making decisions about construction, remodeling, and high-stake financial deals for lunch everyday.

She asked for a set of shell plans on which she could outline what her store would look like inside so Red could tell her if her design was feasible and within the project cost. She talked with Mr. Borderoux about the financial arrangement, and about the offer for similar deals at other major metropolitan malls being part of the contract, not just the verbal offer that had been expressed to her by Ms. Ponder. In the end, Carson was given the contracts to review, but for all intensive purposes, the deal had been struck.

If she signed and returned the contracts, the remodeling would begin within the next two weeks and completion was projected for mid- to late summer. In the interim, she would be checking on the progress of the remodeling, firming up suppliers for her clothing and make-up lines, hiring stylists for the salons and employees for the store, and ordering her needed computer and scanner equipment. It was a lot to do and would take careful planning; it would also take all of the time she would have normally spent working at the center. Within a week she would be working for herself, but with no regular paycheck coming in.

Briefly, she felt a spark of admiration for the work Albert had to have put into ATI to get his dream off the ground. The only trouble was that he never stopped that beginning drive; he never seemed to reach a point of leveling out; he just continued pushing and fighting as if each day was the beginning of his company. He had an insatiable desire to win—at any cost. And with that thought, all of her anger and hurt concerning him returned like a dark cloud over an otherwise exciting and fulfilling day.

After leaving the mall, she and Carson stopped by Donovan's dealership to let her tell him how the meeting had gone, and to introduce Carson to him.

Carson could see the happiness light-up in both their faces when they saw each other, and even though he liked Donovan, he couldn't help thinking that being around him was a bad decision before her official divorce was finalized. Help in her divorce was tough to find and, unfortunately, hindrances were plentiful. Donovan was a crucial hindrance. He could only hope that she was being discreet about any relationship she might have with Mr. Randall.

Friday evening, Katie and Jordan went to Donovan's house in Tampa for a special congratulatory dinner that he had prepared for beginning her store. He had a terrific Spanish style house in the historical district of Tampa. Its warm stucco exterior with black wrought-iron gates and dome-shaped windows gave it the traditional Spanish appeal. He had landscaped the yard himself, using a variety of cacti and native plants as well as rock-lined paths and boulder accents.

They could do no more than smile at each other; physical affection, even a light greeting kiss on the cheek, was out of the question in front of Jordan. They didn't want to give him anything to say innocently to Albert that would fuel his fight even worse than it was. Not that Jordan would have noticed a quick kiss; he was intensely interested in Donovan's housecat, Boots. He spent most of his time chasing, catching, petting and releasing him, only to do it all over again when the cat would saunter away.

"I love this!" Katie exclaimed as she came into the gourmet kitchen. A wrought-iron pot rack was suspended from the bare-wood rafters over a big center island with an old, but very functional and beautiful, gas stove. "This looks as if it came out of the house of a rich family," she said as she watched him skillfully flip the sizzling pan of garlic and herb shrimp and scallops and place it back over the deep blue flame.

"It did," he answered. "This house was built in the 1950's for a Cuban dignitary who ran a local cigar factory. It was high-stylin' back then," he said, giving her a wink.

"How did you manage to afford it?" she asked, a little too bluntly.

He smiled at her question. "It was a wreck when I bought it. I picked it up for $60,000 with only five percent down because I said I'd renovate it according to the historical guidelines, and they were a bear!"

"You sure did a great job. You know, if you ever want to leave the car business for remodeling, I think I know some place you could find work."

He was enjoying her teasing, "I might just do that; you can never tell with a guy like me."

Dinner was delicious, even Jordan asked for seconds, which was a true compliment because he ate like a little bird when it wasn't his mother's cooking. After dinner they watched an animated movie on the television and then said goodnight. All in all, the night seemed to end too soon.

On the way home, she was pleased as Jordan remarked, "I liked Boots, Mama! And Donovan, he's funny and he makes good food, too."

By Monday evening she had signed and returned the contracts and had a farewell send-off at the center. To her surprise even Doctor Phillips came by, not only to wish her well, but also to ask her a question.

"I was wondering if you needed any more investors? I knew you were planning a store, but I had no idea it was so imminent."

"Of course," she replied, "any new venture needs working capitol. If you give me the names of the investors, I'll be happy to explain the plans to them."

"Well, actually, just one investor—me. I'm a brain surgeon, but for all the accolades given to that title, I don't know a lot about business. Could we get together later today and you could explain it to me?"

Instinctively her pulse sped up, months ago she would have jumped at the opportunity to be alone with him, but now? She simply reminded herself that even though he was drop-dead gorgeous, very sweet, considerate and somewhat timid, this was business and that was all it was.

"Sure. I can run the program on the center's computer to give you the general idea of how it works, what the intriguing points are, and how much the other investors have given to the project."

He looked somewhat disappointed in her business-like manner, but still he smiled and said he'd love to if they could get together later that evening. "You could come over to my house, if you don't mind; I should be there by eight." He was flashing his buoyant smile, causing her to momentarily forget what she was going to say.

He took her hesitation in answering to mean that she was uncomfortable coming to his house, "I'm sorry. I hope that didn't sound forward. I suppose we could get together somewhere neutral another time."

"No, your house at eight is fine. I was just thinking I wouldn't be able to run the program for you without the right computer equipment, but I could explain how it works and the concept of the store, if that's all right with you?"

His amber eyes brightened, "Sure, that sounds terrific. I live out on Terra Ceia Island and... ."

"I live on Terra Ceia, too!" she interrupted, "I can't believe that. It's such a small community; I'm surprised we haven't run into each other."

"I live all the way out on the northern tip by Tillet's Bayou. I've lived there for three years, but my schedule hasn't permitted me to become social with the neighbors."

"I live in the old section near the Indian mounds. It's a great little community."

He explained how to get to his house and then left to go back to the hospital.

She was excited about explaining her concept to another possible investor, but she was apprehensive as well. Donovan was supposed to come by to take her to lunch and she knew she'd tell him about her appointment to meet with Gill. The meeting was a little unusual, late evening at a man's home, just the two of them. She didn't think he was a jealous person, but she never really thought Albert was either.

But Donovan was not a jealous man. He listened to her and then asked, "Do you think he's seriously planning to invest?"

"Yes, of course. I don't think he would have asked me over if he wasn't."

"Well, you are a beautiful woman, and I can tell you seem to like this man because you're so nervous about telling me."

She was ready to protest, but it was true. At one time she had a little schoolgirl type crush on him, but this *was* business!

He laughed at her flustered look.

"It's okay," he said, taking hold of her hand. "I don't have any rights of ownership to you as your former husband seems to think he does. I love you and I want you to be happy. I know you can use more investors."

"I did like him," she confessed. "But that was before you came back into my life. You're the only love in my life now, and this meeting is strictly business. I just didn't know if you'd be upset with me."

"Never," he answered. "I do want to be the only man in your life, but if things ever change between us and you feel someone else will make you happier, well, I just want you to know that your happiness is what's important to me." Then laughing at the thought of giving her a rough time, he added, "You might find my truck parked on top the skyway, but hey... ." He easily dodged her as she tried to reach across the table and slap his shoulder.

"Jerk!" she jokingly replied. It was good to be able to laugh again. She looked at him and thought how lucky she was to be in love with him. His sexy, classic Italian looks and the deep, golden Florida tan made him a handsome man, but it was the guy on the inside that was special.

Granny came over that evening to stay with Jordan until Katie got back. She wasn't sure how long she would be there, but she was certain it would be past his bedtime.

The drive only took about five minutes and she was in parked in front of Gill's elegant, three-story home. Before she could gathered all of the items that she brought to show him, he came outside and opened the car door for her.

"Can I carry something for you?"

"Oh, no thank you, I've got it. Wow, you've got a great looking house. I'd always thought this end of the island was just mangroves and mosquitoes."

He laughed, slapping at one as it tried to land on him, "It is, but I don't spend much time outside with them. I think the real killer is when we get a bad swarm of sand gnats in the summertime. They're meaner than the mosquitoes!"

She agreed. They were worse, especially since they usually came in invisible hoards and they were so tiny that they could get through a window screen.

"I'm originally from the other coast," she told him as they climbed the wide stairs to the front door. "I don't ever remember them getting as bad as they do here."

"I'm originally from N' Orleans," he said with a put-on Cajun accent. "And da get baaad down der in dem bayous!"

She laughed at his attempt; he wasn't very good. "You must not have lived there very long with that accent."

He opened the door and they went into the marble tiled foyer. The foyer went all the way up to the ceiling in the top floor with a glittering chandelier suspended above them. She looked all around her and it was opulent and tasteful—reminding her of someone else she knew.

She followed him to the living room. The fireplace was burning brightly, soft instrumental music was playing in the background and the lights were on in the pool area.

"Your home really is lovely."

"Thank you. I hope, for once, I'll get to spend a little more time in it to enjoy it."

"What do you mean?" she said, as she lowered herself to the soft leather couch.

"Ever since I came to the children's hospital as an intern, I've practically lived there. I moved up to head of neurology two years ago and that accelerated the time I spend there even more so. But Dr. Wilhelm from Washington recently relocated and is working at the hospital. He's the man I idolized as a young medical student. I can't believe that he came here because he wanted to study *my* work."

"I can," she said frankly. "Everyone I've talked to that knows anything about you says you're the best in the country."

He sank back against the couch cushion. "Thank you, again," he said with a shy smile. "We have a great surgical team, but I'm always getting called in for consultations, besides my own patients. He's taking some of the workload off of me, so I can relax a little. I'm starting to get burned out and I'm only thirty years old!"

"You must have been a child prodigy," she said, half-teasing, half-serious.

"I've forgotten my manners!" he said, hopping up to his feet. "I didn't offer you something to drink. Would you like some tea or lemonade, or perhaps a glass of wine? I'm not a consumer of the harder stuff, so I'm afraid wine is as strong as it gets around here."

"Me either," she replied. "But a glass of wine sounds good tonight. I'm so keyed up with everything going on I could use something to unwind me a little."

He got a bottle of white wine and two glasses and came back to the sofa.

"So, were you?" she said, re-asking her last question.

He uncorked the wine and poured it into the sparkling crystal stemware.

"Yes, I guess you could say that. My mother and father are both doctors and, even though they married young, they didn't want to have children; they felt there were enough in the world without parents. When they were still in their early twenties they adopted two, a boy and a girl and raised them. When Mom was forty-two she got a big surprise, she was pregnant with me."

"Boy, forty-two?" Katie said, shaking her head. "I have a little boy almost three and I have a hard time keeping up with him at thirty-two!"

"They treated me like an adult from a very young age, giving me a lot of responsibility and expecting great things from me in return. I graduated high school at fifteen because I studied so hard that I was able to skip ninth and tenth grade." He paused, sipping his wine and reflecting, "I wanted to be a doctor just like them, but when my adopted brother was in a car accident and died from brain swelling, I decided to go into neurology, pediatric neurology because I love kids. And here I am today."

"Are your parents still living?" she asked.

"Yes, they're in their seventies and still practicing medicine. They run a little hometown clinic just outside of Jackson,

Mississippi and most of what they do is free, although," he chuckled, "Mom says she still doesn't mind being paid in chickens or fresh vegetables."

"They sound like wonderful people."

"I've always thought so," he answered. "And not just because they're my parents, but because they have a set of values that you just don't find much these days."

"Is that why you're always so polite?" she said. Her keen insight was painting a different picture of Gill Phillips. Instead of the mild mannerisms that Hilda and others had taken as being an indication of being gay, she was seeing a man who was raised in the school of old-fashioned politeness and unobtrusiveness.

He blushed unknowingly as she had pinned him down on the root of his shy nature. "I guess so."

They spent the next hour going over the concept behind Seasons and how it was all coming together. He was noticeably impressed with her business skills and her vision for the future. Then, in an uncomfortable turn in the conversation, he began to ask about her, personally.

He had moved close to her on the sofa when she had shown him her plans, and now she could feel the warmth coming from his nearness. She didn't want to discuss her pain-filled past, but he was intensely curious about her. She was reluctant at first to dredge up old memories that were best forgotten, but she realized that he had become very focused on her as she began to tell about herself.

"Are you sure you want to listen to a 'sob' story after such a pleasant evening together?" she asked.

"Please," he said, genuinely. "I'd love to know more about you—that is if you don't mind my asking." He knew some about what was going on in her life; he'd seen her on television, but he had never asked about her past.

By the end of a long evening together he was even more impressed with the woman who had come to his home. He had not been truly worried about entrusting her with his money because it was only a small portion of his wealth, but he was now very comfortable with her ability to handle the money.

"All right," he said as she finished, "I'd like to make two investments with you."

"Two?" she said in surprise.

"Yes, a hundred-thousand in your company, and fifty-thousand in you."

Surprise turned to shock; she wasn't sure what he meant by that remark.

With her speechlessness, he knew he'd better explain, "I mean, as you said, you're going to be working hard and living on a small savings account, but I don't think you'll be able to work efficiently if you're so pressed for cash. So, I think an investment in you personally, repayable whenever you like, will go a long way in securing the success of my first investment."

His logic was flawless, but she was still stunned by what he said.

"It's okay," he said, reassuring her. "I can afford it. I may not be a Trathmoore, but my income is very substantial."

"I don't know what to say. I certainly didn't come here expecting that from you."

"I'm sure you didn't, and please don't think that I am trying to obligate you to me because I'm not. My father always impressed upon me that a woman is to be respected at all times. And I assure you I don't have any other intention for doing this for you." Then reconsidering for a second, he added, "In all truthfulness, money aside, I have to tell you something. I'm not trying to be forward, but I was disappointed when you said you're romantically involved. I was hoping we might go out sometime. My social life, well, it basically stinks." Then they both laughed at his candor.

"Friendship wouldn't be out of the question," she offered.

His whole expression brightened, "I'd like that." Then, being proper for a moment, he said, "You are an interesting lady, Ms. Danor. I haven't had an evening of good conversation that didn't involve brain surgery in a long time."

She left Gill's home feeling like a weight had been lifted and a prayer had been answered. She had worried about how she was going to survive on the small amount of cash that she had saved, but now she was set. She knew she could have setup a payroll account for herself out of the investment funds because that is where she was going to get the funds for the initial employee payroll, but she didn't want to do it unless it was absolutely necessary; now it was not.

As the next two weeks passed, she talked with suppliers, setup accounts, made initial orders, and met several times with the construction manager. She was totally immersed in the business of business. And, for the first time in what seemed to be such a long time, she was happy. She felt, with the exception of dealing with Albert, who had become sullen to the point of never being around when she dropped off Jordan and never personally returning him to her, her life was going well. She asked Jordan if Daddy was spending time with him on 'his' weekends and Jordan said yes he was.

She was on top of the world. Had she know the future, it would have felt more like the edge of a cliff, with a storm coming to blow her away.

CHAPTER SEVEN

The State Penitentiary in New York is a foreboding place where those who can not live within the law now live behind gray bars and razor wire fences. Some were there because they chose to be the scum of society, hurting and hating everyone that crossed their paths. Others were there because they had made the wrong choice at the wrong moment, tangling the fate-lines of life; they were serving time for mistakes they never intended to make.

Henry 'Jibs' Randolph was one of those who made a bad choice; he killed a man in a barroom fight. It wasn't premeditated and it wasn't something he was thoroughly conscious of doing at the time. Drunk and angry, he picked up a cue stick and brought it to rest, full force, against another man's temple, killing him instantly.

He was sentenced to eighteen years in prison for second-degree murder. The trial was emotional for the family of Hector Gonzales; half the courtroom was filled with his relatives. Jibs sat alone; no one cared about an old, obnoxious, drunkard with a habit of barroom brawls and hard living. But the young man who died had family that cared, and they made it plain that they hated Jibs.

Hector's brother came to the prison as a visitor a few months after Jibs was sentenced. Using an assumed name and dressed like a Catholic priest, he came to deliver a message to Jibs. It was a message of death. He told Jibs they would count the days until he was released. They would find him and would attack him with pool cues. He made sure Jibs could visualize how they would beat him mercilessly until he begged them to stop. Then they would use the sticks to smash his skull into a bloody pulp.

He sat there stunned; he didn't know what to say because he was sober. If he had been drunk he'd have said a lot, but sober and with no chance for a drink of liquor, he could only sit and listen to the plan for his demise. Daytime, nighttime, any moment he was conscious, he thought about the end of his miserable existence when he left the sanctity of the prison.

Nick Randall was in the cell beside Jibs, and he knew he had a pigeon—it was just a matter of timing to pluck him. He knew Jibs had been eligible for parole ever since his sixth year, but he would always become difficult and lose his chance. He wanted to stay in prison because staying there he felt safe. And Nick made sure Jibs knew the outside world was a bad place to be. He told Jibs about the hits he'd seen the Mexican Mafia carry out and they, according to Nick, were the most gruesome. The more he told Jibs the more Jibs wanted to stay in prison.

The guards came and went in the cellblock. It seemed they never lasted very long. Nick began to say his nickname was "Gibbs" and soon the guards began to call him by it. Then one night, long after lights out he pressed his face to the bars next to Jibs cell.

"Jibs, Jibs," he whispered, no louder than the shuffle of a mouse.

Jibs was awake. He would lie in his bed and stare at the ceiling, sometimes until dawn. "What!" he answered, a little louder than Nick wanted.

"Shhh! I've figured out how you can stay in here. You know they are going to make you leave at your next parole. They said the prison is too crowded and people like you gotta go."

"I'll just pull something stupid and get put back in here then," he whispered back.

"Don't you think they are planning on getting you as soon as you get out? Maybe even the same day?"

Jibs mind raced with the fear he had about getting out. His chest began to tighten and a great weight felt as if it had been lowered onto his body. In short quick breaths, he asked, "How—can I—stay?"

"Tomorrow when we get out to wash-up and eat, you and me switch shirts. I'll have your number and you'll have mine. When we get back to the cellblock, we each go into the other's cell. We've got two new guards and they'll never realize we switched. In a few days, I'll take care of the bands." he said, referring to the identification bracelet each prisoner wore.

Jibs thought over the plan that seemed too simple to work, "Then what?" he said, his voice dropping lower.

"Mulcasey and Carter are helping me with the rest of it, but the thing is when they throw you outta here, they'll really be throwing me out. You can stay for as long as you want, I've gotta life sentence with no parole for another twenty-two years."

Jibs laughed insincerely, "Yeah, *buddy*, what if I decide I'd rather be outta here? What if I decide I'd rather take my chances outside someday?"

"That's when you ask the guards about your parole and they discover the mix up. You'll get out and they'll start lookin' for me."

The plan was more interesting to Jibs now because prison life or life on the outside would be his choice. He was quiet for a long time as he turned it over in his mind.

"What if they catch you when you're leaving? You know, figure out that I was being quiet to help you get out."

Nick knew Jibs would ask that question, but the predictability of it was funny to him and he began to laugh quietly from deep in his throat, "What are they gonna do to ya, Jibs? Make ya stay in this place another year or two?"

Finding the humor in getting what he wanted either way, Jibs smiled; he wouldn't have to leave if he didn't want to.

"I'll tell ya tomorrow if I'll do it or not."

Parole was less than a month away and Jibs wasn't ready for the outside, yet. Besides that, he sincerely believed those men would be waiting just beyond the prison, and if he was lucky, since they hadn't seen him in years, maybe they'd beat Nick to death thinking it was him. He didn't like Nick, but then again he couldn't think of anyone he did like.

The next morning when they left their cells to go to the showers, he told Nick he'd do it. When they finished their brief dose of personal hygiene they each took the other's prison shirt. After breakfast and exercise they returned to their cells, but this time they switched. They would know if the plan had a chance if the new guard didn't discovered the mix-up during role check.

Joe Peters was new to the system, but he had adjusted well and didn't seem to get too much guff from the prisoners. But that was somewhat understandable when you saw him; he seemed almost as wide as he was tall and he wasn't fat either. He was an avid believer in being able to physically have the upper hand in any power struggle. He had a friend who shared his medically needed steroids. That, coupled with Joe's obsessive strength training, created a muscled body that had to have tailored clothes because of its odd dimensions.

Peters walked down the cellblock checking off names and numbers. Most of it was done silently, but occasionally he would banter with a prisoner. The Q's and R's were Joe's block. The other guards gave him some good-natured ribbing when he started working there, telling him he had the queers and rears section.

Nick held his breath as he listened to the foot falls of the man in the shiny black shoes—shoes that would play a part in getting him out of there. He heard Peters stop at his old cell and pause. "Shit!" Nick whispered under his breath, "We're caught."

"What are you doing?" He heard Peters say.

"I gotta take a piss!" Jibs growled.

"Take a piss in a minute, I gotta write down your number Gibbs!"

"Like you don't know it. It's on your friggin' clipboard!"

Nick could hear Jibs continuing to urinate in the drain, "Don't blow it you stupid asshole!" he said under his breath.

Peters was muttering something Nick couldn't make out. Then he was standing in front of Jib's old cell. Now Nick and Jibs certainly weren't twins, but their height and weight was close. Nick had had to shun some of his meals to get to the leaner, gaunt look that Jibs had, but it would be worth it if this worked. He also had studied Jibs for so long that he had his grooming habits and mannerisms down pretty well, too. Peters looked at the number on the clipboard then back to Nick's shirt. He looked perplexed for a moment, but the moment faded quickly and he moved to the next prisoner. With a sigh of relief Nick knew the first hurdle was over.

Two days later they both broke and then traded the arm bracelets that had their identification numbers imprinted. It would be too suspicious to have them both replaced at the same time, so they temporarily repaired Jibs bracelet with a piece of clear tape that Nick received from a buddy in the prison library. Nick complained to one of the guards that he had caught his on something and it broke. Without much fuss the bracelet bearing Henry 'Jibs' Randolph's number was replaced—on Nick Randall's arm.

The years of thought and preparation were ready to come to fruition. Just over a month had passed since taking Jibs place and it was time to go. The board met on a Monday and by Tuesday afternoon the last of the plan was put into action.

Mulcasey was a prisoner who worked in the library and he was good with a computer. He knew Nick from the years before prison and was willing to stick his neck out a little for him. Using a simple publishing program, he made a nearly perfect reproduction of a fingerprint card and printed it. The guard, Yoder, had worked so long with Mulcasey that he only occasionally checked what he printed. The card left the library unnoticed inside an Outdoor Life magazine. During his deliveries to the cells, Mulcasey gave it to Jibs. Using a tiny amount of black shoe polished that came from a prisoner in laundry, Jibs carefully put his fingerprints on the card. Then late that evening he put the card back in the magazine and slid it on the floor down to Nick.

Wednesday morning, a nervous and pale man walked with guard Peters to the exit-processing rooms. Truly, Nick was nervous, but that nervousness only served to help him act more like the man he was portraying. Prison systems were not all alike; Nick had been in prison before, but it wasn't this prison. The last time he was released, it was a little different. As long as the prisoners he had talked with about what happens during the release from here were right, his plan should work. They gave him back the belongings that were taken from Jibs years ago: a Harley-Davidson lighter, two ten-year old cheap cigars in plastic holders, a chain-wallet, $17.42 in cash, a little black, beat up address book with very few entries and a bundle of men's clothing.

Nick held his breath; this was the moment the other prisoners said he would be fingerprinted, handed the card and sent to the next step. If they were right, Jibs original fingerprints from the national justice computer database would be pulled up, matched with the freshly inked prints and then he would be released. It was supposed to be a foolproof way to make sure no mistakes happened; this time things would be different. As the guard behind the counter finished making Nick's new prints, Nick saw Peters' hand rising up to take it. Quickly, Nick grabbed it as if he had no idea Peters wanted it, stepping right in front of Peters as if he was anxious to go to the next room. It didn't matter to the other guard or Peters who took it, it was only twenty feet away and what could happen in that distance?

As they headed to the next room, Nick dropped the items he was given. He was no slight of hand expert, but he knew he had to get Peters' eyes elsewhere so he could make the swap.

"I don't wanna go," Nick said in a choked voice, barely louder than a whisper.

Peters, who had stooped to help him pick up the items, stopped and looked Nick in the eye. He'd worked the county jail before going State and he'd never heard that response from someone who was about to be released.

"They're gonna kill me!" Nick continued, still with his voice low. The perspiration had begun to bead on his forehead and his skin was pale. He had Peters' attention now, giving him the opportunity to swap the card with the one in his waistband as he slowly retrieved items from the floor.

"Who's gonna kill you?" Peters said.

Nick wanted to laugh because he could hear the genuine concern in Peters' voice, but he wouldn't end this façade until he was sure he'd get out.

"The man I killed—his family wants me dead. They told me when I get out of here that they are gonna kill me."

"Where are you going to go when you get out of here, Jibs. Do you have family in New York?"

"No—nobody," he said, standing upright with the belongings.

"I think I'd leave New York if I were you. They may have changed their minds, it's been a long time, but just to be safe... ."

"Yeah, I think you're right," he interrupted. Suddenly he looked at ease with his impending release. "I don't think I'll stick around."

He smiled as they punched in the numbers from his bracelet into the computer and Jibs' fingerprints appeared on screen. He watched as the guard compared the prints.

"All right Henry, you can change your clothes and then you're free to go," said the guard in the fingerprint room. "Stop and see the parole officers within a week and let them know your permanent address."

Nick smiled as he stepped outside the gates of the prison for the first time in almost four years. He walked into the snowy landscape in a pair of shoes that were at least one size too large, but he didn't care about that. He didn't have a jacket, just a long sleeved flannel shirt, but that didn't matter either; Florida wouldn't be this cold.

~:~

The week had been great and Katie was looking forward to spending some time with Donovan over the weekend. Everything had been so wonderfully hectic that she was ready for a little private relaxation in his arms. They had carefully restrained themselves; they couldn't enjoy each other whenever they liked, and discretion meant being patient, waiting for the right opportunities that would not often enough come along. Tonight would be the first opportunity since New Year's Eve, and they both eagerly anticipated a romantic reunion.

She had worked the last few days at the mall in a little makeshift office amidst the remodeling mayhem. She hired an architect and they worked over the design with Red Balsinger until a reasonable middle ground between the two had been reached. Donovan had recently bought her a cellular phone as a gift for two reasons: one, to reach her wherever she was and two, so she didn't have to worry about a tap on her home phone line. He called an hour earlier to say he was heading home to shower and change and would be down for dinner after she had taken Jordan to his father.

She was wrapping up and putting away plans and notes when she heard footsteps, looking up she gasped as Albert made his way toward her with a smile on his face. She didn't like the type of smile he was wearing; it said he had something up his sleeve.

"Albert! What are you doing here? How did you know where to find me?"

"I still keep pretty close tabs on you," he said, still smiling.

Her heart started the familiar gallop as she wondered what torment she was getting ready to face to give him such obvious delight.

"I'm sorry, but you don't have any right to keep 'tabs' on me anymore and I don't like… ."

He laughed in her face and then said exactly what his expression had already told her; "I don't care what you like." He was reaching inside the pocket of his coat pulling out an envelope when her cell phone rang.

"I don't have time for your games," she said tersely, picking up the phone.

"Believe me, I'm not playing a game with you, *Darling*," he said as he watched her hit the talk button. It annoyed him that she was answering the phone when he was talking. He wasn't used to that; he always commanded the full attention of whomever he was speaking with.

She put her hand up in front of his face to silence him, and he did, but he was seething mad at her for doing it.

"What? Michael, slow down, I can't understand you. What happened?"

Suddenly the color drained completely from her face, the tears immediately welled over her eyes and she began to tremble violently, "No, no, God, please no!"

Albert was immediately pulled into the conversation. He didn't know who Michael was, but he knew he'd never (even with all the hateful things he'd done to her) seen her react as she did to the news on the phone. Then his heart jumped into his throat as he thought it must be something to do with Jordan.

She dropped the phone to the desk, feeling more helpless than she ever felt in her entire life.

"Katie, what's wrong?" he demanded, "Is it Jordan?"

"No," she said as she crumpled to the chair and slumped her body against the desk, "It's Donovan."

His heart went back to normal rhythm and the ice began to flow once again in his veins. But she would soon melt that icy, cold heart with her plea.

"Albert please, I can't drive like this. Could you have your driver take me to Tampa General, please."

He was ready to say no, when she asked again, "Please, Albert," she said, grabbing his unoffered arm to steady her weak knees. He was unprepared for her to come to him so vulnerably. "He's dying—please help me get to the hospital."

He looked into her beautiful eyes that were flowing with anguished tears, "Yes, of course I'll get you there. Come on." He wrapped his strong arm around her shoulder and guided her out to his waiting limousine. He hated Donovan, but he wasn't so vindictive that he wanted him dead. And then there was Katie, the woman he despised for fighting him, yet the one woman who, unknowingly, had captured his heart for all time. He wanted to destroy her for hurting him, for making him love her so deeply that it became physically painful to know he couldn't have her, but for now she needed him.

Once inside the limousine, Albert asked gently what had been said to her on the phone to make her believe Donovan was dying. Though her heart was ready to break, she told him the man on the phone worked for Donovan and he said there had been a propane gas explosion at Donovan's house. The doctors didn't expect him to pull through.

They rode in silence the rest of the twenty-minute trip from the mall to the hospital; Katie wrapped in her thoughts and he in his. But his thoughts were very different from hers. He thought about the helpless way she pleaded with him to take her to Donovan, the touch of her hands as she held on to his arm for support, the look in her eyes that changed a no to a yes. Perhaps with this ending could come a new beginning for the two of them; instead of destroying perhaps they could build a new relationship from here.

Pulling up to the emergency entrance, she didn't wait for the driver to open the door; in fact, she hadn't quite waited for the car to come to a complete stop before jumping out and running for the emergency room. Albert didn't say anything, but quickly caught up to her. Michael was there, as well as several other people from the dealership. At the look on their faces, Katie's heart seemed to fall to pieces, and she wondered if it was too late.

Michael, openly crying, took her arm and led her back to the doctor who was waiting just beyond the cubical.

"They won't let us in to see him," Michael told her.

Katie looked at the doctor's face and saw the hopelessness written on it.

"I *have* to see him," she said, gathering back some of her lost composure.

"Are you a family member?" he asked cautiously.

"He doesn't have any family left; I'm his fiancée."

At those words she heard someone's choking cough behind her and that is when she realized Albert had walked back with them. She didn't care. She and Donovan hadn't discussed marriage, but she knew when the problems with the divorce were behind her, he would have asked and she would have said yes.

"I'd like to encourage you to wait," the doctor said. "I don't think you'll want to remember him this way. I'm sorry, but it isn't going to be long and I don't think he'll know who you are anyway."

"Let me see him now!" she demanded in a quivering voice. She didn't want to wait and let him die alone.

"Have you ever seen someone with severe burns? I really think… ."

"If you don't let me in to see him and he dies in that room alone, I'll sue you and this hospital. And trust me, damn you, I'll win!" Her voice suddenly had a hard edge that Albert had never heard from her. He realized, as did the doctor, that it was the voice of angry truth; she meant what she said.

Knowing that she would not be dissuaded, the doctor guided her into the clinically cold and sterile room. The air was antiseptic but had a strong sickly-sweet aroma that was overpowering and nauseating. He walked with her behind the curtain; this was one of the worst burn victims he had ever worked with who was still alive, and he felt certain when she saw him she would faint.

A mixture of horror, unbelief and denial hit her hard as she saw the body of a man burned beyond recognition. His skin was charred black with bloody red flesh surrounding each swath of burnt-black skin. A cloth covered his groin, an oxygen tube was placed in one nostril, and a heart monitor was connected to his burned chest.

The doctor led her to the edge of the bed, "He has third degree burns over ninety percent of his body. If you want to touch him, the palms of his hands aren't burnt, but I wouldn't touch him anywhere else."

Gently she slipped her fingers to the underside of his hand to find the smooth, unburned flesh of his palm. She looked at his face and she couldn't recognize who it was. Her heart began immediately to tell her this was a mistake; it was not Donovan. Most of the hair was burned away and what remained was like a melted mass stuck to the almost bare head.

"Donovan," she whispered through the wall of tears. "Donovan, it's me. It's Katie. I'm here, Sweetheart. I know you probably can't hear me, but… ."

At that moment the dark red and black eye lids forced open. Her heart disintegrated in the truth; she was looking into Donovan's beautiful dark brown eyes.

The doctor was visibly shocked as he saw the man respond to her voice; he was cognizant.

Donovan's mouth attempted movement, but it was excruciating and labored, "I love you," came the struggled words in raspy wisps. His lungs were nearly seared and it took all the air he had to say it.

"Oh, Donovan, I love you, sweetheart; I'll always love you."

"Tell—Jordan, I—love him."

"Yes, I will," she answered him. "He loves you too, I know he does."

"Fight—to keep—him," he said, barely audible.

"I will," she nodded.

Trying to swallow, his eyes closed at the pain of it, then slowly reopened.

"Find…" he paused, his speech too painful to continue, but he had to finish what he wanted to tell her. The room was beginning to darken and only her face was visible to him now. He knew his time was ending.

"…someone—to make—you—happy—someone—to love."

"No, Donovan, I love you. Please don't leave me. I'll always love you."

"No. Find—someone. I want—you—happy." His eyes told her he wanted a response, he was holding out for her answer.

She didn't want him to die, but she couldn't bear to see him in this hideously painful state. "Yes," she said softly. "I'll find someone to make me happy, but I'll never forget you. New York is gone and New Year's morning is the place I'll always remember. I love you so much."

His eyes closed again. His breath came in short rises and falls of his chest. She watched it fall, but it didn't rise again. He stiffened a little, squeezed her hand, and then relaxed. The heart monitor suddenly let out a deafening tone and the line went flat.

"No, please, no…Donovan…Donovan… ." It had ended and she knew he couldn't hear her anymore. Her cry came out loud and unrestrained; a wail of deepest painful mourning.

When Albert heard her, he stepped into the cubical to support her, but he had never seen anything like this before; he stood there in shock just a few feet from her, as the cries of despair filled the corridor.

Then, in a moment at the end of her own will, she collapsed. She would never know it was Albert who picked her up and carried her out of the room.

The doctor and nurses rushed over to the gurney where he laid her. Breaking an ammonia vial, they brought her unwilling body back to consciousness.

~:~

It was a dark several days that passed, dark and run together like muddy streams rushing to a river of grief. She had never lost someone that had touched her life in such unforgettable ways; never had she experienced such pain and hollowness that expanded to fill her heart and mind. She ached for someone who was not there to comfort her, for his gentle touch and his gallant smile. She felt an undeniable hole within the confines of her heart, a hole she believed would never close.

She made the funeral arrangements and sat in the front of the church as the only family member. It comforted her that there were many people who came to bid him farewell. Flowers filled the small island church, many with notes of condolence and sorrow and a great many that were anonymous. She hadn't realized how many lives he had touched in his short time in Florida, his sales staff and their families, customers who liked that 'bright young Italian man,' suppliers and friends he had made. His body would be sent to New York to be buried with his mother and his real father.

She worried that his death might have been the result of foul play, someone who knew Nick or one of the crime families Donovan had informed on, but when the official police report was concluded days later it was ruled as accidental. She wept as she read the scenario they put together from shattered remains of his home.

The report stated that when he entered the house that evening, the gas line evidently had not ruptured yet. They believed the coupling to the stove burst apart sometime during his shower, rapidly filling the house with propane gas. It was assumed he smelled the gas and exited the shower, put a towel about his waist and moved down the hallway to the kitchen. Since only the tiniest spark is needed, it probably occurred with something as simple as the flip of the kitchen light switch. The resulting explosion was heard over a mile away, shattering the window glass in six nearby homes and three vehicles.

Albert kept Jordan that week, knowing that the funeral would be hard enough for her without trying to explain the events to a small child. But his third birthday was only another week away and he knew she wanted him home for that.

She appreciated Albert's newfound quiet politeness when he brought Jordan home. She knew that the absence of his previous vindictive state was his way of expressing sympathy over her loss, though he would never have said so.

Construction continued at the mall without her, her architect handling the small problems that came up. She knew she would be back in the thick of things soon because Donovan wouldn't have wanted her to abandon her dream and her passion for what she was creating. Life would continue, she realized; it never stopped its continual flow for anyone, no matter the pain, no matter the loss. And as for her, she had a very beautiful reason to go on, a reason that filled her with a sense of joy and purpose every moment of her life: the sunshine of her days and the starlight of her nights—her son.

A few days after Jordan's birthday, Katie talked with him about Donovan, but she waited for him to mention his name first. She was reading him his nightly bedtime story when he asked if they were going to visit Donovan.

"Why are you crying?" he asked in a voice filled with wonder at her sadness. She closed the book and pulled the covers up under his little chin.

"I'm sad because Donovan had to leave and we can't go visit him anymore."

"Why, Mama?"

"Do you remember what you've learned about Jesus and Heaven in church?" she asked him, wiping back the tears that kept returning to her cheeks.

"Yes," he said, his eyes going wide. "Hebben is a purdy place we go when we die."

"You're right," she said. "Donovan wanted me to tell you that he loves you very much, but he had to leave to go there. He's very happy there."

"We can't go visit him, Mama?"

"No, Sweetheart, but someday we'll get to see him again, when it's our turn to go there."

"We gotta take turns?" He asked, a little annoyed. He was good about taking turns with the other kids at Granny's house, but he preferred to do things when he wanted to.

She smiled, then bent and kissed his button nose, "Sort of, but only God knows when it's our turn."

"Did Boots go too, Mama?"

She hadn't thought about him asking that question. Taking a deep breath, she knew the cat perished in the blast, but she had never thought about animals in Heaven. Finally she answered, "I think he did."

His little eyes welled over as he began to understand why she was so sad. "I'm gonna miss them, Mama."

He reached out for a comforting hug and she pulled him onto her lap and whispered, "Me too, Jordan, me too."

She rocked him gently in her arms until he dozed off to sleep; then she softly laid him down on the pillow and covered him up.

The house was dark and she was ready for sleep. Each night put away another day, and with each passing day she knew the pain would lessen until only a beautiful memory of a special man remained. She wearily shed her clothes and pulled on her silky pajamas. With her head finding its resting place on the downy soft pillow, she drifted off into a deep sleep. It would be a night she would never forget.

In the wee hours of the morning something in the recesses of her mind jarred her from her dream state; something in the darkness wasn't right. Her mind was so foggy that she couldn't determine what it had been: the squeak of a door, the brush of night air across her face, the sound of breathing that wasn't her own. Whatever it had been, it brought her from the unconscious, to the semi-conscious and on the verge of consciousness when that something flew out of the darkness and attacked her.

She tried to scream as the heavy weight of a human form landed on top of her body. A hand, rough and gnarled, painfully covered her mouth, and a voice from the past came out of the darkness.

"You know I thought about burning your house down while you were sleeping inside it; then I thought I'd just come in and shoot you."

She heard the click of a hammer coming back in a gun and she felt the cold steel pressed to her temple. She stopped her struggle out of fear that this person might not only kill her, but Jordan as well if she continued to fight him.

"But you know what I thought to myself? If your hot little box was good enough to get my little brother to turn you loose from that warehouse and come out of protective custody to tap it again, it must be worth trying myself."

Her mind went wild trying to make sense of the confusion racing through it. It couldn't be Nick; she knew he was in prison, but somehow it was him. Before she could decipher the pandemonium that flashed through her thoughts, his hand left her mouth and ripped hard and quick the soft material of her pajama top to exposed her breasts and then returning to cover her mouth. With the gun still at her head she couldn't think what to do; things she had learned in martial arts whirled with the other confused thoughts and she couldn't get a grasp on anything other than the peril she was facing.

His mouth, slobbering and cold, viciously found her breast, painfully sucking and tearing at them. She was screaming "NO!" into the hard palm of his hand; then the hand pressed so forcefully that it seemed her jaw would snap.

"You can try to scream all you want; nobody's gonna hear you!" he spewed in her face.

The gun left her temple and she heard it come to rest on the dresser next to the bed. She wondered for a moment, but then realized he needed his hand free as he began undoing his waistband. She knew this was the only opportunity she would have to stop him and she began to struggle violently, her parted legs trying to close under him so she might be able to force her knee into his groin. She struck his neck with a ridged hand, but there wasn't enough room to put power into the strike. It stunned him briefly, but it only seemed to anger him.

Growling at her like some kind of animal, he used both hands to force her arms above her head, covering her mouth with his own to muffle her cries for help. Once he had her arms above her, he easily held her slender wrists tightly together with one hand and returned his other to her mouth.

"Oh no, you little bitch, you're not going to get away from me! I'm gonna do you and when I'm done I'm gonna kill you, just like I killed Donny. The only difference will be that yours is gonna be a bullet; his was a house full of gas and a broken light bulb to ignite it."

"NO! NO!" her heart screamed out of the depths; he had murdered Donovan! His own half brother had ended his life! Darkness was crowding her mind as she struggled to stay conscious, his weight was crushing her and her breath was being smothered out by his hand. She had to stay conscious, Jordan was in the house and she had to find a way to stop this mad man.

He laughed as he realized she was on the verge of passing out. He pulled his hand lower and lightened himself from her chest, "No Candy-Ass, you're not gonna pass out on me! You are gonna feel everything I do to you; you deserve that for all the trouble you caused me!"

His lower body was exposed now and she could feel his hardness against her silk pants. Letting go of her mouth again, he tried to get his hand to her thin waist string and break it, while trying to put his acrid mouth to hers. But she rolled her head violently from side to side to avoid him. For only an instant he was off-balanced, but that was all she needed. She jerked her knee upward, not hitting his groin but the soft area between the hipbone and appendix, sending them both crashing to the floor.

Scrambling to her feet she tried to reach up quickly and grab the gun from the dresser, but he hit her before her fingers could close on it, sending it somewhere onto her bed. Suddenly a struggle that had been almost silent had become alarmingly loud. She hoped and prayed that it was loud enough for Elaine, the police officer who lived next door, to hear it and come to her aid. Instead she woke someone several blocks away from his sleep when the sounds her sounds of distress came across the speakers; already he was dialing the police and preparing to run out the door to his car and head to her side.

Nick slapped her, open-handed, several times in the face then put both his hands around her neck and began to squeeze as he violently shook her.

"I've always liked a woman with a little fight in her, but you're startin' to piss me off. Now lay still or I'll kill you first and still do what I want with you!"

Yet above his bitter spew, she heard something, something only a mother's ears would hear during such mayhem. A little voice was calling to her.

"Mama—Mama, what's wrong!"

"RUN JORDAN, RUN! RUN TO MISS ELAINE'S HOUSE AND GET HELP FOR MOMMA!" she screamed out.

She heard his little feet hit the floor and take off running to the front door, but as he reached it and tore at the knob with his hands she realized it was locked; he didn't know how to open it.

In her moment of distraction, Nick managed to tear away the cord that held her pants in place as his frenzy heightened to enter her.

"NO," she yelled in his face, "GET OFF OF ME YOU BASTARD!" She tried to push him away, but he only laughed at her efforts and continued toward his vile purpose.

Then once again she heard Jordan's feet take flight as he screamed out, "I'M COMING, MAMA!"

"NO JORDAN, NO! DON'T COME IN HERE!" She cried out her warning, but he was already charging through the darkness to try to save her.

She felt the weight of his little body as he flung himself on to Nick's back, screaming and crying with all his might for the monster that had her to let go.

But he was no more than a small annoyance to Nick, who easily knocked him off of his back. He didn't like kids, and he didn't care for this little brat interfering with his pleasure. He would kill them both, but at the moment he had other plans.

"DON'T YOU TOUCH MY SON, YOU… ."

He smashed his hand hard against her face, disorienting her for a moment and finally putting himself in the position to enter her. It seemed the inevitable would occur and he would take her. But then, once again, Jordan jumped onto Nick's back; this time his sharp little fingernails dug deep into Nick's back and his teeth found a place on the massive shoulder to clamp down. He bit with all the power his jaws could inflict.

Yelling out at the painful bite, Nick reached over his shoulder and grabbed Jordan by this nightshirt and literally threw him like a rag doll into the darkness. He landed with a sickening hard thud, and then there was nothing but stillness in the direction which he had thrown him.

At the moment when he raised up to pull Jordan off him, Katie struggled to slide from beneath him and her hand landed on something under the bed—the wooden dowel!

He turned back to her, sneering in the darkness at the thought of breaking the child's neck, but as he faced the matter at hand, she swung the dowel, catching him across the face with it and he toppled off her.

Cursing, spewing, and swaying he grabbed for the dowel as she tried to hit him again. He wrenched it from her hand, but not quick enough to keep her from getting to her feet. She dove for the bed to find the gun lying somewhere on the tangled bedding, as he swung with all his might hitting across the back of her legs with the dowel. The pain was like a bolt of lightening going off inside her brain, but she kept her mind focused as her hands felt for the gun.

"I'M GONNA KILL YOU!" he thundered. His promise of death screamed out so loudly that it woke the neighbors in both houses bordering hers.

She turned over in the bed, seeing the outline of his body in the light of the sliver of moon. His arms were raised above his head and the dowel, clutched in his hands, was hurling toward her. In a millionth of a second her hand touched steel. She fired toward the form that was almost on top of her. The blast was deafening, lighting the room with the propulsion of the bullet toward her attacker. The force of the shot caused the gun to jerk so hard that it came out of her hands and glanced across her cheek as it fell. Her hands then went up instinctively in self-defense against the body crashing onto her own.

She was prepared to feel the hard dowel sink into her skull, but instead it fell to the floor on the other side of the bed and never touched her. Nick's weight dropped onto her like a rock, knocking the breath from her. She struggled out from under him in fright. He didn't resist her efforts to get away; in fact he didn't even move when she rolled him off her onto the bed. She felt something warm and wet on her chest as she pulled what was left of her top to cover herself. It had an odor she recognized: blood. Nick was shot.

Running for the light switch she flipped it up and illuminated the horror that had taken place in her room. Blood was splattered across her bed and across Nick's chest from a gaping hole in the center of his shirt. The room looked as if someone had turned a tornado loose in it. Then, catching her breath she saw Jordan's crumpled little body on the floor against the cedar chest.

"Nooooo!" she wailed, as she ran to the unmoving body of her son. She heard the front door being kicked down, but she didn't care what happened beyond this point; she had to get to Jordan and make everything all right. Her little hero had come to her rescue and now she was coming to his.

Ever so gently she lifted his tiny thirty-five pound frame onto her lap. Kissing his head and rocking back and forth, "It's okay baby, Mama's here, Mama's here." But his eyes didn't open and his body didn't respond. Trying to wake him, she slipped her hand under his head and that was when she felt his wet hair. Pulling her hand back in disbelief she stared at the blood that covered her palm. Glancing for an instant at the cedar chest she saw the corner had hair and blood on it. The back of Jordan's skull had been crushed when Nick threw him across the room.

Hands were around her, people were there, figures moved about her room, but she wouldn't let him go. She felt the side of his neck with her fingers and, almost undetectable, there was the faint beat of his pulse—he was still alive, but barely.

"I NEED AN AMBULANCE FOR MY SON!" she screamed out to the people around her. She was focused on him and didn't even recognize her own neighbors, though some were faces she wouldn't have known anyway. The police were already there and an ambulance crew was waiting outside for the all clear signal so they could enter the residence. Quickly they were ushered in and a woman paramedic was at Katie's side telling her she had to let go. Reluctantly she let her take him. Another paramedic looked at Katie, and a third at Nick. They were helping her to her feet as she saw them pull the bed sheet over Nick's face.

Her legs were painful and hard to stand on. Already dark red-purple marks had formed across the backs of her calves where the dowel had struck her. Elaine from next door was there helping her get some clothes to cover herself, a pair of slip-on pants and a button-up-the-front blouse was handed to her and she put it on over her torn pajama top. She limped through the house, heading to her son in the waiting ambulance. As she did, she walked past a man who was talking with the police. His face was stored somewhere in the recesses of her memory, but it was long ago and unclear. She heard him say something about being a detective, working for Trathmoore, and hearing the commotion inside her home. She didn't understand it all and she didn't care. She boarded the ambulance with Jordan. Looking out at Elaine who was standing just beyond the open ambulance doors, she motioned for her.

"Elaine, please, you've got to get my friend Doctor Phillips. He lives in the big three-story house out on the northern tip of the island. He's a neurosurgeon—the very best—get him—tell him what happened and have him come to the Memorial Hospital." She choked back the tears as she looked down at Jordan's pale face, "He's going to need the best. Elaine, hurry—please."

The doors were shut and they began speeding down the darkened streets, illuminating them in a spray of colored flashing lights and screaming sirens.

By the time they pulled up to the emergency entrance her leg muscles had swollen so badly that walking would have been impossible except that the will down inside her wouldn't recognize the pain until she knew if Jordan was going to be okay.

She stepped down into a paramedic's arms, before the gurney was unloaded. She looked up and Albert was standing there. He had gotten the call from his informant, and without waiting to wake his driver, took the limousine himself and sped through the almost deserted streets to reach them. She found it hard to recognize him with an unshaven face and disheveled hair, but it was him.

When she emerged from the ambulance he was equally shocked at the state she was in, still covered in blood from Nick and Jordan, purple welts on her legs, and a face that was battered and bruised, she looked as if she had battled Goliath in hand-to-hand combat. But his focus quickly changed when his son, unmoving and pale, was removed from the back of the vehicle.

"MY GOD! JORDAN," he cried out. "What happened to him? I was told someone was in the house, but... ."

The crew said little as they made way for the waiting trauma team. He would have to get his answers another way. They had work to do and this little boy was only hanging on by a thread.

Rushed to an area where they could assess his condition, two doctors and three nurses began to evaluate him. IV's were started and statistics were shouted back and forth. His pupils were dilated and his body didn't respond to stimulus, and all the while he lay there with his sweet angelic face never moving. One doctor tried to look at Katie, but she flatly refused treatment until she knew how her son would fare.

"We have to take him to x-ray immediately. He'll be right back. Please stay here and the let the doctor take a look at you, Ma'am." the nurse was saying, as she gently tried to console her. She was a mother herself and she knew this was the most difficult moment any parent faces, the unknown about their child's ability to pull through something like this.

Numbly she nodded, as they took him on his gurney to x-ray. The doctor looked at Albert wondering who he was. His face was so familiar to him and hers as well. Then, looking back at the paperwork handed him by the ambulance crew, he realized he had a very unlikely pair: the most famous ongoing divorce couple in recent history.

"I need to look at you," he said, gently removing her outer shirt. "Do you want him here?" he asked, referring to Albert. But Albert was too worried about his son to be angry.

"He's okay," she said, still in a state of disbelief over the events of the morning. He asked her if she was able to move to a nearby exam table, but her legs were refusing to work properly. With nothing said, Albert pushed aside the doctor and picked her up effortlessly and laid her down on the table. He had done it before and he was starting to get good at it. They looked into each other's eyes as she released his neck and lay back on the table; they were both afraid.

The nurse used a warm sponge with a betadine mixture to wash away the blood from her chest and hands. To Albert's relief the blood that covered most of her, was her attackers, not hers. But with all the contusions the doctor wanted her to have a full set of x-rays.

"No! I'm waiting until my son's back."

"You need x-rays in case anything is…." the doctor started to say.

But she interrupted him, "Not until Jordan gets back!"

Just then Gill walked into the room. He had no idea the severity of the situation.

All he knew, after Elaine came banging on his door at four in the morning, was that she said Katie and Jordan had been attacked and Jordan had a serious skull injury. He wasn't prepared for anything like this. He acknowledged them briefly and then left with the other doctor to head down to x-ray where Jordan was being scanned.

It was about fifteen minutes before he came back to the room. She had her over-shirt back on and was sitting up on the gurney.

Gill's expression was grave. "Katie, Jordan needs to be flown to All Children's immediately. He's got to have surgery. We can't wait. I've ordered the helicopter, but you've got to give me the go ahead to move him there. I've got the best facilities possible. We're running out of time, let me take him."

Albert didn't like any situation that he couldn't control and he felt completely helpless for once in his life. He looked at Katie as if she should know what he was thinking, and she did.

"It's okay, Albert, I know Doctor Phillips from the center where I worked. He is the best pediatric neurosurgeon in the entire country. If anyone can get Jordan through this, it's him."

"Take him then," Albert said in a choked whisper, the tears beginning to openly flow as the words 'we're running out of time' echoed in his memory.

"Can we fly with him?" She asked.

"I'm afraid not, there isn't enough room to bring you along. Someone will have to drive... ."

"I'll call for my helicopter," Albert said, looking at her and suddenly remembering his social position.

She reached out to Gill and he willingly hugged her as she cried out, "Please Gill, don't let him die, please."

"Shhh," he consoled her. "We're going to do everything we can. You just keep the faith."

Then he was gone; the helicopter came and whisked him and her son into the placid, predawn sky.

When Albert's helicopter arrived at the hospital thirty minutes later, the sun was just beginning to illuminate a clear and cloudless morning. They put Katie into a wheel chair and took her to the helicopter. With much assistance, she boarded it with wonder and familiarity; she had ridden in it many times.

At the children's hospital she and Albert waited for word on their son. Contacted by friends and neighbors who began a prayer vigil, she waited in the Chapel room, her own prayer vigil begun. Albert paced the hallway floors, angry and tearful at his inability to help his son, angry with himself for the foolishness that caused him to throw-out the woman who bore his child.

Her parents arrived from the other coast, shaken and upset. Max drove them over. But even though they made it, there was still nothing to do but wait and support their own battered child.

Eight hours after taking Jordan into surgery, a very tired Doctor Phillips came out of the operating room. He explained in detail the nature of Jordan's injury, the things he could say with certainty and the many things that were not yet known. Tiny fragments of bone had to be removed from his brain where the corner of the chest pierced the skull. He worked diligently to retrieve them, but the damage from this injury wasn't known yet. Swelling was the most crucial concern for the immediate future. He took measures to reduce it. Gill had pioneered some of the most innovative methods in reducing and relieving pressure on the brain, but each case posed something different. Jordan could have partial paralysis, memory loss, impaired mental function, or all of these things. Only the next twenty-four to forty-eight hours would tell the effects of his injury.

"Can we see him?" She begged.

"Yes, of course you can, but only one or two at a time, okay?"

Her parents agreed that she and Albert should go together to see him. Albert pushed the wheelchair quietly into the recovery room. They wept openly as they came up to the bed and saw his head swathed in bandages, tubes and IV's running, it seemed, in every possible place on his little body. One machine showed his steady, but sedated heart beat; another assisted his very shallow breathing; and the third and most crucial, a monitor that showed brain activity. In his comatose state, there was none, except a tiny blip that, far too seldom, caused the straight line to jerk.

Katie reached through the bed rails and touched his tiny hand. Albert sat in a chair he pulled up close to the bed, his knees weak at the sight of his little boy so badly hurt.

"Mama's here little man, my little hero. Daddy's here too and we love you Jordan. You've got to get all better so Daddy can buy you that pony he promised," her voice was weak and trembling. They stayed beside him talking quietly, but he didn't respond. Grief and dread filled their hearts. It was time to leave the room and let his grandparents in to see him.

Albert took Katie out of the room and wheeled her into a tiny waiting room that was unoccupied.

"What happened, Katie? Tell me, please. Who did this to you both?"

"It was Nick Randall," she said, stifling her sob.

"He's in prison, Katie. I would have known if he had escaped."

"It *was* him. I'd know him anywhere. He said he came to kill me just like he killed Donovan."

"Donovan's death was an accident, Honey. The police report said... ."

"I don't give a damn about the report, Albert! He told me he was going to kill me, just like he killed Donovan except I'd get a bullet. Donovan got propane and a broken light bulb to ignite it."

"But why—why did he attack Jordan; he's just a baby?"

The tears ran harder as she told him, "He jumped on Nick's back twice to stop him from attacking me. Nick threw him across the room the last time; it was the only thing that saved me..." Albert seemed mystified, so she completed her sentence, "...he was trying to rape me."

His tears turned to hot rage as he whispered that he was going to see that Nick got the electric chair this time.

She looked at him confused; she thought he knew what had happened, but he didn't. He had left his house the minute his detective called him and said that the 'bug' had picked up someone attacking her in the house. By the time he was almost to her house, he saw the ambulance speed away, so he followed it to the hospital.

"He's not going to the electric chair, he's... ."

"Oh yes he is, if I have to... ."

"I killed him," she said, trying to grasp the reality of the words she spoke.

He didn't say anything; he just looked at her.

"I shot him and he's dead."

"My God," he said looking at her, "Katie, I didn't know." He moved to hold her and she broke down in his arms, sobbing, crying, and screaming for Jordan to live.

"He was trying to save me—my little hero ran through the darkness to help me. He can't die, he can't—if he does—I can't go on—I can't."

Holding her tightly he tried to quiet her, "Don't talk that way. He's going to be okay. I'll find the best doctors in the world if I have to, I'll... ."

Pulling back slightly, their faces close to each other she said, "You can't buy this, Albert. He's been with the best doctor in the country. You can't buy the outcome. You've just got to wait, just like me."

She was right. He always paid for what he wanted to happen, but this time the worth of his entire empire couldn't pull his son through to consciousness if it wasn't meant to happen. And it was then that he realized there was something else his money couldn't buy—and he was holding it in his arms.

She stayed, night and day, in a chair at Jordan's bedside. Albert couldn't take the pressure of waiting, but he returned three and four times each day to check on his son. Two days passed, then three, and then four. Still they waited for an end to their vigil.

She could see the mark of hopelessness in Gill's face after the second day and still Jordan didn't respond. Each day he checked him and each day she waited for him to tell her he'd pull through, but it was still unknown. He had experienced swelling, but his brain activity never went completely off the monitor, which was something good according to Gill and Doctor Wilhelm.

On the fifth day, as she sat holding his hand and staring listlessly out the window, she felt him stir. She looked down and he was staring at her with tears on his cheeks. Quickly she called for the nurse, who paged Doctor Phillips before rushing into the room. Jordan was awake, struggling against the tubes and wires. The nurse removed the ventilator tube that had been helping him with every third breath. Now it registered a normal breathing pattern. And the most beautiful sounds Katie had ever heard were his cries when the nurse took it out.

Then during his cries he said, "Drink!" He was thirsty and he vocalized the request. By the time Gill reached the room, Jordan was quiet and taking minute sips of water through a straw. Checking him over, Gill talked with him.

"Who is that?" Gill said, pointing to Katie.

"Mama!" he answered with a big grin.

"Who are you?"

Jordan looked at him as if he were silly; "I'm Jordan!" he giggled loudly.

"Would you like a Popsicle?"

"Yes!"

After a little more checking Gill asked Katie to join him in the hallway outside of the room. She was smiling at the knowledge that her son had returned to her, yet she was concerned why he wanted to speak to her in private. But, when she looked up into his face he was wearing the biggest grin she'd ever seen.

"I don't know how he pulled through it. To tell you the truth, I felt it was really touch and go there for a while. He's obviously fine and I might even be able to release him to go home after a few more nights of observation."

She let a shout of pure joy escape as she leaped into his arms and hugged him tight. "Thank you, Gill, for everything you did."

Still holding her in his arms and looking down at her; he shook his head, "No, I did what I could, but I think the Man upstairs had a big hand in this one."

"Well, thank you anyway for your wonderful talent." She gave him another long squeeze and then released him.

Albert had come to the hospital to see if there had been any change and he was coming down the corridor as he watched her hugging Gill. Still too far away to hear their conversation he became angrier the closer he got to them and they were still in each other's arms. His old inclination toward heated jealousy was still alive and well.

"I hope I'm not interrupting anything," he said sarcastically, as they broke from their embrace.

She looked at him with undeniable radiance in her still bruised face. "Oh shut up, Albert!" she said to his and Gill's astonishment. Then grabbing him by the hand she led him into see their son.

Jordan was sitting up in the bed munching on a bright red Popsicle. "Hi Daddy!" he happily shouted.

Albert was astonished. He looked at her and her eyebrows shot up as she motioned toward Gill standing in the doorway.

"Well, do you want to hug him too, or what?"

He walked over and put out his hand. "I can hardly believe it!" he said, shaking Gill's hand. "He doesn't even act as if anything ever happened to him." Then in a rare moment he said, "Thank you."

Returning to the jubilant mother and child, he talked at length with Jordan about how he was feeling. The only thing missing was that he didn't know how he got into the hospital; the whole affair of what happened in the wee hours days ago was forgotten. After an hour of everyone quizzing him from where his belly button was to where his nose, eyes and ears were, what sound does the dog make, and on and on, he began to grow tired and was ready to rest again. This time though, as he drifted off to sleep, his parents weren't concerned that he wouldn't wake.

Quietly they tiptoed out of the room and let him have his well deserved rest.

"I can't get over it. He's going to be fine," Albert was saying.

"I am so happy," she said, giving him a spontaneous embrace in her joy. "The waiting has been hell, but to be rewarded with such a total recovery is—well it's just… ."

She looked at him and they both had watery eyes filled with happiness.

But, unfortunately, he wouldn't allow the happiness to last for long. "Can we talk somewhere?" he asked her.

"Sure." At that moment she didn't particularly care. He could have asked her to go to the moon and she would have said sure.

They went to a room near Jordan's that was unoccupied. Closing the door behind him he turned to her, his deep blue eyes penetrating hers as if he was looking down into her very soul. "I want to ask you something, but I don't want you to answer it now. I want you to think about it for a few days and then give me your answer."

Her joy was fading and she was starting to get uncomfortable as he moved closer to her. He had been so kind recently that she had almost forgotten the vicious streak that was in him. She could tell he wanted something they had already decided couldn't be, but now he wanted it even more. Her heart began racing as he embraced her, pulling her body against his own. She knew that look from long ago and it was evident to her that his mind was becoming engulfed with the insatiable want and the physical need to touch and possess her.

"You're still so beautiful, even when you're battered and bruised," he said, caressing her face. His mouth began to seek hers; passionate and light he kissed the exterior of her lips.

"Please don't, Albert," she said, beginning to tremble.

He remembered the way she trembled in his arms when he made love to her; and more than anything at that moment, he wanted her.

She pushed him away gently.

"I didn't bring you in here to make love to you, Katie." He was saying it, but his actions didn't match his words. "I want you back—shhh—don't answer me." He stopped her before she could say anything, resting his fingertips lightly across her soft lips. "I want you to seriously consider it for a few days. Everything will be dropped, including this," he said, pressing a white envelope into her hand. "Don't look at it right now. I was going to give it to you the day I came to see you at the mall. I won't do it if you say yes to me. We can raise Jordan together, the way it should be." Again she tried to say something, but he put his fingers back on her mouth, "No, not now. I've thought it over for so long. I'll divide my company and give you half, if you'll take it." Then slowly and deliberately he said four words, *"I want you back."*

She looked at him, knowing this was wrong; once again he was trying to buy the love he needed. "I never wanted your money," she answered as the tears formed in the corners of her eyes.

"Kiss me," he whispered, pulling her back against him and ignoring what she told him. "Just to let me know you'll at least do as I ask and consider my generous offer."

She didn't want to kiss him. She wanted to cry and tell him to stop torturing her, she'd been through enough.

"Please, Darling, just this once and then you think it over. One kiss."

Her face turned slowly toward his, the tears in her eyes this time were from anguish.

Softly and slowly he pressed his mouth to hers, fanning the flames that were raging uncontrollable inside him.

She tried to break away from the kiss, but he only intensified his hold on her, forcing her lips to part as he pushed her back on the nearby bed.

He had never been so close to the edge in his life. His control over his needs had always been firmly in place, but at this moment there were no boundaries, only desire. His hands were finding their way under her sweater, groping her warm breasts. Pressing his groin into hers, his mind slipped away, leaving her with someone who was no different than the man who tried to force her to submit to him only days ago.

Quickly his hand replaced his mouth to keep her silent as he was finding his way up from the bottom of her jean skirt to the private recess of her body. Then pulling her skirt up, he positioned himself, but when he reached for his zipper, he looked into her face; her eyes were wide in disbelief and astonishment. In that same moment he became aware of the muffled cries of, 'No,' and the tears on her cheeks.

He stopped; his pounding heart slowing and his grip loosening from her face. He could see the red finger marks that he had made on her jaw. Suddenly, he was ashamed and angry at the same moment: ashamed at his inability to control what had always been under his command, and angry that she had reduced him to this point.

"I'm sorry, Katie."

But she turned away and wouldn't look at him.

"It's been a long time and I still…" He couldn't tell her that he loved her. He didn't want her to know that she still possessed his heart, but at this point he thought of it as more of an obsession than anything else. "I'm sorry," he repeated. "We were good together once. I know you still have needs. We can be good together again. Think about it. I know my timing was wrong, but there will be a time when you'll want a man's affection again—and I intend to be that man." Stiffly, he walked from the room, never looking back at the woman he had attacked.

Rolling over on the mattress, she sobbed her pain into it. He had stolen the first joy she had felt in weeks. Jordan's recovery filled her with unspeakable happiness. Why couldn't he let her enjoy it without doing what he did to her? Rising from the bed and wiping her eyes she opened the crumpled envelope. There were legal documents inside and for a moment she wondered if he had given her the original divorce papers. Had he done that, it would have shown he was not completely the beast she felt him becoming, but she was wrong. It was the last crushing blow, and she knew she couldn't take another like it.

The document said that he was formally declaring that he was the rightful owner of the Season's program and, therefore, was the rightful owner of any store bearing the name or using the concept. He'd had his attorney issue a writ to stop work and prevent the opening of her store.

She closed her eyes and crushed the paper in her hand, "I guess you'll just have to sue me," she said to his memory, "because you're not stopping me."

He came to the hospital each day to visit Jordan before his release to go home. But she never returned his gaze. Even when he asked her something directly, she avoided his eyes. He knew that what he had done to her had left an ugly wound that would never close, and he knew it wasn't the papers about stopping her from building her store either.

He realized he would never know the comfort of her body again unless he followed through with what he had tried to do to her when he had her alone that day. And, in considering the consequences, he began to think that if he was ever alone with her long enough he'd face the repercussions of his actions—because the next time he would not stop.

Finally came the day when Jordan could go home. She had spent every day and every night there with him and she was ready to get out of the hospital. Margaret had come from the east coast to help put the house back in order. She, Beth, and Elaine had cleaned the house until it was spotless; removing all traces of the events that had taken place. A carpenter friend of Granny's replaced the broken and splintered front door and installed a new lock on the back door where Nick had jimmied it to get into the house.

Yet, even with all the preparation, Katie still felt a cold tingling sensation when she walked into her room. The mattress had to be replaced, so the bed and bedding were both new. Still the memory lingered.

"Are you going to be okay here tonight?" Margaret asked gently.

"Yes, I think so anyway. If I do find that I can't stay here, I hope you'll understand."

"Oh, Honey!" Margaret said, giving her a warm and tender hug. "Why of course I'll understand! To tell you the truth, I don't know if I was in your shoes, if I could have even come back to the same neighborhood."

Jordan, on the other hand, was completely happy to be back in his room, in his familiar bed and with his toys. For his sake, She would shake the memories and push ahead.

She called Carson the day she brought Jordan home and told him about the writ that was issued to stop her from opening her store, but that only filled him with anger to strike back at Albert.

"Look, Katie, that son-of-a-bitch is playing hardball. Are you going to let me start swinging back or what?!"

"What do you want to do about it," she asked, worried at what he would say in his anger.

"You told me you weren't interested in his business, but I say if he's going to try to take yours then by damn you need to let me file your claim for part of his!"

She had told Carson from the beginning that all she wanted was her son and a divorce. She didn't want his wealth, just as she didn't want it when she signed the pre-nuptial agreement. But it was to Albert's disadvantage now, because the pre-nuptial agreement clearly stated that Albert would, in no part, have any heirs from her and wouldn't provide for such. That was the only reason he hadn't produced the agreement because she hadn't been after his money. Although he could produce it now and end her claim to his business, he wouldn't get his son.

"Well?" He asked impatiently, "Are you gonna give me the go-ahead to take him on where it really hurts, or not? I'll get that writ rescinded because if you can't operate your business then he sure as hell isn't going to operate his either!"

This wasn't what she wanted, but Albert himself left her no choice in the matter. "Do it," she said, suddenly relieved at the thought of slapping his face with this. "Do it right away."

"You got it, Baby!" And he let out a whoop for joy. "Finally, we're gonna fight just as dirty as he has!"

"Just let me know when he's being served with those papers," she added. "I might need a little support when he shows up."

"We can arrange that too!"

That evening a big, handsome looking fellow named Tom Watson from the sheriff's office showed up on her doorstep. He was supposed to be off duty for the next several days and Carson LaBrant had hired him privately to stay with her until the reaction from the papers passed. There was no chance Albert would get the papers tonight, but the courier was set to deliver them the next day, and who knew what would happen after that.

She met with Red and her architect at her home the next day; not wanting Jordan to go to Granny's yet. He still needed to stay close to her until Gill said he was a hundred percent recovered.

By four in the afternoon a limousine pulled up into the yard and a very agitated man got out of the back of it. She'd taken a step against his first love and no one would touch his company. He'd destroy anyone who tried, including her. Pounding on her door, he was thoroughly shocked when a man more than six feet tall and weighting about three hundred pounds opened it.

"Who the hell are you?" Albert demanded, his temple was showing throbbing veins and his jaw was tight.

"Can I help you?" Tom replied quite casually.

"Where is Katherine? Get out of my way."

"No, Sir. Unless you calm down, you're not going to talk with Ms. Danor."

By now Albert was seething to the point of loosing control. It seemed she was provoking that side of him more often these days.

He tried to shove the deputy out of his way, but he quickly realized that was a futile plan and he began a string of obscenities.

"Sir, your son is in the house and I'd caution you to use different language or I'm going to have to arrest you. I don't think you want him to see that, do you?"

Albert stepped back and re-evaluated the man blocking his path; "You're a police officer?"

"A sheriff's officer, yes Sir. If you want to speak with her you'll have to be civil or you'll go to jail, and I mean that," he said leveling an eye on Albert.

"Well, I have visitation with my son this weekend and I'll be damned if you're going to be in the way then."

"No Sir, you don't." Producing papers from his back pocket, he handed them to Albert. "Ms. Danor's attorney petitioned the court this morning that he should remain with his mother until he is completely well. The doctor and the court agreed."

Albert was trying to regain his focus because he was so angry that he had lost the ability to see straight. Things were not going according to plan. He had half expected that she would accept the offer he had given her the other day, feeling that he left her no other choice. The idea of ending her dream about opening her store should have been the last thing he needed to crush her will. But for it to give her more strength to fight him, he would have never believed.

"May I see her?" he said in a much calmer manner.

"Yes Sir, but if you make any move to physically harm her, I'll take you down in a heartbeat. Got it?"

"I would never hurt her," he was saying as the deputy stepped aside and Katie walked out from behind him. He was caught in a lie, and they both knew it. He had already tried to hurt her in the worst way.

"I'm sorry, Albert, but I knew what you were going to be like when you came to see me and... ."

"Where is Jordan? I want to see him now if I can't have him this weekend."

She looked at Tom as if to say it was okay for him to enter the house. He stepped back to allow him in. Jordan was playing with a collection of toy cars on Katie's bed. Saying nothing to her, he walked to Jordan and sat down on the bed.

Looking up, he smiled at Albert, "Hi Daddy! Wanna play cars?"

"He looks fine to me. Why can't he come this weekend?"

"He's been having headaches. Gill doesn't think it's a good idea to... ."

Reaching out and gently touching his son's cheek, he nastily added, "Well, if he'd done his job right then Jordan wouldn't have any headaches, would he?"

"Albert," she said in disbelief. "How can you say that? Jordan's recovery has been miraculous. Gill did a wonderful job saving our child's life!"

"Maybe I'd like a second opinion."

"His health care is my responsibility, and I believe Doctor Phillips is... ."

"I believe you like Doctor Phillips. It's not what's best for Jordan, maybe it's what's best for you?"

She bit her tongue. She was tired of the way he was talking to her; tired of the way he pushed her around whenever he felt like it. She'd had enough of him. "I believe it's time for you to go now," she said as she shot a look at the deputy.

Tom began to move toward him, but Albert got up instead. He kissed Jordan's head and nonchalantly remarked, "See you this weekend, Tiger."

"Okay, Daddy, bye. Wuve you."

She followed him to the door.

He turned to her as he reached it and gave her a wicked look, "You've made a grave error in attacking my company, and this," he said, motioning with his eyes toward Jordan, "I know how to play the game Katie—much better than you."

"Not today you don't," she replied just as acidly as he had spoken to her.

Tom was relieved of duty early because Albert wouldn't return, at least not while he thought Tom was there. There was no sense in trying to stay under someone's protection forever. One day soon, she knew she'd have to face him without that protection, and she'd have to be strong on her own.

~:~

Carson petitioned the courts to allow her to continue with her store until the ownership dispute was cleared in the pending divorce case. She had already met with her board of directors and they unanimously agreed that the project should continue. The court agreed to allow her to continue working on her store and to open it for business if that time came before the divorce was finalized. But, she was warned that all her work and effort might be simply going into someone else's hands if she lost.

Albert, in his irritation at not being allowed to see Jordan until he got a clean bill of health, went back to New York. He had been slightly inattentive to his business with all his effort directed to punishing Katie, and it was time to put his mind back on the company, for a while.

Without the concern of him lurking at every corner, she was able to concentrate on the business of raising a child and birthing a store. And that is exactly what the process seemed like: it grew and grew, seemingly by itself until she felt as if she would explode from the anticipation of realizing her dream.

She was happy with the progress the contractor had made in what seemed like years to her, but in reality was little more than a few months. Red estimated that it would only be a couple more weeks before she could have the suppliers start stocking the store. The advertisements had already started playing on Florida television stations about the exciting change that was coming to the clothing industry. And the response to the ads was phenomenal. Success was so close at last.

Jordan progressed wonderfully, but most of the time she took him with her wherever she went instead of Granny's. He was truly bothered by occasional headaches, they hadn't lied to keep him out of Albert's hands, yet the discomfort was minor and quickly relieved by over-the-counter medicine.

Gill made Katie's house a regular stop on his way home from the hospital to check Jordan's progress. She suspected he was visiting as a friend more than a doctor. He was wonderful to be around. He was so polite and considerate, and gently playful with Jordan. Jordan thoroughly enjoyed the male company.

Jordan often asked his mother where his father had gone. It broke Katie's heart to know that she was intentionally keeping the two of them apart, but in Albert's current state of mind, it was for the best. Tenderly, with all the care a mother has, she explained that he would be able to spend more time with his father after some things had been worked out between them.

Gill surprised her one evening when he stopped by for a visit when he asked if he could join her the next day as she worked at the mall.

"Yeah, sure you can, but I didn't think you got many days off. Are you sure you want to spend it with me at the mall?"

"I don't get many days, but I'd love to spend it with *you*."

They stared at each other; then he smiled and looked away at what Jordan was doing. The moment she had wondered about had just occurred and she was stunned by it. He had finally let her know that he was interested in her. She had been interested in him from the first time she met him, but that seemed like an eternity ago. She thought about what he said for so long that he took her silence the wrong way.

"I'm sorry, I guess I should have said that differently, but I do enjoy being around you."

"No, Gill, you're fine—I was just a little surprised. Maybe we could have dinner afterward—if you want." She had waited a long time for an invitation from the good Doctor Phillips and she wasn't going to miss the opportunity to make the most of being around him.

He smiled. He has the sexist shy smile I've ever seen, she was thinking as she looked at him. And, almost reflexively, she gave a little sigh at the pleasure of that smile. His cheeks warmed a little and he went back to playing with Jordan.

"I'd like that. Where do you want to go? It's my treat," he said, tousling Jordan's hair.

Jordan's ears perked up at the mention of 'treat.' "I wanna go for ice cream," he happily beamed.

Gill and Katie both laughed.

"Fine dining and ice cream? It'll take me a little while to figure out where to go, but okay big guy we'll find a place for ice cream after dinner. Sound good?"

"Yeah," he responded, looking from Gill to his mother with a giant smile for such a little face.

Early the next morning he came by and they rode together to the mall in his Mercedes. It was refreshing, yet amusing, the pains he took to be very proper and gentleman-like, opening the car doors for her and Jordan to get in and out, opening the doors for her at the mall, rising when she left her desk and returned to the room. She was so used to doing things for herself lately that several times she had to stop herself from jumping ahead of his next polite gesture.

And, of course, it had to be one of those days when nothing seemed to go right. When they arrived there was a truck being unloaded with a shipment of merchandise and the specific instructions she had given for the color combinations on the clothing were wrong. The corals looked like hot pinks and the neutrals had definite color shades in them. She had to call her supplier and tell them she wasn't accepting the shipment because of the discrepancies. By the time she finished talking with them she had to threaten to find another supplier for that line because they couldn't seem to understand their error with the colors. They eventually did see it her way.

The truck driver was angry that he had to reload the merchandise, and tried to tell her she would have to wait for another truck to pick it up. After a war of words, the shipment went back on the truck. A make-up order came in that was wrong and had to be returned. Then one of her employees worked on putting up a display rack, but he didn't fasten it correctly and the whole display, products and all, came crashing down.

It was a comedy of errors, but at the moment not at all funny. To end her horrendous afternoon, a petite elderly woman wandered through the construction entrance and wanted to find out what 'all this computerized stuff' was about. Politely and with great finesse Katie explained that they weren't open yet, but she would give her a quick color analysis. She spent the better part of a half-hour with the lady who left happy, saying she would be glad when the store opened because that was where she was going to shop from now on.

By four in the afternoon she looked at Gill and asked if he'd had enough of the life of a retailer and would he like to go to dinner early. He laughed and told her he was ready to go back to brain surgery; it was less stressful. They pulled out of the mall parking lot as Gill was giving her some places to choose from for dinner. She already had a headache coming on and the more she tried to think about dinner the more it ached.

With her eyes closed and her head on the headrest she said, "To tell you the truth, I know what I'd like to do after a day like today, but I'm afraid it doesn't involve a restaurant." She was thinking she'd like to spend an evening on the beach at the little park Margaret had shown her when she first came to the West Coast. Gill suddenly became noticeably quiet. She opened her eyes and looked over at him. His hands were gripping the steering wheel tightly and his eyes had a firm frozen gaze on the road ahead.

He had no idea what she was alluding to, but it sounded like a physical need she wanted to satisfy and he wasn't prepared for her to say anything like that.

Mentally reviewing what she said to him, she quickly realized she should have explained it a little better, but she couldn't help the laughter that started to come up without restraint. "Gill, I guess I should explain, I want to... ."

"Don't say it with Jordan in the car," he quickly interjected.

By this point she was dying with laughter.

Even Jordan wanted to know what Mommy found so darn funny.

The more she laughed the more serious Gill became.

Finally, with tears running down her cheeks from laughing so hard, she blurted out, "The beach, you big dummy; I want to go to the beach!"

His countenance relaxed and he too began to laugh, but even through the laughter his face turned red from the embarrassment of thinking she meant something else.

"I'm sorry, I know it's not a restaurant, but I could whip something together at the house and we could go to a really great spot on the beach that has picnic tables and some big trees for shade. It's really nice," she offered.

He was still smiling, "I think it sounds great, but are you sure after a day like today you don't want to just stop for some fast food?"

"No, I'm used to cooking when I get home, besides fast food is convenient but…"

"Yeah, I know what you mean, before you say it, it's not good for you."

"Be careful," she said with a wink, as he stole a glance at her. "You might misunderstand me sometimes."

They both laughed.

She put together a big salad and added a couple grilled chicken breasts from the meal the day before. She cubed some mild cheddar for the salad as well and she packed a bag of soft bread sticks and dressing. They brought swimsuits, sand toys and a pair of beach chairs and then switched cars at Katie's insistence. It wouldn't matter to her if they got in her car sandy and wet, but Gill's car with its plush leather seats and meticulous interior wouldn't fair as well.

The beach was wonderful. Just as Margaret had told her, the crowd had gone to the other side of the island to see the sunset so they had the eastside of the island practically to themselves. Gill and Jordan splashed and played in the water and built sand forts on the beach with zest and great enjoyment. She relaxed in her chair with her toes in the edge of the water. Her headache never dimmed but she was enjoying herself immensely, especially watching Gill in his beach attire. She felt that she watched him a lot more than he looked at her in her bathing suit. No wonder, she thought to herself, he doesn't have a girl friend already. He just didn't seem interested in the sensual aspect of a woman.

They stopped at the Shake Pit on the way home for Jordan's requested ice cream and it was delicious, except now she added a brain freeze on top of a headache. Gill drove home, more concerned about her headache than she was. She bathed Jordan, though Gill asked to take over so she could relax, but she wouldn't. They read him a story, together (which she found to be extremely sexy for a man to do), tucked him in and turned out the lights. He had played so hard at the beach that it took only a moment for him to be fast asleep.

"Now let's take care of that headache of yours," he said matter-of-factly, taking her hand and guiding her to her room.

It was her turn to be the one to misunderstand. "Well, but I… ." Nothing was coming out of her mouth correctly as the formerly bashful and unobtrusive Gill told her to lie down on the bed. She was the one ready to put the brakes on this time.

"But Gill, I… ."

He smiled and shook his head at her flustered look, "I'm just going to give you a scalp and neck massage—that's all, I promise. Don't you trust me?"

Trust? What an odd thought occurred to her. Trust had been something she'd had to make herself give to Alex, Albert, and even Donovan. She gave it to them unwaveringly, but she had to convince herself first to do it. The first two had horribly broken that trust. A pain stabbed at her heart with even just a thought of Donovan. But what she found so unusual was that she felt no need to *make* herself believe that she could trust Gill; she just simply did, with no reservation or mental preparation to give it. Odd? Yes, she thought, but wonderful to know a person she could feel that way about.

"Yes, of course I do," she replied as she lay down.

He knew intricately the location of each muscle under the surface of the human scalp and his skilled hands and fingertips began to massage away the tension of the day. She could only moan at the extreme experience of literally having someone 'rub-out' a headache. He worked her neck muscles, manipulating the upper vertebra until she felt one carefully pop back into its proper placement. It was one of the most pleasurable experiences she had ever felt—except perhaps one other.

"Oh, Gill," she moaned with her forehead resting on her pillow, "you should hire out for this stuff—ooh, I never felt anything so good. It's almost better than sex." In her extreme comfort she hadn't realize she was getting quite so vocal with what was on her mind.

"All done," he said suddenly. "See you tomorrow."

She was turning over trying to stop his departure, but she realized with a quick glance why he was hurrying to leave. It was obvious he enjoyed giving her the massage as much as she enjoyed receiving it. She wanted to stop him; she wanted him to stay, but he was already out the door and getting into his car.

"Damn," she said to herself as she watched him back out of the driveway. "Me and my big mouth!" She could only sigh and wave goodbye as he left.

But the next step with Gill would have to wait because she was soon to discover the divorce from Albert was more than imminent; it was upon her. She knew that Albert had had enough of the game he'd been playing with her; but what she didn't know was that his lawyers were no longer clogging up the wheels of bureaucracy; they were greasing them fast and furiously.

It was time to end it. And Albert wanted to end it in the worst way. He and Katie had experienced intense pleasure when they were married, and he wanted to be certain that she experience an equally intense pain when he ended it. He would take it all from her: her dignity, her business, and her son. He wanted her life to be so empty that she would feel as if she had stepped into a vacuum chamber when she walked out of the courtroom.

Carson wanted more time, not that he hadn't had enough, but he didn't like Albert's team controlling the pace. But it was beyond the point of slowing down the process by the time they found out about the hastily set date. It was a little unusual that he wasn't given a heads-up before it happened and he wondered how much money Trathmoore was spending to get what he wanted.

Carson came down personally to see her and tell her she'd have to get prepared because the court date was only six weeks away, one week before the grand opening of her store. She sat there numbly at first, realizing Albert had purposely arranged the date, knowing if she lost, as he was certain she would, he would take away her joy of opening the store.

"I'm sorry Katie. We knew it was going to come to this point eventually, but the timing—well, what can I say, it sucks," It might not have been the language a respected lawyer should have used, but it was the only thing appropriate enough to fit the situation.

"No," she said, resolved to beat Albert at his own nasty game. "I'm changing the date of the grand opening."

Carson was shocked. He knew it had been advertised for months and to change the date would be costly. "But, Katie how much is it going to cost to change the date? Is everything set to open if you change it?"

"Yes, I could have it ready to open in a few days if I had to, but I'm going to change it to the week before the court case. I have almost a hundred thousand in the bank, most of it is owed to the mall and part of it is payroll. I can spend a little of it, but I think I know a great attorney who can get me some pre-court press coverage." She looked at him with a smile and a determination that said she was going to find a way to make it happen.

He put an arm around her and gave her a comforting hug. Then he whispered, "Is anything in your life ever easy? I'll get you on television. You're just going to have to turn the interviews into ads for your business."

"I will," she said quietly.

She had been avoiding the press the last several months, but after Carson spread the word, within two weeks she had been on three talk shows, one national news program, and three Florida news programs, and she was to be featured in two weekly national magazines the following week. In each case she managed to turn the focus to how she was rebuilding her life with the opening of her store and she talked candidly about her vision for the future of Seasons.

Albert was wroth at the knowledge that she had circumvented some of the pain he intended to inflict, but he would still inflict it. It would just be after the grand opening instead of before.

"Enjoy the feeling, darling," he said as he sat in the New York penthouse apartment watching her on the television. "It's not going to last for long."

But someone else was watching the actions of the lovely Katherine Danor-Trathmoor, and he was moved to find a way to help her win her case. After all, she certainly could use all the help she could get to defeat the unbeatable Albert Trathmoore.

CHAPTER EIGHT

It had been a long battle and now it had come to a head. Carson and his team spent months preparing, yet it still was no more than her word against his. And if anything was a known fact about Albert Trathmoore it was that if he said it was so, then it was. He had a reputation of being a brilliant, successful businessman. She was some little girl he picked out of the abundance of women available. Although the public seemed to adore her to a certain point, he was definitely the one who had the credibility.

The case, for all the pomp and circumstance that brought it before the court, was still basic. She filed for divorce almost one year ago, claiming that she had signed the divorce papers long before her son was born and, knowing she was pregnant, he willfully threw her out penniless and without even so much as a means of returning home. Since she raised their child alone since birth, she wanted custody of him. She never said she would exclude Albert from visitation.

Albert, on the other hand, said he would give her the divorce she now desired, but it had not been agreed to years ago, and his son belonged with him. He would take full custody of his child because she was not 'stable' enough to rear him.

The matter was complicated with both of them owning corporations to which the other was now laying claim. Unfortunately, Katie's team advised her that he stood a very real chance of taking Seasons. But she had not married Albert before the formation or the astronomical growth of ATI; thus she had only a small chance of doing any significant damage to him or his company. They filed the counter claim more so to anger and aggravate the situation for Trathmoore.

Witnesses for both sides took the stand over two days of testimony. Each person told how, why and what had occurred to make them believe that Katie and Albert were or were not divorced. Albert and Katie each took the stand to tell their side of the story.

Albert calmly and coolly lied, saying that she had taken off not long after the kidnappers had been apprehended. He said the pressure, understandably, had been too great for her and he had given her some space to recoup. He said he never thought that in that time period she might suffer some form of dementia and create a fantasy about a divorce. Out of fear for his son, he said he tried to take the boy home with him to New York, but she cursed and struck him and said she wanted a divorce right away.

She wanted to stand up and call him a liar to his face, but it would only serve to fit the description he was painting of her. But his cruelest blow was when he said to the courtroom that she had reunited with the kidnapper who decided to set her free and began a sexual relationship with him. She could hear the gasp come up from the gallery at the thought of her irresponsible behavior.

During her time on the stand she spoke frankly about what had occurred during the kidnapping, the decision she had made to say the sex was consensual which had ended her marriage, and the way in which Albert had thrown her out the next day. She admitted to the relationship with the late Donovan Randall, who re-entered her life almost three years after being separated from Albert. Carson gave her room to briefly state that Donovan was a caring and kind person who had risked his own life for her. That risk eventually led to his demise at the hand of his half brother. She said she had no regrets about the relationship and, as she spoke, she could see Albert's expression of anger and bitterness as she willingly exposed the truth about her feelings for Donovan.

When it was time for Mr. Rizzona to cross-examine, he wasn't interested in the issue between Katie and Donovan, but in something else.

"Mrs. Trathmoore," he began.

"Danor," she interrupted, "Ms. Danor."

The judge nodded and Mr. Rizzona continued, "*Ms.* Danor, were you married prior to your marriage to Mr. Trathmoore?"

"Yes," she stated.

"You divorced your first husband over an extra marital affair?"

Carson objected, as he would many times during the day, but he was over-ruled more times than sustained.

322

"Yes."

"Did you sign divorce papers and a request for name change with the courts?"

"Yes, I did, just as I did with... ."

"Just answer the question, don't embellish. How did you know that your divorce from your first husband was finalized?"

"I received... ."

"Yes?"

"I received copies of the filed divorce papers."

"You claim that you and Mr. Trathmoore signed divorce papers four years ago?"

"You were there, don't you remember?" she said sharply.

He smiled briefly, "No, I am sorry Ms. Danor, I guess I don't." Low laughing came up from the gallery and the judge banged the gavel for silence. "Just please answer the question."

"Yes, we both signed the divorce papers, just like we signed the prenuptial agreement before we married."

"Did you receive copies of either of these alleged documents?"

"No."

"You've been divorced before and know that you are supposed to receive the court filed copies. Didn't you find it strange that you never received papers confirming this alleged divorce?"

"I thought it was because I moved around. I didn't tell Albert where I had moved to and... ."

"You stated earlier that he came to your house to ask you to come back, didn't you?"

"Yes, but... ."

"Then Mr. Trathmoore obviously knew where you were staying, correct?"

"That was two and a half years... ."

"Just answer the question, Ms. Danor. Did he come to your house?"

"Yes."

"Thank you. What was the media attention like when Mr. Trathmoore announced that he had married you? Light, heavy?"

"There was considerable media coverage."

"Wouldn't it make sense that you would get the same coverage with a divorce?"

"Not necessarily," she said. "I felt his money could assure his privacy if he wanted it."

"Yes, just like the privacy of the current divorce proceedings," he said, mocking her.

"He wanted this to be public!"

"I believe *you* have recently been the vocal public figure concerning the divorce haven't you?"

"OBJECTION!" Carson shouted, rising to his feet

"I withdraw the question, your Honor," Mr. Rizzona quickly said to the judge. "I have no further questions."

Several times during the testimonies and arguments from the legal teams, she felt Albert's hot stare on her. Each time she looked back at him with the disgust and disappointment she felt for someone she once so completely trusted.

The next day the final arguments would be presented and she would know her fate. The newspapers and press were quite convinced that Trathmoore was in the right and would win, taking her son and her business but leaving her with the staggering legal debt.

She spent the early morning with Jordan, preparing herself for the crushing blow of losing him, her business, and every dream she had ever held in her heart. How could it have come this far? How could she have fought differently to save her son? She refused to lie and be hateful as Albert was. If she was going to win it had to be based on the truth. She knew Albert loved Jordan; that was obvious when they were together, but he had to realize it was going to cause his own son pain when he was taken from his mother.

In the beginning she didn't want Albert anywhere near Jordan, but it wasn't because she feared he would hurt him or try to turn him against her. It was more the fact that he had purposely waited two and a half years before reentering their lives. It wasn't enough that he had tried to crush her once when he had her sign the divorce papers, but it seemed he wouldn't be satisfied until he finished what he started to do and she was ground into the dust of the earth.

The bodyguards Carson had appointed came and guided her down to the court room past the throng of reporters clamoring for a comment or an opportunity to take her picture. For some reason though, Carson and his other two team members were not seated in the courtroom yet.

Albert sat confidently with Mr. Rizzona and his team. He was smiling because he knew he was going to win. She would finally get what he so desperately wanted her to have—nothing, except for hollowness inside. That was a feeling he had been living with since he decided to take her back and she refused him and filed for divorce. He wasn't used to refusals and she would pay dearly for it.

But when Carson did appear in the room he didn't stop to sit with Katie, but asked permission to approach the bench. After several quiet moments speaking with the Honorable Judge Harrison, the judge granted a thirty-minute delay to the start of the proceedings. Carson looked over at her with an expression she had not seen on his face before that day. It was an expression that told her she was decisively going to win this case.

"Come on," he said, taking her arm and leading her from the room.

Albert looked only mildly annoyed at the delay and then relaxed in his chair as they exited the room.

Carson took her into a side room. Quietly, yet fervently, he was saying, "We've got him! We can prove it now!"

Her heart began beating faster at the possibility of victory. She saw Carson's team seated in the room with a man. His back was to her, but moving closer to him, her apprehension began to grow. She knew this man somehow. She had not seen his face yet there was something very familiar about him. Then she faced the man who was smiling serenely, but with an underlying dark and evil look.

"Hello Katherine," he said evenly. "It's been a long time, do you remember me?"

"Yes, I know who you are, Mr. Lindquist, but it's why you're here that worries me."

"I don't know why it would worry you—I've got the answer to your prayers." As he opened his briefcase the first thing that caught her eye was the original divorce document signed by both her and Albert, dated over four years ago.

Her knees went weak and Carson caught her quickly as she swayed. A chair was brought up underneath her and she began to openly weep, knowing she could finally prove that she had been truthful and Albert, vindictive and hateful, had been lying.

"How did you get that?" she choked out.

"Oh, I have much more than this," he said, pointing to two large boxes on the floor.

Carson set the first box on the table and opened it, revealing hundreds of cassettes and videotapes. Carson was smiling, but she was mystified.

"Katie," Carson said, "these are conversations taken from your telephone over the last six years. He's been listening in on everything you've done from the time you accepted the job offer in New York up until a few days ago."

"I don't believe it," she said as she stared at the pile of tapes marked, dated and with notations on each. "He spied on me before—before I slept with him, before I knew him. Why?"

"There's more, lots more," he said as he lifted the second box, which appeared to be heavier than the first. The lid came off to reveal stacks of files, reports and records.

"Look at this," Carson said as he tossed a folder onto the table before her.

Slowly she opened it. "My drug test results?" she ventured a guess.

"Look again, Katie. He had you tested for a lot more than drugs. It's a complete blood analysis, he was checking for everything from syphilis to AIDS. Here are notes about all your activities: where you went, who you were with, what you did, pathology reports checking Jordan's DNA with his own. The son-of-a-bitch knew everything. He knew you inside out before you ever even met him for the first time."

"I don't want to see anymore," she said, pushing the files away from her. There was a sick, nauseating flood rushing over her, mingling with the pain of such a complete shattering of the illusion that was Albert Trathmoore.

"Come on, Honey, it's all right. We've got him. With Mr. Lindquist's help we not only have the divorce papers, but the pre-nuptial agreement too, and we can put the sneaking bastard in jail where he belongs."

"What?" She said, looking up at Carson with fear and surprise. "What do you mean?" She looked back at Jon Lindquist. What was it he wanted so badly that he found a way to get all these items?

Jon smiled. "You're going to do me a big favor when you walk into the courtroom with all of this. I want to see him ruined, destroyed and sent to prison. His detective has already provided taped conversations between himself and Trathmoore in which he was told, point-blank, to tap your phone line. And Trathmoore said he didn't care if it was a federal offense or not. Then add to it perjury and invasion of personal medical privacy. It looks like he went well beyond the line this time. And the best part," he said, reaching out and softly stroking her arm with an eerily cold touch, "is that you get to be the one to put him away. He was very fond of you at one point."

She swallowed back the sickness creeping up her throat. She hated Jon Lindquist; he was the only person she could truly say that about. She knew, as Albert did, that Jon was the reason behind the kidnapping though it couldn't be proven. The only link that could have connected him was a go-between who was found floating in New York Harbor the day after she escaped.

She turned to look at Carson; her agony visible, "Carson I need to see you—alone—please."

Carson was confused at the expression on her face. If he was reading her correctly, he had a sneaking fear she wasn't going to accept this 'gift' of evidence.

But Jon continued to smile in his wicked way. She would have to take it. She'd have to destroy him or she'd lose her son. He knew a lot about human nature and there was one thing you didn't do and that was to take a child from its mother without one hell of a dirty fight. He was confident that this time it would be the end of the man he loathed to the point of purest and deepest hatred. He would finally attain his greatest goal in life and get back at Trathmoore for the stunt he pulled in buying all the stocks he could for the total control of ATI. For once in his life, Albert Trathmoore would be, undoubtedly, the loser.

Reluctantly, Carson took her arm and they went into another adjoining small room. Closing the door behind the two of them, he looked at the very obviously torn woman that he had worked so hard to win this fight for. "Don't say what I'm seeing in your face. You *can't* refuse this. What about Jordan?"

"Stop it, Carson!" she sobbed. "Don't you know it's killing me to know I'll lose him?"

"Katie, please." He reached out and held her for a moment. "*You don't have to lose him.* If you can't go out there and do this, then I sure as hell can."

"NO! Please Carson," she begged. "Let me talk with Albert for a few minutes. I can't use Jon Lindquist to do this to him, no matter how badly I want to win. This is wrong."

He had been sympathetic throughout her plight, but this was a golden opportunity to win, and Albert deserved the taste of defeat that he was trying so hard to cram down her throat. The more Carson realized this, the angrier he became with her. Grabbing her by her shoulders so hard that she came close to crying out at the pain of it, he shook her and looked into her eyes. Through clenched teeth he said, "*This isn't the time for your damned morals!* I like you, maybe a little more than I should, but you aren't only losing for yourself and your son; you're gonna lose it for my company, too. We've got to win this!"

"At what price?" she cried out, trying to get him to let her go. "If he has to lose everything and go to prison, it will *kill* him. Carson—please—I know him better than anyone else. I hate what he's trying to do to me because he wants to be vindictive, but…"

"He'd do this to you, you know that?" He hadn't realized how hard his grip had been on her and he slowly released her. "If he had something like this on you, you'd go to prison. I don't think he'd even give it a second thought."

"Yes, I know it, but I'm not like him. I can't destroy without regret and pain. I've got to talk with him. Give me the divorce paper and let me have at least a few minutes alone with him. *Trust me, please.*"

With nothing more said, Carson opened the door and stormed back to where Lindquist was seated and snatched the divorce paper right out of Jon's briefcase before he even had the chance to react. He put it in Katie's hand and gestured toward the door.

Reentering the courtroom, he asked permission to approach the bench again. "Your Honor, if you will please allow it, my client would like to speak in private with Mr. Trathmoore before the proceedings continue."

"Not without legal counsel present!" Mr. Rizzona said, rising to his feet.

But Albert saw something in her face, something that intrigued him. Perhaps she would finally accept his offer to return to him. Whatever it was it distressed her greatly and that pleased him.

"No, Mr. Rizzona, I'll speak with her in private."

They walked to the judge's chambers, just the two of them. The curiosity of the gallery peaked; a murmur traveling through the crowd as she and he left the room.

"I assume this means you're ready to accept my offer, but I think it might be too late for... ."

"Albert," she said softly, causing him to go silent for a moment, "you're going to win, do you know that?"

"I've known that all along," he said, moving closer to her. He liked it now when she was frightened, all her bravery pushed aside. She had given him more of a fight than anyone else had ever been able to do, and there was a certain amount of respect that went with that accomplishment, but she was at the end and he knew it. He might even have her back in his bed by tonight. Her tears were flowing harder now and he knew she was experiencing the pain he wanted her to feel.

"Do you really love Jordan, or is it that you hate me so much?"

"I love my son, don't ever doubt that," he answered honestly. "I don't hate you, Katie. I want you back, but I guess I'm still punishing you for sleeping with Donovan—both times," he added, letting her know that he knew everything about their relationship. "But you don't have to lose, if you change your story."

"No, Albert," she said, taking a deep breath, "you don't understand; I *do* have to lose." She pulled out the divorce paper from the pocket of her suit jacket and handed it to him. "I can't hurt you the way you're trying to hurt me. I never stopped loving you; I just can't be with someone I can't trust, someone who has done what you've done to me. I can't send you to prison."

Her confession of love pleased him, but prison? What was she talking about? He opened the paper and upon seeing it he let it fall to the floor as if his hands couldn't hold onto it.

"Where... How could you have this!?"

"There's more—boxes more. You spied on me before I ever met you. You had me tested for diseases. You tapped my phone lines and bugged my house for years. Why?"

"How did you get all of those things!" he demanded, taking hold of her. He suddenly had the feeling of having his privacy invaded, just as he had invaded hers so many, many times. She was weak in his grip and he could feel it; she was on the verge of collapse.

"You would use anything to hurt me, even the love that I have for Donovan, but I can't use Jon Lindquist to ruin you."

He stood there for a long moment, his eyes bearing down on her. It would take time for what she told him to sink in. He didn't know how his private items got out of his office in New York, but he knew who, Jon Lindquist. But she was refusing to use what Jon was giving her? That he couldn't understand. He deserved to be punished for hurting her. Why wouldn't she do it?

The way he held her changed; the look on his face changed from anger to sorrow. "I'm sorry, Katie." He pulled her to his chest and held her. She was crying and shaking in his arms. Begging him to stop the pain he was inflicting on her.

"*Please*," she cried out to his very heart, "please don't take my son away from me. I can't hurt you. Please stop trying to hurt me, Albert, please."

He smoothed her hair back from her face and kissed her temple. He held her, never wanting to let go. For all his ugliness toward her, he could not damage the very beautiful heart that was within her.

Tenderly he kissed her lips, repeating his words of sorrow. Then passionately he pulled her tighter to him, trying to stop her from quaking so violently. This was the woman who had beaten him; no matter what the outcome of the courts, she *had* beaten him.

"Will you stay with me, Darling?" he whispered, but he knew her too well to even need the reply.

"I can't. There's too much between us."

Taking the last fragrant breath from her hair, he released her and walked back to the courtroom.

She wasn't sure what would happen. She had refused to fight him. She had refused to come back to him. He could end it with one blow.

She walked out behind him, trying to wipe away the tears, not wanting to look into the faces in the gallery. She had almost reached the table where Carson and the other two were waiting when Albert announced to the judge that he was dropping his suit against Ms. Danor and that he would be complying with whatever she requested of him. She stopped and looked at him as the stunned silence gripped the courtroom.

"I'll also be taking care of the legal fees for both sides," he added.

The silence broke and the courtroom went out of control. The pounding of the gavel went unheard and the media from the hallway burst into the gallery when they heard the frenzied noise. Barely aware of what was going on around her, Carson and his teammates were holding her, congratulating her. They released her and she turned to look toward Albert's table. Mr. Rizzona was obviously shaken. She could hear the only words he was managing to say to Albert, "But, Mr. Trathmoore, we had her—we had her." Albert's other two team members were frozen in their seats, looking pale and disbelieving as the shock engulfed them.

Yet above the bedlam a furious thundering shout was heard.

"*NO! YOU IGNORANT, STUPID BITCH!*" screamed out Lindquist. He was close enough to grab her over the gallery gate and the bailiff was too far away to reach her in time. Grabbing her lapel, he jerked her against the gate with his fist pulled back to smash into her face, as Carson scrambled to save her. It was Jon's last chance to beat Trathmoore and if he couldn't have this victory he'd take it out on her before they could stop him. But someone grabbed his arm and spun him sideways—and he stood face to face with Albert Trathmoore. In the blink of an eye, Albert hit him full force with a powerful punch that sent him sprawling unconscious into the spectators.

Cameras were going off as additional officers filled the courtroom trying, unsuccessfully, to restore calm to the room.

"Are you all right?" Albert asked, holding her for a moment.

She was still stunned but she managed to find her voice, "Yes, I'm okay." Then she smiled at him, it had been a long time since she had given him that smile. "You have some private items in the next room. Please, do me a favor, Albert, and get rid of them."

He shook his head and sighed, "You're the damnedest woman I've ever met." Releasing her, he motioned to his team to follow him and they left.

Carson was there supporting her, but she barely heard his words until he turned her face toward him. "We need to meet with him and wrap up the loose ends. Do you want to try it while he is still feeling so generous?"

"I really want to see my son now, so if you don't mind."

"I understand." He hugged her. Holding the embrace for a moment he whispered, "You're tougher than nails, woman. I never thought you'd come out of that room with anything other than another fight on your hands."

The bodyguards had a hard time getting her through the crowded courthouse hallways but finally they emerged from the mass of people and as they did, she broke into a run, heading down to the room where Jordan and a court liaison were waiting.

"Mama!" he squealed with delight. She had told him she might not see him for a while after their morning together so he was pleasantly surprised when she came into the room.

She picked him up and held him tight, kissing his cheek and enjoying the feeling of having him in her arms. "Oh Jordan, Mommy loves you so much," she said with her face muffled against his neck.

"I wuve you too, Mommy." Then looking into her face he remembered she had told him he would get to see his father today. It had been a long time and he missed him. "Where's Daddy?" he questioned.

"Right here," came a voice from the doorway.

"Daddy," Jordan happily chirped, "where you been?"

"Oh, I've been very busy lately, Son. I'm sorry, but I don't think we'll be spending too much time together. I wanted to see you before... ."

"Why?" Katie said with a smile.

"You have full custody now, Katie."

"What is custard-dee?" Jordan asked. It seemed he'd heard a lot about this word lately and no one seemed to like it.

"It means," she said, taking a deep breath, "who you are going to stay with, Mommy or Daddy. How about if we share?"

"You're *suppost-da* share, Mama," he said, looking surprised at her for not knowing that; she had told him he had to do it enough times.

Albert dropped down to rest on his heels as she set Jordan on the floor to go running to his arms. He held him for a long while, rocking back and forth with his eyes closed and tears on his cheeks.

"Why are you crying, Daddy?" Jordan asked in his most serious voice. He'd never seen his father do that.

"I missed you, Son. I just missed you."

She watched as Albert and Jordan embraced. She knew the love for his son was more than genuine; it was completely from his heart, just as his love for her had been once. But she knew, very well, that the bonds between a parent and a child are special and able to withstand more of the pressure that life throws on us from time to time.

Quietly she stood there, waiting for him to look at her. He wiped his eyes and stood, letting Jordan go back to the scattered toys on the floor. Clearly his own emotion over what he thought would be the end of the relationship with his son had been difficult for him. His ego, she knew, was taking a bruising like nothing he had ever experienced before.

"Do you want to take him this week? I mean, I know we need to straighten out the final details as soon as possible, but... ."

"Yes, I'd like to take him—to New York." He waited for her reaction, wondering if Florida was still to be her prerogative.

She didn't like the idea of Jordan flying around the country, but she knew to force Albert to only be able to see his son in her state would be wrong. "New York is fine. He's been so anxious to see it and... ."

"Why, Katherine?"

She was puzzled at what he was asking her. Why was Jordan anxious to see New York?

"Why didn't you send me to prison for what I did to you? I would have stripped you of everything in that courtroom. You could have accepted Jon's help, but you trusted me after—after everything between us."

"Wrongs and rights aren't interchangeable, not for some people." She looked away from him and back to her son, "I wish we could go back and change what's wrong between us, but we can't and Jordan never should have been in the middle of it."

Mr. Rizzona entered the room to tell his employer that the evidence had been removed from the building, but Carson LaBrant was close on his heels.

"Mr. Trathmoore, her lawyer wants to set a time to sign the paperwork, but I think we... ."

"I'll take care of that myself, you can leave and go back to New York, Mr. Rizzona."

"But, Sir... ."

"That's final—leave." There would be no rebuttal.

Clearing his throat, Carson spoke up, "Would tomorrow at the First National Bank's conference room be acceptable with you? In the afternoon perhaps?" He looked at Katie to see if it was acceptable to her and she nodded.

"Four o'clock; just the three of us," Albert stated. He wasn't asking if that was convenient, he was telling Carson when he would be there.

"Yes Sir, that would be fine. Four o'clock okay with you, Katie—I mean, Ms. Danor?"

She said, yes. Then she looked at Albert, wondering why just the three of them, but she wouldn't be able to tell from his face. His steel façade was slipping back over his demeanor; his feelings wouldn't remain exposed in front of these people. He was moving back into his position of control.

~:~

Albert realized he surprised Carson when he said he'd meet with them without his legal staff, but Albert wasn't concerned about the arrangement between the two of them. He did multi-million dollar contracts on a regular basis. This he could handle without any assistance; he had no fear of Carson LaBrant. Besides that, he was hoping for an opportunity to speak privately with Katie and that just wouldn't happen with a roomful of lawyers.

They met at the First National Bank in a quiet conference room on the fifth floor with a spectacular view of the bay and the late afternoon sunshine sparkling off the water.

Carson left her and Albert alone for only a few minutes while he went to retrieve the diamond and her $23,000 cashiers check from the purser's office. Their conversation had been focusing on the end of the trial, when she mentioned that after speaking with him in the Judge's chambers she had to trust that he would do the right thing. He leaned over in the thickly padded executive chair less than a foot from her. Gingerly he reached out to touch her arm. In a moment that she thought might be a tender remark about what he did that day, his fingers trailed lightly down her arm letting his thumb brush the curve of her breast. He startled her with the sexual contact.

"Don't ever trust me." His dark blue eyes flashed, giving away the thought on his mind. "Don't ever find yourself alone with me because I've already decided that I *won't* be able to do the right thing—and I do mean that."

"Please, Albert," she said uncomfortably, looking for Carson to return. "You stopped once when I thought you wouldn't. You couldn't hurt me that way, I know... ."

"Oh yes, I could." And he pulled her chair to butt up next to his. She jumped in fright, her face flaming red, as Carson opened the door and walked back in the room. Albert straightened back in his chair slowly, as if he had leaned over to listen to what she had said.

Right away Carson knew something was awry from the red, flustered look on her face. "Everything okay with you two?" he asked, but he was looking at her.

Katie said nothing, Albert only smiled; Carson worried. He returned her cash and then rolled out the diamond on to the table.

Albert's head cocked sideways a little in surprise. He picked it up before she could. "I didn't buy this for you?" He was prepared to find out from whom such an expensive jewel came from, but she removed it from his hand, their eyes locking as their hands touched.

"My uncle gave it to me, not long after..." she stopped for a moment as she looked at him, "after you threw me out."

"That," he said, with a smile playing the corners of his lips, "I will admit here in private, was the worst mistake I ever made in my life."

Carson shook his head; these two had some undeniable chemistry between them and it was the most evident love/hate relationship he'd ever seen.

They completed the paperwork in amicable agreement. The schedule for the visits with Jordan, the release of his claim to her business, her release to any claim in his, and the agreement for Albert to pay the legal fees, all would be quickly filed in the courts.

Standing up at the finish of their business, Carson extended his hand to Albert, something Albert didn't expect, but accepted.

"I'm famished," Albert remarked looking at Katie. "Would you care to join me for dinner? I know a wonderfully *private* place."

"NO!" she said, a little too loudly. "I mean," she continued, as the red filled her face again, "I have other plans for dinner."

Carson still wondered what in the world had transpired while he had been out of the room and he thought that he should question her about it.

Albert laughed out loud and nodded. She was catching on to this new game quickly, and he liked it.

Then, as if it were a common occurrence, he touched his fingertips to her chin and kissed her cheek, "Goodbye, Darling. I'll come by in a week and drop off Jordan." And he walked from the room.

Carson arched one eyebrow; "He certainly seems—how shall I say—overly friendly today?"

"Too friendly," she responded. "I think I'd rather have him angry with me. At least then I'd feel a little more prepared for him."

It was over now, she and Carson said their good-byes. He would be flying back to Atlanta in a few hours. His firm had a list of cases waiting to be handled since hers turned out to be a success.

"I'll never forget you, Katie. You're a special person. If you ever need a divorce lawyer again... ."

She frowned at him, "No Carson, I like you as a friend. I don't want to need you on a professional basis again. The next time I marry, I hope it's forever and always."

"You sound like you've already got someone in mind."

"I have a wonderful friend who's seen me through some rough spots, but he isn't asking."

Carson chuckled as he closed up his leather briefcase; "I can't imagine someone not wanting to ask you. Maybe he needs to have his head examined?"

She laughed out loud.

He wasn't quite sure that what he had said was all that funny.

"He can do that himself!" she said, with a radiant smile.

~:~

Gill was at home. He'd had a hectic schedule for the last two weeks because Dr. Wilhelm had been on vacation, another doctor had been out with a bad bout of poison ivy, and one was on her honeymoon, leaving Gill, one other doctor and an intern to handle all the injuries that came into the neurology ward. And it seemed as if most of the cases that came through the emergency doors of the hospital for the last two weeks managed to have some type of trauma to the head. He had wanted to be with Katie for the trial, but there simply was no way. Dr. Wilhelm's travel plans had been made a year in advance, so there was no chance to slip away to get to her side. Now with Dr. Wilhelm back and Gill's first two-week vacation in five years starting tomorrow, he was planning on relaxing with a special friend.

He was happy for her and glad that she and Albert arranged Jordan's custody so well. Jordan's love for his father was evident. And by Gill's theory, if the father was worth anything as a man he should help raise his child. He planned a quiet celebration dinner for her tonight at his house and he found a great movie to enjoy afterwards.

She was a very special woman; and he knew he wasn't the only man to ever realize that. He felt fortunate that she was so obviously interested in him. He had some experience dating and yet he had never found a woman that he felt so comfortable around. He'd always felt tongue-tied around women, but he could talk and even joke with her. He had such deep emotions and inner stirring when he was near her. He wanted to hold her in his arms and kiss her tender mouth and tell her that he wanted to fall in love with her, but he couldn't. He hadn't even attempted to kiss her, though he thought several times that she had wanted him to try.

He sighed aloud as he worked on the dinner. He remembered when he was a young man, a senior in high school at only fifteen years of age, a cheerleader named Dianna had turned his head. She was a senior as well, but she was eighteen; and definitely more experienced. She made it clear that she liked him, and it delighted her to no end to embarrass him with public affection. She asked him to take her to the senior prom, not just because she was forward, but also because she realized he was too shy make the invitation.

The truth was that he had no interest in going. He was so busy preparing for medical school that a dance was the last thing on his mind. He agreed to go, but reluctantly.

The day before prom they sat outside the school cafeteria at the picnic tables, just the two of them. She asked him several hard questions, not brain hard—those he could have handled—these were emotional questions. She wanted to know how he felt about her, about them together, and about what would happen to their relationship after they graduated.

He could still picture her in her blue and white cheerleading uniform because she had a pep rally after school that day. The day was warm and breezy, blowing her blonde ponytails back from her face. The sun deepening her golden tan and causing the line of freckles sprinkled across the bridge of her nose to show. Looking at him with her light brown eyes she asked him if he loved her. He didn't know what to say. They had kissed and fondled each other, but love? He wondered if that was all there was to love—wasn't he supposed to feel it from the heart, not his jeans? He fumbled with what to tell her, and then he gave the response that he thought he was supposed to give, "Yeah, sure I love you." Perhaps, he thought, the actual feeling would come along later.

Dianna then proceeded to shock him by saying that she wanted to take the next step in their relationship. She had already reserved them a room at a hotel near the hall where the dance was to be held. She was excited as she kissed him goodbye and said she'd pick him up at seven (he was too young to drive) and that she couldn't wait for their night together.

Gill was sick. What had he done? He had told this girl he loved her, and now she was expecting him to become her lover. This is what most teenagers do, right? He wondered. All that night he tossed and turned. The next morning, with the prom less than a dozen hours away, he went to his dad. Telling his father was nearly impossible; his hands were sweaty and cold, as was his forehead, his stomach was rolling around, and his mouth had become curiously dry. He wondered if he should give up and sleep with Dianna—that would certainly be easier than telling his father what he was planning on doing. But his father sensed the apprehension and brought the subject up before Gill got around to it.

"Son," his father said, leaning back against the creaking, old leather chair in the study, "are you and Dianna planning on anything after the prom—you know, maybe going somewhere alone together for awhile?"

Gill looked at his father. His dad was already close to sixty years old, and he always looked so wise to Gill. Now as he stared at him, he seemed to leap from wise to an out-right deity. But telling a deity what he was going to do was even worse. Gill's eyes dropped to stare at the floor, as he fidgeted in his seat. "Dad, Dianna told me she's rented a room for tonight. She wanted to know if I love her. She wants to take the next step. I—I don't know what to do, so I came to you."

He heard his father rise from the chair and walk around to where he was sitting, but he still couldn't look at him. Then he felt a warm and knowing hand come to rest on his shoulder.

"I'm glad you came to me, Son. We need to talk."

Gill would never forget that talk. They were no longer father and son, but man to man. Though some might have thought their parent's ideas were old fashioned or out-dated, Gill had learned that there was nothing old fashioned about what was right or wrong. His dad asked some hard questions, but telling his dad about his feelings for Dianna was more honest than telling her. When helping Gill understand what love was really all about, his father asked him if he was prepared to make sacrifices for her. Would he be willing to change his chosen profession so he could more quickly support her, especially if anything should go wrong in the night and Gill became a father at fifteen or sixteen years old. Was he willing to marry her, and devote himself to her alone? Marriage was not, according to his father, something to ever be taken lightly. If Gill found a woman that he was willing to take to his bed, then he should be certain that he'd take her to the altar as well.

"I can't make that decision for you, Son," his dad finished saying. "Only you know if this is the girl for you. I just want you know that the impact of the physical commitment should only come hand-in-hand with the true emotional commitment to someone. Ask *yourself*, Gill, if you're ready because I can't tell you that." His father paused and then added, "There is a lot of pressure today for young people to just have sex and worry about the rest later, but never forget that *you* are the one who will be doing worrying, because later comes quicker than anyone expects."

Dianna and Gill never left his driveway together that night. When he got in the car, he told her he wanted to talk for a few minutes before they left. With as much tact as a fifteen-year-old boy is capable of, he explained to her that, in order to respect not only her but himself as well, they would have to wait before their relationship became physical. He told her he wasn't sure if he really understood love, and he didn't want to mislead or hurt her.

Dianna, whom he thought might be upset with him, was smiling as he spoke. He was hoping it was because she understood and agreed with him, but that wasn't it at all.

"Gill, it's not a big deal, really. It's not like it's my first time, you know. I'm on the pill, so don't sweat it; I won't get pregnant."

"But, Dianna... ."

"And it's okay, you could have just said you weren't sure if you loved me yet or not. It's not like I would have went berserk. We'll grow on each other if it's meant to be. If not, hey, it's not like we're married or anything, so loosen up."

But it was a big deal to him. He didn't think like other teenagers and he couldn't throw what he believed out of his head. By the end of the conversation, Dianna said to forget the whole thing and that if he didn't want to go with her to the hotel later than maybe they shouldn't even go to the dance together.

When Gill's father looked out the kitchen window to see why they were still there, Gill was standing in the drive and Dianna was backing out.

He never regretted his decision. He knew with every fiber of his being that Katie was no Dianna. For that matter she wasn't like anyone he'd every known, and with that a pain hit his heart. There were reasons he had never been forward with her and he felt certain when she knew his secret, she would find someone else to fall in love with.

She called him after she left the bank to tell him she was on her way. He knew she'd be there in about forty-five minutes and he wanted to have everything prepared. The tossed salad was chilled in the fridge, the russet potatoes were baking in the convection oven, and the loaf of sourdough bread was almost ready to come out of the bread machine. The only thing left was to throw the Delmonico steaks on the grill when she arrived and then they could relax and enjoy some good conversation. Not half bad, he thought to himself as he considered the meal he prepared.

She pulled into the yard with a song in her heart. Everything in her life was now going the way she wanted it. The store was a huge success and she had already been offered the next two mall projects in Florida. The divorce was finalized and she didn't bear the guilt of separating Jordan from either one of his parents. And, quirky as Albert had acted toward her at the bank, she knew that for some reason she brought out unusual traits in the man who was known to have an iron-will to resist women; except when it came to her. She could only hope and pray that with the official end to their relationship he might find someone to love, just as she was hoping to find in Gill.

To Katie, Gill was the embodiment of a gentleman. Every social grace that a man was supposed to offer to a woman, opening doors, pulling out chairs, standing when a woman entered a room, all of it, he carefully made sure he did. He treated women with respect, and that was wonderful.

The only thing that bothered her about a man who otherwise was perfect in every way was that he didn't pressure her for any type of physical affection, ever. She could understand now why the women who had a brief stint dating the dashing Doctor Phillips excused themselves from the relationship rather quickly. Feelings of being unappealing to him could surface rapidly when he wouldn't even give a goodnight kiss after a date. Which brought her back to what Hilda told her long ago about his sexual preference, but she had never seen him in the company of a man either. He was very solitary for the most part. But he made her feel wonderfully special, and she couldn't deny the fact that he was built stunningly.

As she reached the top step, he opened the door for her. Unexpectedly for him, she embraced him for a long moment. Awkwardly he held her and for the first time ever, kissed the top of her head, but even then it was done quickly.

"I can't believe it's over and done," she said, holding him. "It seems I've been in this fight my whole life."

"Are you hungry?" he asked, pulling away from her.

She didn't want him to step away, but once again he was distancing himself from being physical. She smiled and sighed together, "Yes, actually I am."

"Great!" He said as he headed toward the kitchen. "I'll throw the steaks on and then everything will be done."

Dinner was very pleasant and their conversation flowed naturally and was most enjoyable. Yet all the while in her heart she wondered how he felt about her.

With a little prodding, she managed to turn the conversation to marital relationships and she casually mentioned that she didn't enjoy leading a single lifestyle.

"But you've only been single for two days?" he said in disbelief.

"No, I haven't," she gently corrected him. "I was divorced from my husband more than four years ago. The court making it official just two days ago doesn't change the fact that Albert and I haven't slept together in years."

"That's true, but the public won't see it like that."

"I've learned not to be so concerned about what the public thinks. They don't know what's on the inside of me."

"Diamond I'd say," he remarked, not realizing he struck a cord with what she had been thinking.

"So I've been told," she smiled. "And this fight did a great job shaping the stone."

"I thought my life was tough, but then I watched you that day at the store, handling suppliers with a hard hand, employees with a firm hand, and customers with kid gloves. And then leaving there to take care of a child, all the while under the pressure of a pending court date with a deranged former lover. I'm thinking if I took off your blouse I'd find a big 'S' painted there for superwoman!" He had made the last remark before putting any thought into the fact that he just mentioned undressing her. "Sorry," he added, hoping she understood what he was apologizing for.

She looked at him with a seductive glance and then brought her blouse forward and peeked playfully down at her chest, "No, there isn't anything painted there."

"Dessert?" he asked, trying to change the subject as he quickly rose to take up the plates.

She thought about saying 'maybe' but she had teased him enough and he was obviously uncomfortable with it.

"How about the movie?" she said, replacing her original thought.

They moved to the living room to watch the movie, but she wanted his company.

"Let's stretch out on the floor," she requested, "I've been sitting all day."

They piled the couch pillows onto the floor and stretched out, Katie nestling her head on his extended arm.

Comfortable in his embrace, she relaxed for what seemed like the first time in years. He was someone she could easily spend her entire life with, but she didn't know if he felt the same way; and she wasn't ready to be hurt again. Yet she was ready to know if he felt anything other than friendship toward her. She wanted so much more than a friend right now.

Looking up at the lines of his handsome face, she was absorbed in the warmth of being near him. She was filled with old feelings and desires that began to flame inside her. She wanted him to touch her and love her, to kiss her and moan her name out softly.

Inside her body the flame of passion had begun to burn and she was certain he should know how she felt about him. She studied him for a moment, but he never returned her gaze—she had no idea that he was simply too nervous to look at her.

"Gill," she said, still looking up at his face as he watched the movie. "Have you ever thought about us—as more than friends?"

He stopped looking at the television and looked down at the beautiful woman he held gently in his left arm, but he said nothing.

"I'm sorry." she said, embarrassed that she had let her passion start to speak for her. "I mean, I'm glad we're friends, but—I—I just wondered if you've ever felt something more than friendship for me? If you do," she added softly, "you're hiding it rather well."

Quietly he replied, "I thought you'd have seen it in my face by now. I would like more than just friendship, but... ."

She slowly took her free arm and began to encircle his waist so she could be closer to him. She was ready for a relationship with him, more than ready in reality. She was feeling an uncontrollable desire to be enveloped by him. His body was taunt and muscled, warm and seductive. But then he was pulling away from her. Gently he took her arm from across him and carefully placed it back at her side.

She sensed that she had done something wrong, and with that thought she felt foolish for her actions. The men in her life had always been the ones to take the first step and now she thought, perhaps, she had tried to make the moment occur between them too quickly. "I'm sorry. I thought you wanted to be more than just friends."

"Katie, I've got to tell you something. I've never been close long enough to a woman to say this." His voice sounded unsteady, and he averted his gaze.

"What, Gill? Tell me, please."

"I told you that my dad taught me that a woman is to be respected, but he also *firmly* impressed on me to never become physical with a woman that you weren't willing to ask to be your wife."

Suddenly it seemed clear and her heart sank; he didn't want to make love to her because he wouldn't want her for his wife.

"It's all right, Gill. I understand. I've been divorced twice and you don't want to end up as husband number three, right?"

"No, that's not it at all," he said, sounding shocked that he led her to that conclusion. "I'd count myself as the luckiest guy on earth if you wanted to be my wife, but… ."

She was searching his eyes; there was something that was causing him pain and anguish.

"Katie, I've never kept a relationship going long enough to be comfortable to talk to a woman like we are talking now. I've devoted myself to being the best pediatric neurosurgeon that I can be, and that hasn't left a lot of free time for romance. Every woman I've ever dated has taken my hesitation to mean that I didn't like her, and would break it off before I could explain. Now I'm a man whose only relationship in life has been his work."

"You think your work would interfere in a relationship between us?"

"I guess there's only one way to say this and I know you're not going to want a relationship with me after I do."

Her heart began to pound. What would he tell her that could possibly make her not want him? Every fiber in her body was yearning for his touch, his kiss and his love. Even though their relationship, up to this point, had been devoid of physical affection, she had known for sometime that he was the man she wanted to be with for the rest of her life.

"Don't tell me then!" she cried out. "Because I do want a relationship with you, Gill. I haven't wanted someone to love me since—since Donovan died, but I want you. Every part of me wants you, so if you've got some secret like you're gay or something, don't tell me!

"Gay!" His eyes went wide. "No! I'm not gay, I'm—I'm a virgin," he blurted out.

She sat there completely shocked. She expected him to say something that would devastate her, but never would she have thought it was his virginity. "But you're 31 years old and you've never... ." She was taken back at the thought that this Adonis of a man had never slept with a woman.

"I knew you wouldn't want someone who didn't know how... Someone who couldn't fulfill your fantasies in bed." He got up from the floor and started to walk away from her as he had done before when they became too close.

"Gill, don't walk away from me, please, I don't care about that."

"Yes you will. I don't know what to do to please a woman."

"Gill do you want to be my husband?" The question came out from the words in her heart. "I don't care if you've never been in another woman's arms. In fact, I'm glad you've never had anyone else, but I've been with three other men and I don't know if you want someone like me?"

"*Someone like you?*" he said facing away. He turned and walked to her, softly wrapping his arms around her, "You are the most wonderful woman I've ever known and I want you more than anything else." His embrace tightened, the awkwardness from before was gone.

She could feel the soft trembling of his body; it was the first time in his life that the mystery of a woman would be understood.

"Kiss me, Gill. Let me be the one who shows you."

Softly his lips pressed to hers sending tingles and sensations long dormant inside her rushing through her veins. With only one kiss she wanted him to take her, but she knew he wasn't ready to be in control over her body. It was time for her to show him everything that could please them both.

His breath became quick and he looked at her with eyes that told how much he wanted her, just as she wanted him.

"We're going to take this slowly," she whispered in his ear, "Take me to your bedroom."

Taking her hand he led her upstairs to his room, a place in his home she had never been before.

"Do you have a stereo in here?"

He didn't say anything, but he picked up the remote control on the nightstand and suddenly the room was filled with smooth, soft jazz. Taking her face in his hands he kissed her again, but this time she let the tip of her tongue explore his lips and then further into his mouth. Passionately he returned the searching kiss.

She unbuttoned his shirt and exposed his muscled chest and stomach. His skin was barely tan, but it was hot under her fingers as if he had been in the scorching sun. He helped her take off his shirt, revealing his muscled upper body. She had wanted to touch that sculpted body for so long and, just as she imagined it would be, it was wonderful to touch him. Then leading him to the bed she began kissing his shoulders and down his arms, bringing his sensitive hands, so skilled at other things, to her mouth. She kissed and caresses each fingertip.

He closed his eyes and moaned at the sensation of her caress, but when she placed his hand on her breast, his eyes open and he hesitated.

"Don't be afraid," she whispered. "Take off my blouse."

His fingers trembled as he undid the buttons and slipped it off, leaving only her pale peach, lace bra. She unhooked it and uncovered her full supple breasts. Tenderly he drew her on top of him on the bed, his mouth reaching her breast as she cried out at the sensation that filled her.

"Yes, Gill," she moaned, "Please don't stop."

His confidence growing with each passing moment, he began to caress her firmly and deliberately.

She was engulfed in feeling for him. Reaching down she began to undo the button on his jeans, but his face looked panic stricken and he put his hand down to stop her.

"Katie, I don't know if I can do this. I don't know what to do to give you pleasure, but I feel like I'm already on the edge and we've barely begun."

"It's okay to feel this way. It won't always be like this. You'll be able to control it soon. It won't end if you can stop what you're feeling." She quietly added, "We have all night together."

He held his breath as she finished taking off his jeans and let them drop to the floor.

Kissing down his rippled stomach, she slipped his underwear to the floor.

"Gill, you're beautiful!" she gasped as she looked at his naked form. He was magnificently built; she had never seen a man so well endowed.

His heart swelled at the though of being pleasing to her. Rising from the bed, he tenderly kissed her stomach and unzipped her skirt. Removing her lacy underwear, he stopped and looked at her with wonder and awe. He knew all about anatomy from his medical training, but the grace and beauty of the female body could not be described in books.

Rejoining him on the bed, she brought his hand to her body. She could feel him began to stiffen and tense at the warmth and softness of her secret places. She stroked him with tenderness causing him to cry out as the feeling that had been building within him crested.

Opening his eyes he expected disappointment in her face, but there was nothing but love.

"Katie, I'm... ."

"Shhh, the first time is always difficult."

"But I didn't even... ."

"Gill it's okay; we have all night—if you want me to stay with you."

"You know I do."

Bringing a soft, warm cloth from the bathroom, she washed off his body.

"Come with me," she said, pulling him toward the bathroom.

Stepping into the shower, the hot water rained down over them as they clung to each other.

"I've wanted to be with you for so long," she whispered above the pouring water, "but I was afraid you didn't want me."

"I wanted you with all my heart, but I couldn't tell you. I didn't want to get your hopes up only to find out that I was inept at lovemaking."

"Have you looked in the mirror?" she laughed softly, "I can't believe someone who is built so perfectly for pleasing a woman hasn't found a partner before me."

"You're the only partner I want," he replied, bringing her body against his own. "Katie I'm in love with you!" he said with startling conviction. "I don't mean for what's happening between us now. I've felt this way for a long time. I just couldn't think of how to tell you."

"I was thinking as I drove here tonight," she began, "that I could spend my whole life with you—and I do want to. I never want anyone else. I love you, Gill."

"I haven't made love to you yet, would you accept my marriage proposal before you know if I can please you in bed."

"Sex is a wonderful thing to enjoy with someone you love, but love is the greater of the two. You please me here," she said, placing his hand to her heart.

"Will you marry me?" he asked, looking deeply into her eyes.

"More than anything, I want to be your wife. Yes, Gill, I'll marry you."

They dried each other off. Gill took her hand and led her back to his bed, kissing her with a new boldness and hunger, his passion to be part of her flamed. He was no longer the timid man who had been afraid of his physical needs for a woman.

"Are you ready?" she said, anticipating his thoughts.

"Yes."

"Go slowly. Explore, don't rush it."

Understanding the reserve he would have to employ, he began to focus on the beauty of her voluptuous body. Kissing and caressing the hidden places of her, causing her to moan with the pleasure of his touch.

She wanted him, but she couldn't rush the tender feelings of letting him become intimately aware of everything she enjoyed. Suddenly she felt his heated breath against her thighs. His fingers were beginning to probe within her. She lost her reserve as his mouth began to search out the private place of her womanhood.

"Oh Gill!" she cried out loudly; her hands clutching his thick mass of wavy hair as spasms of pleasure rippled through her

He moved up her body and drew her in so tightly that she felt faint, she heard him whisper, "Now?"

"Yes" she said as tears of joy ran down her cheeks.

"Show me," he said pressing himself to her.

She guided him to the entrance of her body, but he would go no farther.

"I've never made love before, but I know that without any barrier I could get you pregnant tonight, unless you've already taken that precaution."

"No Gill, there is nothing to prevent that from happening, but there is no guarantee that I'll ever get pregnant. It happened once in years of lovemaking. I don't know if I can have any more.

"Would you want another child?" he asked.

"More than anything, I'd want to have a child with you—more than anything."

"I love you," they said in silent unison.

He never took his gaze away from her face as the sensation of entering her engulfed him.

She was also being absorbed in the feeling of uniting, but such an intense moment for her was always something she couldn't share. Her eyes would invariably close as she would become internally focused on the experience. She felt him hesitate; reopening her eyes he was still looking at her.

"Don't close your eyes," he softly whispered, "I want to feel what you feel; share it with me, Katie. I want to go there together."

She didn't know what to say as his body pressed deeper into the recesses of her own. All she knew was that he seemed to be looking into the depths of her heart, and in that moment they not only joined physically, but it seemed their very hearts bonded together. It was an experience beyond sexuality and went into the realm of total emotional sensuality.

Their bodies had become one. She cried out from pain, yet not wanting him to stop. He was more than her body had ever experienced, and in that moment, it felt as if it was her first time too. Her body began to adjust to him, rising and falling with his incredible rhythm. Shocks and sensations coursed through her and she lost track of the number of orgasms that seemed to wash over her. Lovemaking had never been like this.

Calling out her name, crying out his love for her, he didn't want their union to ever end. He fought the sensation as long as he could, but she was begging him to join the pleasure that coursed through her. Finally, at the end of his ability to restrain what he felt, he released himself completely to her. They held each other in the lover's embrace for a long time before either said anything.

The week that followed was filled with tender moments as he grew even more adept at controlling himself and the lovemaking stretched the boundaries of any pleasure she had ever felt. As good as the sex had been with her other lovers, Gill was beyond any thing she had ever known. His body completed her own, and they were an incredible union, not only sexually, but also mentally and emotionally.

When the week ended, she returned home to meet Albert the following morning. She knew he was returning to New York after dropping off Jordan. Gill stayed the night with her, first of all because it was the first time that she had been alone at home since Nick had attacked her, and secondly, because he wanted to be with her. They would not be together again as lovers until Jordan spent another week with his father.

They had set the plans in motion for their marriage, and, to add to the happiness she already felt, he told her he would like to get married in the little church she attended on the island. They had set the date for the week before Christmas, but that only gave them a little more than three months to coordinate everything. With both of them having gargantuan schedules, they decided to hire a wedding consultant to take care of the legwork.

But before anything else, even before telling both sets of parents, Katie wanted a chance to talk with Jordan. He and Gill enjoyed each other, but it would be a change in his life that needed special adjusting. They would move from Margaret's little house to Gill's and, though he liked going there when they had visited before, it would mean leaving the only home he'd ever known.

The limousine pulled into the yard by 10 a.m. Jordan bounded from the car door as quickly as the car stopped. Glancing at Gill she asked if he'd mind waiting in the house. He nodded, knowing she would tell Albert before he left.

"Mama! I missed you!" Jordan said, jumping up at her as she walked out onto the driveway.

She caught him mid-jump and tossed him up in the air, "Mama missed you too! Did you and Daddy have fun this week?"

"Yeah," Jordan answered and began telling her all the things he could remember about his week.

Albert stood quietly listening, but more than that he was watching. She was glowing and radiant with life, the look of sheer happiness permeated her physical appearance. Where had he seen that look on her before? Then he realized it was the way she used to look after making passionate love, and he remembered it well.

She put Jordan down and he ran toward the house. She couldn't help but smile; she was glad he was home on top of everything else. She turned to thank Albert for bringing him when she realized he was giving her a hard look.

"You're sleeping with someone?" It was a question, but he sounded certain what the answer would be.

It only took a split second for anger and suspicion to pop into her mind, "If you bugged my house again, I'm... ."

"No," he laughed at her remark. "I've learned my lesson—one close call was enough." Then he was serious again, "Are you?"

But before she answered him, Gill opened the front door and welcomed Jordan home. She looked back at Albert and saw his jaw go tight.

"You have no right to be angry with me," she said in her defense, although she knew his 'right' or not didn't matter to him. "For once, do you think you could be happy for me? Gill and I are getting married."

It seemed forever that he just stood there looking at her, and she was growing uncomfortable under the silence.

"Of course I'm happy for you," he finally said, giving her a congratulatory hug, but then he didn't let go. She was wedged between the front fender of the car and his body. Holding back a moment of panic, she returned the hug and thanked him.

Still holding her, he whispered in her ear, "We've only been divorced nine days, if you needed someone that badly I would have been happy to... ."

With all her strength she pushed him away, breaking the embrace.

"We've been divorced a lot longer than that and you know it! And as far as you and I... ." She didn't know how to say it, and her face grew darker.

He smiled and opened the back door to the car, "Let me know when the 'blessed' event is planned. I want to kiss the bride."

He laughed at her frustration as he watched her storm back into the house.

~:~

The months passed by quickly; both of them working and preparing for the wedding. Gill's parents were a little concerned when he told them who he was marrying. They had heard so much about her in the news, good and bad. But they trusted his judgment. When they came down several days before the wedding to meet their future daughter-in-law they found a charming, sweet and lovely woman that they both were greatly pleased with, and that they thought Jordan was the most precious little boy they had ever met!

She mailed invitations, but there were those that she called. And among the first, after her parents, were Alex and Crystal. She mentioned to them that if they could come, she was in need of a flower girl.

Cheyenne was willing even though the only way she knew Katie by was a photograph. She was a beautiful girl with pale blond hair like her mother, but she had Alex's eyes, even down to the funny way she could look at someone, exactly like he did. Their newest addition was a son, and he looked like an *exact* copy of his father, so much so that when he was born, Crystal said they had a completely different name picked out for him, but at first glance they knew this would be Alexander Thomas Davidson, the second.

But of all the people that surprised her by accepting the invitation, none was more so than Ruth and Tom Dunochio. They flew down the day before the wedding. When she introduced them to Gill, Ruth took one look at him, turned and looked at Katie and right there in front of everybody, exclaimed, "Hot Damn! No wonder you're marrying him!" It embarrassed Gill to no end, but Katie thought it was hilarious.

Ruthie spent a few hours that afternoon catching up on old times and talking about the changes in their lives. Ruth and Tom had a little boy now whom they left with Tom's parents when they came down because flying was stressful enough without a wiggly two-year old. She told Katie that Marc had recently married a woman from Japan and that they were very happy.

They talked about what had happened to her after Albert threw her out, why she didn't come to Ruth for help, and about Donovan. She had been so happy with the wedding so close, but the memory of losing him was a pain that she still had trouble facing. Ruth was a good person to talk with about it and she made a suggestion that surprised her.

"When my dad died," she said, "I had a really hard time coming to the ending point in my pain. I knew he didn't want me to be that way, but I couldn't stop thinking about what I'd lost."

She had always thought of Ruth as being tough, New York tough, but in reality she was a very tender-hearted person who experienced deep hurts and pains just like her.

"Finally," Ruth continued, "I went to our favorite place in New York—Coney Island. I went to our favorite ride, the roller coaster, and I rode. At first all I did was cry; then I began to talk to him and tell him my feelings. He wasn't there physically, but I could feel his presence. I rode it several times and by the time I stepped off, every hurt feeling I had was replaced with a peace that it was going to be okay. Now every time I think of my dad I remember that ride, what I said in my heart and what I know he answered it with. If you have loved someone Katie, they are never any further away than your heart. Find a place that was special and talk to him. God knows he'll be listening."

The wedding day was perfect with the cool, crisp December air. Sunshine and blue skies seemed to wrap the church like a giant present from God Himself and everything had come together perfectly. The church was filled with family and friends, for both of them. Cheyenne walked down the isle scattering rose petals, then Jordan marched down the isle in his pint-sized tuxedo, and he looked so much like a little man instead of a little boy. Half way down the isle he dropped the pillow, "Oops!" he said smiling shyly, picking the pillow up. The rings were tied on so he continued to the front with a smile on his face.

They didn't designate a maid of honor or a best man. Gill said, other than the children, he didn't want anyone else up there with him except her. The music began and Katie's father carefully took her arm and walked her down the isle. He was handsome, even if he didn't have a hair on his head! Gill was magnificent in his tailored tuxedo, tailored because a suit that fit his broad shoulders didn't fit his arms or waist without an adjustment. Katie wore a simple, yet elegant off-white dress-length gown. She started down the isle; then she looked at her future husband and felt his eyes beholding her with deep love. Her father gave her hand to Gill and stepped back. When the Pastor asked, "Who gives this woman?" He stepped forward again and said, "Her mother and I, but," he added, "he must love her always, no matter what happens in life."

Katie was surprised; that wasn't in the rehearsal. It was something her father felt he needed to say because he wanted, more than anything, for his daughter to be truly happy.

The pastor turned to Gill. Gill turned to face her parents, "*I will.*" he said, leaving no doubt that he was sincere.

They said their vows in simple honesty to each other as the crowd listened silently. And then he was kissing her as a cheer went up in the church.

"Ladies and gentleman," The pastor said loudly, "I give you Mr. and Mrs. Gilleon Robert Phillips."

After the wedding reception, they slipped away in a black limousine for a two-day getaway at a very private, very luxurious beach house on Anna Maria Island. Her parents kept Jordan at Gill's house until their very short honeymoon ended. Two days wasn't a long time, but both of them had commitments to their jobs, a longer honeymoon was planned for the summer. But two days can be enough when the love is so very real and alive.

Christmas passed and New Year approached. Gill sensed something was troubling his new bride. December 30 came with a dark cloud of depression covering her heart. Gill pleaded for her to share what was burdening her, but she didn't know if he'd understand. They had only been married a short time and she knew she shouldn't be this way. Through his gentle prodding that night, she told him everything about what had happened between her and Donovan last New Year's morning. She told him what Ruth told her about dealing with the loss of her father. And about an idea she had to spend New Year's Eve alone this year at the place she had stayed that night with Donovan. Then she waited quietly to see what reaction such a confession would bring.

"You know I want to spend that night with you, but I don't want you to carry this pain inside you." Then pulling her close to him, he whispered, "I love you enough to let go when you need it, if you think this will help. I'm not jealous over something from your past. I want you to go."

She contacted Michael at the dealership the next day and asked if anyone was staying there New Year's Eve, he said no. He gave her the keys, and that evening she kissed her husband and son goodbye, took some very special music that she hadn't listened to in a year and went to the place she and Donovan had stayed.

At first she felt awkward being there, but then she put on the music and opened the patio door to let the gulf breeze fill the room. She could still envision it as if it were occurring that moment; his dashing figure on the balcony asking her to dance, his arms warm and secure holding her, even the smell of his cologne was there with her. Her heart over-flowed and the tears began to spill, the amount of pain inside was so close to overwhelming her that she wondered if she had made the right decision to come here.

She cried and sobbed until it seemed there was nothing left inside her. The fireworks began at mid-night and when the last one faded, she began to speak.

"Donovan, it's been a long year and I've missed you so much. I came here tonight because I can't empty the pain about you from my heart. I left New York behind a long time ago, but I can't—I can't keep New Year's morning in my heart, because I still see you. I still see you lying there. I still see you dying. I wouldn't have changed our last moments together in order to avoid this memory, but I know there is a place beyond this pain. I came here tonight for you to help me with it. Please, I need you to help me."

She tried to wipe back the fresh torrent of tears that welled up from the desert inside her soul. "The divorce is over with. I came close to losing, but I wanted you to know that I have custody of Jordan. Albert still sees him, but he loves him, Donovan. He's really good with him." Suddenly her heart felt as if it was crumbling, and she realized the pain she had been holding inside her was guilt, guilt because she couldn't go through life alone, guilt because of Gill.

"I'm married now, Sweetheart. I wanted to tell you and I'm sorry—I had wished the next time I married it would have been to you, but there just wasn't enough time for us."

As she cried, she suddenly heard his words. She heard them with such clarity that it startled her. The words were coming from her heart and they repeated what he said to her in his last breaths. "Find someone to make you happy, someone to love—find someone, I want you—happy."

"I did, Darling, and I do love him and I am happy. Oh, Donovan, I'm so happy. Thank you, Sweetheart, for reminding me how much you loved me—how much you want me to be loved."

She lay on the bed in the darkness and remembered. It wasn't wrong. It was a beautiful memory of a special moment in her life and suddenly that beautiful memory lifted the last painful thoughts of the hospital and the burns. She could see him again, her beautiful Donovan was no longer burned and in pain. He was just as she had loved him, and *he was happy for her, just as she knew he would be.*

~:~

From that night forward, the joy that filled her heart for her husband was complete. No longer did she feel some hidden guilt that she owed to Donovan over her marriage. She and Gill grew a bond of love that increased its strength every day.

Her store blossomed from its early beginnings to four stores within the first year and they were building and planning openings for another eight stores in the second year. But she had something happen her second year that would slow down her ability to manage her budding empire. It was a beautiful something that increased her happiness more than anything her business ever could. Just over a year of marriage behind them, Katie was pregnant.

She realized her period was late immediately, but she didn't say anything to Gill. She wanted to wait a little bit and be certain before she told him. When she was certain that a miracle existed inside her body, she was ready to tell him.

She prepared a wonderful dinner for him and waited for him to come home. The hospital was an unpredictable place to work and he was often late, as he was tonight. She chased Jordan off to bed. Then, after saying prayers with him and knowing that Gill would know by morning, she shared her secret with her four-year-old. He was thrilled that he would have a brother or a sister to play with.

She stretched out on the couch, eyes dozing as she watched the clock, and she fell asleep. When she heard his keys in the lock, it was 11:30.

He came to the couch and kissed her, "I'm sorry honey, I just couldn't... ."

"Gill, it's all right. I'm used to it now. I married a doctor. I have to share you with the world." She got up and fixed his plate and listened as he told her about the cases from the day.

She watched him eat his dinner; she loved watching him.

"I was wondering if you 'brain surgeons' know anything about the rest of the human body?" she said. She was teasing, but it got his attention.

"I know what to do with your body," he answered with a seductive look, "and I plan on doing it as soon as I get you in the bedroom, too."

She moaned a little, "No, I mean if I'm not feeling well and I tell you what's wrong, can you figure it out, or do I have to go see a *regular* doctor?"

He stopped eating, now he was concerned instead of playful. "What's the mattered, Honey? What's wrong?"

And she began, "I've been light headed."

His face darkened with deeper concern.

"And I have the worst case of nausea. It won't go away."

Getting up, he walked to her where she was sitting. He got out his little pocket penlight and looked into her eyes. He felt her head for a temperature, felt her neck for swollen glands and made her stick out her tongue and say 'Ahhh.'

"My chest hurts, mostly my breasts, and my stomach is tender."

By now he wanted to check her appendix!

"Sweetheart, come over here to the couch and lie down. I want to feel around your appendix to see if it's tender. Some of the symptoms sound like an appendicitis."

"Can I undress? My clothes are uncomfortable?" she said in a pouty voice.

"Yes, of course. Get down to your bra and underwear if you want." He helped her get undressed as she lay down on the couch. She wanted to laugh and tell him the end of her charade, but she had to keep a straight face for just a little bit longer.

"NO!" she said as he tried to probe around her stomach.

Her stomach looked swollen, and by now he was ready to call for an ambulance. "You need to go to the hospital, Honey, I'm not an internist, but... ."

"There is one more thing," she said, slipping from the couch to his arms as he knelt beside it. "I think you can figure out what's wrong if I tell you the last symptom." She couldn't stand the worried look on his face any longer. "I haven't had a period in two months. Do you think that might have something to do with how I'm feeling?"

He wasn't thinking the obvious at first, he was adding symptoms together for a cause and then what she said hit him like a ton of bricks. He looked down at her face as she began to bubble over with laughter.

"You're—you mean we're gonna have a—you're pregnant?"

"For a doctor it sure took you a long time to figure it out!" she laughed.

"I can't believe it! We're gonna have a baby!"

He was kissing her and holding her, tears of joy ran down his cheeks and mingled with hers as he cried out from sheer happiness.

"Oh Katie, I never thought when I married you that I could ever be happier than that moment. Oh, Baby, I can't tell you how happy I am right now. I love you, Baby. I love you."

And they did make love, but Doctor Phillips was a very gentle lover this night.

She was scheduled for a sonogram by her fifteenth week. Her doctor was concerned about some unusual test results, knowing this was either something very good or very bad. He talked with Gill in private before the procedure and told him he had some concerns. Gill's heart sank. He and Katie both were thrilled with the pregnancy and he didn't want anything to end this happiness.

Jordan and Gill jockeyed for a good view on the screen when the doctor noticed something different. Gill had seen many sonogram images in his career, and he immediately noticed two tiny craniums on the screen. Katie watched him jump with surprise before her doctor had a chance to say anything. She thought for an instant something was wrong, but then she saw a huge smile light up his face.

"Do you want to tell her or do you want me to?" the doctor asked, realizing Gill had figured it out.

"Tell me what?" She said.

"Twins," Gill almost whispered, "Honey, it's twins!"

Amidst the shouts of joy and hugging, she realized Jordan was still studying the screen intently.

"What's wrong honey? You should be happy we're going to have twins!"

His face screwed-up in a disgusted look, "Twins!" he snorted, "I wanted a brother or a sister. What's a twin?"

Everyone laughed; no one thought he that he might not know what they were talking about.

"Sweetheart, it means we're going to have two babies instead of one."

Jordan looked thoughtful for a moment, then he smiled and very tenderly leaned over the table and hugged her, "I love you, Mommy."

~:~

Albert became morose with the news of the pregnancy. He would pick up Jordan on his appointed weeks, but he didn't want to speak with her, only look at her as her body expanded to hold the miracle inside. It was still a look of desire, but a different kind of desire. When Dalfina became pregnant with his first child, it was the most sexually intense time of his life. His whole being was infused with the curiosity and pleasure of knowing that she carried his child. The lovemaking was taken beyond any height he'd ever achieved with a woman—except the last, which surpassed every woman he'd ever known. He had missed Katie's pregnancy with Jordan and he couldn't help but feel the pain inside. What would it be like to experience this with her? He knew he'd never know. It was an unbearable pain.

By her seventh month she was on total bed rest. She took two of the best store managers she had and put them in positions to run her business. They took directions from Katie on every major decision, but she trusted their judgment on the daily affairs and problems. She hated the bed rest though; it was *miserable*!

She was thankful that she had enough modern technology to stay in touch with her business from the bed, but her room looked like a pigsty! Placed on small tables next to the bed she had access to her cellular phone, a laptop with infrared connection to her cellular, a fax/copier machine, a mini desktop scanner, and a stack of paperwork that she needed to read and approve. She tried to keep it neat, but it always seemed by the end of the day she had papers and projects scattered from one end of the bed to the other. Gill even teased and said it would have been easier just to put her mattress on the desk back at her office building.

To say she was uncomfortable would have been a gross understatement. As she entered her eighth month she was prone to bouts of crying and depression. Everything inside her body ached so pitifully that Gill was afraid to sleep in the same bed with her for fear of increasing her discomfort.

Her doctor told her she couldn't continue this way to term. It was early but it was time. Once in the hospital, he gave her an injection to mature the babies' lungs rapidly. Gill stood by her side, his nerves going crazy inside him, but he remained calm on the exterior, hoping she wouldn't know how he felt. He watched as she was given the epidural and held her hand as she cringed in the midst of the painful procedure.

Then they were headed to the operating room; he never let go of her hand. He was a surgeon, and he'd cut inside the most delicate area possible in the human body, but this was out of his realm and he was in awe at the miracle of it all. He held her hand, spoke the most encouraging and loving words in his heart, but all the while he watched as her body was opened and the first precious small child emerged.

"It's a girl!" he fairly shouted.

Neither one had wanted to know the sex during the sonogram, but they did know the babies were fraternal twins, not identical. The next child was removed, and a very obvious boy greeted the world with an ear-piercing scream.

"It a boy! We have a girl and a boy, Sweetheart!"

The babies were brought around briefly so she could see them and then they were taken to the side to be cleaned, get their first shot and get their little toes pricked. The screaming mayhem was wonderful music to a very tired and thankful mother.

They were tiny because of the early deliver and cramped living quarters, but they were healthy. Myanna Katherine Phillips weighed in at 4 pounds 4 ounces and Joshua Gilleon Phillips tipped the scales at 5 pounds, 1 ounce.

Later, when mother and children were settled into their room, Gill brought their big brother Jordan in to see his new family. For once in his little life he didn't say anything. He just smiled and smiled as he gently touched the downy soft cheeks of his siblings.

~:~

Life was good. The next few years passed in wonderful bliss. Gill was, as Katie knew he'd be, a very wonderful father. She worried before the babies were born that Jordan might start to feel like an outsider when it came to Gill, Myanna and Josh, but Gill was so careful to make sure Jordan knew he shared an equal portion of his heart.

Jordan had become a handsome young man. He was seven years old and with each passing day he grew to look more and more like his father. His hair had darkened to Albert's shade of light brown and his eyes stayed that same piercing dark sapphire blue. The girls at his school were crazy about him, which (though he didn't admitted it) he enjoyed. Albert tried spoiling him with gifts, but Jordan was good at being level-headed. He was being raised in the affluent upper class, but in his boyish ways he was still the same as the other boys his age.

Joshua had dark curly hair with a touch of red highlights and amber-green eyes. His disposition was good, but he and Myanna were going through the 'terrible two's' and occasionally they were less than kind to each other, fighting over toys and family affections.

Myanna was a little Katie, her hair was straight and auburn, but her eyes were the palest green. She also seemed to have the biggest stubborn streak of any of the children.

One night after a particularly rough time getting them all to bed, Gill flopped down with Katie on the bed and exclaimed, "I think she's made out of the substance her mother is!"

"Would you have her be made of anything less?" She asked, arching a brow.

Rolling over and pinning her to the bed with his powerful arms, he whispered, "Never." And then thinking about it for a moment he added, "But good Lord, what are we gonna do when she starts dating?"

Katie had never been interested in body building like Gill was, but she knew, even with the hectic schedule she had, she would have to make time to get her figure back in shape. She worked out with him every night they were home together in the exercise room he had designed in their house. Having twins had stretched her stomach muscles greatly, and even though she pulled back together in relatively good time, she still felt she could trim up better. So she put an effort into keeping that head-turning shape of hers looking sharp.

Gill was completely turned on by her newfound interest in sharpening her lines by defining her muscles. Sometimes when he watched her working out on the machinery he couldn't wait to get her back upstairs. And, if the kids and their housekeeper were all asleep, he'd make love to her right there in the exercise room.

Albert continued his wicked game of trying to catch her alone when he would either pick up or drop off their son. She pleaded for him to stop making her fear him every time he was around, but he would only smile as he thought of new ways to catch her alone.

She hadn't told Gill what intentions Albert said he had for her, first because she couldn't believe deep in her heart that he would sink so low as to hurt her that way. They had a child together and for Jordan's sake she wanted them to have a civil relationship. And secondly, she had never seen Gill truly angry before, but she knew, with the powerful physique he possessed, he could do some serious damage to another man. Albert was a strong man, but he didn't have the muscle mass that Gill did. And she feared that someday they might clash.

CHAPTER NINE

Albert seated himself in the comfortable office, waiting for her to bring his son to him. He looked about at the furniture and the way she had arranged her office. It was classy and sharp, just like her. He sighed for a moment, every time he saw her it just got harder to bear. He wasn't a young man, but whenever he was near her he felt so alive and filled with desire to love her.

He heard her coming down the hall; she was walking with Gill, laughing and talking together just the way he and she had been once, long ago. Through the glass he observed their parting kiss, the spark ignited and instantly he felt his blood come to a boil. Jealousy reared its ugly head and he was angry with her once again.

She stepped into the coolness of her office, smiling politely at Albert as she did. "Jordan will be here in a few minutes."

"He should have been ready when I got here!" He replied sharply.

She took a deep breath and headed behind the safety of her big mahogany desk. "I apologize. I'll be certain he is ready next time; *you won't even have to come in the building*." She added her own little barb to let him know she wasn't pleased with his attitude.

She watched him cool off, the angry red in his face fading. He was easy for her to read and she knew he was hot under the collar when she had walked into the room.

But he did want to see her each time he came; it was a pain that he couldn't stand, yet didn't want to avoid. In truth, he had become dependant on the pain and it was as much a part of his life as was taking a breath of air. He watched her in silence briefly; she became lovelier every time he looked at her. She had let her hair grow out and it was a few inches past her shoulders now, her figure was more endowed, motherhood had enhanced her bust and the curve of her hips, but her stomach was still flat and her waist petite. He knew she would always keep that lovely figure.

363

His face grew hot again, but this time it was from the thoughts he was thinking about her. He rose and headed toward her desk. Politely he offered, "I'm sorry. It's been a long morning. I really don't mind coming in to get him. Please don't change a thing."

Lightly he seated himself on the corner of her desk, with a wonderful view of the cleavage down the front of her business suit. "How's business?" he said, suddenly smiling.

Her face was beaming, "I've been given an offer I can't refuse and in less than six months, I'm selling it!"

"What?!" He practically choked at her news. "But, Darling, this is what you've always wanted. Why in the world would you sell it?"

"No, Albert, *this*," she said, motioning around her office, "Is not what I always wanted. I wanted to create and bring Seasons to life. That was a goal and I achieved it. I'm not going to kill myself and neglect my family to push it beyond the billion-dollar industry that it's becoming. What I always wanted was a family to raise and love, and I plan on spending my time with them, not this." Then reflecting on the fact that she was refusing to do what he had done with his company, she added, "I'm not getting younger and my children *are* getting older. It's going by too fast and I don't want to miss it."

"How good was the offer?"

She knew the businessman in him had to know, "Four hundred million to let them make it a major franchise, a big stock option and a position on the board if I want it, but I think I've had enough of board meetings," she smiled at him.

He was impressed; "Did you negotiate the deal?"

"Most of it, but as you know it's the legal team that polishes it up."

He admired what she was going to do, but it was still difficult for him to see in his mind. He longed for his children. His daughters were grown and married. His first grandchild was born just the year before, and his son, whom he devoted more time to than the others, were all precious to him.

She saw the look on his face. The hurt and the longing for a family to draw near and love. She reached out and took his hand, "You could do the same you know. You've got more money than you'll ever need. You could spend more time with Jordan and your girls."

It had been a long, long time since she had touched him.

"I can't do that," he answered as if it was a physical limitation instead of a mental one, but he held her hand and slid closer to her.

Her action had been impulsive and now she was wishing she had not touched him. She had come too close to the flame before and been burnt. The scar was still in her heart.

She looked beyond the glass and could see Gill and Jordan coming down the hallway toward her office. Her panic increased as his grip tightened. "Albert, please," she said, trying to distance herself from him, but he only moved closer.

"You see," he said, close enough that she could feel his breath, "If I sold my company then all I would have left would be my obsession for you. And I've discovered that you're something I can't have, but it doesn't end my wanting you. I'll find a way to have you again."

"Albert, please," she repeated. "There are so many wonderful women out in the world for you to be happy with. Find someone and fall in love." She stood up, trying to end the feeling of being dominated as he loomed above her.

"*No*," he answered so decisively that her cheeks began to turn red. "*There will never be another woman like you.*" Releasing her hand, he turned and walked to the door to greet his son, and then they were gone.

Gill stepped into her office, seeing, even from a distance, that she was upset.

Without any discussion he pulled her into his arms. His embrace was safe, warm and filled with the love that soothed her to the very core of her being.

Kissing her forehead he asked if she was okay.

"Yeah, I'm okay," she said, wrapping her arms around his waist.

But he didn't believe her. Looking into her eyes, he could see the tears that were being held back, "What does he do to you when I'm not around?"

"Nothing," she whispered, "that being in your arms can't repair. I love you, Gill. Don't ever leave me."

He kissed her long and passionately. Then, with his mouth still resting close enough to touch her lips, he answered, "I'll never leave you—never." Yet as he held her he could still feel her body shaking, and concern filled him about what had transpired, "What did he say to you?"

"I don't want to discuss it, please."

"I'm tired of him making you upset whenever he gets near you. I have to know what it is. Does he still have some hold over you?"

"No, Gill, no. Please don't ever think that anyone holds my heart but you. It's just…" she sighed and shook her head, "He likes playing games, sick games that I don't like."

"What kind of 'sick' games?" he said. And for once he didn't sound as if he was asking her a question, but demanding she answer him.

They sat down together on the long leather couch. Slowly and with great embarrassment, she explained what he almost did to her the day Jordan came out of his coma. Then, with a heavy heart, she told him what he promised to do with her someday if he ever found himself alone with her.

Gill's body went rigid; every muscle in him turned to rock.

She looked into his face and all she saw was anger. She felt the anger was for her because she hadn't told him before now.

"Why didn't you tell me! I never would have let him get near you!" The anger made the veins on his temple stand out, "He can deal with me from now on when he comes here!"

By this point she was weeping. He had never acted so angry with her. "I'm sorry," she said quietly.

"No, Katie," he said taking her in his arms. He realized the miscommunication. "I could never be mad at you about this. I'm angry at him. I just wished you had told me sooner. I'm going to put a stop to it!"

"Please, Gill. It's got to be handled carefully. Jordan loves his dad. I can't let Jordan be hurt by this."

He kissed her head, "Don't worry. I'd never do anything to hurt Jordan."

When the week ended and Albert returned Jordan home, Katie wasn't there to greet them. It had happened before, when she was away on business, but there was something different this time. Albert could feel the hard look that Gill was giving him. Gill hugged Jordan and told him to go put his bag upstairs, he needed to speak to his father.

Albert looked mildly surprised as Gill stepped out on the front lanai.

"She told me," he said with obvious anger.

"Told you what?" he replied innocently. He didn't fear anyone, but he could play coy if he wanted.

"You're never going to find yourself alone with my wife—ever. And if by some coincidence you ever are, you'd better not touch her, or you're going to need someone in my profession because I'll put your head through a damn wall. You got that?"

Albert laughed briefly, "If you ever assault me, I'll take Jordan from her custody. The courts won't favor letting him stay with an abusive stepfather."

Gill was so mad he was ready to hit him, but he restrained himself, "Well, guess what? I don't think they'd approve of him staying with a rapist, do you?"

Albert sneered as he turned and headed down the steps, "The problem is you'd have to get her to admit I did it, and because of Jordan, she'd never do it, would she?"

Gill stood there seething mad as he watched the car leave the driveway. He'd never met someone so cold and conniving. He'd make sure Albert didn't get around her again.

~:~

Albert didn't like the fact that whenever he came to Florida for his son he rarely ever saw her. Occasionally she would be there, but Gill was always at her side when that happened. He was angry and decided he'd have his staff pick Jordan up and drop him off instead, so when he did come down it would be unexpected. If he was lucky he might even catch her alone.

The summer was rapidly approaching and Jordan would be spending the entire summer with him. Albert had not taken him the previous two summers for the whole time for several reasons, but he cleared his calendar of most major business this summer and planned some great things for the two of them.

He called several times to talk with Katie about when he was going to get Jordan, but she had been jetting all about the country, kicking off the openings for another eight stores. When he did finally get her, she was not the woman he expected. She was angry and snapped at him repeatedly about stupid things that weren't worth the breath it would take to argue over.

"What's wrong, Katie?" he asked point blank.

"Nothing! I have an awful cold and I'm tired. I'll be back in Florida in two days. You can wait until then to get him, can't you?"

"I was going to get him tomorrow."

"Wait until the next day!" she said, anger clear in her voice.

He didn't like that she was taking a commanding tone with him; no one did that. But he though it was a great opportunity to toss a barb at her. "Well, I guess if you insist on being there so I can actually see you then... ."

"NO, ASSHOLE!" she practically screamed at him, "It's not so you can *see me!* It's so I can see him before he leaves!" And she slammed the phone down hard.

His ear was still ringing as he sat there trying to understand what had just happened. Katie had never spoken to him that way. All his senses had tuned in and he was beginning to see a picture. Something was troubling her terribly to put her in such a state. Business he dismissed, he felt she could handle anything in her business that popped up, but her personal life was another story completely. A sly smile came across his face, husband troubles? Perhaps that would be enough to set her over the edge. He needed to pay her a visit, just her—alone. He wanted to find out if her 'wonderful' husband wasn't so wonderful anymore.

He didn't call her anymore and he waited four days before he came down. He had his driver call her office and see if she was in. She was, but she was in a managers' meeting and wasn't expected to get out of there until late. Albert smiled, late was good. He'd wait to see her after the meeting. Then, after he and his driver sat in the parking lot of her office building until the people started leaving, he made another call, but this one was to the children's hospital.

"Yes," he said as, the young woman on the other end answered for the neurology ward, "Is Doctor Phillips on duty this evening?"

"Yes, I believe he's still here. Would you like me to get him for you?"

"Yes, thank you," he answered. When she put him on hold, he hung up. The smile on his face grew broader.

But he was premature in hanging up, because Doctor Phillips had left a few minutes before the call came in and he was on his way to take his wife out to dinner.

The parking garage was now empty, but Katie's Jaguar was still there. He smiled as he headed upstairs. The parking attendant nodded at Mr. Trathmoore as he watched him disappear inside the elevator.

Katie was sitting inside her office, rummaging through her desk for another bottle of aspirin. She felt sick for over a week with what seemed to be the flu. She had suppressed her fever and aches with aspirin, but it was only growing worse. And, to add to her misery, her period started a week early the day prior. She knew Gill was coming to take her to dinner, but she was going to opt for home instead. For a woman married to a doctor she didn't like going to them—this time she would make an exception. Something felt horribly wrong inside her, a feeling that had overtaken her that afternoon, one of deep dread, a foreshadowing of something serious. There was more wrong with her health than a cold.

Finally, seeing the bottle of aspirin, she reached for it as the door to her office opened.

"Honey, I don't want to go to... ." Then looking up, in shock, she gasped, "Albert! What are you doing here?" She was angry, but she couldn't hang on to the anger because her physical body was the area of her concentration now.

He smiled at her, the moment had come that he had been waiting for. No one else was in the building; only the parking attendant was there and he was downstairs. His heart began pounding against his chest; she would be his again even if it was against her wishes. He would possess her, husband and consequences be damned.

"Hello, Darling," he said, low and even, "I guess you didn't expect me did you? And that big, strong husband of yours, were you expecting him? No, he's at the hospital. I know because I called."

Her head was swimming in confusion; Gill had phoned her twenty minutes ago to say he was on his way. None of this was making any sense to her. Then looking at him she watched as he began to loosen his tie, and the way he was looking at her filled her with a new dread

"I don't have time for your foolish games!" she snapped, but there was a slur to her speech. Then in a bold move she got up and went around her desk and faced him. She was tired of the intimidation, she felt horrible and this charade was going to end immediately.

He was definitely surprised that she walked right up to him. But looking at her there was something wrong. Her eyes were reddened and had a glazed look to them. Her skin, even under the make-up, looked pale, very pale. He took hold of her and pulled her to his chest. Her body was hot and her strength was low as she feebly tried to pull back from him.

"What's wrong?" he whispered, close enough to kiss her. Her eyes blinked open and shut a few times and she swayed in his hold. The nearness of her set off the fiery torrent that would take him over the edge. "Something is wrong. Have you been drinking, darling?" He smiled as he thought she had. Husband troubles would definitely be cause for a drink and she could never hold her liquor.

Then he kissed her, and to his surprise, she didn't resist him. Passion went out of control inside him. She wasn't pushing him away, she was clinging to him as he began kissing her with the deep desire that had been building in him for too long.

Gill had been thinking all day about his lovely wife. She had been working far too hard to get everything settled before turning the business over to the conglomerate that was purchasing it. He was glad she was selling, not because he didn't want her to enjoy her dream, but because he was tired, tired of the late nights for both of them. In the last week he only seen her once, between both their schedules, and she was so tired that she fell asleep before he could tell her he wanted to make love. Soon it would be over and they would have all the time in the world to spend together.

He had a surprise for her tonight, she would find out that he had turned in his resignation as chief pediatric neurologist; he was stepping down so they could be together and raise their family. When the company was sold in two weeks, he would be taking her and the twins on a very long, well deserved vacation. And if that snake of an ex-husband hadn't come down to pick-up Jordan by then… Well, he'd just have to wait because they would take Jordan with them!

Pulling into the lot he saw her car, but then over by the elevator he saw a long, black limousine and his heart sped up. Parking haphazardly, he rushed to the elevator.

"Good evening, Doctor Phillips. How are you tonight?"

"Whose car is that?!" he demanded.

The attendant was shocked momentarily, because Doctor Phillips was not the type of man to be angry.

"Aaah—Mr. Trathmoore's car. He's been here about ten minutes."

"Call the police!" he shouted at the man, punching the button for the elevator to open. Before the door closed, he saw the attendant's confused face, "CALL, DAMN IT!" he shouted as the door shut.

The elevator door opened to the office suites and he dashed down the hall to Katie's office. Through the windows he couldn't see anyone there, but as he reached the door he heard loud and labored breathing beyond it. Snatching the door open, he saw them.

Katie was lying unconscious on the carpeted floor in front of her desk, her blouse was torn open and Albert was astride her with his mouth on hers.

"YOU SON-OF-BITCH! GET OFF OF HER!!"

Albert turned and looked as Gill's fist came hurling toward him.

Gill hit him so hard with his closed fist that he sent him crashing against her desk.

Albert struggled to keep conscious after the thunderous blow, and he tried to move back to her.

Gill grabbed him by his shirt, jerking him to his feet with his fist drawn back to hit him again, when something Albert said stopped him mid-strike.

"SHE ISN'T BREATHING, DAMN YOU—LET ME GET BACK TO HER! SHE'S DYING—LET ME GO," Albert struggled from Gill's stunned grip and rushed back to her.

He pinched her nose and tipped her head back and began to blow air into her lungs.

"My God, Katie!" Then Gill was at her side, too. Her face was turning blue as Albert struggled to get air into her lungs. Gill put his head to her bared chest and listened for the sound of her heart, he heard a beat; then he heard the air Albert was trying to get into her; then another beat—and then it stopped.

"Get out of the way and let me take over!" He pushed Albert back and, coming astride her, began aggressive CPR, pumping her chest and breathing for her.

"Come on, Honey! Don't die on me—come on, Baby—you gotta breathe—you gotta live." Then turning to Albert, he glanced to the phone, "CALL 911, HURRY!"

Albert's hands were shaking as he called the emergency number and told them they needed an ambulance immediately.

"Tell them she's in full cardiac arrest!" Gill shouted to him. He could hear the sirens downstairs from where he had told the attendant to call the police.

"Take over the breathing!" he shouted to Albert, "I'll keep her heart going, just get some air into her!"

They began to work as a team trying desperately to keep the one woman alive that both of them loved so deeply.

The police arrived at the chaotic scene, but neither man would let the officers take over for them. They continued CPR until the ambulance crew came rushing down the corridor with the gurney laden with equipment. The officers had to pull both men away to let the crew take over.

Gill and Albert watched in disbelief as the paddles were put to her chest and her body was jolted against the floor with current, again and again until a faint rhythm was restored. They shouted medical terminology back and forth, Gill understanding it, Albert uncertain as to what they meant. One man was bag breathing for her and another started an I.V. Wires were run from her chest to a monitor that showed a weak heart beat. Then they were taking her down the hall toward the waiting ambulance.

They burst out of the elevator into the muggy afternoon heat. Katie was loaded into the ambulance. Albert looked at Gill and Gill back at him; they were both shaking uncontrollably.

"I'll have my driver follow the ambulance. You can't drive like this—come on!" Then motioning toward his car they both jumped inside and began following the ambulance to the hospital.

As they careened through the late afternoon traffic with Albert's driver following dangerously close to the back of the ambulance, Gill asked him what happened.

"I don't know," Albert said, choking back the stinging tears, "She walked around the desk and practically collapsed into my arms! Her eyes were glazed and her face was pale, deathly pale. She was clinging to me and then I saw her turning blue. I tore open her blouse and listened to her heart—it was barely beating. I don't know much about CPR, but I knew something had to be done, someone had to breathe for her."

"Thank God you were there," Gill said, looking with sorrow-filled eyes at the man he attacked. "She'd be dead right now if you hadn't been."

Silence filled the car; neither man able to find the words to break as they pulled up to the emergency entrance.

The emergency team wouldn't let either one into the room as they worked aggressively to stabilize this woman who was so close to death.

After a half-hour of anxious waiting, one of the doctors emerged from the room. "Which one of you is her husband?

They both stood up, but Gill spoke first, "I'm her husband. What's going on?"

"We need your permission to get her into surgery right away. She has a massive uterine cyst that has become systemic. It's ruptured into her intestinal cavity. Her body is filling with fluid. If we don't do an immediate hysterectomy and a transfusion, she's not gonna make it. We've got to get her to surgery now."

Medical school flashed through Gill's mind; uterine cysts often meant one thing. "Cancer?" he questioned aloud in disbelief.

Albert went white.

"We won't know until we get pathology reports back, but surgery has got to be done now if she's gonna have a chance."

"Yes, take her," he said, feeling helpless in a medical situation for the first time in his life. "Don't let her die—please."

The gurney left with a woman on it so pale that she didn't even resemble the woman they loved.

Turning to Gill, Albert swallowed hard, "What does it mean? Does she have cancer? What's happening to her?"

Gill tried to explain that a ruptured cyst was similar to blood poisoning, but it was throughout her body now. It would be touch and go to see if she could pull through.

"But it's unusual to have a uterine cyst unless it's—they're often cancerous. It very serious," he added, with dread in his voice.

Gill called home and told their housekeeper what had happened and asked her to make the calls to his parents and hers, "But," he added, "don't tell the children yet. I've got to see if she's going to pull through. I'll talk to them later."

They both waited outside the operating room, silent for a long time. Then it began to rain outside. A thunderstorm moved in from the gulf and began to pound against the building with a heavy down pour.

Albert shifted uncomfortably as he looked out the window watching the raindrops running down the windowpane. "Katie loves the way it smells outside after a rain storm," he said it as if he was saying it to someone else in the room, but there was no one else but Gill.

Gill looked at Albert; he saw where his eye was beginning to blacken where he had hit him. "Yes, she does. She's always looking for a rainbow when it stops. She was out on the pool deck a few weeks ago looking for one after a storm went through." Gill bent forward and let the anguished sobs flow out of him. "I can't live the rest of my life without her. She can't die; she's so young. The twins are going to have their third birthday soon. How am I going to raise them without her?" His shoulders shook violently from the painful thought of losing his wife.

Albert looked back out the window. The pain in his heart was crushing him. He knew what life would be like for Gill without her. He had lived the last eight years without her in his life and it was a pain he felt deeply every day.

"Life is too short," Albert said quietly. "I made a mistake hurting her like I did. I should have forgiven her that day, instead of telling her to get out. I'm fifty-eight years old and I won't have as long a life to live without her as you, but I'll have more guilt and shame for what I've done to her than I can bear." He cried silently, the tears running hard down his face, but he sat there like stone.

They sat there, one man facing a long life ahead without her, and another man who saw a life wasted on business, jealousy and anger.

Finally the surgeon came out and looked at the two distressed men waiting for word on the beautiful woman he had just tried to save.

"She's in recovery. We'll just have to wait and see," the surgeon said, but he could tell neither man was satisfied with his short response. "Everything looked good. It didn't look cancerous to me, but we can't say for certain until the report comes back. I can't believe she didn't die before we got her on the operating table. She must be one tough woman."

Albert gave a bitter laugh, "You have no idea how tough she is."

"Can I go see her?" Gill asked.

"You can, but she'll be out for awhile. We're going to try to get her into a room as soon as possible."

"She's going to be all right then?" Albert asked, reading the look the doctor was giving him.

"She's not out of the woods. We've got the I.V. pumping the antibiotic in her, but it's going to be touch and go until she regains consciousness."

Gill went in and sat with her for a long time. Albert stayed in the waiting room. They moved her to a room and Gill stayed by her. Her parents arrived and went in to be with her. Still Albert waited. He had no right to ask to go into her room. He wanted to be by her side, but as Katie herself told him once he had no 'rights' to her anymore.

He dozed in the chair and just before dawn, Gill woke him and asked if he wanted to go in and see her. He knew Albert had waited for someone to ask him.

"Is she conscious?" he asked, hoping she was.

"No, not yet."

Quietly Albert walked into the room with Gill, the heart monitor beeped the reassuring sound that her heart was still pumping, and an oxygen tube was in one nostril, feeding her the oxygen she needed to get a little color back in her face.

"I'll leave you alone," Gill said, turning to go out.

Grabbing his arm Albert stopped him, "You said you'd never let me be alone with her."

He rested his hand on Albert's shoulder, "You kept her alive. I think I can trust you now." And he walked out.

Albert pulled a chair up to the bed, then brushed back the hair from her face and neck. "I love you, Katie," he said softly. Regret filling him for every angry action, every callous word, and every crass attempt to punish her. "I'm sorry for the way I treated you." Emotions choked up inside his throat, threatening to stop him from speaking. "If you pull through this—I promise—I won't hurt you anymore."

He took her cold hand in his and pressed it to his cheek and released the bitter tears of sorrow and regret, but when he looked up at her, her eyes were open and she was staring at him.

Happiness filled him and he kissed her hand, "Katie, can you hear me?"

She was still groggy, but she nodded slowly. She swallowed with great difficulty.

He understood that her throat must be dry from the oxygen so he picked up a near by water pitcher and pour some in the little yellow plastic cup. He held it for her as she weakly sipped it.

"Albert," she barely whispered. "What happened to your eye?"

"Your husband knocked the hell out of me. It doesn't matter though, it's all right because you're going to be okay."

"Albert," she continued, "I remember you kissing me and that's all I remember. You didn't—you didn't... ."

"No, Sweetheart, I didn't."

"Are you sure, because it sure feels like somebody raped me—damn it hurts."

He smiled. Her spunk was still there and she'd make it now, he was certain. "You've been through surgery, Honey—that's why it hurts."

"Thank God," she whispered.

She could tell he was momentarily hurt, but then she added, "I don't think I could send you to jail. I couldn't do it before either." She smiled a weak smile, "I knew I could trust you."

He leaned over and kissed her forehead, "No, you were right not to trust me before, but you don't have to worry now. I promise I'll never hurt you again. I'm so sorry that I ever hurt you, Katie, I... ." But he couldn't continue.

"Albert, you're still hurting me," she said as her eyes filled with tears.

He didn't want to see her cry ever again, "Why, Sweetheart. What am I doing to cause you pain?" Whatever it was he wanted to remedy it.

"I can't stand seeing you lonely. Eight years you've chased after me and been lonely and bitter. If you want to stop causing me pain, find a woman and fall in love with her. Marry her." Then she smiled a stronger smile, and said something she thought she'd never tell him since they had parted so long ago, "Don't let all that good sex you're bottling up go to waste. Find some one to enjoy it with."

He smiled the sexy smile that he used to give her when she was his, "You want me in another woman's arms?"

Her eyes closed at the pain in her abdomen, then looking back at him, she said with certainty, "Yes, very much, Mr. Trathmoore, very much."

"I suppose you want to see that husband of yours, don't you?"

Her lower lip was quivering as she nodded yes.

He got up to leave and then turned back, leaning over the bed he gently kissed her forehead, "I'll see what I can do about your request."

When he walked out of the room he looked at Gill with a smile of relief, "She's awake, and she's talking."

Gill surprised Albert by grabbing him and pulling him in for a manly hug, holding him for a moment, he thanked him again for being there when she needed him.

He walked to her bedside and she looked up at him.

"Honey," she whispered, "I don't think I want to go out tonight."

He laughed out loud; "It's a little too late for dinner anyway." But then he became serious as he sat by her side looking at her, "I really though I'd lost you." But he couldn't say any more.

"What happened?" she questioned her emotional husband, "One minute I've got Albert giving me a rough time and then the next I'm waking up in here."

"He saved your life. If he hadn't been there you would have died."

"Why did you hit him then?"

"I thought he was—he was giving you CPR, but it didn't look like it when I walked in."

"CPR? What's wrong with me?"

He didn't want to tell her because he knew it was going to be a hard thing for her to accept, "You had a large, uterine cyst. It became infected and it burst. They had to remove it."

"The cyst?" she said, looking worried.

"No, Honey."

"No, Gill, no," she pleaded as the tears started down her cheeks, "please don't tell me they took my uterus out."

He swallowed hard, "I'm sorry, Honey, they had to. You've had a hysterectomy."

The tears flowed like a river down her face, "No, no, no," she repeated over and over. "I wanted us to have more children. I can't have any more?"

He leaned over the bed, pressing himself gently chest to chest with her. She sobbed and let out muffled screams as she buried her face in his neck. All the while he smoothed her hair with his free hand and spoke softly to her, "It was the only way. We have three beautiful children to love. It's enough of a blessing to have them—and you. I love you, Honey, and I'm sorry."

She wrapped her free arm around his neck and held on tightly, never wanting to be out of his arms again. "You're right." she whispered, "I have so much to be grateful for. Besides the kids, I have you and you're enough to make me happy, no matter what."

CHAPTER TEN - EPILOGUE

Sitting in the waiting room at the hospital, Katie recalled all the times she had been in this place. It was a place of hard memories and suffering about Donovan, and it was a place of letting go and trusting for herself. It was a place of fear when they thought she might have cancer, and a place of relief when the test came back negative. Gill sat beside her quietly. He was deep in thought as well. She wondered if he was thinking about the night she almost left him a widower. He looked over at her and smiled, squeezing her hand; it was time. They stood up and she straightened his tie, with a quick kiss they headed out to the waiting crowd. The cameras flashed, and reporters yelled-out their questions, but they were both oblivious to the press.

The crowd had increased three-fold in size from those who had been there only thirty minutes earlier. The president of the hospital made a statement to the press and then, walking over to Katie and Gill he said they were ready to complete the ceremony. She walked to the podium it a shower of lights going off like fireworks. She smiled at the thought of fireworks.

"We are here this evening to present a gift to the community of Tampa, Florida. We are also here to commemorate a loving and giving man who was an inspiration to those who were fortunate enough to know him. It is with great pleasure that we open the new twenty-eight million dollar Donovan Randall Intensive Burn Unit for use." She turned to Gill and together they cut the ribbon and then shared a brief kiss as the crowd applauded.

"Thank you Mrs. Phillips for your generous contribution to our hospital," the president said, shaking her hand. "Will you and Doctor Phillips be staying for the reception and tour inside?"

"No, I'm afraid we can't," she answered. "We've already had the tour. Please let me know if the burn unit ever needs upgrades. I'm sure the funds can be provided."

The limousine pulled up and they slipped into the back of it quickly and pulled away from the hospital.

Katie looked at the blur of street lamps passing outside her window as they travel down the interstate to return home. She was quiet and Gill wondered if she was crying. Lightly he touched her shoulder and she turned to him.

"You okay?"

"Yes, I was just thinking about what Donovan said. He told me to find someone to love and be happy."

"Are you happy, Mrs. Phillips?"

She reached around his body and held him tight, "Yes, the happiest of my entire life."

He held her in his arms all the way back home. Dropping them off at the house the rented limousine pulled out on to the quiet, deserted streets and sped away.

The children stopped playing when Katie and Gill stepped in through the front door.

"Momma! Daddy!" Mya and Josh yelled out together when they saw them.

Jordan met them at the doorway; "Did the ceremony go okay?" He asked.

"Yes, Honey, it was wonderful," she said grabbing hold of him and ruffling his hair. "Look at this!" she said, smiling at Gill, "He's only got about six inches to go and he'll be as tall as I am—and he's only ten years old!"

"Yeah," Gill added, "he's gonna be a tall one."

Jordan smiled, he liked it went they said things like that. It made him feel grown-up on the inside too.

"I'm getting big too!" Josh said from under his mop of dark curly hair. He hugged his daddy's waist.

"Me too!" Mya added, and quickly switched the pieces around on the board game they had been playing.

"Myanna Katherine!" Katie said loudly, "Don't cheat your brothers. Win fair and square!"

She flashed a pretty smile; "I was just teasing, Momma." Then she winked at her father. He knew she was just having a little fun with her mother.

"Off to bed," Mrs. Penworth, their housekeeper said as she shooed the children toward their rooms. "You have school tomorrow and we don't want a bunch of sleepy heads in school."

Mya ran back and gave her mother a hug, "Are you going to be on television Friday, Momma?"

"Yes, Sweetheart, the awards ceremony is going to be televised. Why?"

"You're going to look so pretty, Momma. I saw the dress you have hanging in your room. I'm gonna tell everybody at school to watch you."

"Go to bed you little imp. Daddy and I will be in to tuck you in soon," and she kissed Mya's little puckered up mouth, "Good-night."

After the bedtime routine, Katie and Gill made their way to their bed.

"Are you tired, Sweetheart?" he asked as he kissed the back of her neck.

"Exhausted!" she said dramatically. She could feel him slump behind her. She laughed to let him know she was teasing. Turning around in his arms that encircled her waist, she faced him and pressed her body to his, "Actually I was thinking that with everyone in bed we might slip out to the pool for a little skinny dip."

He smiled. He loved skinny-dipping with his wife, but tonight he wouldn't wait. He unzipped her dress and laid her back on the bed.

She could feel his heart pounding under her fingertips.

"We'll do that later," he whispered breathlessly, "If we have time after I'm done with you, and that may be a very long time from now. I want you to know how happy I am to be your husband."

Kissing and caressing each other, the passion between them surged into the realm of pleasure that was unique to their lovemaking. As their bodies pressed together, he looked at her with that steady gaze that told her he wanted to see the emotion and love through her eyes. The 'I love you' came in unison as their bodies united in total harmony. He knew how to bring about every pleasure that she enjoyed and he would not stop tonight until she experienced them all.

She had the intimate knowledge of how to intensify his every experience, heightening his pleasure to the point of making him fight to contain himself. It was a unity of love, pleasure, and reverence for each other. Her body beginning the crescendo of uncontrolled pleasure as he brought her to the peak and kept her there until she forced him to submit to her will and join her in ecstasy.

Breathless, they lay together in the lovers' embrace. Neither wanted it to end, but the physical body was limited, whereas the love inside their hearts for each other stretched to the ends of possibility.

They whispered their I love you's and drifted off to sleep, comfortable, secure, and deeply satisfied that the bonds between them would never be broken.

~:~

Gill and Katie were happy raising their family together. He donated two days a week to work with neurology cases that either didn't have insurance or had reached the maximum on their benefits. And Katie had been working on her own project since she left the retail industry. Friday, at Rockefeller Center in New York, the first fruits of her labors would come to bear. She had been excited about it, but when the Memorial for Donovan finished ahead of schedule and fell into the same week, she was rapt by the pairing.

She and Gill flew to New York Friday morning and met with the consultants, director, producers and members of the board to review the order of the evening events. The program would be aired on major network television and had been touted on the airways for the last several weeks as the gala event of the year. She had put her all into the concept and now the concept would become a reality.

The center was filled to capacity as the cameras panned the audience showing the mix that made the evening special. The social elite, movie celebrities, sports figures, singing personalities, and politicians sat interspersed among the families of special guests.

The finishing touches were made to her make-up before she headed toward the stage and awaited her cue. It would be her position to start the event, introduce the celebrities who would take over the presentation and announcement of the musical numbers. Then she would be the one to close the event and thank the sponsor for support and leave the viewing audience with what would become the trademark words of encouragement.

Her heart was pounding furiously as the moment neared for her to go on stage. She had been in the spotlight many times as the wife of Albert Trathmoore, but never in this type of role. Upon cue she began across the stage as the incredible applause came up from the audience, raising them to their feet. She become a household name when she married Albert, and then slipped into brief obscurity only to emerge as the woman with the most publicly debated divorce in history. The line of stores bearing the name 'Seasons' had become a phenomena in the clothing industry under her vision and guidance, and now she was giving something back to the public. She was stunningly poised and beautiful as she crossed the stage in her pale peach colored gown.

"Good evening ladies and gentleman, and welcome to the first annual Heart of the Diamond awards ceremony." The audience again broke into deafening applause. She paused as it died down, "I have found in life that the road we travel is rarely ever smooth. We navigate down a course that, in retrospect, will seem to have been predestined, but during the journey, we believe that we are engulfed in the whims of the world. But I tell you this evening, we have come together to honor a select group of women who have stayed true to their course and themselves to emerge victorious over the circumstances of life." Again the applause rocked the building. "Tonight we will present these ten chosen women with a token of esteem for their ability to do what was right in the face of adversity, proving to the world that beating with in each of them is not a heart of gold, but a heart of purest, and clearest, unflawed diamond."

The applause came up again and didn't die down as she announced the celebrities who would continue the program. She exited the stage as the program began. Gill was waiting at the base of the stairs as she descended to special seating they had at the front of the audience. He held her briefly and told her how incredibly proud he was of the event she orchestrated. She was shaking with the nerves that she restrained on stage when he put his strong arm around her and took her to her awaiting chair.

The event unfolded beautifully. A short video preceded each recipient's appearance on stage, giving the circumstances surrounding their achievement, and the recipient was then brought out of the audience to receive the beautiful Heart of the Diamond award and a check for $25,000 dollars.

Katie had designed the award herself, and with the help of the professional glass masters of Murano, Italy, it came to life. The award was the glass image of a woman on her knees, to show humility, a balance in her right hand for the search for truth, a dove in her left for the peace of heaven to go forward and, miraculously enveloped in the center of the glass image was a one carat, heart-cut diamond that represented the incorruptible true heart. The image was attached to a large, polished, black granite base that was etched on the top with the verse: 'Fighting the good fight for all that was right – No one else could know where my heart had to go – No one else could fight this battle for me – When God gave out diamonds, He put one in me.' Attached to the front face of the award was a fourteen karat gold plate with the recipients name and date and the phrase: 'Surviving Life's Test By Giving My Very Best'

Some of the recipients had come from the depths of poverty to a life of affluence by their determined struggle, and those recipients had already pledged their checks to their favorite charities. But some, like the grandmother who had lost her grown children to gang violence, but went on to raise, support, and put through college eight grandchildren while fighting against drugs and crime in her community were glad to accept the check award.

As the last of the ten recipients accepted her award, Katie took the stage again. She spoke about the example set before everyone this evening and how, when it least seems possible, we can all reach within us to uncover a heart of diamond and rise above insurmountable odds.

"I would like to take a moment to acknowledge and thank our sponsor for this year's ceremony, ATI founder and president, Albert Trathmoore."

The crowd cheered as he came on stage. This was a New York crowd and New York loved its number one savvy businessman and resident. He stepped up to the podium beside her, "Thank you very much." he said above the applause. "It has been an incredible night for everyone, and we have all been inspired by the women honored here this evening. I was privileged to sponsor this year's event and I encourage the sponsor for next year, World Media Conglomerate, to rival the presentation we have given tonight. Heaven knows they have made enough money from of the stories about me, my business and my personal affairs to do it," he said looking at Katie. The crowd broke in to thunderous applause and cheers of laughter. "I'm sorry, Darling," he said, looking again at Katie, "I just had to throw that in."

She couldn't help but laugh herself.

"I also would like to take a moment to recognize the driving force behind the awards that have been presented here tonight: Mrs. Katherine Danor Phillips." He stepped back from her and faced her as he applauded her, along with the audience that once again came to its feet.

She did not expect him to recognize her. That had been done at the start of the ceremony, and she was humbled at the response.

"I know you would not have wanted to receive one of your own awards tonight. That simply would not have been up to protocol, but even my lovely wife Patricia will attest to the fact that anyone who has ever had to put up with me deserves some award for courage in the face of adversity."

The crowd responded and Katie turned flaming red. Live on national television he had deviated from the script!

He sighed briefly, looking at her as he reached into his pocket. Once again they were together in the limelight, but it was much different than it had been in the past. The day her heart stopped beating and he thought her life would end, he took a long hard look at the man he had become. She taught him so much about love and sacrifice, and more importantly, he accepted the lesson in his heart. Ten months after she lay in a hospital bed pleading for his happiness, he married Patricia Hargrove, a widow of nine years who had no interest in finding another husband—until he came along. She was a petite, fine-boned, attractive woman who was only eight years younger than he was.

Albert had met Katie and Gill that morning when their flight arrived, just as he had when they had come to New York for the program rehearsals, but this time he made a point of opening his heart and speaking frankly about his feelings for her. He admired and loved Patricia, but he admitted, with Gill at her side, that Katie would always have a most special place in his heart. He said that all along he had treated the love he had for her as an obsession, a game to be played, a battle to be fought, and a conquest to be made, but when he finally realized it was *true* love, it was too late. With that realization came the hard fact that when it isn't a possibility anymore for the person you love to be yours, love learns to let go. He shook Gill's hand and said he couldn't think of a finer person to entrust with such a special woman.

He withdrew his hand from his pocket producing a stunning heart-shaped diamond necklace and walked around behind her to fasten it about her neck. The diamond was familiar and suddenly she realized it was the six-carat stone that Uncle Patty had cut for her. She looked out into the audience at Gill who was smiling from ear to ear. It was then that she remembered how insistent he had been that she shouldn't wear a necklace with her gown; he said she was perfect in the gown alone. He had been in on it the whole time and had given the stone to Albert to have the necklace made. She cast a glance to her producer who was standing just off stage. He was smiling also from the secret they had kept well hidden from her.

She stood there for a moment; her parting lines left her as her hand reached up to feel the diamond draped about her neck. Albert kissed her cheek and exited the stage to join his wife of two years, Patricia.

"That wasn't rehearsed," she admitted to the audience's merriment. Then, finding her voice and remembering her closing remarks, she spoke, "I encourage every person out there this evening, man or woman, if you have been inspired by the people and the actions that have been presented to you tonight, fight to achieve what is right with all of your might—and discover the diamond inside of you."

The applause went up as she descended to her husband's arms. She looked into his eyes, and he looked deep into hers. They loved each other with all the strength they possessed. Together they were one; there was no flaw between them to separate their love. Together they were one heart—one heart of the diamond.

ABOUT THE AUTHOR

Lindsay is a Florida native and lives with her husband and two daughters in a quiet log cabin on the central west coast. Her son is currently serving in the United States Army in Afghanistan. She is a network administrator for a local high school, and she has written eight full-length novels.

Novels: Heart of the Diamond
         Untouchable (book I)
         Unforgivable (book II)
         Untraceable (book III – coming soon)
         Kingdom Hill (coming soon)
Erotic Novelette: The Substitute

Thank you for purchasing this novel. If you found it to be an inspiration, please post a review so others will know it is worth the small investment and time spent reading.

Lindsay enjoys hearing from fans. You can contact her at: Delagair@gmail.com

You can also find her under Lindsay Delagair on Twitter.

Made in the USA
Columbia, SC
24 December 2023

29412327R00236